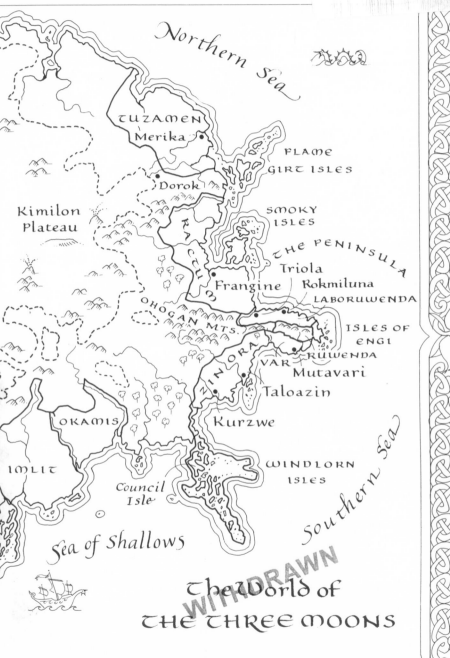

Northern Sea

TUZAMEN
Merika

FLAME
GIRT ISLES

Dorok

SMOKY
ISLES

Kimilon
Plateau

RACCUS

THE PENINSULA

Triola
Frangine   Rokmiluna

OHOGAN MTS.   LABORUWENDA

ISLES OF
ENGI

RUWENDA

VAR

ZINORA   Mutavari

Taloazin

OKAMIS

Kurzwe

IMLIT

WINDLORN
ISLES

Council
Isle

Southern Sea

Sea of Shallows

The World of
THE THREE MOONS

BLOOD
TRILLIUM

Also by Julian May

BLOOD
TRILLIUM

Julian
May

Bantam Books
New York • Toronto • London
Sydney • Auckland

BLOOD TRILLIUM

A Bantam Book / August 1992

All rights reserved.
Copyright © 1992 by Starykon Productions, Inc.

Book design by Guenet Abraham.

Library of Congress Cataloging-in-Publication Data:

May, Julian.
Blood trillium / by Julian May.
p.   c.m.
ISBN 0-553-08851-3
I. Title.
PS3563.A942B57   1992
92-2888
813'.54 — dc20   92-2888
CIP

Published simultaneously in the United States
and Canada

PRINTED IN THE UNITED STATES OF AMERICA

BVG   0   9   8   7   6   5   4   3   2   1

For Betsy Mitchell,
who knows

1

Springtime and the end of the winter rains were long overdue that year in the world lit by the Three Moons. Lingering monsoons had flooded the lowlands of the Peninsula and piled the snowdrifts high round about the Tower of the Archimage on the southern slope of Mount Brom. And on the night that the small fugitive named Shiki came, there was sleet.

The lammergeier that bore him through the shrieking gale was too weary and battered to use its mental voice to call ahead to its fellows at the eyrie of the Archimage, so its arrival was a dismaying surprise. The gigantic bird had no sooner landed upon the slippery Tower roof than it collapsed and died, and the servants of the White Lady at first did not even see the burden it had borne so steadfastly southward. All parts of the great black-and-white body save the wings, tail, and head were sheathed in a glaze of ice. The leather cloak of Shiki, which had shielded him as he crouched on the bird's back during the awful journey, was as stiff as armor and all but welded to the huge corpse. The fugitive himself was so near death that he lacked the strength to creep out of his shelter, and he might have perished had the Archimage's voorkeepers not hastened to his rescue. They saw at once that he was a man of the Mountain Folk, of the same aboriginal Vispi race as they themselves, but by dint of his small stature obviously belonging to some unknown tribe.

"I am Shiki. I have news for the White Lady," he managed to say. "A terrible thing has happened in the north country — in Tuzamen. I — I must tell her — "

Before he could say more, he fell bereft of his senses, dreaming of his dead wife and two dead children. They seemed to beckon Shiki in his feverdream, urging him to join them in a golden realm of peace and warmth where sacred Black Trilliums bloomed under cloudless skies.

How he longed to follow his loved ones there! To be freed at last from pain and the relentless press of duty! But he had not yet delivered his portentous message, and so he begged the phantoms to wait for him only a little while, until he fulfilled this last mission and informed the Archimage of the great danger. Even as he spoke his family seemed to drift away smiling into a bright mist, shaking their heads.

And when he woke, he knew he would live.

He found himself abed in a dim and cozy chamber, tucked beneath a fur coverlet and with both frostbitten hands thickly swaddled in cloth. The small lamp beside the bed was strange, giving off a bright yellow light from a kind of crystal, without any trace of flame. Freezing rain rattled on the window of the room, but the place was very warm, even though there was no hearth or brazier of coals to be seen. A subtle perfume filled the air. He struggled to sit up and saw on a table at the foot of the bed a row of golden urns, and in them bloomed magical Black Trillium plants like those he had seen in his dream.

Standing in the shadows beyond them was a tall woman. She was cloaked and hooded in a shimmering white fabric that had fleeting blue glints like those in the ice of the great inland glaciers. Her visage was hidden and at first Shiki caught his breath in foreboding, for an aura of surpassing mystery and power seemed to emanate from her, unmanning him and setting him trembling like a terrified child. He had encountered a person having this kind of aura only once before, and he had nearly died of it.

The woman threw back her hood and came to his side. Gently, she pressed him back against the pillows. "Do not be afraid," she said. The fearful aura seemed to recede then, and she appeared to be only a handsome black-haired young female — human, not of the Folk — having eyes of opalescent blue with golden glints deep within, and a sweet mouth gravely smiling.

His fear changed to wild anxiety. Had his voor brought him to the wrong place after all? The legendary Archimage he sought was an ancient, the protector and guardian of the Mountain Folk from the days of the Vanished Ones. But this woman looked to be scarcely thirty years old—

"Be at ease," she said. "From time out of mind, one Archimage has followed another as was decreed in the beginning. I am the Archimage Haramis, the White Lady of this age, and I confess to you that I am yet a novice in using the powers of my great office, which I have held for only twelve years. But tell me who you are and why you have sought me, and I will do my best to help you."

"Lady," he whispered. The words came slowly, like the last drops wrung from a sponge. "I asked my faithful voor to bring me to you because I sought justice — the righting of a terrible wrong done to me and my family and the people of my village. But during my flight, as I came near to dying, I realized that we are not the only ones who need your help. It is the whole world that does."

She regarded him in silence for a long moment. Then he was amazed to see tears appear in her eyes, but they did not spill onto her pale cheeks. "So it is true!" she whispered. "All throughout the land there have been rumblings of unease, rumors of evil reborn among both the Folk and humankind — even contention between my own two beloved sisters. But I sought mundane reasons for the disturbances because I did not want to believe that the very balance of the world was once again threatened."

"It is indeed!" he cried, starting up. "Lady, believe me! You must believe me! My own wife would not believe and she was slain, as were our children and scores of our Folk. That evil one who came forth from the Sempiternal Icecap now holds all Tuzamen in his thrall. But soon — soon — "

He had a fit of coughing and could speak no more, and from frustration began to thrash about the bed like a demented thing.

The Archimage lifted her hand. "Magira!"

The door opened. Another female entered, came swiftly to the bedside, and regarded him with enormous green eyes. Her hair was like fine-spun platinum, with the upstanding ears adorned with sparkling red jewels. In contrast to the austere white dress of the Archimage, the newcomer was magnificently attired in gauzy but voluminous robes of a rich crimson color, and she wore a golden collar and bracelets all studded with multicolored gemstones. She carried a crystal cup of some steaming dark liquor, and at the command of the Archimage administered it to him.

His coughing eased, as did his panic. "In a moment you will feel better," the one named Magira said. "Have courage. The White Lady does not turn away those who petition her."

Magira wiped his pallid, beslimed forehead with a soft cloth, and he noted with relief that her hand bore three digits like his own. It comforted him to know that this person was of the Folk as he was, even though she was of human stature, and her features more finely drawn than his own, and the accents of her speech odd. It was in humankind, after all, that the impending calamity had its source.

The taste of the medicinal drink was bitter, but it both soothed and strengthened him. The White Lady seated herself on one side of the bed and Magira sat on the other, and in a few minutes he relaxed and was able to tell his story:

My name is Shiki [he said], and my people call themselves the Dorok. We dwell in those parts of far Tuzamen where glacial tongues of the Sempiternal Icecap thrust forth from the frozen center of the world and nearly reach the sea. Most of that land is treeless and grim, a place of windswept moors and desolate mountains. We Folk have our small settlements in deep valleys beneath the frozen crags. Geysers spout there, warming the air and soil so that trees and other vegetation may grow, and our cave-homes are simple but comfortable. Humans from the coastal settlements and the Flame-Girt Isles visit us only rarely. We also have little contact with other tribes of the Mountain Folk, but we know that we have kin living in the highlands in many parts of the world, and like them we cherish the far-flying voor, and associate with these great birds, and ride them.

(I realize now that the Lady Magira and those servants of yours who took me in must belong to an exalted branch of my race that is privileged to serve you, White Lady. And now I begin to understand why my poor departed voor Nunusio was so determined that I should bring my dire news to you . . . But forgive my digression! I must get on with the tale itself.)

I earned my living as a trapper of the black fedoks and golden worrams that live only in the highest mountains, and betimes I also guided human seekers of precious metals into the remote ice-free enclaves where the great volcanoes mitigate the terrible cold.

Over two years ago, during the autumn Dry Time, three humans came to our village. They were not prospectors or traders, but said they were scholars from the south, from Raktum. They had been sent forth by Queen Regent Ganondri, they said, in search of a certain rare herb that would cure their boy-king Ledavardis of the malignant languor afflicting him. It was a plant alleged to grow only in the Kimilon, the remote Land of Fire and Ice that is a temperate island surrounded by glaciers, lying amidst rocks newly cooled after being belched forth from the belly of the world.

The First of our village, old Zozi Twistback, told the strangers that the Kimilon lay over nine hundred leagues west, entirely encompassed by the icecap. It is inaccessible by land, and only those great birds that we Folk call voor and the humans call lammergeiers can reach the place. The journey is all but impossible because of the monstrous storms that lash the Sempiternal Icecap. No other Mountain Folk save the Dorok have ever dared to venture to the Kimilon on voorback, and we ourselves have avoided the place for nearly two hundreds.

The three strangers promised an enormous reward to the Dorok guide who would take them to the Kimilon; but none would go. Not only was the expedition deemed too perilous, but also there was an ominous mien about the trio of humans, a smell of dark magic, that made us loath to trust them. One was dressed all in black, another in purple, and the third wore garments of vivid yellow.

The three then demanded that we sell voors to them so they could fly to the Kimilon themselves!

Our First restrained her outrage and explained that the great birds are free beings, not property, and carry us only out of friendship. She also reminded the strangers very courteously that the voor's talons and sharp-toothed beak make it a formidable creature to those who are *not* its friends. At this the trio renewed their offers of rich rewards for any Dorok guide who would accompany them. But no one would listen, and the humans finally mounted their fronials and seemed to quit the village.

Now, it is well known among the Dorok that I am the best guide of all, and the strangers no doubt found this out. One day when I returned from my traplines I found my home-cave deserted. My wife and two young daughters had disappeared, and none of the Folk could say what had become of them. I was mad with grief that night, and near drunk to the point of insensibility on mistberry brandy when the stranger dressed in black tapped at my door and said he had an important message for me.

Yes, you have guessed it: the human scoundrels had abducted my family in order to force me to be their guide! I was warned that if I spoke to any of my people of the deed, my wife and children would be killed. On the other hand, if I took the three men safely to the Kimilon and back, my loved ones would be returned safe to me, and the humans would pay me with a bag of platinum that would equal ten years' earnings.

"The dangerous trip could all be in vain," said I, "if we fail to find the medicinal herb that you seek."

At this the villains laughed merrily. "There is no herb," said the one garbed in purple. "But there is something else awaiting us that will brook no delay. So summon a flock of your sturdiest lammergeiers — four for us to mount and ten to carry certain supplies that we require — and we will leave before dawn."

I could only comply.

I shall not tell you of that horrible flight into the Sempiternal Icecap. It took seven days, with only a brief rest on the stormy surface of the ice allotted to the valiant voors each night. When we came at last to the Land of Fire and Ice, the volcanoes were in full spate, with molten lava pouring down their flanks and the sky full of black smoke all smeared with crimson, like a vision of the ten hells. A rain of ash was falling, whitening the ground and coating the meager vegetation like poisonous snow.

And there we found a lone human male.

He appeared to have built himself a sturdy house from blocks of lava. The place was as large as two ferol-barns and emplaced against a great cliff, and it was not only well made but even handsome. But the man's only food would have been the lichens encrusting the rocks, roots and berries from the few shrubs growing in the thin soil, and the slugs and shelled creatures inhabiting the hot springs. The ashfall was doubtless depleting these, and he had no more flesh on him than a skeleton when we first encountered him.

He was a man of tall stature, nearly twice my height. His filthy yellowish hair and beard reached nearly to his knees. His face was seamed and scarred and his eyes — of the palest blue, with a spark of gold deep within the dark pupils — peered out from deep caverns in his skull and had the glitter of madness. He wore clumsy sandals to protect his feet from the sharp lava rocks, and a stiff patchwork robe woven of plant fibers which served him well enough, since the subterranean fires render the Kimilon much warmer than the surrounding icecap.

I immediately understood that the purpose of our expedition had been to rescue this man, whose name was Portolanus. He was beyond doubt a powerful sorcerer. I must tell you straitly, White Lady, that he had about him the same awesome atmosphere of enchantment that invests your own person — but his magic evinced nothing of benevolence. Instead Portolanus seemed almost to glow with suppressed fury, as though his inner self were a sump of incandescent emotion. It seemed to me that this might gush forth as destructively as the red-hot magma rages from a volcano if he should ever unleash his soul's full power.

When we first found this Portolanus he was scarce able to utter human speech. I never learned how long he had been marooned in that hideous place, nor how he had managed to summon his three rescuers — who treated him with the most profound respect, commingled with fear. They had brought rich new snowy-white garments for him; and after he was well fed and cleaned and his hair and beard trimmed, he could not be recognized as the poor wretch who had bellowed like a triumphant beast when the voors first landed us near his dwelling.

The "supplies" that the henchmen of Portolanus had had me pack upon the extra voors were, in addition to our food and the tiny tents we slept in upon the icecap, nothing but sacks and ropes. The purpose of these wrappings soon became clear. While the voors rested and I remained outside with one villain to guard me, the sorcerer and the other two men busied themselves within the stone house. They eventually emerged with many packages, which they loaded onto the birds. Then we returned to Tuzamen by the same dangerous route we had come.

We did not fly to my village, however. We went to the coast, to the squalid human settlement of Merika at the mouth of the White River that calls itself the capital of Tuzamen. There the villains disembarked with their mysterious freight at a ramshackle place called Castle Tenebrose that overlooks the sea. I was discharged and given a small pouch of platinum coins, less than a tenth of the sum I had been promised. The balance of my fee, Portolanus said, would be paid "when his fortunes mended." (A likely story, thought I. But I wisely held my tongue.) The lackeys of Portolanus told me the location of the remote lava tube where they had walled up my family. I would find them safe enough, they said.

The voors and I returned to the mountains, and I rescued my wife and daughters. They were hungry, cold, and dirty — but otherwise unharmed. You may imagine the happiness of our reunion. My wife was overjoyed to see the bag of platinum, and immediately made fine plans on how we were to spend it. I commanded her and the children to tell no one of their ordeal, for when one is dealing with humans — especially those who are wielders of dark magic — no precaution is too great.

Then, for nearly two years, we dwelt in peace.

News of human affairs comes slowly to the remote mountain valleys of the Dorok. We did not realize that Portolanus, claiming to be the grandnephew of the mighty sorcerer Bondanus, who had ruled forty years earlier, swiftly put down Thrinus, the nominal potentate of Tuzamen, and took over the country himself. It was said that he and his followers used weapons of sorcery that made ordinary armor useless, and were themselves invulnerable to hurt, and that they could seize the very souls of their foes and turn them into helpless puppets.

I did not encounter Portolanus again until this winter's Rain, about twenty days ago. He came in the dead of night and burst into our cave in a thunderclap of wizardry, nearly tearing the stout door from its hinges. Our little daughters awoke screaming and my wife and I were shocked nearly out of our wits. This time the sorcerer held his aura in check somehow, and I would not have known him — except for his eyes. He was dressed like a king beneath his muddy riding-cloak. His body had regained its flesh and his voice was no longer harsh but smooth and compelling.

He said: "We must go again to the Kimilon, Oddling. Summon voors for yourself and me, and one more to carry our necessary supplies."

I was full of indignation and great fear, for I knew — even if he did not — that we had barely managed to escape with our lives the last time we had ventured across the icecap, and that was during the Dry Time. It was lunacy to attempt such a journey now, when the snowy hurricanes were at their worst, and I told him so.

"Nevertheless, we shall go," said he. "I have magic to command the storm. You will suffer no harm, and this time I will leave your reward with your wife so the thought of it will cheer you as we travel."

And he pulled forth an embroidered leather pouch, opened it, and spilled a pile of cut gems onto our eating-table: rubies and emeralds and rare yellow diamonds all asparkle in the guttering light from our hearth.

I still refused. My wife was with child and one of the girls sickly, and in spite of the wizard's assurances I feared that we two would not return alive.

To my dismay, my wife began to remonstrate with me, pointing out the good things we would be able to buy when we traded the gems. I was in a rage at her silliness and greed, and we shouted at each other, and the children wailed and sniveled until Portolanus barked: "Enough!"

His awesome magical aura suddenly enveloped him. He looked taller and supremely menacing, and we shrank away from him as he drew a dark, metal rod from a pouch at his belt. Before I knew what was happening, he touched my wife's head with this thing and she fell to the floor. I gave a cry, but he did the same to my poor little daughters, then brandished the rod at me.

"Demon!" I screamed. "You have slain them!"

"They are not dead, only bereft of their senses," he said. "But they will not wake until I touch them once again with this magical device. And that I will not do until you and I travel to the Kimilon and back."

"Never!" said I, and I concentrated my mind and sent forth the Call to my Dorok tribesmen. They came racing through the stormy night to my aid with swords and hand-catapults ready, gathering in a howling crowd beneath the rocky overhang that shelters my cave door.

Portolanus laughed. He opened the door a crack and threw some small object outside. There was a bright flash of light — then all the loud voices fell silent. The magician opened the door and strode outside. My stouthearted friends lay there in the rainswept darkness, blinded and helpless. One by one, Portolanus touched them with his rod, and they were still.

The families of the fallen now began to appear at the doors of their cave-homes, calling and crying. The tall sorcerer turned to me, and his aura froze me like the glacial wind and his terrible eyes had become blazing diamonds set in black obsidian. When he spoke, his voice was very calm. "They will all die — or they will live. It is your choice to make."

"You've killed them already!" I cried, beside myself. "I'll call the voors to tear you to bits!"

Whereupon he touched *me* with the rod.

I felt as a candle must when it is snuffed out: swallowed into utter nothingness. An instant later I came to myself again, limp as a new-born vart, lying on my back in the mud with the rain pelting my face. The magical rod was poised a finger's breadth from my nose and Portolanus glared down at me.

"You Oddling blockhead!" he said. "Can you not understand that you have no choice? I stunned you senseless, then restored you with my magic. The rod will restore your family and friends also — but only if you serve me!"

"The voors cannot fly long distances in the storms," I muttered. "During this season they mostly remain in their eyries."

"I have a way to gentle the storm," said he. "Call the birds and let us be off."

Having lost both courage and hope, I agreed at last. The wives and older children of the settlement came forth to bear their stunned husbands and fathers to shelter, and Portolanus directed them in the way to care for their loved ones and for my own family until I should return.

When we finally lofted into the air, he had the three voors fly closely together, with his own mount at the center. In some miraculous fashion he softened the force of the windblast, and we soared as if in calm weather. When the birds tired, we landed upon the interior icecap as before and sheltered in tents while the birds huddled around us. The same enchantment fended off the snow and wind while we rested, and then we took off once more. It took only six days to reach the Kimilon this time in spite of the incessant blizzards, and I arrived hale in body and resigned in spirit.

The magician retrieved only a single thing from the lava-rock house: a dark coffer about the length of my body, three handsbreadths wide and the same in depth. It was made of some slick material like black glass and had a silvery star with many rays embossed upon the top. All jovial now, with his aura once again in check, Portolanus opened the box to show me that it was empty.

"A simple thing, is it not, Oddling?" he asked me. "And yet it is my key to the conquest of the world"—he pulled from his fine jerkin a battered and blackened medallion on a chain, formed like the same kind of star—"just as this was the salvation of my life! There are powerful sorcerers in the southern lands who would forfeit their souls' immortality in order to possess these two things, and kings and queens who would gladly give up their crowns for them. But they are mine and I am alive to make use of them, thanks to you."

He began to laugh madly then, and his aura enveloped me like the bone-freezing fog of the Sempiternal Ice, and I feared I would die of despair and self-disgust on the spot. But in my mind I heard the voice without words of my beloved voor Nunusio bidding me to have courage, and I remembered my family and the others.

We must go, Nunusio told me, *for a vast storm approaches that will challenge this evil one's magic to the fullest. We must be away from the Kimilon before it breaks.*

Haltingly, I told Portolanus what my voor had said. He uttered a strange oath and began quickly to wrap up the precious star-box. He lashed it to the back of his own bird, rather than to that of the third voor who carried our supplies. Then we were off, just as the volcanoes vanished in impenetrable snowclouds.

Our homeward journey was so ghastly that my memories of it have all but vanished. The wizard was able to stave off enough of the wind so that we were not hurled to our deaths on the icecap, but he could not keep out the monstrous cold. On the fifth day the storm finally blew away. We camped on the ice that night under the brilliant light of the Three Moons, and Portolanus slept like a dead man, exhausted from his storm-fending.

I dared to send a Call to our village, inquiring about my family and the others stricken by the sorcerer's spell. Old Zozi Twistback responded to me with dreadful tidings. Those who had at first seemed only to lie in enchanted sleep had by the second day clearly surrendered their spirits and gone safely beyond. The signs had been unmistakable. And so the sorrowing Folk had consigned their bodies to a single great funeral pyre.

I could not help but howl my grief aloud. The sorcerer woke, and I berated him for a liar and a foul murderer, and made to draw my hunting knife, desisting only when he threatened me with the magical rod.

"When used upon humans, it has the harmless effect I described," he said. "And you yourself recovered easily enough, having been senseless for only a minute. There must be some unforeseen effect. You Oddling aborigines have bodies of a different sort from humans, and perhaps you are more vulnerable to the rod's magic."

"Perhaps!" I cried. "Is that all these murders are to you? A riddle to be pondered?"

"I did not mean to kill your people," he said. "I am not a heartless monster." He paused, thinking, as I continued to curse him impotently. Then he said: "I will make it up to you by tripling your reward

and taking you into my service. I am the Master of Tuzamen now —
and in time I will rule the world. I would deem a voorman a most
valuable servant."

A scathing refusal was on my lips, but prudence made me choke it
back. Nothing could restore my wife, my children, or my friends. I
would have my revenge upon this dark wizard one way or another,
but he was apt to kill me out of hand if I defied him now. We were
only a single day's flight from the icecap's edge, and my village lay an
hour or so beyond.

"I will consider your offer," I growled, turning away from him in
the tent. I pretended to snore, and soon he was asleep again himself. I
thought about what to do. When I had been afire with grief and fury, I
would gladly have slain him. Now I could not do the deed in cold
blood. There were the voors . . . but I could not deliberately order
them to attack him, either. If I murdered him, I should be no better
than Portolanus himself.

I crept from the tent, came close to Nunusio, and addressed my
great friend in the speech without words, asking his advice.

He said: *In days long gone, when the Mountain Folk were sore perplexed,
they sought counsel of the Archimage, the White Lady, she who is the guardian
and protector of all Folk.*

I said I had heard tales of her as a child, but surely she dwelt in
some distant corner of the world and would care nothing for the plight
of a poor Dorok of Tuzamen.

We voor know where she dwells, Nunusio said, *and it is a far ways. But I
will take you there if my strength allows, and she will grant you justice.*

I bespoke the other two voors, telling them to take the wizard safely
to the edge of the ice but no farther and then return to the village. The
bereaved Folk might divide among them the gems that Portolanus
had left and my household possessions. I told the birds my further
wish: that all voors should leave our village forever, so that no other
luckless guide would bring calamity upon our people as I had, should
Portolanus return and command further service. Without voors, the
Folk were useless to him.

Then Nunusio and I flew away.

And at length came to you, White Lady, with this story.

2

Haramis and Magira left the little bedroom and went down the spiral staircase toward the Archimage's library.

"Surely it could not be him!" Magira exclaimed. "He died! Blasted into nothingness by the Sceptre of Power!"

The Archimage's face was clouded with uncertainty. "As to that, we will see. It is sufficient for now that we know that the Master of Tuzamen is a sorcerer who is quite possibly capable of upsetting the balance of the world . . . and the name of the place where he was marooned: Kimilon. I know I have come across that word before, but it seemed in a different context."

The library was a huge, book-crowded chamber that was a full three stories high. Haramis herself had caused it to be built, expanding the original study of the old wizard's Tower. It was here that she most often worked, poring over books of magecraft, history, and a hundred other topics that she hoped would assist her to carry out the difficult office she had chosen. Opposite the door was a cheerful hearth where a true fire always burned, for Haramis found inspiration in staring at the flames, even though they were less efficient in warming than the hypocaust system employed throughout the rest of the Tower. A pair of spiral ramps coiling up from opposite sides of the room gave access to the bookshelves, and there were tall, narrow windows piercing the wall along the spirals as well, which lit the place brightly during the day. After dark, the magical lanterns flanking the windows gave soft illumination. On her large worktable by the fire was a curiously wrought candelabrum, using the same ancient science, which blazed brightly or went dark if one but touched a certain spot on its pedestal.

Standing now in the library's center, Haramis closed her eyes and rested her hand on her talisman, the white-metal wand with the circle at one end that hung on a chain about her neck. Her eyes flew open and she went dashing up one of the ramps, to pluck a certain book from the shelf.

"Here! This is the one! It was among those that I found in the ruins of Noth, where the Archimage Binah dwelt for so long."

She returned to the worktable and plopped the dusty volume onto a table and tapped it with the Three-Winged Circle. The book flew open and certain words seemed to glow. She read them aloud:

" 'It shall be an immutable law among the Folk of Mountain, Swamp, Forest, and Sea that every artifact of the Vanished Ones found in the ruins shall be shown to the First of their place, and studied to ascertain whether or not it may have a harmful action, or one not easily controlled, or one mysterious and perhaps pertaining to powerful magic. It is forbidden to the Folk to use such artifacts or trade them. They shall be gathered in a safe place, and once a year they shall be dispatched unto the care of the Archimage, who may store them in safety at the Inaccessible Kimilon, or otherwise dispose of them fittingly . . .' "

"Now we store the dangerous devices here on Mount Brom," Magira said, "in the Cavern of Black Ice."

Haramis nodded. "And I assumed — wrongly, it seems — that this Kimilon was a place in the tower of the old Archimage. The one that vanished at her death. But if our friend Shiki has it right, then the Kimilon out on the ice must be the place where the Archimage Binah had her cache . . . and perhaps even other Archimages before her."

Haramis stood frowning down at the open book, still tapping it idly with her talisman. She had neglected to light the candelabrum and the drop of fossil trillium-amber enclosed within the small wings at the circle's top shone with an interior radiance of its own; but the magical device offered no further assistance.

"If the man found there is who we think he is, then he could only have come to the Inaccessible Kimilon because the Sceptre of Power *ʃent* him. Sent him after we Three besought it to judge us — and judge him."

"But — why?" Magira cried. "Why would the Sceptre do such a thing rather than destroy him? Was its action not intended to restore the balance of the world?"

But Haramis was staring at the glowing amber and spoke as if to herself. "He would have had years to study all those wondrous ancient artifacts. And then, somehow, he was able to summon his minions to rescue him. He seized control of Tuzamen with the aid of the Vanished Ones' devices."

Magira's perplexity was now frankly fearful. "But why? Why did the Sceptre allow this awful thing to happen?"

Haramis shook her head. "I do not know. If he is truly alive, it must be because he has a role yet to play in the restoring of the great balance. We thought that balance had been achieved. Recent events show that we were wrong."

"In my opinion, *he* is the one who is at the root of all the recent troubles!" Magira asserted. "His agents of dark magic could be fomenting the human border unrest, and the turmoil among the Forest Folk, and even the sad antagonism between Queen Anigel and the Lady of the Eyes — "

Wearily, Haramis held up her hand. "My dear Magira, you must leave me. I must think and pray and decide what is to be done. Care for our guest, and when he is stronger, I will speak to him again. Now go."

The Vispi woman obeyed.

Alone, Haramis stared sightlessly at the library window streaming with rain, remembering not only the appalling evil that had been wrought twelve years before, but also the lineaments of a certain face that she had tried to banish from her memory and her dreams. She had managed to forget him, believing that he was dead, and she had also forgotten the turmoil he had engendered in her soul, that confusion she had mistaken for love —

No.

Be honest, she commanded herself. You wanted to believe the lies he told you — that he had not inspired King Voltrik of Labornok to invade Ruwenda, that he had never demanded the murder of your parents, Ruwenda's rightful King and Queen, nor conspired to slay you and your sisters. You believed him because you *did* love him. And when his deceits were made plain to you, when he showed you his dark plan for ruling the world and asked you to share it, you feared and despised him. You rejected his monstrous vision and rejected him.

But never hated him.

No, you could never bring yourself to do that, because deep within your secret heart your love for him still abided.

And now, faced with the prospect that he lives after all, you are filled with the most profound fear, not only of the havoc he might wreak upon the world, but also of what he might wreak upon you . . .

"Orogastus," she whispered, feeling her heart turn over as her lips dared once more to pronounce his name. "God grant that you be dead. Safely dead, and consigned to the deepest of the ten hells!" And having cursed him, she began to weep, and she found herself retracting the wish for his damnation at the same time that she still besought heaven to let him not be alive.

It was only after a long time that she managed to collect herself. She seated herself in front of the fire, then concentrated again on the talisman, holding the wand with its circle upright, as one would hold a handmirror, and looking into the silvery ring.

"Show me who or what most threatens the balance of the world," she said firmly.

A shimmering mist began to fill the circle. At first its colors were faint, like the nacre that lines seashells, but then they brightened and formed a central blur that was at first pink, then rose, then crimson, then vivid scarlet. The blur clarified, became tripartite. She saw that it was a three-petaled flower: a trillium the color of blood, such as had never bloomed in the world of the Three Moons. The image held for only a moment and then the circle was empty.

Haramis felt as if her body had turned to ice. "We Three?" she whispered. "Are *we* the danger, rather than him? What is the meaning of this thing you have shown me?"

The silver circle reflected the flames from the library hearth, and the inset amber with its fossil Black Trillium gave forth its usual faint glow. The talisman replied:

The question is impertinent.

"Oh, no, you don't!" Haramis exclaimed. "You shall not fob me off as you have done so many times before. I command you to tell me if we three Petals of the Living Trillium threaten the balance of the world, or if the threat comes from Orogastus!"

The question is impertinent.

"Damn you! Tell me!"

The question is impertinent.

Ice-pellets from the sleet storm rattled against the windowpanes and a burning log shifted in the fireplace with a thud and a brief hiss of sparks. The Three-Winged Circle remained inert, seeming to mock her, reminding her once again how little she actually knew of its working, for all her studies.

Haramis discovered that her hands were shaking — either with anger or with fear. Forcing them to be steady, she besought the talisman: "At least show me if Orogastus lives or is dead."

The silvery circle filled again with pearly mist, the faint colors making agitated small whorls, as if trying to form an image. But no face appeared. A moment later the Three-Winged Circle was empty.

So. It was to be expected. If he did live, he would shield himself from observation through sorcery. There was one other way she might try to view him . . . but first, a final request of her talisman.

"Tell me what manner of thing Portolanus took from the Kimilon on his second journey there with Shiki the Dorok."

This time the vision was clear, showing the shallow dark box as Shiki had described it, with a star upon its lid. But now the box was open, revealing a bed of metallic mesh inside and a square at the corner of this having several sparkling jewels mounted upon it. Haramis was puzzling over the star-box when the talisman spoke:

The box breaks bonds, and it enables new ones to be formed.

"Breaks bonds? What kind of bonds?"

Bonds such as that binding me to thee.

"Triune God! Do you mean it could unbond the three talismans of the Sceptre of Power from me and my sisters, and transfer their power to Portolanus?"

Yes. All that is needed is to place a talisman in the box, and finger the gems one after the other.

Her heart consumed with dread and foreboding, Haramis went to her own chambers and procured furs and warm gloves in preparation for a visit to the Cavern of Black Ice. The special vestments Orogastus had always donned before entering the place, and the duplicates he had made especially for her, were part of a futile ritual intended to placate his dark gods and quite unnecessary. But then he had failed to understand so many things about his sources of power, mistaking ancient science for sorcery and coming to depend overmuch upon it, while neglecting the genuine magic he had learned at the feet of his mentor Bondanus.

"And, by the Flower, I am thankful that he did neglect it," Haramis said to herself. "For if he had been able to use true magic against us, he might have prevailed after all."

Bundling up, she went down to the lowest level of the Tower, to a long tunnel that led deep into the flank of Mount Brom. The rough-hewn rocky tube was lit by the same wonderful flameless lanterns found in the rest of the Tower, but there was no heat. Her breath formed a trailing cloud as she hurried, clutching the furs tightly about her. She had not visited this place for years, so disturbing were its resonances. But it was not any aura of dark magic that had repelled her: it was the memory of him.

She opened the massive, frost-covered door at the tunnel's end and entered into what seemed to be a large cave with walls of rough granite all veined with white quartz. Its floor was paved with glassy tiles as dark and slick as the black ice that intruded through cracks in the cavern walls and ceiling. All about the chamber's perimeter were open niches with peculiar, complexly shaped objects in them. Glassy black doors opened into more rooms filled with strange things. It was Orogastus who had told her that the cavern was a repository for instruments of sorcery vouchsafed him by the Dark Powers. But Haramis had suspected even then that the things had to be machines of the Vanished Ones — some collected by Orogastus through trading with the Folk, others that he had found when he first discovered this place. He had built his Tower here to protect the Cavern of Black Ice and have easy access to its trove of marvels. When he died, Haramis had taken the Tower for her own use, but she had never utilized the contents of the cavern, which had been slowly augmented over the years by other forbidden devices collected by the Swamp Folk from the ruins.

Many of the things hidden in the Cavern of Black Ice were weapons.

Not the thing she had come to use tonight, however. She opened one of the obsidian doors and came into a shallow chamber with one wall thickly encrusted with hoarfrost. Inset within it was a gray mirrorlike circle, an ancient machine that had the potential of locating and overseeing any person in the world. The machine was in very poor working order, and indeed the last time Haramis had tried to consult it, seeking the whereabouts of the Glismak witch Tio-Ko-Fra, it had only sputtered weakly and then extinguished itself, muttering incomprehensibly about being exhausted. However, it had enjoyed many years of rest since then, and there was at least a small chance that it might have restored itself. She would have to frame her query carefully, though, since it was likely that her first request would also be her last.

She faced the mirror, took a deep breath, and intoned in a loud voice: "Respond to my request!"

Only her own image stared back at her, and after a time she repeated her words in a tone more highly pitched.

And it woke! A dim glow replaced her reflection and she heard a faint whisper: "Responding. Request, please."

She was careful to reply in the same unnaturally high tone she had used before, in the truncated language Orogastus himself had taught her when he showed her his most precious secrets in order to win her love.

"View one person. Locate present position of person on map."

Slowly — so slowly! — the mirror brightened. It hissed: "Request validated. Name of person."

She conjured up his image in her mind, dismayed at how easily his face came to her, austere and beautiful, framed by long silver hair. But this time she dared not speak his former name. Whoever this newly empowered sorcerer was, it was necessary that she behold him so that she would know the one who was her great enemy.

"Portolanus of Tuzamen," she said.

"Scanning," said the mirror, as faintly as a dying breath. The mirror's surface became a kaleidoscope of wan colors that almost parodied her talisman's working, and its voice sibilant gibberish that she could not understand. Haramis wanted to cry out in frustration, but she restrained herself, knowing that any word she spoke now would be construed by the ancient machine as a command and might bring about an undesirable result or even cause the mirror to extinguish itself.

The jumping mass of broken colors steadied, and the dim image that formed could just barely be distinguished as a map of the sea in the vicinity of the Isles of Engi. There was a tiny blinking dot of light far from land. Haramis felt a giddy sensation invade her mind. Her heart was thudding behind her ribs like a captive beast trying to escape a cage.

First the machine would locate a person. Then it would show a face.

The map disappeared and a new image formed, this one even more indistinct than the last. It was certainly a man's visage, but the features were so bleared and shadowed that they might have belonged to anyone. She felt a rage of disappointment, and then castigated herself for being a silly fool.

The picture vanished. The mirror sighed a few more incomprehensible syllables and then the light in its heart died. Haramis knew with a terrible certainty that the machine would never work again. She withdrew from the chamber and closed the door, shivering from the abominable cold and from the strength of the inner feelings she sought to conquer.

Portolanus was at sea, doubtless traveling south with the Tuzameni delegation toward the same destination that her two sisters would soon reach. He owned a nation. He had access to treasures of the Vanished Ones that might be far more dangerous to the world than those secreted within this cavern. He also had the star-box that might grant him ownership of a talisman, could he but wrest it from its owner. Perhaps Portolanus was only some upstart magician who had come upon the secret cache of the Archimage by accident. If so, he was menace enough, and she would have to organize a careful campaign to deal with him. But if the sorcerer was in truth Orogastus, then her task would be infinitely more difficult — and not only because of her own emotional involvement.

She reminded herself that he would have been banished to the Inaccessible Kimilon by the Sceptre of Power itself, for some unfathomable reason. And it was entirely possible that Orogastus, having spent twelve years of exile in the icebound solitude, had finally learned to master the true magic within himself.

As she had yet to do.

Kadiya's conference with the Aliansa leaders had taken many months to arrange, and it was so important that she had even consulted with the Teacher in the Place of Knowledge before deciding upon the strategy she would use. These Sea Folk were not like the aborigines of Ruwenda, accustomed to obey the laws of the White Lady and freely accepting Kadiya as their leader. The Archimage was a half-forgotten myth to the Aliansa of the Southern Sea — and the Lady of the Eyes a personage unknown, and quite possibly not to be trusted.

Now Kadiya sat on one side of the great hut on Council Isle with the Sea Folk on the other, glad of the light breeze blowing through the loose weave of the lown-leaf walls. Her talisman, the Three-Lobed Burning Eye, lay on the grass mat in front of her, bound about with flowers and green fragrant vines in the symbolism of peace. The sword of the Aliansa High Chief, similarly adorned, was beside it.

Behind Kadiya, Jagun the Nyssomu and the sixteen Wyvilo warriors who were her escort stirred restlessly. They had been in the council hut for nearly three hours without a recess. But as long as Har-Chissa and his thirty chieftains showed a willingness to talk, Kadiya would give them her full attention. She had already explained her own proposal to them at length. As the Lady of the Eyes, the Great Advocate of the Folk of the Peninsula in their dealings with humankind, she had come to offer her services also to the Aliansa in their long-standing dispute with the kingdom of Zinora. She had come to make peace.

The Sea Folk had listened to her words in stony silence. Then Har-

Chissa gestured for the subchiefs to detail their grievances against
Zinoran humanity, and one by one, they had cataloged the atrocities
committed by human traders against the Folk. Kadiya had been
dismayed at the way their tales contradicted the story she had been
given by the smooth-tongued King Yondrimel of Zinora, who had
pooh-poohed any need for her intervention. It was obvious that
matters were at a much worse pass than she had suspected.

A female chieftain of the Sea Oddlings from one of the smaller
islands was winding down her harangue. Her great yellow eyes with
the vertical pupils were popped out on their short stalks and her fangs
gnashed as she gave vent to her anger. She came from a poor place,
and wore only two strands of misshapen pearls about her neck and an
unadorned grass tabard. The scales on her back and upper limbs were
unpainted, and the weapon at her belt was a crude stone axe with a
shell tassel.

"You say we should make peace with the humans of Zinora!" She
waved one webbed hand to encompass the squatting company of
aboriginal leaders. "We — the proud Aliansa! — who have lived free in
these islands from the time that the Big Land was still locked fast in
the grip of the ice! But why should we listen to you? The Zinorans
come to our islands and always cheat us in their trading. If we refuse
to trade our pearls and kishati and perfume oils, they steal! They burn
our villages! They even kill us! My own son was slain by them! You
have heard the words of many other chieftains, Lady of the Eyes,
attesting to the wrongs committed against us. We no longer want to
have anything to do with the Zinorans. We do not need their trade.
We will sell to the nations of Okamis and Imlit across the Sea of
Shallows. Tell this fierce new King of Zinora that we spit upon him!
We know he dares to claim these islands as part of his kingdom, but
he is a liar and a fool. The Windlorn Isles belong to the Sea Folk who
live upon them — not to a braggart human who dwells in a fine palace
on the Big Land."

The assembled Aliansa roared approval.

"If his traders come again," the chieftain went on, "let me tell you
what we will do to them! Our warriors will lurk in their canoes among
the outer reefs, and as the ships come creeping in to despoil us we will

pierce their hulls and sink them without warning. When the sea gives up the Zinoran bodies, we will skin them to make our drums! Their skulls will be piled in heaps upon the sea-stacks, and the griss and pothi will make nests in them! Zinoran flesh shall be the food of fishes, and their broken boats the abode of the sea-monster Heldo!"

All the other chieftains gave a great bellow of assent as she crossed her scaly arms and resumed her seat.

Now the High Chief Har-Chissa rose up at last. He was a splendid creature, a head taller than a stalwart human, though not quite so tall as a Wyvilo. His face with its short muzzle, gleaming tusks, and gold-painted scales was a sight to stop the heart of the most bloodthirsty Raktumian pirate. He wore a kilt of fine blue silken cloth woven in Var, and his steel cuirass with its bejeweled baldric could only have been made by the royal smithy of Zinora. He was a taciturn and dour individual, preferring to have his minor chieftains voice the injuries done to the Sea Folk. Now that they had finished, he addressed Kadiya in deep, croaking tones:

"Lelemar of Vorin has summed up the feelings of us all, Lady of the Eyes. We have listened to what you had to say, and you have listened to us. You tell us that you are the Advocate of the Folk, one of the Three Petals of the Living Trillium, the blood-sister of the great White Lady. You have showed us that magical talisman called the Three-Lobed Burning Eye that you carry, and we know that certain landly Folk — Nyssomu, Uisgu, Wyvilo, and Glismak — name you their leader and follow your counsel. You ask us to do the same. But I say that you are also the blood-sister of Queen Anigel of Laboruwenda, who with her consort, King Antar, oppresses those Folk who refuse to do her will. And you are also *human* . . ."

The other Sea Folk nodded and murmured and growled. Chief Har-Chissa continued:

"You have urged us to make peace with Zinora. You tell us that we are fewer in number than the humans of that country and not so clever in waging war. You say that our women and children will suffer if we fight the Zinorans, and it is best that we compromise with them . . . But did not the once-proud Glismak give up their fierce ways at the behest of you and your sisters? And did they not suffer thereby, being forced to work in road gangs in the swamps of Ruwenda rather than living free in the Tassaleyo Forest? And are not they, together with the Nyssomu, Uisgu, and Wyvilo, treated as inferior beings and subjected to the will of the humans who dwell among them?"

Again the gathering of Sea Folk nodded and shouted their furious indignation. The Chief silenced them.

"I say to you, Kadiya of the Eyes, that the Aliansa will never make peace with Zinora, nor will we submit to the will of any *other* human. We are free, and we will remain so!"

There was a great tumult of cheering. Finally Kadiya rose and the Sea Folk quieted. It was nearly dusk and the interior of the council hut was dim. The only illumination came from the warm glow of the trillium-amber inset in the pommel of her talisman and the great shining eyes of the aborigines: those of the hostile Sea Folk and of Kadiya's own loyal Wyvilo friends.

"Let me first refute your beliefs about the Glismak," Kadiya said. "If you will not take my word, you may consult with my companion Lummomu-Ko, who is Speaker of Let and chief among the Wyvilo, and who honored me by accompanying me on this mission. In former days, the Glismak lived by preying upon the Wyvilo, their neighbors. When they gave up their immoral ways, they had to find other means of surviving. Some Glismak became foresters like the Wyvilo, but others agreed to labor on the Queen's Mireway in the Ruwendian swamps, a great new road sponsored by my sister Queen Anigel. The wages she offered were more than fair. Many thousands of Glismak went north during the dry seasons to work on the road. But last Dry Time some of them became surly and discontented. They demanded that their wages be doubled and asked for other things the humans could not grant them. They rioted and killed some humans — and humans killed some of them. Then they returned to the forest. The proud and greedy ones among them now prevent those who would work from returning to the road. This is a sad matter, but I am working to resolve it. I also seek to resolve the inequalities and injustices that still prevail between other Folk of the Peninsula and humanity. I would willingly work with you also, to mediate your grievances with Zinora. My talisman, the Three-Lobed Burning Eye that is part of the great Sceptre of Power, will ensure that justice prevails."

The Chief grunted, noncommittal. Others of his fellows gave derisive hoots and snarls. Kadiya seemed not to notice, but sat in calm dignity at the front of her small entourage of landly Folk with her gaze now fixed upon her talisman. It seemed to be only a dark pointless sword with dull edges — just as Kadiya herself seemed only a human female of medium stature with bright russet hair, wearing a tunic of golden milingal-scales emblazoned with an Eyed Trefoil. Every one of the Aliansa had heard tales of how the hilt of her talisman was possessed of three similar magical Eyes — and how it could kill with flameless fire those who were the Lady's enemies, or even anyone who touched it without her permission.

And so Chief Har-Chissa silenced the disrespectful among the Folk and carefully concealed his own contempt for this weak-bodied human witch. So she wished to appoint herself advocate of the Aliansa! Who had asked her to meddle in their affairs? Beyond a doubt it was the King of Zinora himself, her fellow human! She was no friend of the Sea Folk. She had never even deigned to visit them until young King Yondrimel laid claim to the Windlorn Isles. The High Chief had only agreed to the meeting when Kadiya pledged to help the Aliansa — and it was now becoming clear that the kind of help she had in mind was surrender.

This Lady of the Eyes was nothing but a dangerous busybody. But she would have to be treated with caution, lest she impose her will on them by force. That magical talisman . . . If she no longer had it, she would be harmless. And the talisman itself —

But now the High Chief was obliged to respond to her, and the honor of the Aliansa demanded that he speak the truth.

"Lady of the Eyes," Har-Chissa said in a voice gravely courteous, "we thank you for being concerned about the Sea Folk. If you would truly help us, warn King Yondrimel of Zinora not to molest us. Tell him that we reject his claim of sovereignty over the Windlorn Isles, and we will not trade with him again for so long as the Three Moons ride the sky. Warn him that death awaits his sailors if they venture into the reefs and shoals and sandbanks that guard this place. Tell him this and make him believe that it is true. Then you will be a true friend to the Aliansa. Now my speaking is at an end."

He took up his sword, stripped the flowers from it, and thrust it back into its scabbard with ominous zest. "Outside, my people are preparing a farewell feast for you and your followers. Come to the feast at third moonrise. With respect and firmness, we ask you to leave these islands before the sun appears tomorrow and hasten to Zinora."

Only the clenching of Kadiya's fists betrayed her reaction. She retrieved her talisman and gestured for her delegation to rise. They all inclined their heads to the gathering of Sea Folk, then filed out of the council hut into the blue twilight.

When they were beyond earshot of the Aliansa, down on the shore beneath the tall, gently rustling lown-trees, Kadiya said: "My friends, I have failed in my mission. I was not persuasive enough. I may even have made the situation worse than it was before. Har-Chissa made it plain that he rejected me, just as he rejected my proposals."

"To demand that we leave before sunup." Lummomu-Ko wagged his head, remembering the High Chief's thinly veiled order. "Among the Wyvilo, this is a mortal insult. I think it may be the same among the Sea Folk, our cousins."

Kadiya uttered a sound that was part exasperation and part despair.

"Do not be downcast, Farseer," said the little old Nyssomu, Jagun. He was Kadiya's friend from childhood and her closest adviser. "This conflict between the Sea Folk and Zinora is an ancient one. You must not blame yourself for being unable to resolve it at the first attempt."

"If I had only been able to bring them some concession from the King of Zinora!" she said bitterly. "But Yondrimel is as stubborn as an overloaded volumnial, and thinks only of putting on a brave show for the other rulers who will be attending his upcoming coronation."

"You did your best to persuade him," Jagun insisted. "In times to come, if the Aliansa prove to be truly intractable in the matter of renewing trade, the King may be willing to listen to you. He is young, and perhaps capable of learning wisdom. The liquors and precious corals of the Windlorn Isles are highly valued in Zinora, and the pearls constitute an important part of their trade with other nations as well."

The band of Wyvilo warriors who were Kadiya's bodyguard went off to stretch their legs before the feast, but she and little Jagun and Lummomu-Ko sat down on the sand together looking out at the sea. The monsoons had ended and the waters around Council Isle were like a mirror of dark metal, with the first-risen of the small half-moons reflecting in it. Here and there on the horizon other smaller islands and lofty sea-stacks and rocky arches thrust up in black silhouette among the brightening stars. The Varonian ship that had carried Kadiya's delegation lay at anchor a league or so out among the reefs, brightly lamplit. Its human crew had been forbidden to come ashore.

"Will we return to Zinora, then, as Har-Chissa bade us?" asked Lummomu-Ko. In physique he closely resembled the Aliansa, being tall and robust and with a face less humanoid than the aborigines of the Mire and Mountain. He was dressed in handsome garments in the latest mode of Laboruwendian nobility, for the Wyvilo were as vain as they were brave and honest.

"It would do us little good to go to Zinora, old friend," Kadiya said. "The coronation gala would be in full swing by the time we reached Taloazin, and I am not eager to parade my failure before the world's royalty. No, it would be better if I simply sent Yondrimel a letter. I can confront him in person later, when my failure can do no harm to my sister Anigel's prestige."

"But how could that happen, Farseer?" Jagun was bewildered. "Surely there is no connection between the grievances of the Aliansa and faraway Laboruwenda."

Kadiya uttered a laugh without humor. She was stroking the three black lobes of her talisman's pommel, and the trillium-amber embedded within shone more brightly, and its light began to throb. "That young King of Zinora is a man of vast ambition. He would take special delight in crowing over my failure in front of the other rulers, pointing out that I have also failed thus far in conciliating the other Folk in their disputes with Laboruwenda. He would talk about his own grandiose plans for smashing the Aliansa, slyly affronting Queen

Anigel and King Antar for not dealing as harshly with the Folk of
their realm. King Yondrimel would curry great favor with the powerful Queen Regent of Raktum by making my sister and her husband
look incompetent and me powerless."

The Wyvilo leader said, "I still fail to see how this would do your
sister hurt."

"Queen Ganondri of Raktum would like to expand her own kingdom at the expense of Laboruwenda," Kadiya explained. "It might be
possible for her to subvert the thrones of Anigel and Antar if certain
human factions in Labornok perceived the co-monarchs to be weak-
lings. The union between Labornok and Ruwenda is a fragile one,
held together largely by the humans' awe of the Three Petals of the
Living Trillium. If two of those Petals seem impotent and the third is
far away in her mountain tower, concerned mostly with occult affairs,
the kingdom's unity may be fractured."

"Could not you and Queen Anigel subdue your human foes with
your magical talismans?" the Wyvilo leader asked.

"No," said Kadiya. "No more than I could force Yondrimel and the
Aliansa into peace with mine. The talismans do not work that way."

Lummomu-Ko rolled his huge eyes. "Human politics! Who can
understand it? Nothing among you is ever what it seems. Actions that
appear simple and straightforward have deeply hidden motives. Nations are never satisfied to live and let be, but must always scheme
against each other and jockey for additional power . . . Why cannot
the humans deal with each other openly and without dissembling, like
honest Folk?"

"I have asked myself that question often" — Kadiya sighed — "but I
do not know the answer." She got up and dusted the sand from her
garments. "My friends, I beg you to leave me now until the last of the
Three Moons rises and we go together to the feast." She indicated the
pulsating amber of the magical sword at her side. "As you have no
doubt seen, my talisman signals that one of my sisters would converse
with me across the leagues."

Jagun and Lummomu-Ko made ready to go, but the Wyvilo leader
said: "We will remain close by, keeping you in sight. I liked not the
soul-tone of the Aliansa at our parting."

"They would not dare to attack me!" Kadiya said, drawing herself erect and taking hold of her talisman's pommel.

Lummomu-Ko lowered his head. "Of course not. I beg your pardon, Lady of the Eyes."

He and Jagun went off together down the shore, the tall clan-leader slowing his gait to accommodate the diminutive huntsman. They took up a stand at a rock outcropping not fifty ells distant, and she could see that their faces were still turned toward her.

"Ridiculous," she muttered, then lifted the Three-Lobed Burning Eye and asked quietly, "Who calls?"

One of the black lobes of the pommel split and opened, revealing a brown Eye, identical in color to Kadiya's own. Immediately her mind beheld a vision of her sister Haramis.

"By the Flower, it's about time, Kadi! Why did you not answer at once? I feared some disaster had overtaken you down there in the Windlorn Isles!"

Kadiya uttered a rude word. "I am perfectly well, except that my mission has been an utter fiasco." And she tersely summed up what had happened at the meeting. "I shall not go back to Zinora. My presence there would only make things more difficult for Ani and Antar. I doubt that I could even be civil to the two of them myself. We have come to a stalemate in the matter of enfranchising the Folk of Mire and Forest, and I am furious at the clumsy way that they handled the Glismak revolt. They *know* that the Glismak are imperfectly civilized. If the insubordinate road-workers had been dealt with more tactfully, they never would have resorted to violence."

Haramis made a dissuasive gesture. "We can talk of those matters some other time. I have more important news for you. But first . . . think this over very carefully, Sister: Have you lately perceived through your talisman or in any other manner an upsetting of the balance of the world?"

"Certainly not," said Kadiya shortly. "I leave such subtleties to you, Archimage. The balance of the Aliansa and Glismak were my worry up until now, and I have had little time for anything else. Having failed here, I shall return to the Mazy Mire by way of Var and

the Great Mutar River and try to propitiate the Glismak as I pass
through their lands. Then I will go again to the Place of Learning and
seek counsel of its Teacher."

"Yes. Of course you must do that. But I had good reason to ask
about the world-balance. Kadi . . . I have received news that makes
me suspect that Orogastus is still alive."

"*What?* But that is impossible! The Sceptre of Power blasted him to
smuts twelve years ago at our victory over King Voltrik."

"So we all believed. But one of the Folk from far Tuzamen, a little
man named Shiki, risked his life to come to me with a strange
story. He was forced to guide a party of humans on lammergeierback
to a place deep within the icecap. There they rescued a magician
who had been marooned there for years. This man calls himself
Portolanus, and he is the same one who has seized the throne of
Tuzamen."

"Such as it is!" Kadiya laughed scornfully. "I have heard of this
Portolanus of Tuzamen. He seems to be nothing but a parvenu with a
certain flair for minor sorcery. The Triune God knows that it would
not require much magecraft to take over a wretched vart's-nest like
Tuzamen. Has your talisman verified that the Master Wizard is
indeed Orogastus?"

"No," Haramis admitted. "It will not tell me if Orogastus is alive or
dead, nor will it vouchsafe me any vision of this Portolanus. It has
never failed me in this way before. But even if Portolanus is not
Orogastus, he may very well be a great danger to us and to our
people."

An emotion that Kadiya had not experienced for long years seemed
to surface within her like a hideous Skritek slowly emerging from its
drowning pool, and that emotion was fear. But no sooner had she
identified it than she denied it.

"If Orogastus lives, we will deal with him again as we did before,"
she declared. "We Three will merge our talismans into the Sceptre of
Power and return him to the oblivion he deserves!"

"I wish it were so simple." Haramis's eyes were bleak. But then she
smiled at Kadiya. "Still, this Portolanus has yet to confront us directly, and at least we are forewarned. Take care, Sister, and bespeak

me immediately if you should perceive any hint of imbalance in the world."

"I will," Kadiya promised, and the vision of Haramis disappeared.

Long past midnight, Kadiya, Jagun, Lummomu-Ko, and the fifteen Wyvilo warriors returned to the shore and embarked in the two small boats that would take them back to their ship. The sea was dead calm and the black sky spangled with stars and the three half-moons. The delegation had all eaten too much and drunk too much of the delicious but highly intoxicating kishati liquor. Instead of cheering them, the feast had made them feel more melancholy than ever. The Wyvilo longed to be back in the Tassaleyo Forest, and Kadiya and Jagun were homesick for the beautiful Manor of the Eyes, which the Nyssomu had built for their human leader and her counselors and servants on the upper reaches of the River Golobar in the Greenmire of Ruwenda.

Feeling dizzy and ill, Kadiya steered with the rudder at the stern of one boat while Jagun did the same work in the other. Lummomu-Ko plied an oar along with his fellows and led the Wyvilo in a lugubrious rowing chant. The guttural bass notes of the singing and Kadiya's general wooziness prevented her from hearing certain ominous tiny noises, and she noticed nothing until the rapidly rising warm waters were nearly ankle-deep in the bottom of her boat. At the same moment that she cried out, Jagun did also from his craft.

"Farseer, we're sinking! Come to our aid!"

"We're sinking, too!" she exclaimed. "Quickly! Head to one of the reefs!"

They were still more than half a league from the ship in a region full of sharp rocks with deep water between. The Wyvilo rowed like fiends, beating the water to foam. Kadiya heard Jagun's relieved shout: "We're on the reef!" Everyone seemed to be yelling. Then the keel of her own boat grated on something and the craft heeled over violently. The Wyvilo dropped their oars and splashed and scrambled overboard.

"I'm all right!" Kadiya cried. "Save yourselves!" But then she found herself suddenly trapped, her feet held fast in some way as the boat disappeared beneath the black water. Struggling grimly to pull herself free, she did not think to scream until it was almost too late, and then her cry was only a strangled gasp before she was forced to hold her breath. The last thing she saw before she submerged was Lummomu-Ko and one of his warriors diving off the rocks and swimming toward her.

She plummeted down, weighted by her ironshell cuirass and the talisman, still seeming to be entangled with the sinking boat. Frantically, she strove to free her legs from what held them. It was not wood and it was not rope, but instead something rough and hard, imprisoning her ankles. She clawed at it as she sank, but it continued to hold her tight. What was it? If only she were sober and able to think straight! The water was full of tiny luminous sparks — glowing jellyfish — and strands of luminous seaweed waved and rippled all round her. It was very beautiful . . . and she was drowning.

Her chest burned like a cauldron of molten metal and the air began to be forced out of her lungs. There was a roaring, hissing sound in her ears. She could hold her breath no longer. Shining bubbles streamed from her nostrils and mouth, tumbling upward through the palely gleaming water-life. The talisman in its belt-scabbard also glowed — not golden, but a rich effulgent green that reminded her of the little trillium root she had followed through the Thorny Hell so many years ago on her great quest.

Kick! Kick harder! Break away from whatever shackled her . . . Finally she did and for a moment swam free. But then one of her legs was caught again and she was dragged deeper — realizing too late that something — or someone — had a tight grip on her ankle. Sharp claws dug into her flesh through the straps of her sandals, and powerful muscles tensed to foil her attempts to wriggle free.

A surge of anger flooded through her. The Aliansa! Lummomu-Ko had been right about them planning treachery! Kadiya's wits seemed to have deserted her, but she continued to writhe with all the strength that her body could muster. The burning in her chest was now unbearable —

And then the pain suddenly ceased. Her anger faded. She stopped struggling and felt only peace as she continued to drop through the field of glowing weed. Her eyes were wide open, but the world was becoming darker and darker.

In one last flash of reason, she tugged at the Three-Lobed Burning Eye. If she could use it . . . if she could only think what was to be done with it . . .

She had it in her hand.

The death-grip on her ankle abruptly loosened. She was free, drifting in the dark.

There, she thought happily. That's better.

Now she could relax.

Her fingers opened and the talisman fell away. She watched its green glow become smaller, smaller, and finally disappear.

After that she knew nothing.

Kadiya opened her eyes. Her head hurt as if compressed in a vise and she saw only a colored blur. Her throat was parched and sour with bile and she did not seem to have a body or limbs. It was some time before sensation returned below her neck and she dared to move her arms and legs. She felt very cold, even though she was dressed in a soft nightgown of wool challis. Little by little her vision cleared, and she realized that she was in a bunk in her cabin on the Varonian ship. The door swung gently open and shut with the sea's motion. By the creaking of the rigging and the hiss of waves along the hull, she knew they were traveling at full sail.

After several futile tries, she was able to call out for Jagun. Her old friend came tumbling down the companionway steps and into her cabin, his mouth wide in a grin that showed his pointed front teeth. He was soon followed by Lummomu-Ko and the human captain of the Varonian vessel, Kyvee Omin. They fussed over her, putting many pillows behind her so that she could sit up. Jagun made her drink some ladu brandy to give her strength.

"What happened?" she asked at last.

"It was the Aliansa," the Wyvilo chief said somberly. "They are fine swimmers, the treacherous devils, even better than we are. They holed our boats with braces and bits, then dragged you down. I saw you go under and dived after you with young Lam-Sa, and we realized at once what had happened. When you finally brandished your talisman, the Aliansa who clung to you swam off, and Lam-Sa and I were able to take hold of you and draw you to the surface and onto the rocks. You seemed to have passed safely beyond, but Jagun was unceasing in his sharing of breath with you."

"Thank you," she said, turning to her Nyssomu friend with a grateful smile.

"In time, the Lords of the Air bore your spirit back into your body," Lummomu-Ko said. "Humans from the ship heard our cries and rescued us."

Kyvee Omin thrust himself forward. He was a gray-haired citizen of Var with the face of a prissy bookkeeper, who was nevertheless famed as the most intrepid skipper in the Southern Sea. Kadiya had had to pay him nearly a thousand platinum crowns to get him to take her to the Windlorns when no one else would dare the voyage.

"I commanded that we up anchor and quit that ill-omened place as fast as the galleymen could row," said he. "The Sea Oddlings were building bonfires on the beach and beating the war-summons on their sacred drums. If we had delayed, their large canoes might have caught up with us before we escaped the windless regions near the islands and gained the open sea."

"How long have I slept?" Kadiya asked weakly.

"Twenty hours," Jagun replied.

"The wind is light but fair, now that we are out of the lee of those wretched sea-stacks," the captain added. "We should reach Taloazin Harbor in Zinora in less than seven days."

"Not there! No, we must turn back!" Kadiya's voice broke, and she moaned and put a hand over her eyes. Her head ached as if it would burst asunder. Why must they turn back? She knew there was a reason. A compelling reason —

"There is worse news, Farseer." Jagun came closer to her bunk and she saw that he held something in his hands: her belt and scabbard. "Your talisman — " he began, but could say no more.

Her befuddled wits finally cleared. She realized that the scabbard was empty, and remembered.

"We cannot return to the islands," Kyvee Omin was saying. "I will not risk my vessel in a battle with savages. I am a trader, not the captain of a warship. I agreed only to take you to Council Isle in the Windlorns, and then back to Var. If you have some reason for avoiding Taloazin, then we can put in at Kurzwe or another Zinoran port to replenish our food and water before voyaging easterly. But there can be no turning back."

Kadiya levered herself up to a full sitting position. Her eyes were ablaze and her face contorted with anger as she spoke in a low, grating voice. "We *must* return. I have lost the Three-Lobed Burning Eye! Do you know what that means?"

The captain took a step backward, as from a madwoman. "No, I do not, Lady. Your friends have indicated that it is a calamity, but the mishap is your fault, not mine, and you must see to its redress yourself. I will not risk my ship and crew in a futile attempt to recover your magical sword. While you lay senseless, your Wyvilo friends and I went back briefly to the place where your boats were holed. We quickly determined that your talisman is lost in a great trench between two reefs where the water is thirty fathoms and more in depth. Not even the Aliansa can dive so deep. The talisman is lost forever."

"No," she whispered, her dark eyes closing in pain. "Oh, no!" Beads of sweat glistened on her forehead, and for a long time she was silent. Jagun knelt beside her, holding one of her limp hands in both of his own, his head bowed.

The captain exchanged glances with Lummomu-Ko, then abruptly left the cabin.

When Kadiya opened her eyes again, her expression had changed to one of resolution. She said: "My dear friends, Kyvee Omin was right. I cannot demand that he help me. If he will not return to the Isles, I shall have to find another skipper who will. Fortunately, I still have plenty of money. I will have Kyvee Omin drop me off at this place called Kurzwe. You, of course, may continue the voyage to Var, and then on up the Great Mutar to Ruwenda—"

"No," said the big Wyvilo leader flatly.

Jagun's upstanding ears quivered with indignation and his huge golden eyes were wide. "Farseer, how can you believe that we would abandon you?"

She stared first at one, then the other. "Without my talisman, I am no longer the Lady of the Eyes, no longer worthy to call myself Great Advocate of the Folk. I am no one. Only Kadiya."

She swung her legs over the side of the bunk and lowered them to the deck. The bruises and claw marks of the frustrated assassin discolored her ankles.

"There is only a small chance that I will succeed in recovering the talisman — and an excellent chance that the Aliansa will attempt to finish the murderous job that they bungled on the first try."

"Nevertheless," Lummomu-Ko said, "my Wyvilo brothers and I will stand by you."

Kadiya's eyes were bright with tears. She wobbled a bit as she stood up, and the tall aborigine and the smaller one each took her by the hand. She made her way to a small table in front of the porthole and sat on its bench.

"Thank you, my very dear friends. In time, my sister the Archimage will discover what has happened, even though I can no longer call her. She will surely find some way to help us. Until then, let us busy ourselves by politely picking the brains of Captain Kyvee Omin and his crew. I will begin by making copies of the captain's charts of the region. I can do that even though I am still too shaky to get about."

She looked up at the Wyvilo leader. "Lummomu, you and your warriors interview the seamen about ways one might eke out a living in the Windlorn Isles — the natural foods that grow on the land, the edible sea life and what things are poisonous or dangerous, anything at all they might know about the islands or their people. We will pay those seamen who cooperate."

"And I, Farseer?" Jagun asked.

Her grin was wry. "Learn what you can about the art of sailing, old friend, and I will do the same. For I fear that the only way we will return to the Windlorn Isles is by ourselves."

4

The royal galley rounded the headland into the Bay of Pearls, and immediately the three children were up in the rigging, scrambling as nimbly as tree-varts while their Nyssomu nurse Immu looked on apprehensively from the deck below and made futile appeals for them to come down.

"More ships! The bay is full of great ships!" Crown Prince Nikalon, who was eleven years old, had custody of the small telescope and had climbed the highest mast. "There's two from Imlit, and one from Sobrania, and three flying the banner of Galanar — and look! Four from Raktum! See that big black trireme all arrayed with gilt and flying a hundred flags? It must be the ship of wicked Queen Ganondri of Raktum herself!"

"My turn for the glass!" whined Prince Tolivar. "Niki's had it all morning! I want to see the wicked Queen!" He was eight years old but seemed much younger because of his frailty. When Nikalon refused to relinquish the telescope, he began to weep. "Jan, Jan, make him give it to me!"

"You children come down at once!" Immu called up to them. "You know your mother has forbidden you to endanger yourselves!"

But the royal youngsters ignored the nurse, as they ignored many of Queen Anigel's attempts to restrict their behavior, cheerfully accepting the consequent punishment.

Princess Janeel, who was ten and very mature for her age, said: "Don't cry, Tolo. I'll deal with Niki — the selfish woth!" She clambered close to her older brother and began to tickle his ribs, and the two of them swayed together in the ropes ten ells above the deck, and poor old Immu down below shrieked in horror. But it was the work of an instant for the agile Princess to snatch the telescope from the giggling, helpless Nikalon. Then she swung back to Tolivar, and the two of them shared the instrument while Prince Niki laughed good-naturedly and began to climb higher, toward the crow's nest.

The telescope, a special present for the voyage from their father, King Antar, was not a mere seaman's spyglass. It was a rare magical artifact of the Vanished Ones. Its tube was of a black material that was neither metal nor wood, and on the side were three colored warts that brought the scene viewed close — closer — closest if one pressed them. A larger silver wart enabled the glass to be used at night, although the images seen then were blurry, little more than greenish silhouettes. The telescope seemed more like a living thing than an inanimate object, for it had to be left lying in sunlight, like a plant, if it were to work. Once during the voyage Prince Tolivar had hidden it away in his trunk for a whole day, pretending it was lost, hoping to play with it all by himself without sharing it with his older brother and sister. But when he next tried to look through it, he saw only black-ness, and ran wailing to the King. After chiding him for selfishness, his father had explained how the telescope fed on sunlight, as did many other mysterious devices of the Vanished Ones.

Now Tolo studied the great ship of Queen Regent Ganondri of Raktum. It had three banks of oars — not two as did the flagship of Laboruwenda — and was at least twice as long, with a huge snout at the bow that could be used in ramming enemy vessels. Its mainsail and foresail were painted with the emblem of the pirate state, a stylized golden flame. Tolo was disappointed to see no trace of the dreaded war-machines that flung molten sulfur or red-hot rocks at the ships of Raktum's enemies. Instead, knights in flashing armor and ladies dressed in brilliant colors lounged about the poop royal, where there was a golden awning raised over a gilt chair.

"The wicked Queen must still be abed," Tolo said to his sister. "I see her throne there at the back of the ship, but it's empty. Take a look, Jan."

Princess Janeel peered through the magical tube. "What a beauti-ful ship! The Raktumians must be very rich."

"They're pirates," Tolo pointed out. "Pirates are always rich. I'd like to be a pirate."

"What a silly thing to say. Pirates kill people and steal, and everybody hates them." She turned the telescope toward the exotic Sobranian ship, from the uttermost reaches of the Far West.

"Ralabun the Master of Animals says you'll have to marry the wicked Queen's crookback goblin grandson when you get older." Tolo grinned with naughty satisfaction. "When you're queen of the pirates, you can make me a pirate, too."

Princess Janeel lowered the instrument and glared at her little brother. "I'm never going to marry anyone! And if I was, I certainly wouldn't marry a horrid thing like Ledavardis. Aunt Kadiya says that I can come and live at her secret manor in the Greenmire when I grow up, if I want to. And I do!"

"Oh, no you won't! Princes and princesses can't do as they please like ordinary people. Niki's going to be King of Laboruwenda, and he'll have to marry another royal. So will you. But I'm only an extra prince. I can be a pirate if I want to! . . . Now give me back the telescope. I want to see if the Sobranians really have feathers like Ralabun says."

Janeel thrust the thing at him angrily and began to climb down the shrouds. Boys! What did they know? All the same, when she reached the safety of the deck and Immu, she brushed aside the Nyssomu nurse's scoldings and also her suggestion that they go into the saloon for a cool drink, and drew her over to the ship's rail behind some lashed-down boxes of cargo. There the elderly Nyssomu woman and the Princess had complete privacy, and Janeel asked:

"Is it true that I'll have to marry Ledavardis of Raktum when I'm older?"

The aboriginal nurse broke out in peals of laughter. "Of course not! Who's been filling your head with such tosh, sweeting?"

"Tolo," Janeel growled. "He had it of Ralabun."

Immu's inhuman face creased in indignation and the upstanding ears above her lawn headdress trembled like windblown leaves. "Ralabun Ralabun Ralabun! I shall box his skull until his eyes pop! That flaplip fool should tend to mucking out the royal fronial-stalls and leave matters of state to his betters!"

"Then it isn't true?"

Immu took gentle hold of the Princess's face with her three-digit hands. The two of them were almost the same height, and the nurse's enormous yellow eyes looked straight into the hazel eyes of her young charge. "I pledge to you by the Lords of the Air that your dear parents would rather die than see you married to the Goblin Kinglet of Raktum. The rumor that silly Ralabun passed to your little brother is one put about by enemies of the Two Thrones — Lord Osorkon and his ilk. It is a lie."

And she kissed Janeel, then began fussing with the girl's plaits, which had come loose from their pinning during her tarriance in the rigging. Jan was not an exceptional beauty like her mother, but her face was pleasant, dusted with freckles, and her eyes wide set and intelligent. She had unusually lustrous hair, the rich golden brown color of a blok-nut shell, which fell nearly to her waist when it was not braided to keep it out of the way.

"Is it true that princesses cannot choose their husbands?" Janeel persisted.

Immu was brisk. "As to that, some do and some do not. When your aunt Haramis was Crown Princess of Ruwenda, before she became the White Lady and before the Two Thrones were united, her hand was sought by the evil King Voltrik of Labornok. This match was refused by King Kreyn and Queen Kalanthe, since it would have meant the swallowing up of Ruwenda by Labornok — which is a far different thing from the Union of Two Thrones. Princess Haramis agreed to marry a Prince of Var, even though she did not love him, because this Prince was willing to become co-ruler of Ruwenda. Thus, your aunt placed the welfare of her country above her own happiness, as was her duty."

"But Aunt Haramis renounced the throne!"

"Yes. And the crown passed to your Aunt Kadiya, who also renounced it, and then to your dear mother, who was far better suited to be Queen than either of her sisters. By then the brutal Voltrik was dead and Antar, your father, was King of Labornok. Your mother and father loved each other very much and married, and now they rule both kingdoms, spending the Dry Time at the court of Ruwenda at the Citadel and the Rains in the Derorguila palace in Labornok."

"But will Niki be able to choose a princess of his own to love and make his queen? And may I choose my prince?"

Immu hesitated. "I hope that it will be true, little darling. I hope it with all my heart. But the future is known only to the Triune God and the Lords of the Air who are his servants, and it is best for little girls not to worry over such things. You will marry no one for a long, long time . . . But now, let us go to the wardrobe cabin! We will be docking in Taloazin Harbor in only a few hours, and we'll pick out a beautiful gown for you and dress your hair with a jeweled diadem. We must show the haughty citizens of Zinora that the royal house of Laboruwenda is far more splendid than that of their puffed-up little kingdom."

Crown Prince Nikalon shared the lofty perch atop the foremast with a young sailor named Korik who had become his friend during the two-week voyage from Derorguila. Unlike the rest of the Labornoki crew, who bowed and scraped and styled him High Lord—while at the same time calling him a sore pest behind his back and denying him access to the more interesting parts of the ship that Queen Anigel had forbidden to the royal children—Korik had taken pity on the bored lad and showed him everything from the chain locker in the forepeak to the sternpost gudgeon. He had surreptitiously taught the Prince how to climb the rigging (and Niki had taught his sister and little brother), and welcomed him to share secretly his watches in the crow's nest, keeping an eye out for rocks and shoals and other vessels as the flotilla sailed through the Isles of Engi, along the coast of Var, and down to Zinora. Korik had explained how the ropes and sails worked, and why the ship tacked when the wind blew from a certain direction, and why they lowered sail during storms, and why free men made better galleymen than slaves, and answered a myriad other questions as best he could.

Niki, in gratitude, had told Korik that he would make him an admiral when he became King. At this the young seaman laughed, saying that admirals had to spend too much time at court, and going to boring council meetings and drawing up tedious papers. All he wanted was to be captain of his own ship.

"And then," he told Niki, "I would be the first to sail to the farthest parts of the known world — beyond Sobrania, even beyond the Land of the Feathered Barbarians. I would sail completely around the world, through the frozen islands of the terrible Aurora Sea, skirting the edge of the Sempiternal Icecap, until I reached the cold deserts above Tuzamen. And then I would come down through the Flame-Girt Isles, and defy the pirates of Raktum, and return safely home again to Derorguila."

Niki had gaped at him. "Has no one ever done this before?"

"Nobody," Korik said proudly. "They are all afraid of the icebound Aurora Sea and the sea monsters. But I am not afraid." Then he had given Niki an intent look. "A voyage of exploration like that would cost a lot of money, but the king who sponsored it would be remembered forever. And I would bring him back rare plants and animals and other fine things — and perhaps even knowledge of some secret new ruined city of the Vanished Ones having more wondrous treasures than any yet discovered."

"I will sponsor the voyage!" Prince Niki had declared. But the sailor had only laughed, pointing out that the boy would not be King for years and years, since King Antar was a young man in robust good health, and by the time he got old and died, Nikalon would surely forget his promise.

"I will *not* forget," the Crown Prince had said . . .

Now, as Niki stared out over the bright water toward the shore where the capital of Zinora lay, he mused over what it would be like to be a youthful king like Yondrimel of Zinora, who could commission explorations or do other great deeds. What must the King of Zinora be feeling, on the verge of being honored at his coronation by all the world's rulers? Of course, eighteen-year-old Yondrimel was already ruler of his nation and the crown was his by right of inheritance. But the ceremony was intended to affirm his reign in the eyes of the other nations, and show them all that he was a true sovereign — not a wretched puppet like the boy-King Ledavardis of Raktum, who was nearly as old as Yondrimel but denied his throne by his powerful grandmother. King Antar had explained that the Zinoran King also hoped to make alliances at this coronation that would strengthen his throne.

Even though he was only eleven, Prince Nikalon already understood how important alliances were. Laboruwenda had alliances with Var and the Island Principality of Engi on the Peninsula. They traded freely, and combined to fight pirates that threatened each other's ships, and refused to give sanctuary to criminals crossing borders. King Antar and Queen Anigel hoped to make a similar alliance with King Yondrimel of Zinora. But so did Raktum, the greatest enemy of Laboruwenda, and it had already sent Yondrimel thousands of platinum crowns and many caskets of jewels as coronation presents. Niki wondered whether the young monarch of Zinora would succumb to the blandishments of the pirate Queen. She was so very rich!

They were sailing nearer to the Raktumian flotilla now. The gilded wood on the flanks of the huge trireme flagship shone brilliantly in the sun and the hundreds of colored banners hung on its rigging made a brave show. The other three black vessels were almost as handsomely decorated. Oh, yes. Raktum was rich! Following the coronation, there was to be a tremendous banquet and lavish entertainment, and it was rumored that most of the cost was being borne by wicked Raktum.

Niki had asked his father and mother why the other rulers did not ostracize the pirate nation. But they had only sighed and told him that great matters of state were not so simple as everyday affairs, and he would understand better when he was older.

Somehow, Niki doubted very much that he would.

Prince Tolivar finally tired of looking through the magic telescope while hanging uncomfortably from the scratchy rigging and had a grand idea: He would climb down and offer to let his mother borrow the wonderful toy. For some reason the Queen had seemed very sad at breakfast time, and this might cheer her up. Holding the narrow tube safely in his teeth, the little boy slid down the ladderlike web of rope, hopped onto the deck, and went dodging and skipping toward the stern. Rounding the midships saloon, he nearly ran headlong into

Lord Penapat and his father the King, who were fishing. Uncle Peni's big arms scooped him up as he tried to escape and held him high in the air, wriggling like a sucbri freshly plucked from its shell.

"Have you seen Mother?" the little Prince asked the King. "I thought she would like to look at the other ships and at Zinora through my telescope."

"She is on the fantail with Lady Ellinis, working away on some official papers, as usual. You may give her the telescope, but do not stay long and distract her with your chatter."

"I won't, Sire."

The child went galloping off, his fair hair streaming in the breeze, and bluff Penapat shook his great head fondly. "What a spirited lad. He and his royal brother and the little Princess have led the ship's crew a merry chase on this voyage, my Liege."

Laughing, the King agreed. He rebaited his hook and cast it out again. Then his face darkened. "I hope we have not made a mistake bringing them to the coronation. I did not want to do so, but Anigel insisted, saying it was their duty to meet the other royals and learn to socialize with outlanders . . . But there is always a certain danger connected to any affair in which Raktum is involved. And it *is* involved very deeply in this celebration, as we know."

Penapat nodded in agreement. "Zoto be thanked that Queen Ganondri has only an ill-favored grandson and not a granddaughter she might marry off to Yondrimel, or their alliance would be predestined!"

"Raktum is a long way from Zinora, so the matter is of little concrete concern to the Two Thrones, no matter how much Ganondri may sneer at us. But I still have uneasy feelings about coming here with the children."

Penapat rested his elbows on the rail and looked across the water to the Raktumian ships, which were now less than two cable lengths away. The small figures of the seamen and passengers on the Queen Regent's flagship could clearly be seen gawking at the Laboruwendian flotilla.

"Not even Queen Ganondri would be brazen enough to move on us with the royalty and nobility of seven other nations as witnesses to any outrage," Penapat said slowly. "Nor would she chance antagonizing King Yondrimel at his very coronation by causing an incident."

"You are doubtless right, Peni. We should probably be more concerned that the Master of Tuzamen will be there."

The hulking Chamberlain uttered a surprised oath. "Tuzamen? Then it is sending a delegation after all?"

The King nodded. "I had news from our captain before breakfast. That fast little Engian cutter that overtook us early this morning signaled that a single Tuzameni galley trails leisurely behind us. The so-called Master of Tuzamen is beyond doubt aboard. His star-ensign was flying aloft. I think we may safely conclude that an unexpected guest plans to honor young King Yondrimel with attendance at the coronation."

"Zoto's Stones! This explains why Queen Anigel looked so downcast."

"Indeed. This bad news, following upon her hearing from the Archimage that her sister Kadiya had lost her talisman, has filled my beloved wife with foreboding. And I for one can't blame her. She has gone so far as to remove her own talisman from its place inside the Queen's Crown of State and hidden it more securely within her clothing. She says she will not be parted from it day or night for so long as we are in Zinora."

"Sire, might it be possible — in spite of the assurances of our spies to the contrary — that this Portolanus of Tuzamen is the sorcerer Orogastus returned from the dead?"

"God have mercy on us and our people if it is so. Do you remember how the vile magician subverted my father? Changing him from a hard but honest man into a maniac driven by unholy ambition? The sorcerer insinuated himself into the position of Grand Minister of State — but I think he really intended to have himself proclaimed Voltrik's successor after killing me. Even now, his legacy of treachery and subversion persists in the intrigues and uprisings secretly fomented by Lord Osorkon and his friends along the northern marches bordering Raktum. If the sorcerer Orogastus really does live, then Tuzamen can no longer be counted a barbarous backwater. He is sure to use his dark arts to turn it into a powerful nation—"

"—and Queen Ganondri will link with him against us," Penapat finished, grimly.

"Perhaps." Antar studied the great Raktumian galley with narrowed eyes. "But she is no fool, the Queen Regent. And she plays the game by her own rules." The King straightened, smiled, and clapped his old friend on the shoulder. "Cheer up, Peni. A week of feasts and parties and high maneuvering and low skulduggery awaits us in Taloazin. Let's put an end to this profitless fishing and go roust out our brave lords from their gambling and drinking. I would make certain that they all have their armor well-polished and their swords sharp."

Queen Anigel thanked her youngest son warmly for lending her the telescope, then kissed him and commanded him to go to Immu for a bath and fresh clothes. When the lad had gone gloomily on his way, she sighed and lay the instrument aside, unused. "Tolo forgets that I have no need of such things to see afar."

Lady Ellinis, the Domestic Minister of the Two Thrones, looked up from the document she was studying and remarked: "Your talisman, of course, fills that function. As well as others." She was a venerable dame of great common sense, the widow of that Lord Manoparo of the Oathed Companions who had laid down his life in futile defense of Anigel's mother. Ellinis and her three clever sons were the courtiers closest to Anigel, as Lord Penapat and Chancellor Lampiar and Owanon the Lord Marshal were to Antar.

Now the Queen drew forth from her simple blue gown the magical talisman called the Three-Headed Monster, and set it upon her coiffed head. Belying its fearsome name, the talisman was a tiara of bright silvery metal having six small cusps and three larger ones, wrought with designs of flowers and shells and three grotesque faces—one a Skritek howling, another an agonized human with mouth agape in agony, and the third and central face a fierce grimacing being with stylized starry rays for hair. Beneath this was embedded the faintly glowing drop of amber with a tiny fossil Black Trillium in its heart that had been her protective amulet from the moment of her birth until the time she had fulfilled her life-quest and found the talisman.

"Shall we gaze together upon the Pirate Queen?" Anigel suggested to Ellinis. "The talisman will share its clairvoyance if I so request. Only the vision will not be a long one, as its summoning for two requires deep concentration."

The dark eyes of the Lady Minister sparkled with interest. "I would welcome the chance to descry Ganondri, my Liege. I have not seen her in the flesh since four years before your birth, when her late son King Ledamot wed the unfortunate Mashriya of Engi. Ganondri was a beautiful creature then, proud but retiring in demeanor. I know this latter seems incredible, given her reputation today."

"Take my hand," Queen Anigel commanded. Then she closed her eyes and called upon the talisman's magic.

They saw a ship's stateroom hung with costly feather tapestries of Sobrania and furnished with elegant chairs and carved chests inset with mother-of-pearl, polished coral, and semiprecious stones. Some of the coffers were open, spilling costly garments onto the thickly carpeted floor. The Queen Regent sat at a lacquered dressing table with a mounted gilt mirror, frowning impatiently as she tried on necklaces handed her one after another by a timorous lady-in-waiting. Anigel and Ellinis did not hear the Queen or her companion speak, for the vision came only to their mind's eye.

In her old age Ganondri was still a handsome woman, although her gaunt face was seamed by a network of tiny lines and excessively painted with cosmetics. Her mouth was tight set in a peevish purse and her eyes, fringed by long lashes, were green and glittered with malice. Her hair, still abundant and dressed in the overintricate style favored by the women of semibarbarous Raktum, was the pale red of freshly scoured copper, shot through with dramatic white streaks. She wore a gown of sea-green tissue velvet, embroidered with threads of precious metal and edged with rare golden worram fur.

After discarding half a dozen gorgeous pieces of jewelry and mouthing what might have been impatient curses, Ganondri seemed to decide upon a heavy collar of golden gonda-leaves all inset with hundreds of emeralds, with diamonds scattered here and there in imitation of dewdrops. The quaking lady-in-waiting then offered her large pendant earrings to match, but the Queen refused them curtly and took instead smaller ear-studs of gold with a single diamond each.

At this point Anigel let go of Ellinis's hand and the vision that they shared dissolved.

"Ganondri's taste in jewelry remains exquisite," Ellinis remarked in an arch tone, "but I would not care to meet her alone and unarmed in a dark corner of Taloazin Castle. She looked ready to devour her poor handmaid, should the girl offer one more unsuitable necklace."

Anigel was somber. "She is a formidable enemy of our nation whether her temper be good or ill, and she has incited much mischief along our northern frontier. I wonder if young Yondrimel will be foolish enough to trust her?"

"If he does, Madam, he may learn the lesson of the simpleton who thought he could safely roast sausages over the volcano!"

Anigel sighed and gathered up the papers she had finished with. "I beg you to take these to Lord Lampiar for me, Elli. Remind him that Antar and I have yet to sign a message of felicitation that must accompany our gifts to Yondrimel. If the scribe has not finished drawing it up, he must be made to hasten. The presents must be sent on ahead of our party as soon as we dock in Taloazin."

Ellinis rose and collected her own work, as well as that of the Queen. It was clear to her that Anigel was troubled and deeply depressed at the prospect of the upcoming visit. She laid a gentle hand on the younger woman's shoulder. "Shall I send Sharice with some sweet wine and wafers to refresh you?"

"Thank you, but no. I must think over certain matters with a clear head."

The old dame smiled sympathetically. "Do not think me tiresome, Madam — but I must urge you to take time before our landing to freshen yourself and put on fine robes."

"Yes, yes," said Anigel impatiently. "I will not disgrace our nation by appearing a royal frump."

"You would be radiantly beautiful if you appeared in a tattered shift," Ellinis said, unquelled. "But our people would be disappointed, and our foes would rejoice." She bowed and departed, leaving the Queen alone at the little table beneath the striped awning.

No seamen or other persons were visible from this part of the fantail. The wind had dropped off almost completely once they had rounded the headland, and now two great banks of oars propelled the Laboruwendian galley through the calm Bay of Pearls. The other ships were also using their oars, and the Raktumian trireme and its three accompanying vessels had pulled far ahead.

"And what of the Tuzameni?" Anigel asked herself. Again she closed her eyes and commanded the talisman. This time the vision was much broader in compass and included all natural sounds. She seemed to be a seabird skimming the waves as she approached a solitary four-masted vessel painted white. Its snowy greatsails bore no device, but atop the mainmast flew a black banner with a multi-rayed silver star.

"Show me Portolanus!" Anigel besought her talisman. The vision focused on the quarterdeck of the Tuzameni ship, where the captain and several officers were grouped behind the helmsman.

In the midst of the officers was a blurred shape having the contours of a man.

"Show me Orogastus!"

The ship image faded—but what took its place was a chaotic whirlpool composed of different shades of gray. As Anigel exclaimed in frustration this began to brighten and shrink until at last there was only a single dazzling spark of white light, which blinked and went out.

"Show me Kadiya."

Another ship, this one a fast merchant-trader flying the flag of Var. It was fast approaching the dingy little Zinoran port of Kurzwe, which lay some four hundred leagues west of the capital, Taloazin. Kadiya was lying prone along the bowsprit, holding a rope with but a single hand, while the sea rushed by many ells beneath her. Viewed from a nearer vantage point, Kadiya looked more like a poor castaway than the indomitable Lady of the Eyes. She wore a salt-stained leather gambeson and her hair was uncombed and stringy from sea-spray. But her swollen eyes and the runnels of moisture on her cheeks were not a consequent of spray, and Anigel's heart nearly broke as she commiserated with her forlorn sister.

Poor Kadi! She was the most fiery and courageous of the three of them — never vacillating or doubting her own abilities like Haramis, never preoccupied with work or stodgy like Anigel herself. It was true that Kadiya often proposed overly simple solutions to difficult problems, and that she sometimes let her temper get the better of her. But no human being loved the aborigines more, nor stood ready to lay down her life for them if it were necessary.

And now she was humiliated by the loss of her talisman, in despair as she faced the prospect of returning to the dangerous islands with companions who were brave, but knew almost nothing of sailing or survival in a maritime clime. Unable to communicate with her sisters yet certain that they had discovered her terrible loss, she did not know that Anigel and Haramis had already worked out a scheme for retrieving the lost talisman once the coronation was over and done with.

Have courage, dear Kadi! Hara and I will help you recover your Three-Lobed Burning Eye.

Did the dejected figure lift its head? Did her face lighten? Was it possible that she heard? Anigel prayed that it were so. Kadiya wiped her eyes and hauled herself up, so that she straddled the bowsprit instead of lying perilously along it. Her tears stopped flowing and a new thoughtful expression came upon her countenance.

Yes, Kadi, yes! Remember that we are Three and we are One!

Then Anigel commanded her talisman a final time: "Show me Haramis."

Lifting her head from a great chart she studied in her library, the Archimage looked at her youngest triplet sister and smiled.

"Feeling woeful, Ani?"

"I confess I have just been descrying Kadiya, and the vision of her bitter remorse pierced me to the heart. I hope that you are right — that my own talisman, taken to the place where hers sank into the sea, will command the Three-Lobed Burning Eye to return to its mistress's hand."

"All will be well," said the Archimage. "Our sister did not lose her talisman through carelessness but only through misadventure. No guilt attaches to her, and the magic that infuses her talisman and bonds it to her remains intact."

"Still," Anigel said, "I feel uneasy not going after it at once."

"We argued and settled this point before. Your presence is required at the coronation for the sake of your country's honor. Kadiya's talisman is safe enough in the depths. Anyone who attempts to touch it without her permission will surely die, and Portolanus with his star-box is nowhere near to it. Very likely, he does not even know that Kadi has lost it."

"Yes. You are surely right."

"It will take some time for Kadiya to return to the islands, even if she is able to hire a Zinoran boat. If she and her companions go by themselves, they will have to proceed with great caution, remaining within sight of land until they reach the northernmost of the Windlorns and then threading their way down to Council Isle. The place is over eight hundred leagues from Kurzwe even by the shortest route. You will certainly be able to overtake them in your fast ships even if you stay the entire coronation week."

"Yes, I agree. It will be easy enough to track her with the Three-Headed Monster . . . I presume you still have had no success in bespeaking Kadi."

"Unfortunately, no," Haramis admitted. "I have tried time and again without result. My predecessor, Binah, was certainly able to bespeak humans and Folk across the leagues, but she had many more years of practice than I. When Kadiya is without her talisman, I cannot speak to her, although I can see and hear her clearly."

Anigel was hesitant. "As I viewed her just now I could not help but share her misery and wish her good cheer. She — she seemed to have some inkling of my thoughts."

"Is that so! Perhaps it is your deep love and sense of compassion that give impetus to your mental speech. I confess that I have been vexed with Kadi of late, and no doubt this affects my concentration. Sometimes I despair that I shall ever learn to be a proper Archimage. I study and study, but when it comes to using magic, I fail too often."

"What nonsense! The old White Lady *chose* you."

"Perhaps she only picked the least flawed in a basket of unpromising fruit . . . But I should not bother you with my plaguey self-doubts. I shall keep a sharp eye on all of the participants in the upcoming drama, and I will inform you if any nefarious schemes seem about to blossom. Blessings on thee, little Sister, and fare thee well."

As the vision of Haramis faded, so did Anigel's glow of good humor and hope. In a brown study, she stared over the ship's stern, beyond the three other Laboruwendian vessels and on to the horizon and the tall headland they had recently rounded.

Another ship was just now entering the wide Bay of Pearls. A ship so white that it was easily visible even though it must be five leagues distant. She could not take her eyes off it, and followed its progress as though mesmerized, until King Antar came a quarter hour later, to kiss away her unease and take her off to the midday meal.

5

Little Prince Tolivar, out of sorts after enduring the lengthy Zinoran coronation ceremony at the Temple of the Mother, flew into a wild temper tantrum and refused to let Immu dress him when he learned that his older brother, Nikalon, would wear a miniature sword at the coronation ball, while he would not.

"Niki always gets the best things, just because he's Crown Prince," the eight-year-old wept. "It's not fair! If I can't have a sword, I won't go!"

Then he ran away, forcing the domestic servants to pursue him upstairs and down, and in and out of the scores of rooms in the Laboruwendian embassy at Taloazin, while the coach waited outside and the King and Queen fumed at the delay. A pair of valiant footmen finally hauled the boy out of his hiding place in the wine cellar and held him tight, still shrieking, as Immu put him into his purple brocade suit. By then King Antar was so angry with his rebellious little son that by way of punishment he declared that Tolo would not get to use the magic telescope on the voyage home.

"You hate me!" the furious boy cried out to his father, tears pouring down his cheeks. "You always treat Niki better than me. I'll run away to Raktum and be a pirate, and *then* you'll wish you'd let me wear a sword!"

The distraught parents bustled Tolo and the other two children into the coach and had the driver whip up the fronials. As it was, they were the last royal party to arrive at the new riverside pleasure palace where the ball was to be held. In the crowded antechamber of the ballroom, Anigel and Antar put the children temporarily into the charge of Lord Penapat and his wife Lady Sharice, then hurried off with an anxious Zinoran usher to find their places in the Procession of Felicitation.

"Why can't we go in with Mama and Papa?" Tolo demanded petulantly.

"Because it's not our turn yet," retorted Prince Nikalon. "Stop acting like a spoiled brat."

"You three royal children will go in after the kings and queens and other leaders," Lady Sharice said brightly. "Now come along with me and Uncle Peni. We have a special place where we can stand and watch the new King of Zinora greet his most honored guests."

"That doesn't sound like much fun," Tolo muttered.

"It's not supposed to be fun," Princess Janeel told him. "It's your duty. After the procession is over, we can eat and dance and enjoy ourselves. But first you have to behave yourself for a little while."

The Princess took one of Tolo's hands and Lady Sharice took the other, and between them they dragged the little boy into an enclosure fenced off with blue satin ropes. There, a crowd of other gorgeously dressed royal siblings and exalted nobles had gathered, both children and adults, most of them chattering and giggling. Tolo, his face set in a black glower, plumped himself down on the polished marble floor in the midst of the oblivious throng.

"I'm going to sit right here," he said, ignoring Lady Sharice's scandalized pleas.

Lord Penapat bent over and began scolding the boy, but an instant later he broke off and straightened, Tolo and his naughtiness forgotten, as someone hissed loudly:

"The sorcerer! Look — it's Portolanus of Tuzamen coming in!"

Tolo was on his feet in an instant. "Uncle Peni, lift me up! I want to see the sorcerer!"

"Certainly, lad." Penapat swung the boy to his shoulder. "There he is, just coming in the door. Zoto's Tripes! What a sight he is!"

"Ohhh!" Tolo had gone wide-eyed with awe. "Will he do magic tonight?"

"I'm sure he will," said Lady Sharice, uttering a giddy little laugh. "Oh, yes. I'm *quite* sure he will!"

"It must be very fine to be a sorcerer." Tolo sighed. "Nobody could ever make a sorcerer do something he didn't want to . . . Perhaps I'll be a sorcerer when I grow up instead of a pirate."

Lord Penapat put the boy down, laughing. "What an outlandish notion!"

"Just you wait," Tolo said. But then he was caught up in the excitement of the coronation ball's beginning, and he forgot all about what he had said.

Portolanus had deliberately refrained from attending the preliminary round of galas and parties that had preceded the coronation, and he also stayed well in the background during the ceremony itself, so surrounded by his aides and courtiers that few people got more than a brief glimpse of him. Only at this lavish ball, where the rulers of the various nations would come forward in a solemn parade to offer good wishes to newly crowned King Yondrimel, would the self-styled Master of Tuzamen finally make a public appearance.

All alone, dressed in fantastic and inappropriate garments, he now shuffled to a place at the very end of the glittering Procession of Felicitation, seeming not to hear the whispers, nor to notice that the eyes of the dignitaries and nobles in the ballroom were fixed mostly upon him, and not on King Yondrimel.

An orchestra of a hundred musicians was playing. The huge room had walls of wine-red damask, gilded pilasters, and huge mirrors framed in semiprecious bloodstone, jasper, and onyx. The scene was illuminated by great golden chandeliers bearing thousands of sparkling tapers. Tall casement windows on either side of the hall were thrown wide open to admit perfumed breezes from the gardens.

It was early evening. Nearly a thousand special guests had come to the pleasure palace situated on the bank of the River Zin, which had been constructed especially for the occasion. Most of the attendees were noble Zinorans, decked out in the costly pearls that were the nation's pride. Among the visitors, the Raktumians were most numerous. Many of the pirate men and women wore ornate helmets and cuirasses studded with jewels, rather than formal robes.

Queen Anigel and King Antar were among the last to take their designated places in the procession.

"I see no resemblance to Orogastus in this man Portolanus," Antar murmured to his wife as he studied the bizarre figure of the Master of Tuzamen. "The sorcerer I knew twelve years ago was handsome of face and stalwart of body. This fellow has a stooped and awkward mien, and his features are twisted in a manner almost comical. There is nothing commanding or menacing about him at all. He looks more like a mountebank than a sorcerer, wearing that silly pointed cap with the diamond star perched on top, pressed down so far on his head that his very ears are bent!"

The Tuzameni ruler was indeed far from imposing. His scraggly beard and ridiculously long mustaches were bright yellow and excessively curled and pomaded. He was clad in a gaudy green robe with orange stripes, so capacious that he seemed to be wearing a tent. Half the ballroom was snickering at him, but he was supremely unconcerned, grinning and winking clownishly at those on either side, and wiggling his gnarled fingers in an arch gesture of greeting.

"Portolanus did not conquer Tuzamen through sleight of hand," Queen Anigel whispered with some asperity. "I agree that from this distance he does not seem to resemble the old Orogastus, and he shows no aura of dark enchantment such as Haramis bade me watch for. But many years have gone by and he must have suffered great privation out on the icecap. His appearance could have changed greatly. I must get a closer look at him after we've spoken to King Yondrimel. Thus far, Portolanus has been as elusive as a lingit in a lamplit closet."

A loud fanfare rang out.

"Oh, dear, here we go." Anigel sighed. "Is my crown straight? It's so heavy, I can hardly wait to take it off."

"You are the most glorious Queen in the room," Antar assured her. He had declined to wear the ornate parade armor and bejeweled monster-helm that were the traditional royal regalia of Labornok. His platinum-and-diamond diadem was small and almost modest in comparison with the great Queen's Crown of Ruwenda, which blazed with emeralds and rubies and was surmounted by a diamond sunburst centered with a great nodule of amber. In the amber's heart was a fossil Black Trillium, emblem of the little swampy country that had so improbably gained victory over its more powerful neighbor — resulting in the Union of the Two Thrones. Anigel and Antar were both wearing blue — his robe as dark as midnight, girded by a sapphire-studded swordbelt, and hers the rich azure of the Dry Time sky, with traditional lattice-smocking and seed-gem embroidery on the sleeves, bodice, and train-panels. She wore a necklace of smaller pieces of trillium-amber, decorated with cabochon sapphires that exactly matched her eyes.

The rulers now advancing toward the young King of Zinora were lined up according to a strict order of precedence, with the most ancient nation leading and the newest — Tuzamen — coming last. First to pay their respects were the Eternal Prince Widd and the Eternal Princess Raviya of the tiny Island Principality of Engi, a nation so scantily endowed and sparsely populated that even the pirates of Raktum scorned to raid it. Engi nevertheless prided itself upon being the most venerable royal house in the known world. Its sailors were also the most skillful, and the Eternal Prince, for all his eccentric airs, was a shrewd old buffer who had mediated many a Peninsular dispute.

Anigel smiled as she noted that dear old Raviya wore the same slightly tatty maroon brocade gown she had worn to Prince Tolo's name giving eight years earlier. Widd had his coronet jauntily askew and calmly gave his princely fundament a good scratch as he offered Yondrimel a few pithy words of advice.

Next came King Fiomadek and Queen Ila of Var — he rotund and pompous of manner and she sweetly maternal — both of them so stiff with jewels that Anigel marveled that they could stand straight. As the neighbor immediately east of Zinora, prosperous Var had looked with apprehension at the young King's dalliance with Raktum and Tuzamen. Fiomadek was nervously cordial and nattered on overlong, while Ila caused the young King's smile to harden when she urged him not to delay choosing a bride.

Then it was the turn of Anigel and Antar. Because Ruwenda was the elder nation, Anigel spoke first, confining herself to brief good wishes. Antar was more specific:

"We wish you a long and prosperous reign, Brother, and we wish nothing more than to maintain the good relations that prevailed between Zinora and Laboruwenda during the reign of your late father. The Two Thrones, together with the monarchs of Engi and Var, would gladly welcome you into the Peninsular Concord if such be your wish."

Yondrimel was tall for his eighteen years, with watery blue eyes that darted from side to side as if he expected the immediate arrival of someone more important. He had an annoying habit of continually moistening his thin lips with the tip of his tongue. Anigel and Antar had disliked him at first sight. He had been cool in his welcome to them six days earlier, and clearly disappointed that they had not brought more costly gifts. For his coronation he was dressed all in soft white leather and cloth-of-gold, and his diadem was also gold, inset with countless pearls of different colors. Pearls also ornamented his baldric, the scabbard of his sword, and the sheath of his dagger. On a chain around his neck he wore a magnificent iridescent pink pearl nearly the size of a griss egg.

"I thank you for your kind words," Yondrimel said blandly. "Although my Royal Father of happy memory declined to join your alliance for reasons that seemed valid to him, I will ponder most carefully your worthy invitation and give it the same deliberate consideration that I give to the proposals of other nations of good will."

Antar and Anigel nodded, still smiling, and began their recessional to a small alcove where the rulers were being offered refreshment. Behind them, the barbarian chief Denombo who called himself Emperor of Sobrania strode up, clad in amazing robes of multicolored feathers, and began to harangue the young King. The music was deliberately loud, so that spectators more than three or four ells away could not hear the exchanges between the King and his royal well-wishers.

"Yondrimel did not seem to welcome your invitation to join the Concord overmuch," Anigel whispered to her husband. "I fear Prince Widd and King Fiomadek were right when they suggested that he has dangerous ambitions."

Antar's face was grim. "If Zinora is truly denied trade with the

Windlorn Isles by hostile aborigines, then its fortunes will greatly decline. Var is a tempting consolation prize."

"Would Yondrimel be such a fool as to defy the entire Peninsula and invade Var?"

"Not on his own, surely. He does not have enough ships, and to go by land is impossible. But if Raktum should join with him —"

"Then we of the Peninsular Concord would have to fight beside our ally." Anigel's fingers tightened upon her husband's arm. "Oh, Antar! We have enjoyed peace for so long . . . I fear the people of Ruwenda would have scant heart for fighting a war on behalf of wealthy Var."

"And if we send our loyal Labornoki knights and men-at-arms south, then our northern frontier would be an open door, with only Osorkon and the other marcher lords of dubious loyalty left to defend us from possible invasion by Raktum. The land forces of Queen Ganondri are insignificant compared to her great armada of ships, but who can tell what armies equipped with magical weapons the Master of Tuzamen might put at her disposal?"

"My darling, we shall have to do something about Osorkon and his two-faced faction as soon as we return to Derorguila," Anigel decided. "We must postpone the court's seasonal move to Ruwenda Citadel until matters in Labornok are settled."

They had reached the refreshment alcove, but instead of partaking of the elegant display of food and drink, they joined the rulers of Engi and Var, who were unashamedly gawking at the continuing procession and whispering among themselves.

The vulgar Sobranian Emperor had completed his felicitations and stomped away with a smug look on his red-bearded face. Behind his back, Yondrimel was licking his lips like mad and seeming to shrink into his coronation robes as he confronted a stout, middle-aged woman with a kindly smile. Queen Jiri of the prosperous western nation of Galanar still had six unmarried daughters, in addition to the three she had already married off to the rulers of Imlit and Okamis.

"Now he's in for it," hissed the Eternal Prince Widd in unconcealed delight. The King and Queen of Var joined in making snide comments about Yondrimel's prospect of remaining unwed for long in the face of Jiri's redoubtable matchmaking. The Queen of Galanar spoke long to the young King, who was seen to wipe sweat from the royal palms and brow with a silk handkerchief after she finally kissed him on the cheek and took her leave.

Then came the two simply dressed Duumvirs of the Imlit Republic and the President of Okamis (with their gorgeous Galanari wives), whose remarks were mercifully brief. They were followed by the Queen Regent of Raktum and her grandson King Ledavardis, who was making his first appearance at a Zinoran function, having been "indisposed" earlier.

"Oh dear, he *is* an ill-favored lad, is he not?" Queen Jiri whispered to Anigel. "I could not make up my mind whether to honor Raktum with a betrothal proposition — they *are* pirates, after all, and one must uphold one's standards. But seeing the Goblin Kinglet in the flesh makes me bless my indecision."

Ledavardis was a dismaying sight, all the more so for standing at the right hand of his splendid grandmother, who wore crimson velvet encrusted with gold, diamonds, and rubies, and a crown twice as massive as that of Ruwenda. At sixteen, the King of Raktum was sturdy but very short, with broad shoulders and a twisted spine. His head, crowned with a simple golden circlet, was too large for the thin neck that bore it, and his features, except for sad brown eyes as large and luminous as those of a night-caroler, were coarsely made. He was dressed all in shining gold-shot black silk, which served only to emphasize his deformities, and said nothing as Queen Ganondri and Yondrimel greeted each other effusively. When the other young King attempted to draw Ledavardis out, he murmured only a few words, made an awkward gesture of salute, and moved with surprising agility toward the alcove. Ganondri, clearly vexed with him, perforce had to cut short her own conversation and follow.

She sailed into the refreshment room with her chin high, ignoring the knot of other rulers who swiftly made way for her, and went directly to the crystal wine-ewers, where she filled a large goblet. The uncouth Emperor of Sobrania, the only one who had thus far partaken of the refreshments, ceased stuffing his mouth with broiled fowl and studied Ganondri's contempt-filled face for a moment. Then, seeming to lose his appetite, he joined the others watching the Master of Tuzamen.

Portolanus took his time approaching Yondrimel. The diamonds topping his pointed hat flashed in the candlelight as he tottered and slouched across the white marble floor with aggravating slowness, continuing to bestow mocking salutes and droll grimaces upon the spectators. They were now openly chuckling and giving other evidence that they were glad that the tedious opening acts of the festivity were over, and the star turn finally come on stage.

King Yondrimel frowned, then immediately recomposed his features, moistening his lips over and over again as if to prevent their cracking as he smiled at the approaching apparition. He lifted both hands in a gesture of warm friendliness shown theretofore only to Ganondri and Ledavardis.

Portolanus suddenly lifted his right arm.

The music mysteriously stopped, cut off in midphrase.

The crowd gasped and held its breath.

The sorcerer held a golden rod with a faceted crystal at the end that gave off prismatic flashes. This he thrust at the King in a parody of a sabreur's lunge, grinning all the while. Yondrimel drew back in astonished apprehension.

"Ah-*hah!*" cackled the Master of Tuzamen. "Afraid, are you?"

He lunged again, and there was a bright flash and a puff of smoke. A knee-high mound of small, shining platinum coins appeared before the surprised young monarch, tinkling as the occasional crown slid to the floor. The watching rulers and the crowd of nobles and courtiers exclaimed in amazement.

Yondrimel had swallowed the indignant words he was about to utter when the sorcerer impugned his courage. Smacking his lips, he began to thank Portolanus for the great heap of money — but he fell silent as the zany Master suddenly began to whirl like a top, his bulky green-and-orange garment ballooning around him. The spinning wizard seemed to become a blurred ball — except that his conical hat surmounted by its diamond star remained motionless. Then the ball collapsed into a perfectly flat puddle of fabric, and the hat sat ridiculously upright at the center.

Portolanus had disappeared.

"Zoto's Teeth," muttered Antar. "He is nothing but a carnival conjurer!"

Something was happening under the striped cloth. The pointed hat trembled. The fabric began to ripple in concentric waves, and then it humped up in great irregular puffs, inflating again like a balloon while the hat was tossed wildly about at the top of it. The striped sphere became twice the height of a man and the crowd shrieked with delighted anticipation, mingled not a little with fear. Inside the balloon a light waxed and waned in brilliance and the bouncing hat abruptly inverted itself, so that the sparkling diamond star was poised above the cloth.

The star thrust down, puncturing the glowing balloon. There was a dazzling flash and a loud explosion. Everyone shrieked—and when they regained their sight, they beheld Portolanus again, dressed as he had been in the beginning, slapping his knees and crowing with laughter. After a stunned moment King Yondrimel began to grin and applaud, and the nobles and courtiers hastened to follow suit.

"A cheap charlatan's ruse," Antar said to Anigel, and he turned away and would have gone to get a glass of wine.

But the sorcerer cried: "Stop!" And pointed his crystal wand.

All eyes in the ballroom followed the wand's lead to King Antar. There was abrupt silence. Antar turned slowly and regarded Portolanus with a face immobile and forbidding as stone. One hand rested upon the pommel of his sword. "Did you address me, magician?"

"Indeed I did, great King of Laboruwenda." The tone was wheedling. "If you would condescend to approach, the Master of Tuzamen will most happily demonstrate marvels that might impress even your regal skepticism."

Anigel took hold of her husband's arm, whispering anxiously: "No, my love! Don't go!"

But Antar shook free of her and strode back into the center of the ballroom, where Yondrimel stood amid the welter of scattered treasure, his mouth hanging open and his darting eyes for once riveted with attention. A sudden strong gust of wind made the gauzy window-drapes billow, and there was a distant rumble of thunder. Another much louder thunderclap occurred immediately, and then a great stroke of lightning lit the riverside gardens, and the pleasure palace shook with the teeth-rattling crash of thunder that accompanied it.

The sorcerer smiled. "Besides the small amusements I have already shown, I am prepared to bring you more spectacular demonstrations of power. For instance, this storm out of season."

Another series of lightning bolts revealed the garden as bright as day. Along the formal paths bounced eerie glowing globes of blue fire the size of melons. More fireballs danced about the masts of the tall ships moored along the riverside quay. Before the astounded crowd could react, one of these things flew in through a window, hissing loudly, and leapt to poise itself on the uplifted wand of Portolanus.

"By the Flower!" gasped Anigel. "He commands the storm!"

The sorcerer's twisted face beamed upon her, lit hideously by the ball of crackling blue lightning above him. "Oh, yes. And much more besides, proud Queen. I command rewards for my friends and the very opposite for my foes and detractors. I admonish all of you to remember that."

Then, casually, he tossed the fulgurant ball at Antar.

With an oath, the King drew his sword and struck a mighty blow at the uncanny missile. At the moment the blade met blue fire, both Antar and Portolanus vanished in twin clouds of smoke.

Anigel screamed and rushed forward, pulling her talisman coronet from her gown and holding it before her with both hands. "Stay, Portolanus! I command you to stay and restore my husband to me!"

The palace was assaulted by yet another great blast of lightning and thunder, and all within were shouting as the rising wind buffeted the chandeliers and the tapers began to blow out. Anigel suppressed a sob as it became evident that the talisman was not going to bring Antar or the sorcerer back. She turned furiously toward King Yondrimel. The royal youth had gone white with terror and his courtiers and guards began rushing to his side.

Anigel stood before him, talisman held high. The trillium-amber inset in it blazed like a tiny sun, and the amber atop her great Crown of State and in the necklace she wore glowed scarcely less bright.

"Order Portolanus to bring King Antar back!" she shouted in a terrible voice to Yondrimel. "You treacherous wretch! I command you!"

"I can't bring him back!" the young King wailed. "Don't hurt me! I didn't know — I had no idea — they never told me that —"

"Behold!" bellowed the Emperor of Sobrania. "Out in the river! The Raktumian pirate ships have set sail! And the wizard's craft as well! I'll lay you platinum crowns to plar-pits they've kidnapped Antar!"

Everyone rushed to that side of the ballroom to look. The almost continual flashes of lightning showed five galleys moving into midstream and heading down toward the estuary, their sails swollen by the storm-wind. Four of the ships were black and one was white. It took only seconds for the crowd to realize that the Tuzameni and Raktumian guests had all melted away during the magic show.

"After the bastards!" cried redoubtable Queen Jiri of Galanar.

The nobles and knights of Laboruwenda, Var, and Engi took up the cry, followed immediately by the indignant worthies of Imlit and Okamis. There was a great commotion. Emperor Denombo and his feather-decked Sobranians flourished their two-pronged swords and went out the ballroom windows howling their war cry, trampling through the flower beds on their way to the docks. Others followed after by more conventional routes, heedless that their fine clothes were being soaked by the heavy rain that had begun to fall.

Anigel, with Lady Ellinis and Eternal Princess Raviya and Queen Ila of Var trying to comfort her, still stood transfixed in the center of the emptying ballroom. King Yondrimel had disappeared, as had most of his compatriots. Some of the younger royal children began to whimper. The elderly guests, as well as those women who had not gone off with the warriors, gathered in a sympathetic group about the Laboruwendian Queen.

Anigel still held her talisman high. "Show me my husband, Antar!" she commanded it. Those round about her exclaimed in awe as the coronet in her hands seemed to become a mirror swirling with light. Then the image of a man clad in dark blue appeared. He lay senseless on a cramped small bunk that was obviously in the hold of a ship. His limbs were bound and three hulking pirates, still in court dress, guarded him with bared blades.

"Show me what ship carries Antar!" cried Anigel.

The talisman showed the huge trireme of the Queen Regent of Raktum.

"Show me Portolanus!"

The scene changed to the poop deck of Queen Ganondri's flagship. On it were the Queen Regent herself, red robes flying in the wind, several ship's officers, and the now familiar blur having the contour of a man.

"Show me the manner of running of the Raktumian and Tuzameni ships all together," Anigel commanded.

The area within the coronet showed the five vessels strung out as they raced down the river. The big black trireme brought up the rear, all three banks of oars flashing in the storm-light. The vision winked out a moment later.

"Be of good cheer, lass," the venerable Princess Raviya told Anigel, giving her shoulder a pat of encouragement. "In this wind, our fast little cutters will soon run the villains down, and foul their oars and rudders."

"And good old Emperor Denombo and his barbarians will be close behind," Queen Ila added. "His ship is nearly as big as the pirate flagship, and better equipped to ram."

"The Raktumians won't be able to use their brimstone catapults in the rain," Lady Ellinis said. "With luck, we'll have the scoundrels before they reach the open sea —"

"No," said Anigel bleakly. "See here, in my talisman."

As many as could pushed closer to look over her shoulder at the new magical depiction. The first of the speedy Engian cutters had just come into view behind the big trireme and was rapidly closing in. All at once a titanic flash of lightning lit the river, and those watching saw a strange columnar thing hovering in the water in front of the Engian, dead black and fully twice as tall as the trireme's three lofty masts. The tiny Engian vessel, racing before the wind, tried to veer aside. But the column writhed directly into its path and smote it head-on, and the cutter vanished as if it had never existed.

Those who saw cried out in horror.

"What is it?" asked one of Queen Jiri's daughters. "A sea serpent conjured up by the sorcerer?"

Raviya of Engi, tears streaming down her withered cheeks, said: "Nay, it is a waterspout — a kind of tornado that forms over the sea. We encounter them around our islands sometimes during the summer monsoons, but never during the Dry Time. Alas! There comes another one! Our brave seamen will soon break off pursuit, as will the others following. No vessel, no matter how stout, can survive an encounter with one of those devilish things."

Across the ballroom, a fresh tumult broke out among the Zinoran guards at the main door. A voice shouted: "Madam! Oh, Madam, what a calamity!" A man in dripping Labornoki finery broke free and ran toward Anigel.

She lowered the talisman. The vision within it disappeared and the glow of its trillium-amber faded, as did the radiance in Anigel's other jewels. Her face bore a haunted expression but she did not speak until Lord Penapat came pounding up to her, his eyes wild and his broad face so reddened that he seemed about to fall in a fit.

"Oh, Madam!" He sank to his knees before the Queen. "How can I tell you? The shame of it! . . . The treachery! . . . How could she have done such a thing?"

"Calm yourself, Peni. There now, old friend! We know already that the King has been abducted by the foul sorcerer —"

"But that is not all!" The big man flung his arms out in an agony of despair. "My wife! My own wife, Sharice! She sent me on a fool's errand from the ballroom during the Procession of Felicitation, giving me a note she said was most urgent, that I was to deliver to Marshal Owanon. But the message seemed to make no sense, and when I returned to my wife, others told me she had gone, taking them with her, and I did not understand, and — oh, God! I ran after them, but it was already too late!"

Anigel's heart seemed to stop. "My children," she said in a dead voice. "My children."

"Sharice has spirited them away," the weeping Chamberlain said. "All three of them, and my wife as well, were seen boarding the galley of the Pirate Queen."

"This note to Lord Owanon," Lady Ellinis said sternly. "What did it say?"

"There were two words only," Penapat replied. " *'Your talisman.'* "

6

In the Flame-Girts and in the Smoky Isles, the marine volcanoes were erupting. Dormant fire-cones on the mainland had begun to smoke ominously as well, and the lands round about them were trembling. The Ohogan Mountains and the other nonvolcanic ranges south of the Peninsula that bordered the Sempiternal Icecap began to experience unseasonal blizzards. In the lowlands and on the high swampy plateau of Ruwenda, extraordinary thunderstorms raged, and the southern and eastern seas were churned by screaming gales.

When the calamitous weather and the stirring of the world's fiery bowels first started on the night of the abduction, Haramis knew about it almost at once. The special sensitivity she had cultivated over the years — that mystical perceptiveness that alerted the Archimage when all was not well in her land or among her people — caused a profound unease to afflict her that was not completely attributable to the shocking events at the coronation that Anigel had informed her of.

In the hours following, after Haramis had ascertained that there was no immediate thing she could do to help Antar or the kidnapped children, she used her talisman to scan the countries of the Peninsula, and then the other nations beyond. She studied the unseasonable storms, the earthquakes and landslides, the belching volcanoes, the agitated behavior of the wild animals, and knew that they were not merely side effects of the magical tempest engendered by Portolanus to aid his escape from Zinora. Something else was happening: something much worse.

She demanded that the Three-Winged Circle give her an explanation.

The talisman again showed her a vision of a blood-colored trillium — and it also spoke:

"Now is the balance of the world truly undone, for the reborn heir of the Star Men has within his grasp two elements of the great Sceptre of Power. Beware, Archimage of the Land! Seek the good counsel of others of your kind and mend your imperfections. Take action and eschew your bootless study and inadequate scrutiny. Otherwise the Star Men will triumph after all, and the healing of twelve times ten hundreds go for naught."

The voice fell silent and Haramis stared at the vision of the Blood Trillium in frozen disbelief until it melted into nothingness. Then indignation took the place of her earlier feelings of dread, and she rose up from her table in the library and began to pace angrily back and forth in front of the fireplace.

Seek good counsel of whom? Of her silly triplet sisters?

Mend her imperfections?

Her life that she had dedicated to study and service — futile?

Her continuing loving oversight of Laboruwenda and the parts of the world affecting it — inadequate?

How dare the talisman insult her so! She was doing her very best and had done so for the twelve years of her tenure as Archimage. Ruwenda and Labornok were united and peaceful, the humans prospering and the aborigines . . . well, most of them were far better off than they had ever been before. If the world was out of balance, then the evil sorcerer Portolanus was certainly to blame, not she!

And why, instead of ordering her to consult with them, had not the talisman pointed out the imperfections of her sisters as well as Haramis's own, when their flaws were so much more blatant?

Consider Kadiya! Always rushing about impatiently, always proposing simple-minded solutions to the complex problems affecting relations between humans and Folk. Arrogant in her righteousness, ever stirring pots that were better left to simmer quietly. She had lost her precious talisman through carelessness and stupidity — and now it was within the grasp of Portolanus.

Then there was Anigel, that lovely, worthy Queen — ruling with a cheerful caution so dedicated that it was stultifying, ignoring the malcontents of Labornok and the manifest injustices in Ruwenda, blithely certain that they would heal themselves. Her husband, more sensible, had tried to warn her what was afoot, but again and again she had dismissed his worries as unfounded. And he, loving her past reason and not wanting to chance discord between them, had convinced himself that she was right. Poor King Antar, so blinded by devotion!

And the three royal children, taught that life was a lovely tapestry of peace and joy, cosseted and overprotected — except when they had needed protection the most! And now King-husband and children alike abducted and held for ransom, their lives forfeit unless Anigel gave up her magical talisman to Portolanus.

And she would *do* it! She was weak and sentimental enough to do it!

Lords of the Air, what a pair of imbeciles her sisters were! What had possessed the Archimage Binah to think that they were worthy to carry instruments of profound magical power? Why had not all three talismans been placed in *her* care?

Haramis knew she would have been able to safeguard them. And having the three pieces, she would now be able to reassemble them into the Sceptre of Power to deal forthrightly with this Portolanus, whoever he was. But with the present impossible situation . . . she might as well surrender as wait fearfully here in the Tower for the sorcerer of Tuzamen to come against her, armed with the other two talismans.

"Great God and Lords of the Air defend me," she whispered, feeling her eyes begin to burn. "The world indeed is coming undone — not only this little Peninsula which I have guarded — and I am behaving like a contemptible fool, blaming my sisters for the disaster and ready to give in to Portolanus without even a struggle!"

Take action.

Haramis stopped short, near to weeping with futile rage. "Action? What kind of action? Shall I fly on voor-back to the South and confront the sorcerer on the Pirate Queen's ship? Long before I reached him, he would almost certainly have Kadiya's talisman in hand — bonded to him through that damned star-box! Why did you let him have that thing? Why did you let him find the Kimilon? *Why did you let Orogastus live?*"

A great blast of wind roared down the chimney, flinging a barrage of sparks at her like a divine admonition. One stung her hand and she dropped the talisman on its chain and screamed. The burn was insignificant. Muttering under her breath, she set about to stamp out the live embers that smoldered on the hearth rug, trying at the same time to regain her composure. Then she adjusted the flue damper and sank down on the rug, staring into the flames while tears blurred her sight.

The storm winds moaned about the battlements of the Tower like choristers singing a funeral hymn, and the thought of music brought back to her a sudden poignant memory of good old Uzun, the Nyssomu harper and flute-player who had been the dear friend of her youth. Whenever she was downhearted, he had worked tirelessly to cheer her. Funny, wise old Uzun, with his bottomless bag of tall tales, who had accompanied her faithfully on her talisman-quest until his own bodily frailties had forced him to turn back. Uzun, who had gone safely beyond these five years, leaving her now with no one to confide in, no one to accept her and love her for all her imperfections. She had not a single true friend. Her only companions were the overawed Vispi servants who called her White Lady and believed that, because she wore the old Archimage's cloak, she also had Binah's power and wisdom.

How laughable . . . Despite all her study, she still knew so very little of her talisman's powers. It seemed she would have to blunder on for endless years, slowly discovering how to use it. The Archimage Binah had lived to an incredible age and wielded great magic even without a talisman, but she had left no manual of magecraft for her successor. Haramis had done her best — but now, at the time of greatest crisis, she was helpless, her efforts mocked by the enigmatic thing that hung about her neck.

Others. Seek the good counsel of others of your kind.

Others? . . .

Her brow furrowed, then cleared. For the first time, the words the talisman had spoken penetrated her mind and took on meaning. Others? Not her sisters then, but — but — It was not possible! Binah would have told her!

But what if Binah had not known?

Haramis turned away from the fire, dashed the tears from her eyes, and lifted the talisman again with trembling hands. She asked: "Am I the only Archimage in the world?"

No.

She gasped. "Quickly! Show me another! Any other!"

The circle filled with pearly mist. But once again there came the peculiar whorls that had earlier indicated to her that Portolanus was shielded from scrutiny by strong magic. She groaned. "Of course. They would also be shielded, as I am myself." She addressed the talisman again: "How many Archimages are there?"

One of the land, one of the sea, and one of the firmament.

So! She herself was certainly of the land, and so that left two others. "Would—would any of them speak to me? Help me?"

Only if you went to them.

"How can I find them?"

There are two ways: The first is through their invitation. The second way is to be found at the Inaccessible Kimilon.

Haramis uttered a cry of joy. "Thanks be to the Triune God! I will go there at once!"

The library door opened and Magira peered uncertainly inside. Several other tall Vispi were behind her. "White Lady? Did you call? We seemed to hear a cry of pain . . ."

Now radiant with excitement, Haramis shook her head. "It was only a spark from the fire striking my hand. A trifle. But I am glad you are here. Notify the voorkeepers! At first light tomorrow I will fly to the Kimilon. Send our guest Shiki to me at once, so that I may ask if he will accompany me. Prepare foodpacks, portable shelters, and whatever else will be needed for the journey, plus a sojourn of at least ten days in the icy wilderness."

"But, Lady!" Magira cried, dismayed. "This magical storm! And if the volcanoes of the seacoast are belching fire, might not those of the Kimilon also be erupting?"

"Any storm Portolanus can conjure, I can withstand," Haramis declared. "I have learned *that* much in my study of the talisman. As for the volcanoes and the other disturbances, I am confident that I can calm them also if they threaten me or mine. This trip is essential if I am to counter the threat that Portolanus poses to the world. Go now, and do what I have told you."

She sat again at the table and held her talisman before her. Before she went off adventuring herself, she must survey again the chaotic situation in the south and advise Anigel how to proceed. Acting on her own, the Queen would very likely make a botch of it! But first, the middle sister.

"Show me Kadiya," the Archimage commanded.

She saw a rainswept narrow street in a shabby town — Zinoran by the style of the buildings, and a seaport by the extraordinary number of taverns thereabouts, many with nautical motifs on their sign-boards. Kadiya, Jagun, and a troop of more than a dozen tall, fierce-looking Wyvilo were tramping along the cobbles, bearing their dunnage in sacks over their shoulders and wearing grim faces. It was obvious that they still had not secured a boat to take them back to the Windlorn Isles.

Haramis placed two fingers upon the inset trillium-amber in her talisman and closed her eyes. The vision of her sister and her friends now filled her entire mind. She could feel the battering rain in Kurzwe, and hear the tavern wind chimes and the melancholy croaks of grounded pothi-birds, and smell the sea-wind and the stench of the squalid alleys.

"Kadiya! Kadiya! It is Haramis who calls. Can you hear me?"

The expression on her sister's face did not alter. It was obvious that Kadi's thoughts were fully occupied with her own problems and not at all receptive to mental contact with Haramis.

The Archimage sighed, opened her eyes, and banished the vision. "Perhaps I can try to bespeak Kadi in her dreams. There must be *some* way to communicate with her over the leagues, even if she does not have her talisman."

Now to look again at the pirates and Anigel. Haramis reached for a nearby parchment bearing a chart of the Zinoran Coast, unrolled it, and weighted down its corners with a book, the candelabrum, a black cube of the Vanished Ones that sang mysterious songs if one pressed its wart, and an empty tea-mug. Then she made a request of the talisman.

"Show me clearly Queen Ganondri's ship in a view from high above, that will also show me whatever land or islands are nearby. Orient this vision so that the southerly direction is toward me and the northerly away."

Again she closed her eyes. The vision that sprang to life in her mind was not so easily comprehended as the elegant map displays of the now defunct ice mirror of Orogastus had been. The talisman had resisted her attempts to teach it to indicate physical scale and to label landforms, rivers, or other identifying geographical features. But years ago she had learned how to interpret the more anonymous overviews that the talisman did vouchsafe, using the library's great store of maps and charts to distinguish the exact region descried.

This was the second time she had spied on the position of the Pirate Queen's trireme this night. Because it was dark and stormy, she saw a depiction without the bright colors that daylight would have shown, a vision in tones of gray and black. The Raktumian flagship was a dot between two small islets, barely visible and now evidently far ahead of the four other vessels that had accompanied it earlier in the evening. A portion of a large landmass was partially visible on the left. It was necessary for Haramis to fix the terrain shapes in her mind, then study the chart until she determined the ship's location.

"Aha! Got you!" The vessel was more than a hundred leagues southwest by south of Taloazin. Just as she had feared, it was *not* heading for home, but was on a direct course for the Windlorn Isles, with Portolanus and the captives aboard. She marked the position of the Raktumian flagship on the chart, then ordered the talisman to show her the other Raktumian vessels, and the Tuzameni ship belonging to Portolanus, and also Anigel's flotilla of four that chased them. The deadly waterspouts had discouraged the other nations from joining in pursuit.

The slower Raktumian ships and the lone Tuzameni were twenty leagues or so behind the trireme, with the distance widening as the Pirate Queen's vessel raced along on the storm-wind. Anigel's flagship was fifteen or sixteen leagues behind the pirates, with her three escort vessels trailing.

"Now show me King Antar," Haramis commanded the talisman.

Her vision of him was all but unchanged from the one she had seen three hours earlier. He still lay senseless on a rough galleyman's bunk in some filthy part of the ship's hold, bound hand and foot, guarded by a pair of ruffians. Shaking her head for pity, Haramis ordered a view of the three children.

They were no longer in the cabin assigned to the perfidious Lady Sharice, but had been put into a cramped, dark compartment with a barred door. The vision of them rose up and down violently with the movement of the ship in the storm, and there was a periodic booming sound, as well as a constant noise of creaking timbers. Great piles of wet, rusted chain with huge links loomed over the thin mats where Nikalon, Janeel, and Tolivar lay sleeping. Their festive garments were stained with dirt and rust.

"The chain locker at the ship's bow: that is where they are confined. Poor little things! Ani's heart must be breaking as she views them through her talisman. Still, they seem to be unharmed."

She summoned a vision of her sister. The Queen was a pathetic sight, wrapped in a leather seaman's cloak as she clung to the quarter-deck rail of the Laboruwendian flagship, face to the storm. Her talisman, the Three-Headed Monster, was on her head and it was evident that Haramis had interrupted Anigel's own scrutiny of her lost loved ones.

"Hara! How far are we from them?" the Queen asked. "I can make no sense of what my talisman shows me of their distance."

"You must tell your captain to change course slightly," the Archimage replied, and she described the exact position and course of the Raktumian flotilla. "The sorcerer and the pirates are hell-bent for the Windlorns, not heading for home as we first thought. They are after Kadi's lost talisman, and this devil's wind Portolanus has whistled up will likely bring them to Council Isle in less than three days, if it holds."

"We shall never catch them." Anigel's eyes betrayed hopelessness.

"There is a chance. Once the trireme crosses the reach of open sea between the mainland and the islands, it will be caught in the calms that prevail there. They are not called the Windlorn Isles for nothing! I doubt that even sorcery could conjure up a reliable breeze in that maze of sea-stacks and islands and rocks and reefs. Your ship is less massive than the Raktumian and your oarsmen free and willing. You might overtake them rowing."

"Has Kadi set sail from Kurzwe yet?"

"Unfortunately, no. She seems still to be trying to hire a ship. I tried again to bespeak her, but without success. Ani, you must try. You are closer to her heart than I — "

"Don't say that! She loves you as much as she loves me, and I know your own love is as strong."

Haramis sighed. "At any rate, try your utmost. If she left Kurzwe at once in a fast ship, she could reach the site of her talisman's loss before Portolanus."

"But we had originally planned to use my own talisman to summon Kadi's from the depths. How can she retrieve it without my help?"

"I don't know. It would suffice if she could find some way to deny it to Portolanus until you and your ships arrive. Try to bespeak Kadi in her sleep. She may be more susceptible then. She *must* reach the talisman before the sorcerer!"

"Very well. I shall try with all my strength. But keep watching over us and guiding us, Hara."

The Archimage hesitated. "I have a new plan for confounding Portolanus — but I do not wish to talk of it yet. Do not be dismayed if I do not bespeak you frequently from this time on. If you have true need of me, however, call upon me at once."

Anigel's face brightened. "A new plan? Oh, Hara, tell me!"

The Archimage shook her head. "It may be futile if Portolanus should get hold of Kadi's talisman — or your own. You will remember that the sorcerer returned a second time to the Kimilon and took away only a mysterious box. I asked my talisman what this box might be — and it told me that the thing was capable of *unbonding* the talismans from their owners. All that is needed is to place them inside this magical box and cast the appropriate spell."

"Do you mean that the sorcerer would be able to touch our talismans without being harmed?"

"It is perhaps even worse than that: he might be able to bond them to himself and use them, once they are released from you."

"By the Flower!"

"Ani, dear, I know you are heartsick over the fate of your dear husband and children. But you must not be tempted to pay the ransom Portolanus demands. He would surely lie about returning Antar and the children unharmed in exchange for your talisman. Our only hope is to rescue the captives. Swear to me that you will not give in to the sorcerer!"

"I — I shall be steadfast. Lord Owanon and his brave knights will help me to save Antar and the children from the pirates somehow. Ah, if I could only get close enough to the whoreson wizard so the Three-Headed Monster might smite him! He would never have been able to seize my loved ones if I had realized what he was about."

Haramis spoke more words of reassurance to her sister, then let the vision fade. Rising from the table, she went to a set of pigeonholes that contained many rolled charts and commanded her talisman to find one that would show the icecap region to the west of Tuzamen. But evidently no such map existed. Haramis rummaged through the compartments, discovering maps of Tuzamen itself (although none with much detail) and a single map of the mountain range where the Dorok Folk lived. There was nothing at all showing the Inaccessible Kimilon.

Haramis had descried the place through her talisman, of course, flinching at the view of the glacier-bounded little enclave all crowded with smoking volcanoes. But in no way had she been able to obtain a bearing upon its exact location, nor did any book in the vast library offer any hint of it. It seemed obvious now that the Archimage Binah had not used the Kimilon as a depository after all. Perhaps it predated her term of office and was of an antiquity unimaginable. Or perhaps the place belonged to one of the others, the Archimage of the Sea or the Archimage of the Firmament . . .

There came a soft scratching at the library door.

"Enter," said Haramis. She abandoned the maps and went to welcome Shiki.

The sturdy little aborigine was almost fully recovered from his ordeal of seven days ago. His enormous eyes were bright gold, free from blood-webbing, and his face with its near-human features and his hands were healing nicely from frostbite. He had lost the tips of both upstanding ears to the cold, and these were still bandaged. The Vispi retainers of the Tower had made him new garments, and he proudly wore a medallion with the Archimage's Black Trillium emblem on a chain around his neck, having dedicated himself to her service.

"Magira says you would travel to the Kimilon, White Lady."

"If you are willing to guide me, Shiki. My maps and magical arts give me no clear picture of where the place might be. It must be guarded by some enchantment, as well as by leagues of encircling ice."

The little man nodded, his face solemn. "I will lead you there gladly, and lay down my life for you if the Lords of the Air demand it. No task would give me more happiness than helping you to bring down the foul sorcerer who murdered my family and my friends. Will others of the Mountain Folk accompany us on voorback?"

"No. Only you and I will go. And we may . . . have to travel even farther than the Kimilon before our journey ends. To places no one of the Folk or the human race has ever seen. Fearful places."

Shiki held out his three-digit hand, smiling. "I am willing, White Lady. We are strong, both of us, and we will go wherever we must and return safe together. I know it."

Haramis clasped Shiki's hand in her own, returning his smile. "You will know exactly what supplies we will need. Will you go to the voorkeepers and see that everything is ready for our departure early tomorrow?"

"I will." He bobbed his head cheerfully and was gone.

Take action.

Thus had the talisman commanded. No more studying, no more observing or pondering. She had been forced into strenuous physical activity earlier in her life, drawn along through perilous mountains by the flying Black Trillium seeds that had guided her toward her talisman. But there were no magical seeds to help her now — only a single vulnerable little man who had come by fortuitous accident to her Tower.

Accident? Oh, Haramis . . .

"Silence," she said firmly. She tucked the talisman into her robe, turned out the candelabrum, and started to walk out of the library.

But suddenly a thought struck her. How to bespeak Kadiya? Of course! She cried out loud: "Haramis, you simpleton!"

Then she lifted her talisman and began to command it.

They huddled together in the street across from the last unvisited tavern but one — Kadiya and Jagun and the fifteen tall natives of the Tassaleyo Forest, while the thunder cracked and grumbled and the bamboo wind chimes dangling from the public house's signboard clonked and bonged in the gale, announcing to even the most illiterate wayfarer that food and drink were available within.

Kadiya said: "Perhaps our luck will change for the better at this milingal-hole. We must secure a ship soon, for I have a feeling of dire foreboding that urges me to go quickly after my talisman. Jagun, you will bring up the rear as always and keep a sharp eye for the town watch. Our reputation may have preceded us. Lummomu-Ko, please order your warriors to restrain their tempers this time if the rascals in the tavern tease or insult us. At the least, command them not to start a fight until I have had a chance to query all of the skippers inside."

The most massive of the Wyvilo, whose once-elegant clothes were now bedraggled from the thunderstorm assailing Kurzwe Port, replied: "If the Zinoran slime-dawdlers persist in refusing to hire us a ship, we may have to fall back on our alternate plan and sail off on our own."

"I would hate to do that," Kadiya said. "With this weird stormy weather, our chances of making it to the Windlorns alive are slender without having experienced sailors aboard."

The young Wyvilo named Lam-Sa, who had helped Lummomu-Ko to save Kadiya from drowning, said: "They, too, might be persuaded." His sharp tusks gleamed in the erratic lightning and his fellow-warriors chuckled ominously at his words.

"No," Kadiya admonished them. "Taking a vessel and leaving payment for it is one thing, but kidnapping a crew is quite another. Better my talisman be lost forever than I retrieve it by base means. I have prayed to the Lords of the Air to succor us. Somehow we will find a ship."

Without warning, Jagun the Nyssomu uttered a sharp cry. He stiffened, the pupils of his yellow eyes wide, and stared up at the sky while rain beat at his flat, wide face.

"Old friend, what's wrong?" Kadiya exclaimed.

But the little man only stood as if paralyzed, gazing fixedly at something no other could see. Finally, after several minutes had passed, he slowly came to himself, his eyes lost their glaze, and his body relaxed. He regarded Kadiya with a look of great amazement and whispered: "The White Lady! She bespoke me!"

"What?" cried Kadiya, aghast.

Jagun clutched his own head in both hands, as if trying to prevent his brains from escaping. "Farseer, she spoke! You know that we Mire Folk can bespeak others of our kind in the speech without words, although we are not so adept at it as our cousins, the Uisgu and Vispi. And you with your talisman have talked to me across the leagues many a time. But never have I heard the White Lady until now."

"What did she say?" Kadiya was almost beside herself.

"She — she accused her own sacred self of being a fool. She had urgent need to bespeak you, yet could not, now that you have lost your talisman. Only this minute did she think to bespeak *me* so that I might transmit her message to you. She had forgotten I was with you, and thought you traveled only with the Wyvilo, who are less keenly attuned to the speech without words that comes from a great distance."

"Yes, yes . . . but the message!"

"Alas, Farseer! The foul sorcerer Portolanus is on a fast ship, sailing south to claim your talisman."

"Triune God!"

"The White Lady says that if we set sail from Kurzwe immediately, we may still have a chance of getting to the talisman ahead of him."

"Did she say how I might retrieve it?" Kadiya asked eagerly.

"Your sister Queen Anigel is also in pursuit of the sorcerer. If you two can somehow reach the site of the lost talisman together, the White Lady thinks that the Queen's talisman will summon yours to you."

"Jagun, if this could be —"

But at that instant the door of the tavern across the street opened abruptly. A blaze of light and a great uproar of discordant music, drunken laughter, and shouting poured forth, startling Kadiya and her friends. A moment later two burly humans wearing dirty aprons appeared, having in their grip a struggling, shrieking patron. This man was dressed in exotic garb — black silk trousers stuffed into high red boots, a vest that was a patchwork of multicolored leather, a fine red cloak, and a broad-brimmed hat with black plumes, tied at his nape with scarlet ribbons and knocked forward so as to blind him and obscure his features as he strove in vain to escape his captors.

"Help! Thieves!" he screamed. "Swin — swindindlers! Lemme loose! The bones're loaded, I say!"

The two tapsters lifted and flung him over the threshold, then slammed the door. The ejected man landed on his face in the center of the muddy high street, his hat masking him and saving him from a mouthful of filth. He lay there moaning piteously while the rain pelted upon his cape and wilted his feathers.

Kadiya knelt beside him, turned him over, and freed him from his headgear. He exhaled a great gust of alcohol-laden breath and opened bleary eyes.

"H'lo, pretty one. Whass a nice lass like you doin' outside on a nassy night like this?" But then all at once he caught sight of the overlooming crowd of inhuman Wyvilo behind Kadiya, and he resumed his drunken shrieking: "Look out! Help! Bandiss! Monssers! Sea Oddlin' invasioners! Help!"

Kadiya calmly thrust a fold of his cape into his mouth. He sputtered and choked and fell silent.

"Be still. We are not going to harm you. We are only travelers from

Ruwenda, and these are not savage Sea Oddlings but civilized Wyvilo Folk who are my friends. Are you hurt?"

The man grunted. His reddened eyes ceased their panicked rolling. He shook his head.

Kadiya nodded to Lummomu-Ko. Together, they hoisted the fellow to his feet, the improvised gag falling from his mouth. He stood there swaying and mumbling. Jagun fished the sodden hat out of a gutter, where it was floating away, and proffered it.

"I am Kadiya, called the Lady of the Eyes, and this is Jagun of the Mire Folk, and this is Speaker Lummomu-Ko of the Tassaleyo Forest Folk and his band of warriors, who are my friends. We were preparing to enter this tavern when you made your sudden exit."

The man gave a bitter snort and clapped the hat back on his head. He plucked a large handkerchief out of his sleeve and began to mop his face. His voice was so thickened by drink they could barely understand him.

"When . . . dirty diddlin' scounders threw me out, y'mean! Skint me like a nunchuk . . . rigged game o' dance-bones . . . cheated me outta my noga, they did, after cheatin' me outta the price of my cargo! Ohhh . . . gonna be sick . . ."

Lummomu and another warrior held the man's head while he disgorged. The wind howled, the rain beat down, and the tavern wind chimes rang merrily. When the victim seemed somewhat recovered, Kadiya asked:

"Who are you, and what is this noga you say you were defrauded of?"

"Ly Woonly's m'name . . . hones' sailorman of Okamis." He peered at her suspiciously. "You know Okamis? Greates' nation inna known world! Republic — not a zach-bitten kingdom li' Zinora. Damn the stinkin' day I ever sailed to Zinora. Shoulda taken my stuff to Imlit, even if they don't pay as much."

Kadiya's eyes brightened. "So you are a seaman!"

Ly Woonly drew himself up and swirled his soaked cloak about him in a proud gesture. "Masser mariner! Cap'n of good ship *Lyath*, trig li'l noga. Named affer m'dear, dear wife." He hiccuped and then burst into maudlin tears. "She'll kill me, Lyath will! She'll salt-pickle m'stones an' sell me to the Sobranian slavers!"

Kadiya's eyes met those of Lummomu-Ko. He nodded slowly, then surveyed the other aboriginal warriors, who grinned in happy anticipation.

"Our new friend Ly Woonly has been bilked in a dishonest game of dance-bones," Kadiya said solemnly. "It is sad that such things can happen — and here in a benighted place like Kurzwe, the authorities would probably side with the local tavernkeeper, rather than seek justice for a stranger."

"That is very likely so." Lummomu's voice rumbled like spoken thunder. "It is shameful, and cries to the Lords of the Air for vengeance." His companions growled assent. Their eyes, with the vertical pupils that betrayed their race's infusion of Skritek blood, glowed like paired golden coals in the stormy night.

Kadiya took both the skipper's muddy hands in her own. "Captain Ly Woonly," she said earnestly, "we would like to help you. But we would like you also to help us. We have been seeking to hire a ship for a journey . . . of some eight hundred leagues. The cowardly Zinoran captains fear to sail in this unsettled weather. If we do get your noga and your lost money back for you, will you let us charter your ship? We will pay a thousand Laboruwendian platinum crowns."

The Okamisi's eyes bulged. "A *thousan*'? An' you'll thrash those Zinoran scoun-scounders an' get back m'poke to boot?"

"Yes," said Kadiya.

Ly Woonly wobbled on his feet, then painfully knelt in a puddle at Kadiya's feet. "Lady, you do that, I'll take y'to the frozen Aurora Sea or the doormat o' hell — whishever's farther."

"Very well. Would you like to accompany us into the tavern as we set forth your just claim?"

Ly Woonly staggered to his feet and retied the ribbons of his hat. "Would'n miss it for the world."

To the great disappointment of the Wyvilo warriors and Jagun's relief, there was no brawl. The very sight of the awesome Forest aborigines, with their fanged muzzles agape and their taloned hands hovering near their weapons, was enough to convert the dance-bone cheaters to instant integrity. Tossing the loaded bones from one hand to the other, Kadiya shook her head sadly at the three terrified

Zinoran gamblers who sat at a back table. They had been interrupted in the act of sharing out the spoils of Ly Woonly's losses.

"Good men," she addressed them, "it is obvious to me — although perhaps you did not notice — that some unknown rogue has substituted bones subtly charged with lead for the honest ones that would surely be used in an upright establishment such as this."

"That — that is possible, Lady," muttered the best dressed of the rascals, a skinny man with iron-hard eyes. "It could have happened without our seeing it."

The other two gamblers nodded eagerly, their grins frozen, as the Wyvilo fondled their sword-pommels and the hafts of the war-axes they wore at their backs.

Kadiya bestowed on the trio a confident smile, then cast down the bones amidst the piles of small gold coins. "How relieved I am to hear that. I was certain that no honest gamesters such as yourselves would take advantage of a poor Okamisi stranger far gone in drink. You see, my Wyvilo comrades and I would be very unhappy if Captain Ly Woonly were unable to sail tonight, for we have chartered his ship."

"Here! Here is the deed to the noga!" said the leading gambler, hastily pulling a paper from his belt-purse and slapping it onto the table. "Take it with our best wishes, Lady, and good voyage to you and your friends."

"And the cargo money!" Ly Woonly put in stubbornly. "Seven hunnerd and sis-sixteen gold Zinoran marks."

When the gambler hesitated, Lummomu-Ko gently took hold of the man's shoulder with one betaloned three-digit hand and began to squeeze. "The cargo money," he boomed.

Uttering a strangled yelp, the gambler swept the piles of coin on the table toward the skipper and said: "Take it and be damned!"

Ly Woonly giggled and began shoveling the gold into his own purse.

Now the tavern's proprietor came bustling up, obsequiously begging the Okamisi's pardon for his earlier mistreatment. The waiters who had thrown him out, the man said, would be severely punished.

"We would be more certain of your good will," Kadiya said sweetly, looking him straight in the eye, "if you would set forth a fine supper and drink for all of us. Then we will take away with us nothing but happy memories of the beautiful port of Kurzwe. In other taverns that we visited this night, the keepers were unfriendly. My aboriginal companions were insulted — and I fear they took restitution according to their own custom."

The Wyvilo all growled and grimaced, again fingering their weapons.

"What a shame!" cried the proprietor, sweat breaking out upon his bald head. "The hospitality of Kurzwe is famed throughout the Southern Sea! Be seated, all, and I will spread you a feast."

"On the house," said Lummomu.

"What else?" said the tavernkeeper.

It was to be their last decent meal for many days.

Ly Woonly fell blissfully asleep while Kadiya and her companions ate, and they roused him only with difficulty and had to half carry him to the wharf where *Lyath* was moored. There, with the rain still pouring down, they found a rakish little vessel with a sharp bow and stern and two masts, rocking in the ugly chop and pounding its rag-rope fenders against the dock. Access to its heaving gangplank was blocked by two glum-looking men, heavily armed.

"Officers of the Kurzwe Wharfinger, Lady," one of them told Kadiya. "No one leaves or boards this vessel until port fees and the overdue ship-chandler's bill are paid."

Kadiya examined the bill of charges beneath a guttering dock-lamp. "These seem straightforward." She took the refilled purse from the snoring skipper's belt and counted out one hundred and fifty-three gold pieces.

The wharf officers saluted and went off hurriedly to get out of the rain. Lummomu-Ko threw Ly Woonly over one shoulder and led the way on board.

The *Lyath* was shabby and in need of paint, less than half the size of the Varonian vessel that had originally carried the negotiating party to the Windlorn Isles. Her metal fittings were unpolished and her deck rough and splintery. But she seemed well found, and the rigging was new and so were the furled sails, shining white in the gloom and neatly secured to the booms. Not a soul was to be seen. There was a single darkened midships cabin, and a companionway leading below, through the glass port of which dim lantern light gleamed.

Kadiya opened the companionway door. "Anybody here?" she called. After she shouted a second time, a young man clad only in a pair of torn pants appeared at the foot of the companionway ladder, rubbing his eyes.

"Cap'n Ly? That you? We 'bout gave you up — *oh!*" His eyes flew open in shock as a bolt of lightning lit up Kadiya, with the fearsome Lummomu beside her bearing the unconscious skipper. "God's guts! Who're you? What's happened to the cap'n?"

"Your captain is safe and well, my man," Kadiya said. "We have brought him back from his night's carouse. I am Kadiya, Lady of the Eyes, and this is Speaker Lummomu-Ko of the Wyvilo. We have chartered this ship, and Ly Woonly has agreed that we are to set sail at once — "

"Nay, nay," said the seaman, shaking his tousled head. He was perhaps five-and-twenty years old, with dark curly hair and a pleasant face. "We don't go nowheres 'thout a crew, Lady. Only me 'n Ban 'n old Lendoon left on board since the others went away on that big Varonian merchantman that touched in this afternoon."

Kadiya and Lummomu looked at each other. She said: "Kyvee Omin's ship, that brought us here."

The young man came up on deck, heedless of the rain, and beckoned Kadiya and the burdened Wyvilo Speaker to follow him to the skipper's cabin in the deckhouse. "See, Cap'n Ly's a bit of a coin-clutcher if a crewman ain't related to 'im, like me 'n Ban 'n old Lendoon is. That Varonian ship was short-handed and just snapped our ten boys up. Glad to go they was, hot for the big money in the eastern ports. Cap'n was ready to pop his eyeballs when they quit. Said he'd try somehow to get more men t'morra, but tonight he was gonna get stewed."

Lummomu dumped the snoring Ly Woonly onto his bunk. The young man stripped off the skipper's soaked boots and muddy outer clothing, took charge of the heavy purse, then led Kadiya and the Wyvilo back below. He produced a bottle of ilisso and three glasses and introduced himself as Ly Tyry, the captain's nephew and first mate.

"Now, what's this 'bout you charterin' *Lyath*?"

"We are very anxious to leave this place tonight," Kadiya said. She sipped fiery spirit from one glass while Tyry drank from the second, Jagun from the third, and the mob of Wyvilo shared the bottle amongst them. "What chance of our hiring other sailors?"

"Slim to naught," Tyry admitted. "That's why the cap'n was so mad. Only lazy Zinoran trash in this hole. None of 'em eager to go to dear old Okamis. Can't think why."

"My fifteen companions and I are not completely untrained," Kadiya said. "The Wyvilo foresters are accustomed to sailing giant log rafts on Lake Wum during the winter gales in Ruwenda, and we have all learned something of the sea since coming to the South. We are willing to help you work the *Lyath* — in addition to paying the one thousand platinum crowns your uncle and I agreed upon for the charter."

"Where're you off to, then?"

"Council Isle in the Windlorns."

The young mate swore and surged to his feet. "Lady, you lost your wits? Bad enough y'wanna set sail in this out-o'-season storm! But to go there — "

"The Aliansa natives will not be hostile to you," Kadiya said. "I have just come from the isles, having conferred with the High Chief Har-Chissa. He has broken off trade with Zinora, saying its people have cheated him. He declared that from now on he would only trade with Okamis or Imlit."

The young man's eyes were shining. "Say y'true?"

"I swear it by the sacred Black Trillium of my people," Kadiya replied. "Now, will you take us?"

Tyry was thinking hard. "The cap'n's out till t'morra. But we got Ban for steersman and Lindoon for second mate. And these Odd — these tall lads of yours look strong and ready, and the little fellow can make himself useful. By damn — I think we can do it!" But then he pulled up short, staring at Kadiya uneasily. "Except . . ."

"What is it, my man?"

"Lady, don't take offense. But, can you cook?"

"Yes. And so can Jagun."

"That's a weight off my mind," Tyry said. He grinned. "Or off my stomach. Old Lindoon's the only one among us who knows a pot from a porthole — but his messes would send a Skritek running to the rail. You and your little friend keep us fed, and we'll do just fine."

Kadiya sighed.

The young mate tossed off the rest of his ilisso, plunked the glass onto the wardroom table, and seemed to notice for the first time that he was half-naked. He blushed. "I'll go put some clothes on and wake Ban and Lindoon. If you and your crew can follow orders, Lady, we'll be off within the hour."

8

The three children of King Antar and Queen Anigel were first confined in a sumptuous cabin of the Raktumian flagship, with Lady Sharice in charge of them and two Tuzameni warriors and the sorcerer's Black Voice on guard. As soon as Sharice admitted that they were indeed prisoners, as was King Antar also, Crown Prince Nikalon and Princess Janeel had demanded to see their Royal Father. When this request was continually denied, they refused to eat and devoted themselves to making life miserable for the traitorous Sharice, berating her without ceasing and giving her no peace as the trireme sped southward through the stormy sea.

Finally she went weeping to the great stateroom set aside for Portolanus and burst in without ceremony.

"Great Lord! I must speak with you. Oh — "

Even in the depths of her distress, Sharice saw immediately that the man sitting at the worktable wearing the sorcerer's garments was very different from the superannuated dotard she had known. He was Portolanus . . . and yet he was not, and she blinked her tear-swollen eyes and wondered if she were losing her mind.

He was tinkering with a strange device that had been taken apart, its innards spread out before him, polishing the tarnished tiny metal pieces of the machine with jewelers' rouge. His fingers were so red-stained that they seemed to have been dabbling in blood.

Sharice could only stammer: "Is — is it you, Master of Tuzamen?"

He lifted his eyes, and they were an inhuman silver blue with very wide pupils, and in the depths of them shone tiny points of gold. A palpable malignancy seemed to emanate from him, delving into her soul's shame and woefulness and dismissing them with icy contempt. Sharice knew she should flee. But from somewhere she dredged up courage to whisper:

"Master—Prince Nikalon and Princess Janeel refuse to eat. And—and they upbraid and despise me, and I can no longer bear to stay with them."

"If they will not eat," Portolanus said curtly, "let them fast. They will cease their obstinacy when their stomachs pain them enough."

"Nay, Great Lord." Sharice was twisting and wringing a fine lace handkerchief into a rag, and her face was ravaged and hollow-eyed. "The Crown Prince is a strong-willed boy and his sister hardly less resolute. They will starve themselves into illness rather than submit. And—and they abuse me so! They reprove me endlessly for my treachery, and for the past two days, whenever I would sleep, one or another of the pair slyly pinches me awake. Between my seasickness and the lack of rest I am harassed unto death! Lord, I can bear it no longer!"

"Silly fool. We will simply give you a separate cabin at night. But during the day you will watch the children and see to their needs. Now get out of here and leave me to my work."

"I cannot stay with them!" Sharice cried wildly. "They are right to call me vile and dishonored. Their reproachful faces pierce me to the heart! Oh, what an idiot I was to succumb to the temptation of your Black Voice and aid in their abduction! No wealth you can offer me and my brother Osorkon can compensate for the evil deed I have done."

Portolanus rose up from the table and pointed a scarlet-stained finger at the disheveled woman. "Out!" he thundered. "Or I will have the Queen Regent's pirates beat some sense into you!"

Sharice crept away, moaning.

For an hour or so the sorcerer worked in peace, mending a certain balky magical contrivance that would be able to peer underwater and locate the exact position of Kadiya's sunken talisman. Then there came a knock at the door, and the short, wiry acolyte called the Black Voice entered, his face flushed with anger.

"Master, the miserable woman Sharice has jumped overboard into the sea. She was seen by a lookout, but in this storm there was no question of heaving to. She must have drowned almost immediately."

Portolanus cursed. "Then put one of the pirate women in charge of the royal brats."

"There is worse news. During Sharice's absence Crown Prince Nikalon set fire to a pillow with one of the oil lamps, and when the guards and I came to investigate the smoke, he and Princess Janeel tripped us up and escaped. Of course, they were immediately recaptured — but we shall have to take greater precautions in confining them."

"Yes, we shall." The sorcerer's tone was ominous. He began to wipe his hands clean with a rag. "And since you, my foremost Voice, seem unable to deal with this small matter competently, I will see to the new arrangements myself before having my conference with the Queen Regent."

As Portolanus left his workroom with the Black Voice, his aspect underwent a change. His body, which had seemed that of a normal well-built man when he was within his private sanctum, now seemed to shrink and become deformed by extreme old age. The fingers that were strong and sure when working on the machine of the Vanished Ones became gnarled, and the fingernails ridged and split. His eyes turned rheumy and his face was no longer firm but furrowed and wattled and as repulsive as a swampland fungus. He limped slowly along the corridor to the cabin where the royal children were imprisoned, bracing himself against the walls when the ship rolled in the heavy seas.

Entering the cabin, which stank of scorched feathers, he found Nikalon and Janeel tied to chairs. The Tuzameni guards supervised a frightened-looking steward who was changing the soaked and sooty bed. Little Prince Tolivar, unbound, sat watching on a couch, eating a cluster of sweet hala-berries. When the sorcerer appeared, he forgot the fruit and stared openmouthed.

"Now what is all this hurly-burly?" Portolanus demanded in a querulous voice. "Setting fires? Refusing to eat? We can't have that, you know. I want to be able to return you children to your Royal Mother all healthy and happy when the ransom is paid."

"We demand to see our father," Prince Nikalon said.

Portolanus flung up his hands and rolled his eyes. "Alas, young

Lord, that is not possible. He is no longer on this ship, but on another that is speeding toward Raktum. But as soon as his ransom is paid, he will be returned safely to his own country, as will you three royal children."

"I think," the Crown Prince said in a level tone, "that you lie. We had it from the traitor Sharice that the King was taken prisoner by you at the same time that she lured us away from the ball and onto this ship. She says that he is chained in the hold with the galley slaves and treated no better than they. If you will agree to give our father the respect due a royal prisoner, my sister and I will call off our fast and give you our solemn word not to attempt escape."

Portolanus began to tut-tut and bluster denials, and pointed out how sensible young Prince Tolivar was to continue eating, at which Tolo had the grace to put aside his fruit and look ashamed.

"He is too young to understand," Princess Janeel said. "But *we* understand all too well that your aim is to take our mother's magic talisman, and use it for evil."

The sorcerer laughed merrily. "What a fabric of lies Lady Sharice spun for you! It is true that the talisman is the ransom, but false that I would use it for evil. No indeed, young Lady! I would use it to restore the lost balance of the world, which your mother does not know how to do. She has never truly understood her talisman, and neither have her two sisters. And so our poor world is poised on the brink of a great catastrophe, with humans scheming to fight humans, and Folk kept in pitiful subjection, and dire enchantments threatening to tear the land asunder and topple the Three Moons from their place in the sky!"

"And you could fix it?" little Prince Tolivar said, overawed.

The sorcerer nodded and folded his arms, striking a pose. "My knowledge is vast and my powers are far greater than those of your Aunt Haramis, the Archimage. She herself seeks to restore the balance, but she cannot do it without help. Help that only I can give her."

Crown Prince Nikalon was skeptical. "I have heard no rumors of wars. And the only Oddlings who are oppressed are those who are rebels or troublemakers."

"And the balance of the world was restored," Princess Janeel added, "when our mother and her sisters conquered the evil magician Orogastus. They are the Three Petals of the Living Trillium. The three magical talismans that they hold in trust ensure that there will be peace forever."

"But your Aunt Kadiya has lost her talisman!" Portolanus hissed, his bloodshot eyes bulging. "Did you not know that?"

"No," Nikalon admitted. For the first time his confidence seemed to waver.

"Is that why this awful storm is blowing?" Tolo asked, tentatively.

Portolanus beamed at the little boy. "Clever lad! Ah, what a brain you have! Of course the storm is a symptom of the world's lost balance, and you knew it while your older brother and sister did not."

Tolo smiled shyly.

But the sorcerer whirled about then, glaring ferociously at Niki and Jan. "I will waste no more time with you two. If you do not give me your solemn word that you will abandon your stupid fasting and behave yourselves, then I will have you confined in a miserable dark place infested with ship-varts."

Tolo was aghast. "Me too?"

Portolanus patted the boy sadly on the head. "Alas! You too, dear lad—if your stubborn brother and sister persist in their naughty ways."

"But I'm afraid of ship-varts!" the little boy wailed. "They bite! Niki—Jan—say you'll do what he wants."

Crown Prince Nikalon drew himself up as straight as he could, being bound. "Tolo, be still! Remember that you are a Prince of Laboruwenda." Then, to Portolanus: "If our Royal Father suffers, it will be our honor to share his pains."

"So say I also." Princess Janeel's face had become very pale, but she set her lips tightly and kept her chin high, even when Tolo began to weep in terror.

"Take them to the chain-locker," Portolanus commanded the Black Voice. "They may bring nothing with them but the clothes on their backs. And give them only bread and water to eat—or not eat, whatever they please—until they come to their senses."

°   °   °

The two green-faced knights guarding the door with the royal crest of Raktum mounted upon it drew their swords reluctantly as Portolanus came tottering along the sterncastle corridor, bent nearly to the waist, reeling from one side of the passage to the other and waving his arms to keep his balance as the ship wallowed in the storm.

"She will not see you, magician," one of the men said in a strained voice. "Did her lady-in-waiting not pass the message?"

"Oh dear, oh dear," Portolanus bleated. "But I *must* speak to the Queen Regent. My business is very urgent!" He was without his pointed hat, wearing a hooded robe of purple and pink stripes having scattered silver stars.

"Come back when the weather moderates," ordered the second pirate-knight. His eyes were sunken and his lips a livid bluish color. "Queen Ganondri is abed with a stomach even queasier than ours, attended by her Lady Physician. We would lose our heads if we admitted anyone."

"We have already lost our lunch," said the first knight, nodding at a bucket nearby.

"Oh dear, oh dear! Seasick, are you?" The sorcerer began fumbling in a large purple wallet hanging from the belt of his gaudy robe. "I have here a sure remedy for what ails you, and it would quickly cure poor Queen Ganondri, too—"

The first knight scowled. "We want none of your vile potions, Master of Tuzamen, and neither does the Great Queen. Be off!"

Portolanus pulled from the pouch a short rod fashioned of dark metal having ornate carvings upon it and also several inset gems. Smiling eagerly, he approached the knights with this object held in the palms of both hands. "No potions! See? One touch from this magical instrument of benevolent healing and your miseries would be over."

The qualmish pirates rejected his offer, and persisted in refusing him entrance, crossing their swords in front of the door. Portolanus whined and drooped and turned away, seeming to give up his efforts, so that the knights were taken completely unawares when the old cripple whirled about and leapt at them with the agility of a fedok, touching first one man, then the other upon the cheek. The swords fell to the carpeted deck with dull clangs and the eyes of the men rolled up into their skulls. Slowly, they slid down the bulkhead on either side of the door, to end sitting with their legs thrust out and their heads sunken on their breasts, quite unconscious.

The sorcerer wagged a chiding finger at them. "I said my business was urgent." Then he took from his pouch another object like a golden key without a bit, and used it to unlock the door.

He came into the Queen Regent's elegantly appointed saloon, which was deserted and dimly lit, the ports shuttered against the unnerving sight of the gigantic waves. With startling ease, he pulled the two heavy armored bodies inside and relocked the door. A tall woman dressed in black suddenly appeared at an inner door leading to the Queen's stateroom.

"What's this?" she exclaimed sharply. "What are you doing here?"

"Oh dear, oh dear!" the sorcerer piped. "A great disaster, Lady Physician! Come see! I found these good fellows sleeping at their posts, and could not awaken them."

He danced about flapping his hands as the doctor knelt to examine the nearest man. But no sooner had she lifted the knight's eyelid than Portolanus touched her bare head with the rod, and she fell prone across the bodies of the earlier victims.

"Koriandra? What is it?" called a fretful voice.

The sorcerer scuttled through the door into the royal stateroom and sketched a bow, whereupon the Queen Regent cried: "You! What have you done to my servants?"

"We must confer, Great Queen. Your people sleep peacefully. I have not harmed them, only rendered them senseless with my magical rod. Another touch from it will restore them — after our little talk."

Ganondri lay in a great round bed, propped up with lace-edged pillows and covered with a handsome wadded-silk comforter. Her coppery hair was in disordered braids and her face had the pallor of death, but in spite of her illness her emerald eyes blazed with fury. She reached for the bell-cord.

Portolanus lifted it out of her way with his rod, wagging his head and clucking his tongue. "We must confer *without* interruption."

"Lowborn rogue!" croaked the Pirate Queen. "How dare you force your way into my chambers?" The ship gave a mighty lurch. Her seasickness overcame her and she fell back with her hand pressed to her forehead.

Calmly, Portolanus cut the bell-rope with his small dagger. Then he pulled up a chair beside the bed and threw back his hood. His damp hair and beard fell in snarls and his features were ludicrously distorted, with the nose twisted like a root and the lips loose and creased as the opening of an old leather pouch.

"Gracious Lady, we must continue that conversation begun two days ago at the start of our flight from Taloazin, which was unfortunately interrupted when you became indisposed. I have pondered that little chat of ours, and fretted over certain of its implications. I must insist that you clarify certain puzzling remarks you made — and you must do so at once."

Ganondri turned her head away. "I am near dying with this miserable tempest you have conjured up, wizard. Make it stop, and then I will talk to you."

"No. It is this gale that will bring us to the Windlorn Isles ahead of Queen Anigel so that I may take for my own the magical talisman of her sister, Kadiya. You know this well enough, Great Queen."

Ganondri groaned. "I know! . . . *Now* I know it, you dissembler! But it was never part of our original bargain. The first I heard of this cursed voyage south was when we all came aboard with the captives. I have puzzled over and pondered it ever since! Our original agreement concerned only the abduction of King Antar and his children so that you might secure Queen Anigel's talisman. We entered into that alliance as declared equals, even though your upstart little nation is puny in trade resources and lacking in money or armed might. Great Raktum took you under its wing because you assured me we would conquer the world together once you secured Anigel's talisman as ransom. And I believed you — the more fool I!"

"You may believe me now. Nothing has changed."

"Liar! There was nothing in our compact about helping you to get a *second* talisman!"

Portolanus shrugged and smiled disarmingly.

"When you first made your offer," the Queen went on, "I had our sages in Frangine determine just what kind of magical device you coveted. They told me that Anigel's talisman is but one of three, and that together they make up an invincible Sceptre of Power. With one talisman in your hands, you would have Queen Anigel's nation helpless, and Raktum and Tuzamen together would conquer it. This was acceptable. But having two talismans of power, you would inevitably use them to obtain the *third*."

"Nay —"

"Do not deny it! You covet this all-powerful Sceptre. And once you have it, great Raktum would shortly be reduced to a vassal state of Tuzamen, and its Queen become your slave."

The sorcerer's hands fluttered in dismay. "You misunderstand —"

The sick woman rose up from her pillows, strengthened by rage. "Silence, wretch! Do not presume to patronize me. If I had not been prostrated by illness, I would have fathomed your scheme earlier. Now that I understand it, I have taken measures to ensure that Raktum does not fall under your devilish enchantment."

Portolanus wrung his hands. "No, no! We are allies! Never would I contemplate such perfidy! You misjudge me!"

"I judge you accurately and find you wanting." The Queen spoke in a harsh whisper. Her green eyes burned. "That you and your three loathsome henchmen still live is due to my clemency. My knights had orders to slay you in your sleep last night, but I reconsidered. I have decided to fulfill our original bargain — helping you to obtain one talisman."

She fell back, once more overcome, but after a moment continued to speak. "And do not think you can win out by killing me or disabling me with magic. I made plans against *that* contingency before we ever set sail for the coronation in Zinora. The great pirate fleet of Raktum has its orders. If any harm comes to the Queen Regent through you, our fighting ships will interdict every port in Tuzamen. You will never be able to return to your country by sea — and if you return by land, our armada will box you in so that your dreams of world conquest will come to naught."

Portolanus bowed his head. "The Queen Regent is a brilliant strategist."

"Mock me if you must," she retorted. "But remember what I say. If I do not each morning give my Admiral orders to continue southward, this vessel will immediately change course and head for Raktum with my dead or senseless body. You will lose Kadiya's talisman. Queen Anigel is hot on our trail and knows what you are after. She surely also knows a way to deny her sister's lost talisman to you, through using her own."

"Are you so certain that I cannot coerce this ship's crew to obey me, once you are dead or rendered powerless?" Portolanus said in a new voice. "My magic can force anyone to do my bidding!"

His enfeebled persona had melted away, and his face, although still grotesque, had changed. There was now about him a halo of enchantment so menacing that the Queen Regent thought she might swoon from fear; but she spoke resolutely:

"If you had not needed great Raktum, you never would have made a pact with us in the first place. As to commanding this ship — you may think you have thought of a way to seize it. But I remind you that three other armed Raktumian vessels follow us, along with your own ship. Before we left Taloazin, I did not comprehend your new scheme in full — but I knew enough not to give you a free hand. The three captains of my escort will not permit you to return to your Tuzameni ship unless I give the order. If you reboard clandestinely and attempt to flee, they will overtake your slower vessel and bombard it with their fire catapults."

The sorcerer said nothing.

Ganondri's eyes gleamed in triumph. "You have power, magician, but your power is not invincible. That belongs only to the one who joins the three talismans of the Ruwendian triplet sisters into the Sceptre . . . You may *have* Kadiya's talisman. My subjects and I will help you to obtain it. But when it is safe in your hands, bonded to you through your magical box, you will be put ashore on one of the Windlorn Isles to await rescue by your own Tuzameni ship. You will leave the star-box with me. King Antar and his brats will also remain in my custody, and I will claim their ransom from Anigel. *Her* talisman is mine!"

"You seem to have thought of everything."

The Queen gave a soft, painful laugh. "I have lived by my wits for many years, magician. How else do you suppose that a poor old dowager became ruler of the Kingdom of the Pirates? . . . Now get out. And restore my servants as you go."

The glittering eyes slowly closed. For a long time Portolanus stood

beside the bed, looking down at the sick Queen, gripping the paralyz-
ing rod in one hand and with the other fingering a battered star-
shaped pendant he wore concealed within his robes. But in the end he
shook his head in frustration and went out, after first touching the
unconscious doctor and the knights, so that they moaned and slowly
began to regain their senses.

There was a potential solution to the impasse. But it lay not in
Queen Ganondri but in another person, whom he hurried off to see.

Under gray skies from which the rain had finally ceased falling,
Portolanus sidled along the tossing deck, maintaining a firm grip on
the safety lines to keep from losing his balance and being washed
overboard. Waves breaking over the ship's sides drenched him with
spray. The huge Raktumian trireme seemed to writhe like some great
beast in torment for all that it was racing before the wind at a league-
gobbling speed, carrying only a few rags of sail. The galley slaves, of
course, were unneeded. In such a high wind, their oars would have
impeded the ship, not assisted it. Most of them were violently seasick
anyway, as were the majority of the passengers, and the Yellow and
Purple Voices.

The illness of the latter pair had been a vexing inconvenience to
Portolanus. At least two of his acolytes were needed as adjunct
sources of mental energy if he was to be able to scan the sea over long
distances, descrying the enemy vessels in pursuit. Without the help of
two or more Voices, the sorcerer could only survey the waters with
another small machine of the Vanished Ones. It was an excellent
device, showing the position of other ships or of landforms as far as
the horizon, working as well at night as in daylight; but it could not
see below the horizon-line as his magical Sight could.

Not once did Portolanus consider tempering the force of the storm
he had called up. Time enough for spying out Anigel when they
reached the doldrums among the islands and the final sprint for the
talisman.

Gaining the wheelhouse at last, Portolanus hauled open the door
and staggered inside, tittering and hooting inanities about the terrible
weather. Admiral Jorot, standing behind the helmsman, gave the
sorcerer only a swift, distasteful glance. But two other pirate officers

hastened to help the distinguished passenger into a chair before the chart table, offering towels to mop the seawater streaming from his face and hair and a warm, dry cloak to wrap him in. Strangely, young King Ledavardis was also present in the wheelhouse, standing aside and staring at the ridiculous, drenched wizard with mingled anxiety and fascination.

"You should not have endangered yourself coming on deck, Great Lord!" one officer said.

Portolanus waved him off, simpering. "It is most necessary that I convey to the Admiral an urgent message I have just received from the lips of Queen Ganondri. I pray that all others leave us for a time" — he bobbed his head and bestowed an oily smirk on the boy-King — "including you, young Sire."

"Not my helmsman!" Jorot snapped. His hair and beard were snowy and his face weather-beaten and brown as an old boot. He was tall and wasted of body, and it was said he suffered secretly from a mortal illness; but he ruled his men with steely authority and even Queen Ganondri spoke to him respectfully rather than with her customary hauteur.

The sorcerer's tone was lilting but insistent as he replied to the old seaman's objection. "Yes, the helmsman must also go. Unless you are unable to steer your own ship, noble Admiral."

"That I can, Master of Tuzamen," Jorot said, through clenched teeth. He bade the others leave, and stood at the wheel with his back to the sorcerer. "Now, what is this bilge about a message from the Great Queen? She does not confide in dubious foreigners."

Portolanus laughed softly. "And yet you seem interested enough in what this dubious foreigner might have to say to you in private."

"Say it, then, and begone."

"Do not be so abrupt, Admiral. I have had my eye on you. You are a man of strength and intelligence, and one moreover with a fine piratical turn of mind. These are qualities to be prized, and I would like to share a few of my thoughts with you, and perhaps discuss certain matters important to us both."

"Save your knavish japes for the gullible Laboruwendians. You are wasting your time."

"I think not. To demonstrate my good will, I shall show my true self to you — as I have done to no other man on board save my own three faithful acolytes."

Portolanus had thrown off both the sea-cloak and his bulky wet magician's robe and now stood straight, without a trace of the senile infirmity he had always displayed. Jorot flung a glance of astonishment back at the transformed sorcerer and growled an oath, for Portolanus now proved to be a man much taller than himself. Dressed in close-fitting hosen and a simple shirt, with a battered silvery star of many points hung about his neck, he seemed as stalwart as an athlete. Even his face, framed by tangled yellow hair and disfigured by its scraggly mustache, had changed from that of a hideous ancient to one belonging to a man barely middle-aged, and comely enough now that the features were no longer contorted.

"So!" said Jorot. "You have more cheap tricks up your sleeve than any of us suspected."

"Believe that if you wish, Admiral." The voice of Portolanus had altered along with the rest of him, and was now resonant and virile. "But of my magical powers have no doubts, for they are even more formidable than you can imagine. This great storm was commanded by me, and if I wished, I could banish it in an instant — or cause it to wax to a fury that would engulf your ship."

"And yourself!" Jorot sneered.

"I would not die, nor would my three Voices, nor the royal captives I hold for ransom. Only you and your crew would perish, and the passengers, including Queen Regent Ganondri and her Goblin Kinglet — if I but wished it."

"And do you?"

The sorcerer came around to the side of the wheel so that Jorot might more readily see him. "That, Admiral Jorot, rests entirely with you. Are you a man who serves the Queen Regent so faithfully that he would lay down his life for her?"

The old pirate gave a shout of laughter. "That vainglorious harridan? She has been a plague upon our nation for seven years, and not a man in my crew would weep to see her breathing seawater. Only the knights of her personal guard are loyal to her here, and her own faction of relatives back in Raktum." He looked aside at the sorcerer, his brow darkening. "But dare to harm young King Ledo, conjure-man, and the mariners of the Northern Sea will hunt you to the uttermost parts of the known world, and feed your tortured corpse to the sea-monster Heldo."

Portolanus chuckled. "Well, well! So the lad is your pet, is he? I wondered why we so seldom saw the ugly young qubar about the royal quarters."

"Ill made his face and body are," Jorot said quietly. "But his spirit is that of a great prince. One day the world will know better than to despise him . . . if he can but survive to his majority."

Now Portolanus was interested. "And why should he not?"

"His royal grandame is two-and-sixty years of age and in robus-tious good health. She is not eager to give up the reins of power two years hence, as she must according to our law. Not when she might rule another twenty years herself—should the King be declared in-competent, or suffer some fatal misadventure."

"You are correct in your assessment of Ganondri's ambition, Admi-ral. She is an intelligent and courageous adversary. She has also fatally underestimated me—for which reason I have come here to-night to confer with you."

Jorot's eyes lit with sudden understanding. "I have it! The Queen is not afraid of you! She has faced you down, wizard, and in some manner now threatens your crooked schemes."

"So she does," Portolanus admitted. "Although I am paramount in magic, I do not yet command a multitude of followers, nor has my small nation of Tuzamen a powerful army or a fleet of fighting ships to equal that of Raktum. Ganondri and I entered into an alliance before sailing to Zinora for the coronation, but I have lately come to realize that I cannot trust her. Let me be perfectly frank. I embarked from Taloazin with my royal prisoners on this ship instead of my own because the Queen convinced me at the last minute that this was the fastest vessel having enough armament to repel the Laboruwendian pursuers. That is true enough—but I did not reckon she would be foolish enough to repudiate the terms of our original agreement and attempt to extort additional concessions from me."

"We pirates have our own quaint notions of honor, it's true. But none of us sail so close to the wind in sharp dealing as the Queen Regent! . . . If she threatens you, why not simply smite her dead with your sorcery?"

"If I did, would you and the captains of the other Raktumian ships follow my orders?"

Jorot guffawed. "Not for a moment, trickster. Black magic has its limits. It cannot force loyalty or love—or even respect. Sink us all with your storm if you dare. Your cranky Tuzameni vessel would also very likely founder, since it is poorly designed for heavy weather. You and your precious prisoners would be cast adrift in the midst of the open sea, over six thousand leagues from your home. You would soon die, even in a flat calm—unless you know how to take to the air and fly like the pothi-birds."

"Alas, I cannot," Portolanus admitted sourly. "If that were so, I would not be aboard your wallowing scow at this moment."

Jorot's face was becoming ashen, and the cords in his neck stood out from the exertion required to keep the huge trireme on an even course. He clung now to the wheel with hands white-knuckled.

"Wizard, I'm tired of fencing mentally with you, and I'm physically exhausted as well. I'm not a young man nor a well one, and my job is conning the helm, not wrestling with a balky wheel in a full gale. I shall have to call the steersman back soon or else risk losing control of the ship—which could very well dismast us in this high wind. You must have had a reason for coming here. Spit it out, or go back and play your games with the Queen Regent."

The sorcerer began to reclothe himself in his damp robe. "Very well. If Queen Ganondri should die and King Ledavardis rule truly, would you and all the pirate fleet accept his sovereignty? Would you obey his orders?"

"Wholeheartedly," said Admiral Jorot. "But if you think you can force your will upon the lad, think again. He only pretends to be a dunce so as not to provoke his grandmother."

"I suspected as much. If he is clever, so much the better. Perhaps he will avoid making the fatal mistakes of Ganondri."

"Fatal?"

"I intend to usher the Queen Regent safely beyond just as soon as she is no longer of use to me."

"I could warn her of your evil designs."

Portolanus laughed. "You could, but I think you won't. Tell the royal brat instead. If he cooperates with me when he wears Raktum's crown, he will soon possess riches equal to a thousand years' worth of pirate loot, and more strong galley slaves than he can count. And you, Admiral Jorot, may have whatever *you* desire — up to and including the post of Viceroy of Laboruwenda."

"But, when the ransom is paid — "

"King Antar and his children will never return alive to their land, ransom or no ransom. And Queen Anigel, deprived of her talisman and family, will soon see her land conquered by my magic, and by the combined forces of Tuzamen and Raktum. Oh, yes. It will happen very quickly once her heart and will are broken . . ."

Now dressed again in his voluminous robes, Portolanus seemed to diminish in stature, and his body grow twisted with age. His face resumed its repulsive aspect. He opened the inner door of the wheelhouse and called out in quavering accents for the others to return. The helmsman and the two officers hastened inside, but King Ledavardis was no longer there, having left by another door.

"Do give the dear lad my best wishes when next you see him," the sorcerer said to the Admiral. "And tell him I look forward to having a little talk with him very soon."

He pulled his hood up and went out into the storm. But this time he did not pretend to be battered by it, but instead walked slowly away, easily maintaining his balance, as though the ship were at anchor in some calm harbor and he out for an afternoon stroll of the deck.

From below, Prince Tolivar called: "Can you see anything?"

"Big waves and an angry sunset sky full of fast clouds," Prince Nikalon said. "First one, then the other as the ship rises and falls."

"No land," Princess Janeel said. "Only ocean."

"That's funny," Tolo said. "On your side, you should be able to see the shore if we're heading back toward the Peninsula. Maybe the pirates aren't taking us to their home in Raktum after all."

The only illumination in their new prison shone from twin openings eight ells above the slimy planks of the chain-locker floor. The furnishings of the place consisted of three thin pallets with musty old blankets, a covered slop-pail, a crock of lukewarm water, and a small basket of stale bread-rolls. Niki and Jan had decided that fasting would no longer help their cause, and they had already eaten half of the bread.

When they were certain that their captors were not coming back, the two older children each mounted one of the two great piles of anchor chain that mostly filled the tall compartment. They clambered up the hanging sections of giant links, past the great double winching mechanism with its iron gears that raised or lowered the anchors, to the hawse-pipes through which the chains passed to the ship's bow. They had forbidden little Tolo to follow. Whenever the trireme nosed into a particularly high sea, there was a ringing boom and seawater sprayed through the two openings and all over Niki and Jan. But the water, like the air, was warm, and they no longer even bothered to shriek when they were hit by a fresh drenching.

"The anchors outside are so monstrous that they hide most of the view," Niki said.

"Do you think the holes are big enough for us to crawl through and escape?" Jan asked.

"It would be a tight squeeze with the anchors in the way," Niki replied. "And even if we succeeded, we would only fall straight into the water and be sucked under the ship."

"Come down," Tolo pleaded. "I think I hear those nasty ship-varts scratching in one of the dark corners again."

"Cowardy-cush," Niki said with more kindness than contempt. "They can't really hurt you."

"But I hate them. They are so ugly and dirty. Come down and drive them away, Niki. Please!"

The Crown Prince began to descend, and after a few moments' hesitation, his sister did also. The chains were caked with wet, evil-smelling river mud and entwined with strands of Zinoran water-weed that made them very slippery.

"When the ship finally stops in some harbor and they drop the anchors," Niki said to Jan, "I'm going to escape! Right out one of those holes and down the chain into the water."

"The pirates aren't idiots," Jan said. "They'll move us out of here before then."

Her eyes were wide in the gloom. Without fear, she clung tightly to a huge iron link as the ship plummeted downward like a falling stone, then pointed its bow up and soared toward the sky. The heavy chains, each wound once about its winch drum, swayed only a little. When next she spoke, Jan made sure to whisper so that the little boy below would not hear. "Niki, do you think they're going to kill us?"

"Not if Mother pays the ransom."

"What about Father?"

Niki turned his face away. His sister was a brave and sensible creature and he usually confided in her completely; but now he could not bear to tell her what he suspected was the truth about the King's kidnapping. Without Antar on the throne, Raktum might well think it could attack its wealthy southern neighbor with impunity, seeking to conquer it outright rather than simply raiding its ships on the high seas. Niki had often heard his father and mother speak of the danger posed by the ambitious Pirate Queen.

But now, in answer to Jan, he could only say: "The pirates will certainly want a ransom for Father, too. They will probably ask a shipful of platinum and diamonds for him in addition to Mother's talisman — but only a few coffers of gold for us."

Jan grinned. "Maybe only a chamber pot of silver for Tolo."

Below, the younger prince uttered a squeal. "I hear something again, but it's not ship-varts! Someone is coming. Oh, come down quickly!"

Niki and Jan began to slide, tearing their hands and clothing on the rough metal in their hurry. They had barely tumbled off the chain piles and onto the thin sleeping-pallets when a succession of thuds announced the unbarring of the chain-locker door. It opened. Outside was a dark hold, a place cluttered with odds and ends of rope, lumber, metal, worn canvas, and barrels of tar. A man stood there, holding a lantern high in one hand and a bared short-sword in the other. He was not one of the scowling pirate-knights who had imprisoned them, but another who had the look of a seaman.

"Stand back," he ordered Prince Nikalon, who had sprung up and rushed forward. "Away from the door, you whelp." He thrust the lantern in and looked about with an expression of repugnance. "A sorry place this is to stow three youngsters, even if they are Labornoki trash."

"Laboruwendian trash," said Niki coolly. "Who are you and what do you want?"

"I'm Boblen the Quartermaster, and I've brought you a visitor." He stepped back outside, still holding the lantern high, and a shorter figure dressed all in black materialized out of the gloomy hold and stepped into the chain-locker.

"The Goblin Kinglet!" shrieked Tolo. "He's come to torture us!"

Jan gave her little brother a swift punch in the side.

The youthful King Ledavardis had flushed at Tolo's thoughtless insult, but he said nothing, only looked at the three, one after the other, as though they were creatures the like of which he had never encountered before.

"Well, you've seen them, young Sire," the Quartermaster said gruffly. "Now come away before someone discovers us. You'll only rate a royal scolding and bed without supper if the Queen Regent finds out you've been down here — but she'll likely have my liver chopped up for fish-food."

"Good!" cried Tolo. "I hope she slays both of you!" And he stuck his tongue out.

"Be silent," Niki ordered. And to Ledavardis: "My brother is an uncivilized infant and I apologize on his behalf for his rudeness. However, he is not used to being treated like some animal in the royal zoo. Neither are my sister and I. Or is this type of accommodation the usual thing for royal passengers on the ships of Raktum?"

"No, it is not," said Ledavardis, speaking low. Hesitantly, he held out a sack to Princess Janeel. "Boblen told me you are to be fed only bread and water now. I am sorry. Here is a roasted waterfowl and some nut-pastries I was able to find."

Jan took the sack without speaking.

Niki said: "Thank you, King."

"Well," Ledavardis muttered, turning away. "I'd better go now."

"One thing," Niki said. "Can you tell us of our father, King Antar? Is — is he alive?"

"Yes. I have not seen him, but I know they have him chained with the galley slaves."

"We had heard that from Lady Sharice."

"The King is certainly not forced to row," Ledavardis hastened to say. "The sweeps are not manned in such a high wind."

"Will we all be held for ransom in Raktum?" Niki asked.

"I do not know. First we must sail south to the Windlorn Isles on some mysterious errand of the sorcerer's."

"South!" cried Niki.

"Come away and say no more!" said the Quartermaster from out in the hold. "What if that lothok-spawn of a Black Voice should find us and report us to the sorcerer?"

"Be silent, Boblen. Nothing is going to happen to us." And the boy-King continued to brush aside the man's urgings, and began to ask many questions about the life the three captives led back home in Laboruwenda. He wanted to know how the courtiers treated them, and if they were allowed to leave the palace and travel about their country, and how they were tutored, and if they had friends of their own ages, and whether they ever envied children who were not royal.

Both Nikalon and Janeel quickly lost their suspicion of Ledavardis, and treated him with civility and even sympathy, not only answering his questions but also asking many of their own. But little Tolivar could not overcome his revulsion over the Raktumian youth's ungainly appearance, and would not speak to him, except once to ask him if he liked being a Pirate King.

Ledavardis did not seem to notice the lad's hostility. He replied that he had been happy enough while his fierce father, King Ledamot, lived. The Raktumian monarch made his pirate fleet the scourge of the Northern Sea, and he was ruthless to any person who threatened him. He had loved his son dearly and had dealt savagely with any Raktumian nobles who dared to hint that Ledavardis might be unfit to succeed to the throne.

But then King Ledamot died untimely in a shipwreck, and Queen Mother Ganondri proved quickly that she would brook no rival as regent for her grandson. Several important fleet-captains who opposed her died of mysterious illnesses, Ledavardis said, and others she vanquished openly through clever political ploys, depriving them of their fortunes as well as their power. The boy-King's mother, Queen Mashriya, was reduced to a pathetic invalid who never left her bed.

Ledavardis was matter-of-fact as he spoke of the way his own life changed for the worse during the seven years of his grandmother's regency. Even though the boy-King tried to make light of his misfortunes, it was evident that he was lonely and despised at the Raktumian court. Only when he was allowed to go to sea did he find some happiness with several of the older pirate captains, who had escaped the Queen Regent's purge and were still his friends. At sea his twisted body had grown strong, and he felt he was a true king and not a helpless child.

When Ledavardis finally left the chain-locker, Niki and Jan admitted to each other that they were sorry to have thought him a goblin. But young Tolo mimicked the hunchback's odd walk, and pulled faces to make fun of his ugliness, and called him a crybaby and a coward and no true pirate at all.

Jan opened the bag of food. "Who cares about that? It was kind of him to bring this to us."

"It's probably poison," said Tolo, making a face. "I don't trust that rotten Goblin Kinglet!"

Niki lifted out the small fowl, unwrapped it from its napkin, and sniffed. "Nay, it seems wholesome enough." He spread the napkin like a tablecloth on the dirty deck and set out the food upon it. "It was strange that Ledavardis should visit us, though, and even stranger that he should open his heart to us." He looked up at his sister, who still stood holding the empty sack. "What do you think, Jan?"

"I — I think that the King of Raktum is a very unhappy person," she said. "More than that, I cannot say."

Niki broke apart the fowl and shared it out, and they all three began to eat.

9

Queen Anigel was in her cabin, alone with her grief and misgivings. The captain of the Laboruwendian flagship, as well as Owanon and Ellinis and Lampiar and Penapat and the other high officers of the court, had prevailed upon her not to conduct her talismanic surveys out on the deck even though she felt closer to her loved ones under the open sky. There was too much danger of a heavy sea sweeping her overboard while she was in her trance.

For four days now she had eaten almost nothing and slept only fitfully, letting only Immu attend her. Almost all of her time was taken up with watching over her lost children and husband through her magical coronet, reassuring herself that no new hurt was done to them. On occasion she would also descry the sorcerer Portolanus; but she had failed to view his crucial meetings with the Queen Regent and Admiral Jorot, and so she knew nothing of Portolanus's plan to murder the captives once the ransom had been obtained.

Anigel did see King Ledavardis's first visit to her children, and she was surprised and touched by the young man's unexpected kindness. She also saw him come again, this time alone, on the fourth day of the voyage, bringing more food. He stayed over an hour, questioning Niki and Jan about the way they had been lured unsuspecting from the coronation ball, and asking them what they thought of Portolanus. Ledavardis was a rather naïve boy, for all that he was sixteen years old. It was evident to Anigel that he was very dubious about his grandmother's Tuzameni ally, and frightened of what the future might hold for him.

Ledavardis also made casual mention of the way that the sorcerer had stunned the Queen Regent's guards and physician with his magical rod, later restoring them by touching them again with the same instrument. Anigel could not contain her excitement as she listened to this, for it now seemed certain to her that the rod had also been used upon her husband, Antar. He was not in a death-coma after all — as she had feared when she saw that he did not wake for days — but was only under some enchantment that could be lifted at the sorcerer's will.

King Ledavardis seemed eager to talk to other young people of his own rank. The life of a royal child was unnatural even under the best of circumstances, but this boy with his twisted spine and repellent features was particularly unlucky.

Anigel was sadly vexed at the way little Tolivar continued to mock Ledavardis and call him the Goblin Kinglet. But Tolo was only a baby after all, and puny and unsure of himself as well. Although Tolo had never suffered the cruel rejection the Raktumian boy had, Anigel knew that he envied his strong, handsome elder brother. Despising Ledavardis made Tolo feel better about his own imperfections.

When I have little Tolo back, the Queen said to herself, I must keep him with me more, and tell him I love him and reassure him and build his confidence. And I will urge Antar to do so as well —

Antar . . .

Love and anxiety for her husband put all thought of Prince Tolivar out of her mind. She bade the talisman depict the King, and saw that he lay still sleeping on a plank bed in the foul quarters of the galley slaves. As always, she prayed for his welfare and safe return. Now that she was certain that he was not in a mortal stupor, she felt thankful that he was unaware of his own desperate situation and that of their children. Antar was a proud man and impetuous, and he would be tortured by rage and humiliation if he were conscious. Who could say what the pirates might do to him if he antagonized them or tried to escape?

Or if she refused to pay his ransom.

What will I do, she asked herself, if Portolanus threatens Antar with some terrible hurt, or even death?

She had mulled over the awful possibility many times before, worrying the thought as one touches a decayed tooth, knowing that there will be pain, yet unable to let it be. Tears came, even as she strove to forbid them, and she faced again the dilemma that had assailed her from the first moment she had read the two words spelling out the price of his freedom:

Your talisman.

Could she remain steadfast, as she had told Haramis she would, if the price of retaining the Three-Headed Monster was Antar's tortured screams, his ignominious dying? If she gave in to Portolanus, she was a false queen, laying her country open to conquest by black magic. But if Antar were taken from her, she knew she would die herself, and the devil take Laboruwenda.

For a long time she only studied her husband's face and gave way to sorrow. Then the vision of Antar dimmed, although she fought to hold it clear, and she heard the impatient voice of Haramis in her mind:

"Ani! Listen to me! Look behind your flotilla and rejoice!"

She seized her leather sea-cloak and dashed outside at once, not even bothering to respond to her sister.

The rain had stopped but a high wind still roared from the north. The mountainous swells coming up behind them looked as though they would surely curl over and smash the four ships down to the bottom of the sea. But somehow the huge waves never broke, and the ships rode up and down their dizzying slopes like wheeled carts rolling backward over hills. Earlier, the peculiar motion had nauseated her. Now she was almost used to it, and she clung firmly to the quarterdeck rail and commanded her talisman to give her a long view of the sea behind the Laboruwendian ships.

The Sight revealed another vessel overtaking them.

Breathless, she ordered the talisman to show the other ship more closely. It was much smaller than her bireme flagship, with two masts slanted back at a saucy angle, and having only four very small sails set. It streaked through the heaving sea like an arrow shot from a crossbow and was already nearly abeam of the last Laboruwendian vessel. Certain of the tiny figures working on deck had a strange form, and when she looked even closer, she saw that these were Wyvilo aborigines. Among the humans was a slender woman with flying auburn hair, who wore the image of an Eyed Trefoil upon her jerkin.

"Kadi!" the Queen cried. "You've come! Oh, thanks be to the Lords of the Air!"

The vision of Kadiya disappeared, and Anigel's mind's eye saw the face of her other sister, Haramis, wrapped in a fur-edged hood and silhouetted against a stormy sky.

"Listen to me, Ani! Now you and Kadiya must work closely together. Both your ships and those of the enemy have nearly reached the latitude of Council Isle. At around midday tomorrow, the pirate trireme will turn westward into the Windlorns to reach the place where Kadi's talisman was lost. Portolanus is so far ahead of you that I fear your flagship can never catch up. You will have to go onto Kadi's smaller boat. It is very swift and it will likely overtake the Raktumian before the strong winds fall away among the islands."

"But in the calms," Anigel protested, "the pirate trireme will be able to speed along so much faster with its oars —"

"Most of Queen Ganondri's galley slaves are deathly seasick. The corsairs of Raktum mostly ply the coastal waters, and the Northern Sea is sheltered by the Peninsula from the worst ravages of the monsoons. I suspect the Queen's men have never encountered anything like this magical storm of Portolanus."

"Our brave Captain Velinikar says that *he* has never seen its like. In spite of the tremendous waves, the wind maintains itself on the fine line between propelling the ships at high speed and blowing the masts and sails away."

"Never mind that," Haramis said impatiently. "The important thing is that the oarsmen on the Raktumian trireme will not instantly recover from their malaise. It will take some time before they are well enough to pull stoutly. Meanwhile, you and Kadiya in the smaller ship can keep ahead of them. In the light and erratic winds that prevail among the Windlorns, you will have the advantage — for a time."

"Then it is not certain that Kadi and I will reach her talisman first?"

"No," said Haramis. "But you must beseech your own talisman to help you, besides praying hard to the Lords of the Air to speed your ship along."

Anigel flung up her hands in exasperation. "I cannot command my talisman the way you command yours! Sometimes the thing obeys me in ways other than the Sight, but most often it does not. I am no Archimage!"

Haramis sighed. "I know that the talismans' action remains mostly a mystery to you and Kadi. My own Three-Winged Circle is only slightly more cooperative. But I am on a journey now that may solve this problem for us —"

"Hara, you must tell me what you are up to! I have spied you out flying over the high mountains on a lammergeier —"

"Little Sister, I can accomplish nothing useful in time to help you retrieve Kadi's talisman. Forget me. Use all your wits and all your strength to bring up the Three-Lobed Burning Eye from the depths. Every hour you delay, the world falls further out of balance. Farewell now, and may God and the Lords of the Air defend you from Portolanus."

The Laboruwendian flagship hove to and tried to launch a longboat that would carry Anigel to the *Lyath*. But the seas were so rough and the wind so strong that the craft was tumbled over before it could even be released completely from the lines on the boat booms. It foundered almost at once, and one of the crew who had volunteered to man it was lost.

"This way is hopeless, Madam," Captain Velinikar told Anigel, when the surviving seamen had been rescued. *Lyath* lay a quarter of a league away from the flagship, half the time invisible behind the colossal swells. Anigel had bespoken her intentions to Jagun, and he had relayed the news to Kadiya and Captain Ly Woonly.

"Then we must find another way for me to transfer to Kadiya's ship," Anigel retorted. She had dressed in a seaman's oilskins, and wore her talisman pinned immovably to blond braids wound about her head.

The Labornoki captain shook his head. "Madam, I do not know one."

"Then let us ask Jagun to consult the skipper of the *Lyath*," Anigel said. She closed her eyes, using the talisman again, and when she reopened them a few minutes later, she said: "The Okamisi captain suggests a breeches buoy — whatever that might be."

The other seamen standing about uttered exclamations of horrified dissent. Velinikar himself cursed, then made clumsy apology to his Queen. "Madam, I have heard of such a contrivance, but it is madness to even suggest that you might use it."

"Describe it."

"We would have to get under way again, running before the wind on nearly bare poles. The small Okamisi ship would have to trim its storm sails with the utmost skill so as to match our speed exactly, then come alongside as close as she dared. We would shoot a line to her with a catapult. This line would be used to haul over a strong hawser with a block-and-tackle apparatus attached. Our two ships being connected safely, you would have to get into a kind of lifebuoy-ring fastened to the block riding the hawser. Those on *Lyath* would then draw you across the gap between the vessels by pulling on the first rope."

Anigel's face went white during the captain's recital, but she managed a smile. "I am willing to do it."

"No, my Queen, you will not!" cried Velinikar. "If the two vessels should happen to drift apart all of a sudden, or one get ahead of the other in a rogue blast of wind, the ropes could break, dropping you into the sea. And if the boats were thrust suddenly close together, you would also go into the water as the ropes sagged — perhaps being crushed between the two hulls."

"I must do it," she said simply. "It is our only chance to save the King and the children. Make preparations, Captain, while I bespeak Jagun and have the *Lyath* do the same."

First the flagship's carpenter had to construct the breeches buoy, which was nothing but a cork-bark ring less than an ell in diameter, with a cutoff pair of canvas breeches firmly attached to it, and ropes to suspend it from a running block. Then it took nearly an hour for the boats to get into position, and by that time it was nearly dark. Velinikar took the helm of the royal bireme himself so that its course would remain steady as rock. *Lyath* edged into position somewhat more clumsily, standing off some twenty ells from the larger vessel and bobbing wildly up and down in the troubled waters, never precisely matching speeds.

Now the mates of the two ships shouted back and forth through hailing horns, their voices almost lost in the great wind. The work of installing the breeches buoy began. Kadiya came to the rail of the noga with Jagun and a tall Wyvilo at her side. She and Anigel shouted only a few encouraging words to each other. It was not a time for relayed conversation via the speech without words.

Anigel watched with Immu, Ellinis, and Owanon standing close by her side as the first line was shot across. Then the rest of the equipment was carefully put into place: a winch, and the hawser for the block to run along, and the lighter block and tackle that would pull the Queen across. The first mate of the flagship assured Anigel that small variations in distance between the ships could be accommodated by the apparatus. It was only sudden, violent motions that might endanger her. Three strong seamen came up and knelt briefly at Anigel's feet for her blessing, then went to stand by the all-important winch that could tighten or loosen the connecting hawser if such aberrant motion occurred.

On *Lyath*, whose deck lay nearly ten ells below that of the tall bireme, the other end of the hawser was made fast to the mainmast. The block and tackle were affixed below it, with Lummomu-Ko himself ready to pull Anigel in as swiftly as possible. The ropes creaked and the winchmen strove to keep the hawser taut. The wind seemed somewhat abated, and finally the first mate decided that the breeches buoy was ready. Anigel kissed Immu, Ellinis, and Owanon. Then she stepped into the thing, clung to the ring about her waist with all her strength, and was pulled off her feet, into the air, and over the ship's rail.

The bireme surged downward and *Lyath* rose up. For a moment the hawser from which the buoy was suspended was nearly at a level, while the foam-streaked gray waters made a roughened hill slanting below. Anigel was moving — riding above the waves, splashed by spray, flung from side to side like a doll hanging on a clothesline. Then the bireme rose and *Lyath* went into a trough. The hawser above the Queen's head twanged with strain, then eased. Anigel came to a sudden, jarring halt and then began to move slowly again. The ships were now maintaining a miraculously identical speed and direction despite the heaving waters, like pair of oddly matched but expert dancing partners.

The buoy was moving quickly again, and Anigel was more than halfway to the noga. She managed to wave at the people along the smaller ship's rail. Momentarily, the sea flattened beneath both hulls as they came to the bottom of a great trough. Anigel slid easily in the buoy down the slanted hawser, drawn along not only by the powerful muscles of Lummomu but by gravity as well. Side by side, the ships appeared to glide backward up another mountainous swell.

And then the wind shifted abruptly. It seemed to Anigel as if *Lyath* were rushing toward her. But the hawser that supported the buoy had gone ominously slack, and instead of sliding along it she began to drop sickeningly toward the water. She heard shouts from the *Lyath* and the shrill scream of a female aborigine from her own flagship. The two ships were closing together, driven by the shifting wind. In another instant she would be in the water.

"Talisman, save me!" she cried.

The wind roared, shifting direction again. There was a mighty *twung!* as the hawser snapped taut. Lummomu had lost his grip and lay sprawled on the deck. Anigel was being propelled as if by a catapult toward the smaller ship. She knew that in another instant she would be dashed to her death against it —

She stopped in midair.

There was no wind.

There was no tossing sea, no heaving small ship. Both *Lyath* and the waters were motionless, as if they had turned to stone.

Anigel seemed suspended in calm air, the ropes all in a tangle above her head but unmoving, frozen. She dared not breathe. Life itself had come to a halt.

And then only she, in all the world, was permitted to move. She floated to *Lyath*, passed above its rail and descended gently, still gripping the ring of the breeches buoy. Her feet touched the deck. Around her were petrified Wyvilo, Jagun like a small statue with wide yellow eyes and mouth agape in amazement, and Kadiya...

Almost as soon as it began, the eerie experience ceased. Anigel fell heavily to her knees, all enveloped in loose rope and cumbered by the buoy. Kadiya and the others were howling with relief, and there were faint cheers coming from her flagship.

When Anigel was freed from the mess, she stumbled into her sister's arms, weeping for joy. "It was my talisman! It saved me! Kadi — Kadi — "

"Yes," Kadiya agreed. "Beyond doubt it did. One moment you were plunging toward the water, and the next moment you were here."

Behind the two women, the mate Ly Tyry was directing the crew to quickly cut loose the ropes that bound the noga to the Laboruwendian flagship. At once the two ships began to draw swiftly apart. *Lyath* had been moving under two small sails. A third was unfurled to the howling wind and the noga took flight, moving faster now than the bireme. It went faster yet as a fourth tiny piece of canvas was raised.

"Let us go below," Kadiya said, leading her sister like a child.

The Queen was trembling violently now, soaked in spite of her oilskin garments, and her face and hands were bloodless. But she smiled still, and tried to wave good-bye to those on the flagship.

"The talisman," she said again. "The talisman *did* save me!"

Kadiya opened the companionway door. "Let us hope," she said in a voice gone flat, "that it will save me as well."

10

The Archimage and Shiki the Dorok flew westward over the Ohogan foothills of Labornok on the first leg of their journey to the Kimilon, each mounted on a huge black-and-white lammergeier. Two additional birds carried their supplies. The Archimage mitigated the storm that swirled around them even more efficiently than Portolanus had done, and Shiki marveled at how warm and comfortable he was — and how swiftly the voors were able to fly — within the magical bubble of calm that the great enchantress spun with her all-powerful talisman.

At first, Shiki was so overawed by the Archimage that he hardly dared to speak to her. He kept reverently silent during their time aloft so as not to disturb her mystical contemplation and was humble and self-effacing when they descended that night to rest on the ground. She produced warm food for both of them from a magical contrivance; and later, with the giant birds nestled round about the two tiny sleeping-tents, the talisman continued to shield them all from the elements.

Shiki half awoke in the middle of the night, thinking that he heard strange sounds like those a human person makes when sore distressed. But when he called out, the faint noise ceased, and he told himself that he was imagining things, hearing only the moaning of the wind. In the morning he had forgotten all about it, and his sleep was undisturbed on the other nights that they camped in the mountains.

By the time they had overflown Raktum's Latoosh Mountains and reached the border of the Sempiternal Icecap itself, the unnatural storm generated by Portolanus finally came to an end and the sky cleared. The flying steeds continued to flap tirelessly across dazzling snowfields, which were broken only rarely by mountains upthrust through the silent immensity of the world-continent's interior.

The Archimage guided her own voor as expertly as Shiki did the new bird who had taken the place of his late friend, and without thinking he ventured to congratulate her on her skill. She took no offense at his familiarity, but instead seemed perfectly willing to converse, telling him that it was her custom to travel on voorback, on the infrequent occasions when she left her Tower to visit her two sisters or to confer in person with humans or Folk who requested her help. She said she had been taught to guide voors long ago, before she was the Archimage, and her teacher had been the Vispi woman Magira who now served as the housekeeper of the Tower.

Here was another surprise for Shiki, who had assumed that the White Lady was a goddess who knew everything without learning. She laughed at that, and told him something of the story of her life, that she had been Archimage for only twelve years and was still only beginning to learn how to do her job properly. Timidly, Shiki then asked her what kinds of work she undertook on behalf of her clients. She responded in a straightforward manner, telling how she adjudicated disputes, and helped to find lost persons, and counseled leaders who were seriously perplexed, and gave warning of impending natural calamities, and in a myriad other ways guided and guarded those who called upon her and trusted her.

Shiki was astounded when she admitted that there were problems to which she had no solutions. (This amazed him almost as much as his early discovery that she ate and drank as did ordinary people, and tended to her body's relief, and sometimes even overslept.) He was further shaken when she confessed that she did not know exactly what she expected to find in the Inaccessible Kimilon, only that it was important; and she dreaded having to go to the place and was exceedingly glad to have him accompany her.

It now began to dawn on the little Dorok that he had been mistaken in his earlier judgment of the White Lady. A wielder of magic she was indeed, but she was not a forbidding goddess or even one of the legendary sindona, too lofty to suffer fear or misgivings like ordinary mortals. This Archimage was instead a person of flesh and blood with emotions very like his own, who was unsure of herself and in need of comfort and friendship. And so he dared more and more to converse with her in a commonplace manner and even made little jokes. She in turn asked him details about his life in the Tuzameni mountains, and he told her how he and his wife had tended scattered plots of ferol-plants that thrived in the geyser-warmed valley where his village lay, yielding both nutritious tubers and fruits that made a cheering beverage. During the snowy season he had trapped worrams and other pelt animals, while his wife spun and wove zuch-wool into fine scarves and shawls that could be traded along with his furs to the lowland humans. With sadness, Shiki spoke of how his people had been the friends of the giant lammergeier birds from time out of mind, speaking to them through the speech without words and riding them when they wished to visit other villages of the Folk in the mountains of Tuzamen.

"But now, as I have already told you," he added, "we Dorok and the voors can be friends no longer because of the foul sorcerer." And he waited for the Archimage to reassure him, to tell him that she would mend the situation by bringing down Portolanus.

But she said nothing, only fingered her talisman and stared out over the desolate icecap that the voors traversed, her face somber and unreadable. That night Shiki again heard the faint sounds that reminded him of weeping, but could not be.

Seven days after they had left the Archimage's Tower, the travelers saw what looked like a lofty dark hill of peculiar rounded form, rising on the horizon beyond the almost featureless expanse of ice and snow. As they drew closer the mass seemed more to resemble thunderclouds, partly gray and partly black as ink, roiling and swirling and yet seeming much more dense than the ordinary clouds that harbored rain or snow. Occasional lurid flashes of crimson lit their depths.

"It is the Kimilon," Shiki said to the Archimage, "the place we Dorok know as the Land of Fire and Ice. Usually the great cloud that enshrouds the plateau is largely steam, with only a little smoke and ash, but I fear that now many of the volcanoes are erupting. We must pray, White Lady, that molten lava has not engulfed the interior basin. It is there that we will find the strange building that you seek, in which the sorcerer Portolanus lived. Can your talisman tell if the basin is safe to enter?"

Haramis pulled forth the wand from beneath her cloak and bade it show her a clear Sight of the Inaccessible Kimilon. When she had tried to view the place back at her Tower, details of the interior were always masked by thick clouds, and she could get no close view of what lay on the ground. Now, once again, the picture within the Three-Winged Circle was an obscure one that showed little more than she might see with her naked eyes had she been directly overhead, peering down through the turbulent smoke.

"I am afraid we shall have to wait until we get there to see what has befallen the ancient storage building," Haramis said. "The Kimilon is a place infused by powerful magic. I am amazed that your people knew of its existence."

The little man shrugged. "The Land of Fire and Ice is spoken of in our most ancient legends as a place sacred to the Vanished Ones. From time to time one of our Dorok heroes would be impelled by some irresistible inner urge to visit it on voorback, but he knew he must touch nothing there lest he never see his home again. Those who resisted temptation came back safely. A few of the heroes were never seen again, and it was said that they had succumbed to the lure of the forbidden magic of the place and remained there, turned to ice-statues. Thus the old tales were refreshed in the minds of the Dorok, and the way to the Kimilon confirmed again and again in folk-memory."

"I wonder," Haramis mused, "whether your people might once have been the servants of some long-forgotten Archimage, who transported at her behest dangerous old artifacts to the Kimilon. You are close kin to the Vispi Folk of the Ohogan Mountains, and they served my predecessor, the Archimage Binah, from time immemorial."

"White Lady, I know nothing of any such duty. We Dorok believed that the Archimage lived far away from our land and had little to do with us. It was my late beloved voor, Nunusio, who reminded me that you are the guardian and protector of all Folk, and who urged me to come to you."

Haramis felt a portentous tingling at the base of her scalp. The lammergeiers! She had never thought to consult them . . .

Hiluro!

I hear, White Lady, and respond.

Speak to me so that Shiki and the other birds cannot hear.

Very well.

Hiluro, do you know of other living Archimages besides myself?

Yes. There is the Lady of the Sea, who lives in the fastness of the auroras, and the Lord of the Firmament, whose home is in the sky. These two and yourself are the only ones remaining of the great Archimagical College established by the Vanished Ones to oppose the evil Star Men. I can tell you nothing of these other two Archimages save their titles and dwellings, and the fact that they will live and continue their mission for as long as the Star threatens the balance of the world.

Thank you, Hiluro.

This was at least a little more than the talisman had already told her, and Haramis pondered it as they flew closer and closer to the Kimilon. Finally, as the declining sun cast a rose-colored veil over the Sempiternal Icecap and gave spectacular backlighting to the ash-clouds, they arrived.

The Inaccessible Kimilon was a small plateau about three leagues in diameter, hemmed in by a dozen or so tall volcanoes. Five of these, standing shoulder to shoulder in the west, were pouring forth black smoke, with occasional blobs of lurid scarlet lava hurled skyward. Narrow rivulets of molten rock streamed down their flanks. Two more mountains merely steamed, their white vapors mingling with the dark plumes of their neighbors, and the rest were dormant. The active volcanoes were a fearsome sight, and their rumbling was like constant thunder. Shiki was surprised to note that the Archimage's hand holding her talisman was trembling.

"The wind is blowing the smoke and ash away from the interior of the Kimilon," Haramis told Shiki. "That is good news at least."

The four lammergeiers flew through a steep cleft on the eastern side of the plateau, where the extinct volcanoes were covered with massive glaciers streaked by ash and soot. The valley floor was solidified lava—some of it blocky and full of holes like clinkers, and some smoother, with an appearance of huge dark ropes or piles of pillows or poured batter turned to black rock. A sizable lake that reflected the angry sky occupied the center of the depression, fed by torrents of melt-water from the ice fields of the inactive cones. Fumaroles spouted and hissed beyond the lake's western shore, a region where the ground was cracked and steaming, and hot mudpots bubbled like caldrons of multihued paint. On the eastern lakeshore the ground seemed solid, although deep in drifts of white ash, and the rocks had lichens growing upon them. There were also a few stunted shrubs and other kinds of plantlife, their green leaves withered and discolored by the poisonous exhalations of the volcanoes.

At the base of a great black cliff stood the building.

The four voors circled the lake once, then glided down to land next to the structure. A sharp stench of sulfur, vile but bearable, pervaded the atmosphere, and the air was humid and very warm. A light rain of ash fell constantly, whirled about the ground by erratic breezes. Small nodules of pumice crunched underfoot as the Archimage and her small companion alighted. The ground seemed to vibrate, and a low, almost musical roar mingled with the hissing of the fumaroles and the sound of rushing water.

"We cannot stay here long, Shiki," Haramis decided. "I will try to hurry with my explorations."

"Would — would you like me to accompany you?" he offered. "If there are demons guarding the place, as our legends say, I will gladly defend you with my life." He drew his long knife from its sheath and held it up with both hands, so that the blade shone redly in the lava-light.

Haramis looked down at him, deeply touched. He hardly knew her at all, and he was surely more frightened than she. And yet she was certain that he had made his offer through friendship, not merely in fulfillment of duty.

She lay one hand upon his shoulder. "Dear Shiki, in the kindness of your heart, you have discovered that I am afraid of what I might find within this place. You must understand, however, that I do not fear monsters or demons or any other form of external danger to my life. This building was built by an Archimage like myself, after all. It is right that I enter and explore it. The unknown thing that I seek — that I will recognize when I see it — is dreadful to me because it pertains to my inmost heart and soul, and within that inner realm no one can accompany me but myself. Still, I would be happy to have you come with me as far as you can. But put away your weapon, my friend."

He slipped his knife back into its scabbard. "We Dorok have a saying: A monster fought with a good companion is smaller than one encountered alone."

But she only smiled at that, and approached the mysterious edifice with Shiki close by her side.

The place was made entirely of black lava rock, as was the cliff it merged with, and about the size of a barn, with a steeply slanted roof of flagstones that would shed both snow and falling ash. Only at the front, on either side of the narrow door, were there windows, deep set into walls nearly an ell thick and having many small panes set in leading. The door was of metal, with neither latch nor knob, and it refused to yield to her touch.

She drew forth her talisman on its neck chain and tapped the door gently, saying: "Talisman, protect us two from all harm and grant us access to this place."

Immediately the door swung open. The area inside was utterly black. Haramis stepped inside and commanded illumination. At once a series of wall sconces lit, having as their light source the same type of flameless glowing crystal found throughout her Tower. Shiki trailed behind as she entered. The room was obviously the place where the exiled Portolanus had made his home. A robe of stiff fiber and a pair of worn sandals still lay abandoned on the floor, and a cape and wide conical hat of the same material had been tossed in one corner. In contrast to these rude garments, the furniture in the room was extraordinarily beautiful and sophisticated. A table, two chairs, a bed, and several cabinets and chests of an unfamiliar gleaming tawny material were fashioned in a style that Haramis had never seen before, all graceful curves without a sign of joints, as though the things had *grown* into their proper shapes rather than having been made by an artisan. The bed had pillows that resembled two huge soap bubbles, and blankets of very strong, gossamer-thin transparent stuff strangely luxurious to the touch, fastened somehow to the bed so that they could not be removed. Beside the bed stood a peculiar narrow cabinet made of a substance slick as polished bone but unyielding as metal, having on its slightly slanted top surface a large gray square and many smaller squares of different colors, each of these decorated with peculiar symbols carved in low relief. On the other side of the room, next to the table and chairs, was a waist-high blocky object with many rectangles of different sizes apparently drawn upon it. Ten circles smaller than a platinum crown were clustered within a frame on the front, and these also sported mysterious glyphs.

"Surely these marvelous things were made by the Vanished Ones!" Shiki whispered.

"You are doubtless correct. And now we will find out what the mysterious contrivances do." She touched the odd bedside cabinet with her talisman and a simultaneous mental query, in the way she had learned when investigating other ancient artifacts in the Cavern of Black Ice. The talisman spoke:

This is a library. One consults it in the following fashion —

"Pray hold," Haramis told it. She next touched the blocky thing near the table.

This is a kitchen unit. It includes an assortment of containers and implements and will cook food, heat or chill it, and store it in wholesome condition indefinitely. One opens the compartment containing the utensils —

"Pray hold," said Haramis. She touched an object the size of a large chest. Its top immediately sprang open, revealing glittering polygons and circles arranged in incomprehensible patterns.

This is a musical creator that can reproduce the sounds of any instrument, and orchestrate them according to the composer's will —

"Pray hold," said Haramis.

She went to an inner door, which opened easily. Lights went on as she stepped into an enormous room that apparently took up most of the space within the building. Ranks of open shelves reaching to the high ceiling were arranged with narrow aisles between, and the shelves were crowded with oddly shaped mechanisms and boxes of all sizes. The shelving and their contents were furred with a layer of dust nearly half a finger-span thick, and here and there were clean empty spaces revealing where some object had been removed.

Haramis and Shiki began to stroll the aisles, looking upon the devices and marveling. From time to time the Archimage touched a machine with her talisman and identified all manner of amazing things — every imaginable kind of tool, horrific weapons, strange scientific apparatus, devices for manufacturing (but of course these lacked the raw materials that would have made them useful to the exiled sorcerer), machines that would teach, entertain, and even heal.

"How wonderful!" Shiki exclaimed. "Portolanus must have been very sorry not to be able to take all of these things with him."

"I think we should thank the Lords of the Air that he did not," Haramis remarked grimly. "Heaven only knows how the larger devices were brought here in the first place."

As they made their way toward the cliffside wall of the building, she again consulted her talisman: "Is this truly the secret storage place of some Archimage?"

Yes.

"Who built it?"

The Archimage of the Land Drianro had it built after the original storage place used by previous Archimages of the Land was engulfed in a lava flow and became no longer usable.

"Tell me when Drianro lived, and why this place was not used by the Archimage Binah."

Drianro was born two thousand three hundred and six years before the present day. He died suddenly, neglecting to inform his successor, the Archimage Binah, of the location of this cache of ancient artifacts within the Inaccessible Kimilon.

Haramis caught her breath. The talisman, reading her mind as it often seemed to do, gave the answer to her next unspoken question:

The Archimage Binah lived one thousand four hundred and eighty-six years, and held her sacred office for one thousand four hundred and sixty-four of those years.

"By the Flower! And am I fated to live so long?"

The question is impertinent.

Haramis's lips tightened. How often had the talisman chided her with that wretched phrase when she asked a question it could not answer! But in an instant she forgot her vexation. Wonderment reasserted itself as she gazed about at the thousands of mysterious contraptions, and she questioned the talisman again. "All of these things . . . were they considered potentially harmful, that they had to be banished here?"

Some of them the Archimage Drianro only considered inappropriate to the indigenous culture, while others he deemed hazardous.

"Are the devices magical, or only machines?"

They partake of an ancient science some would deem magical.

"But is there true magic?" Haramis demanded.

The question is impertinent.

"Bah!" cried Haramis. "When will you ever stop mocking me when I seek to get to the heart of the matter? To the very essence of my duty as an Archimage?"

The questions are —

"Pray hold," she interrupted in exasperation, and let the wand drop on its chain around her neck.

Shiki had listened to her dialogue with the talisman with his mouth wide open and his eyes glazed with incredulity.

"Do not be scandalized, my friend," she remarked tartly. "Magic can be awesome — but it can also be dreary and frustrating, especially to those forced to learn its ways without a teacher. I came here hoping to remedy that very lack."

Shiki smiled uneasily. "Did you hope to find a magical book or machine that would instruct you?"

"No. I am looking for something more special. And since it has not condescended to show itself to me, I shall have to command it." She lifted the talisman again and spoke in a loud voice: "If there is a contrivance in this place that will let me communicate with other Archimages living in the world, then reveal it!"

They heard a small sound.

It was like the vibration of a crystal glass struck by a fingernail, high, pure, and ringing. Haramis looked wildly around her at the ranks of shelves packed with enigmatic objects. Where was the sound coming from? It began to fade even as she tried vainly to pin down its source.

Shiki had torn off his leather cap so that his upstanding ears with their frostbitten tips could listen more keenly. "This way!" he cried, and dashed away with the Archimage close on his heels.

They were moving along that part of the wall farthest from the entrance, which was of raw lava-rock and obviously part of the cliff-face. Shiki finally fetched up at a spot that looked no different from any other, pointed down at the floor, and said: "Here!"

Haramis tapped the dusty rock surface with the talisman. Again the note chimed — and a section of the floor became as transparent as thin smoke and then vanished, leaving a hole over an ell in diameter, impenetrably black in its depths. Musty air gushed forth from this, stirring the dust of the storage chamber and making Haramis and Shiki sneeze.

She ordered that the inside of the hole be lighted, but nothing happened. It remained completely dark, and there was no more wind from it, but only the musical note still sounding faintly in their ears.

Haramis addressed her talisman: "What is this opening? Where does it lead?"

This is a viaduct, and it leads to where one is summoned.

"Am I summoned to enter it?"

Yes. The Archimage of the Land is summoned to the Archimage of the Sea, for an instructional sojourn of thrice ten days and thrice ten nights.

Haramis let out a long breath. Her face was radiant. "This is what I expected — what I hoped to find! Thanks be to the Triune God!"

She would have stepped into the viaduct opening at once, except that Shiki piped up forlornly: "What about me? Shall I wait here until your return, White Lady?"

Haramis was ashamed of her thoughtlessness. She addressed the talisman sternly: "I cannot leave my good servant Shiki alone here in this awful Kimilon for thirty days. And there are also our faithful lammergeiers to consider."

Shiki the Dorok is summoned elsewhere, where his presence is required, and he shall enter the viaduct ahead of the Archimage of the Land. The four voors that bore you here have already taken wing for home.

"Ohh!" cried Shiki. "We are marooned — just like the evil wizard!"

"Hush," Haramis chided him. "We are nothing of the sort . . . Talisman, where are you sending Shiki?"

Where he must go.

"Oh, you maddening thing!" Haramis exclaimed. Then calming herself, she said to Shiki: "Try not to be afraid. I am certain that the talisman means no harm to either of us. I — I can only presume that there is some place where you will be usefully employed while I am engaged in my studies, and this place is not with me, and that is why we must be separated. Will you go forth bravely into the viaduct, and do whatever the talisman bids you?"

The little man bowed his head. "It is your talisman, and I am your servant, White Lady." He took one of her hands and kissed it. Then he settled his leather cap firmly atop his ears and stepped into the dark opening.

There was a very loud bell-sound, and Shiki the Dorok disappeared. Haramis called after him, but there was not even an echo of her voice, only the lingering reverberation of the chime.

Now it is my turn, she said to herself. And then a sudden terrible thought struck her. Had Portolanus also been summoned?

Had he been summoned twice? . . .

Was there some purpose in the Threefold Sceptre, and the individual talismans that formed it, that lay far beyond anything she had ever dreamed? She experienced a powerful yearning to seek the advice of her triplet sisters, to tell them all about this mystery, to ask them to lend her their strength and resolution as she stepped into the unknown. Valiant Kadiya! Loving, steadfast Anigel!

And I am the faltering one — who should be the leader.

No, she decided. I will not add to their burdens in order to lighten mine. I will cease this cursed wavering and follow the example of good old Shiki . . .

She took hold of the talisman with both hands and stepped into the hole called the viaduct. For an instant she was enveloped in suffocating darkness, hanging suspended in a void. Her brain seemed to explode painlessly with a huge, musical throb.

Then immediately she felt matter beneath her feet. Shifting pebbles. It was still dark all about her, but she knew that it was only nighttime, not some magical banishing of light. As her eyesight slowly accommodated she saw that there were even stars, barely discernible in a sky that seemed flooded with a peculiar dark red glow. And a noise, the lapping of small waves upon the shingle, gently rustling to and fro. A sharp breeze bearing a breath of profound chill touched her face.

A seashore.

Out in the water enormous things were floating, glimmering like ghostly ships but more immense than any man-made object. They were as big as islands, as big as small mountains, and each had a faint greenish or electric-blue phosphorescence. The little waves were edged with a foam that was luminous, too.

And now the red-black sky was changing. From the far horizon a beam of pearly opalescence grew up — and then others materialized slowly until there were five in all, wavering like spectral fingers. They widened, became a bright fan of pink, white, and green light, then expanded into luminous draperies. The sky-light shone on the gigantic icebergs offshore and lit up the strange landscape behind Haramis, a desolate expanse of barren treeless hills, occasionally patched with gleaming snow. The wind was rising.

"Where am I?" Haramis whispered.

On the shore of the Aurora Sea.

So that explained the fantastic light in the sky! It was the aurora, a rare natural phenomenon she had read about but never expected to experience, seen only in the far northern parts of the world. The everchanging colors were so glorious that she nearly forgot why she had come . . .

But you must not do that, Haramis. You have so much to learn.

She uttered a sharp cry. The one speaking without words was not her talisman. "Is it the Archimage of the Sea?" she called out. "Where are you?"

Follow the Way of Light.

The aurora's splendor was brightly reflected in the sea now, and in one particular place near where she stood it almost seemed as if the water were solidifying, turning to a firm surface that sparkled like clear ice strewn with a million tiny diamonds. As she watched, the icy patch lengthened, extending out from the shore toward the tallest of the glowing icebergs.

Will it hold my weight? Haramis asked herself. She shivered in the keen wind, then extended one foot. The ice gave forth a gentle tinkling but remained solid. She took another step. On either side of the narrow glittering path the black waters rippled; but the Way of Light itself was as firm as iron.

Drawing her Archimage's cloak around her, Haramis began to walk out to sea.

11

I f this mapsheet you scrawled up is true, Lady," Captain Ly Woonly said to Kadiya, "we're likely only a couple o' leagues or so from the place where your magic talisman got dropped."

Kadiya and Anigel, having just awoke, had hurried up onto the deck of the *Lyath* when summoned by the vessel's master. They found that the ship was moving slowly southward along the ragged shore of Council Isle, keeping well away from the land.

For the past three days, ever since *Lyath* had begun to thread her way through the Windlorns, a lookout had been posted to watch for signs of the Raktumian pirates or hostile natives. But thus far there had been no other craft sighted on the waters, although smokes were visible from the many Aliansa village sites and a small group of aborigines was spied netting fish in the shallows.

Anigel's talisman had proved to be of little use in tracking the pirate trireme through the maze of islands. The Queen could descry the big vessel well enough, but she found it impossible to pinpoint its position on the chart through simple observation; so many of the islands looked alike to her, and the chart was obviously none too accurate. Whether the pirates were ahead of them or behind them remained a mystery.

The talisman did confirm that there were large numbers of Aliansa natives watching the passage of *Lyath* from places of concealment. Since the Sea Folk on the various islands communicated with each other via the speech without words, they doubtless knew exactly where the pirate ship was. But the Aliansa refused to respond when

Kadiya's Wyvilo companions bespoke them; and while Queen Anigel could eavesdrop upon them through her talisman, she learned to her dismay that when the Sea Folk talked among themselves they used their own incomprehensible language, not the universal trade dialect based upon human speech that they had spoken during the abortive conference with Kadiya.

Deprived of any knowledge of their enemy's whereabouts, the two sisters could only urge Captain Ly Woonly to sail on as fast as possible in the fitful wind, while they prayed that they would reach the site of the talisman's loss before Portolanus did.

"You did well to reach Council Isle so quickly, Captain," Anigel said to him warmly. "I am amazed that you were able to travel at night through the labyrinth of reefs and rocks that surround it."

Throwing a glance over his shoulder at one of the Wyvilo, who was trimming a sail, Ly Woonly whispered: "We owe it to those Forest Oddlings, great Queen. The big-eyed boogers have some kind o' special sense that helps 'em get around obstacles in water. Night and day are pretty much the same to 'em, and navigatin' in a shallow sea is no different than travelin' their home rivers."

"The bay where the High Chief Har-Chissa has his large village seems to be located just beyond that headland," Kadiya said, poring over the wrinkled chart. "I cannot understand why no native boats have come to intercept us. When last we came, large numbers of canoes carrying twenty or more paddlers swarmed out to meet and escort us to the anchorage when we were much farther away than this."

"Mayhap the Sea Oddlings have good reason for remainin' ashore," Ly Woonly observed, his usually jovial face gone grim beneath his plumed hat. "Great Queen, give a peek through your farseein' coronet again to find out what might be goin' on around the other side o' yon point."

"Very well." Anigel closed her eyes and touched the silvery circlet braided into her fair hair. "Oh! The pirate trireme is there, with its sails taken down! . . . And I can see that its anchors are in the water."

"Thunderin' blazes!" Ly Woonly exclaimed. "All hands on deck!

Helm! Ready to heave to!" He ran off shouting more orders, and in minutes the small ship slowed and stopped.

"Quick!" Kadiya said to her sister. "Look more closely at the pirate ship. Are they putting out boats with grapples, or doing anything else that smacks of a try for my talisman?"

Anigel was silent for a moment, her eyes unfocused. "No, I see nothing like that, only sailors coiling ropes and tying down the furled sails, and the Raktumian Admiral talking to one of his officers . . . He says that they have just arrived at Council Bay. They could not sail at night for fear of running aground. It seems Portolanus has a magical device that is supposed to show the depth of the water, but it has not worked properly and this forced the trireme to lie at anchor each night . . . By the Flower! Portolanus himself and his acolytes are shortly expected to come on deck!"

"Show me!" Kadiya demanded.

Anigel asked her talisman to share the vision, and the scene dimmed somewhat and became bereft of its natural sounds. Nevertheless, Kadiya saw clearly three figures emerge from a stern companionway on the Raktumian ship — a man of medium stature wearing a hooded robe of purple cloth, a stockier individual in similar yellow garb, and a third, quite short, clad all in black. Following them came the all-too-familiar blur that signaled the presence of Portolanus. Coming last of all were Queen Regent Ganondri, wearing sea-green silken robes and evidently fully recovered after the three days of calm weather, and the hunched young King of Raktum, glum-faced and pale.

The enchanter's assistants ranged themselves close together along one of the ornamental side railings of the poop royal, seeming to look directly at Anigel and Kadiya. The concealed sorcerer came up behind the three — and abruptly became visible. His robe was pure white and he was hatless, his tow-colored hair and beard stirring in the faint warm breeze. As the two sisters gasped he waggled his fingers in an ironic gesture of greeting, evidently knowing full well that they descried him. The Queen Regent and her grandson moved as far away from the thaumaturgic quartet as they could get, but did not take their eyes from them.

Portolanus's face lost its clownish grin. He seemed to straighten, becoming tall and wide of shoulder, and his face was somehow less grotesque. He uttered a short word of command and the three acolytes fell to their knees. With startling force, the sorcerer tore back their hoods, revealing shaven heads, which he swept close together as a fruit-merchant gathers melons. Then he spread his bony hands wide so that the fingers touched all three pates, and closed his eyes.

"Great God," Kadiya whispered. "The minions! Do you see, Sister?"

Anigel only nodded, astounded. The eye-sockets of the three kneeling men had turned into empty dark pits, and they were as motionless as statues. Behind them, Portolanus slowly opened his own eyes, letting his hands fall to his sides. Beneath his tangled yellowish brows two tiny white stars shone with dazzling brilliance.

"Well met, Queen Anigel, Lady Kadiya!" said he, and they heard him as clearly as if he had been standing beside them.

"He sees us!" Anigel said.

"Of course I do," Portolanus replied, grinning. "With the help of my three powerful Voices, I can descry to the uttermost ends of the world, and see virtually anything or anyone, and bespeak them as well! . . . Isn't it a lovely morning? I confess that I prefer calm weather myself, and it was a great relief to me — and to my servants as well — to have done with conjuring tempests. Let me congratulate you and your captain upon the fine turn of speed your little vessel managed to achieve. Our Raktumian galley slaves are quite prostrate after laboring since dawn to bring us here ahead of you via a shortcut."

"You should have kept your magical gale blowing," Kadiya retorted.

"Alas." Portolanus shrugged. "My power to command the storm is not subtle enough to influence the erratic light airs that prevail among the Windlorn Isles. Nevertheless we have won the day through natural means, as you see. I must warn you now to come no closer. Do not attempt to enter this bay or approach the site of the sunken talisman, or the consequences will be most grave."

Portolanus snapped his fingers, and from out the companionway came two armored pirates, supporting a limp body between them. A third brute followed after, carrying a drawn sword.

"Antar!" cried Anigel.

The star-eyed sorcerer laughed. "A fine figure of a king, is he not? And lazy, too, napping away the days of our journey from Taloazin. But now it is time for him to wake up. Through my magic, you may speak to him."

He touched the King of Laboruwenda with a small rod. Immediately the unconscious man stirred in the arms of his captors and lifted his head, and when he recognized that he was held prisoner, he began to struggle violently and call down curses upon Portolanus.

The sorcerer shook his head mockingly. "Tsk, tsk. The royal guest repays our gentle hospitality with harsh words. He must be taught better manners."

One wizened finger thrust forward toward Antar's face, and at its tip there burst forth an orange flame. Portolanus spoke softly to the Raktumian warrior with the sword. Both Anigel and her distant husband cried out in unison as this man took hold of Antar's hair and pulled back his head, so that the King's blond beard met the enchanted fire. There was a sizzling sound and a puff of smoke, and Anigel burst into tears of horror. But when Portolanus drew his finger away, only the hair was burnt and not the King's flesh.

"You foul bastard!" Kadiya cried, taking weeping Anigel in her arms.

Portolanus made an airy gesture. "I may well be, for I knew neither my father nor my mother — and there are no bathtubs on Raktumian ships, for all their trumpery ornamentation. But I advise you to hold your tongue, Lady of the Eyes, lest my next demonstration be more painful to your brother-in-law."

"Do not hurt him!" Anigel pleaded.

The twin stars in the enchanter's skull flared and his voice boomed in the Queen's mind. "I will set him free at once — and your three children as well — if you give me the talisman called the Three-Headed Monster."

"No! You are a foul liar! I — I do not believe that you will free them! You wish the death of all of us!"

Portolanus sighed. "Silly woman. Who has told you this? Your sister Haramis? She is naught but an incompetent dabbler in mysteries she will never comprehend. She knows nothing of my plans. Pay the ransom! Your coronet is of small use to you — a mere convenience for spying and a symbol of . . . heaven knows what."

"Do not listen to him, beloved!" King Antar cried. "Command your talisman to slay him!" A sword was placed at his throat to compel silence, but the sorcerer made a commanding gesture and the pirate knight reluctantly lowered his weapon.

"Only think about it, Queen Anigel," Portolanus said earnestly. "Of what true use has the Three-Headed Monster been to you during the past twelve years? Yes — it has let you communicate with your two sisters across the leagues. But I will give you three small machines of the Vanished Ones that will do the same service!"

Kadiya spoke hotly: "And what will you give me, trickster, to take the place of my Three-Lobed Burning Eye? And will the Archimage Haramis also give you her talisman in exchange for a magical gimcrack?"

Portolanus's amiable expression melted away and he scowled. "I am addressing the Queen, Lady, and not you! . . . Anigel, if you do not pay my ransom, your husband and children will surely die. This is how you can save them: Place your coronet in a small boat and let the boat be cast adrift. I will at the same time put Antar and the children into a boat here. The King can row around the headland and reach you in less than two hours in these calm seas. I will draw the boat with the talisman in it to me through my magic. Then, if you set sail for home at once in the *Lyath,* I swear by all the Dark Powers that I will not follow or otherwise harm you."

Anigel hesitated, her eyes brimming with tears as she beheld Antar, shaking his head, urging her refusal. The King was a woeful sight, with his eyes sunken deeply into his head and his face gaunt from over seven days without food. The talisman seemed a small price to pay for his safe return and the return of the children. Still, he had told her not to give in . . . urged her to use the talisman to kill. But she had never deliberately given the magical device such an order, and even now, with her husband's life at stake, she hesitated.

Kadiya seemed to be aware of the struggle going on in her sister's mind. "Do what you think best," she said, her speech laden with hidden meaning.

Anigel closed her eyes. *Talisman! By the Lords of the Air I command you to strike dead that evil man who holds my husband and children captive! I command it! I command it! . . .*

The Queen opened her eyes again to the talisman's vision. Portolanus stood unharmed. Nothing at all had happened.

Kadiya's eyes met hers, and Anigel shook her head imperceptibly. The muscles of Kadiya's jaw knotted as she swallowed a bitter exclamation, in her heart blaming Anigel as much as the talisman for the magic's failure.

Speaking in a voice barely audible, striving to conceal her own misery and disappointment, the Queen said to Portolanus: "I cannot give you my talisman."

The sorcerer did not seem overly disappointed. "An unfortunate decision, my Queen. But in time, you may change your mind. For now, to show my good faith, I will forbear harming the King any further if you will but keep your distance. Will you swear to me on the Black Trillium that you and your sister Kadiya will not approach any closer?"

"Do not swear!" shouted the King, struggling anew. But he was helpless in the grip of the burly pirate-knights.

"Yes!" cried Anigel at once. "I swear!"

Kadiya's response was more reluctant. "Yes," she finally growled. "We swear to you by the Flower that we two will not stir from this place. But if you do the least hurt to King Antar, this oath is void. And we will watch him unceasingly."

"Do so, by all means." The sorcerer laughed. And he said to the Raktumian knights: "Chain him again with the galley slaves, and feed him a small bowl of their swill. Take care, for his stomach cannot hold much after his long fast."

When Antar had been hustled below, Portolanus gave a tremendous yawn, and stretched. When he settled himself, Anigel and Kadiya saw that his eyes had resumed their normal human aspect. At the same moment the three minions of the sorcerer moaned and seemed to suffer brief convulsions. Their faces then also became as before, with their eyeballs rolling whitely, and they slumped down onto the deck.

Portolanus turned and bowed sweepingly to Ganondri and King Ledavardis and then quit the royal poop deck. The Queen Regent spoke sharply to her grandson, who had been listening awestruck to the sorcerer's exchange with the invisible sisters. They two also went away, and a number of crewmen came up and carried off the unconscious acolytes.

Anigel banished the vision. "Now what are we to do?" she wondered. She wiped her tearstained face and went to sit on a water cask, for she was still very shaken.

Kadiya remained at the rail for some minutes, silent, looking toward the shore of the large island. It was heavily wooded, with beaches of shining white sand broken by tumbled outcroppings of reddish-black rock. The sea was a brilliant azure lightening to pale green nearer the land, with creamy breakers forming complex patterns as they marched shoreward through hidden reefs. On this side of the tall headland there were no signs of habitation.

"Haramis's original plan called for you to summon my talisman through your own," Kadiya said, turning at last to face her sister. "Try it, even though we are still at a distance!"

"Why, I never thought to do that," Anigel said. "Of course I will try." But her expression was more dubious than hopeful as she closed her eyes and pressed both hands to the trillium-amber inset at the coronet's front.

"Talisman," she whispered, "I command you to bring me the lost Three-Lobed Burning Eye."

For half a dozen heartbeats nothing happened; and then Anigel's talisman spoke to her:

This I cannot do, unless you suspend me directly above the place where the Eye lies.

"Oh!" cried the Queen. "Did you hear it, Kadi?"

"Yes." The face of the Lady of the Eyes had become both determined and ruthless. "You could do it by rendering yourself invisible and making your way somehow to the pirate ship. There is nothing else to do but break the oath —"

"Do not even think of it!" Anigel rebuked her. Dressed in rough seaman's garb and with a smeared face, she still looked a queen. "I will not break my oath, nor will I allow you to break yours."

"Don't be a fool, Ani!" Kadiya's brown eyes were battle-lighted. "If we do not retake my talisman before Portolanus gets his hands on it, we forfeit all chance of rescuing Antar and the children! Do you think he will simply turn them loose once he bonds my talisman to himself?"

"I don't — "

"Or do you plan to meekly hand over your own talisman as ransom for them after all?"

"Of course not! But there must be an honorable way to save them."

"Honor! You are as simpleminded as a volumnial calf! How can you prate of honor when the lives of your family are at stake? And my talisman?"

Anigel sprang up from the cask. "Your talisman! That's all you really care about, isn't it? Without it you have no power. The Swamp Folk and the other aborigines will no longer revere you and follow you and call you their Great Advocate if you are without it, will they, Lady of the Eyes? Well and good, say I! You will then no longer be able to stir up dissent among them — "

"There would be no dissent if human rulers like yourself were not blind to the injustices inflicted upon the Folk! You and Antar have consistently ignored my petitions to give them full citizenship."

"And for good reason!" the Queen responded furiously. "It would destroy our economy if the Oddlings were allowed to trade directly with other nations, rather than through us. You know this full well, and yet you have persisted in encouraging seditious schemes among the Wyvilo and Glismak, as well as urging the Nyssomu and Uisgu to hold back their trade goods in order to force a price increase."

"And why should they not get higher prices? They work hard, for a pitifully small return. You call them Oddlings! I say they are *persons* and as worthy as any humans. You have no inborn right to exploit them!"

"Who told them they were being exploited?" the Queen demanded. "Who filled their simple hearts with discontent? You! Their so-called advocate! Oh, I did not want to believe what Owanon and Ellinis and the others said of you — that deep in your soul you regretted having given up the crown, and envied me my queenly power, and so stirred up the aborigines to enhance your own self-importance. But they were right!"

"What a monstrous notion!" Kadiya cried. "It is you who have become self-righteous and arrogant, forgetting how the Folk helped us to defeat King Voltrik and Orogastus! You think only of the welfare of your human subjects and merely *use* the poor inhuman peoples who also look to you for justice! You defer to your Labornoki husband, who was brought up to believe that the Folk are animals! He has poisoned your mind — "

"How dare you speak of my darling Antar so! Heartless one, you know nothing of true love! All you have ever had is the vain adulation of your pathetic throng of savages. They are like children, and you also have the mind of a child! You are filled to the bursting with the kind of reckless anger that drives naughty brats to troublemaking. With you, the simpleminded solution to a problem is always the only one! What do you know of the ruling and safeguarding of nations?"

"I know what is just and what is unjust," Kadiya said, in a voice suddenly gone quiet and dangerous, "and I know the difference between a true oath and an invalid one extracted under duress. You may do as you will, Sister, and withhold your coronet's help from me if you must. But if you attempt to stop me from retrieving my talisman in my own way, then the Lords of the Air have mercy upon you — for I will not."

She strode away, calling for Jagun and Lummomu-Ko to attend her, and would not respond when Anigel called out apologies for her angry words and begged her to return.

Too defeated even to weep, Anigel stumbled up to the bow of *Lyath* and sat amidst the coils of rope. For all the rest of the day she watched over King Antar and her children through her talisman, and spied also upon the sorcerer, even though his body was once again a blur. With leaden disinterest, Anigel saw Portolanus and his three acolytes within their cabin, chanting and uttering incantations and performing strange rituals she did not understand. Aside from this, they made no attempt to go after Kadiya's talisman.

Nor did Kadiya herself. After her conference with her aboriginal friends (which Anigel did not deign to spy upon), the Lady of the Eyes went below to her bunk and slept all day.

Toward the end of the afternoon, bored with the inaction on the pirate trireme and lulled by the warm sun and the gentle motion of the noga, Anigel left off her vigil. Jagun brought her a cooling drink of ladu juice, and she fell into a doze. She did not awaken until long after dark, when it was too late to prevent the calamity.

12

"There is something strange happening on deck,"
Prince Nikalon called down to his brother and
sister. It was full night and the chain-locker
was dark except for filtered moonlight shining through the hawseholes. Niki was hanging half in, half out of one of these large openings. "I hear chanting," he said. "It is in a language I cannot
understand."

"It must be the sorcerer," Prince Tolivar said, with unseemly
delight, "casting a spell on the people chasing us. How I would love to
see him toss thunderbolts or conjure up monsters!"

"Ninnyhammer!" Princess Janeel said to him. Then to Niki: "Can
you see anything on the shore?"

"A single flickering fire back among the trees. There are no boats of
any kind in the water. Two of the Three Moons are shining brightly,
however, and we would very likely be seen if we attempted to escape
now."

"If we wait, this ship may sail away!" Jan said. "Let us go while we
can."

"It is true," Niki mused, "that the trireme has anchored closer to
land this time than it ever did before. We would only have to swim
about half a league."

"How far is that?" Tolo asked apprehensively.

"A thousand ells," Jan told him. "But you needn't be afraid, sprog.
Niki and I can tow you whenever you get tired."

"I don't want to go," the little boy wailed. "I hate swimming. The
water always goes up my nose."

"You'd hate being tied to a mast and used for knife-throwing practice by the pirates even more," Niki said heartlessly.

Tolo burst into tears and Jan hastened to comfort him, glaring up at her older brother. "Now look what you've done, Niki! . . . There, baby, Niki was only teasing. No one's going to hurt you."

"I hate it in here," the little Prince sobbed. "Why doesn't somebody come and rescue us?"

"I'm sure Mama is trying — " she began, but at that moment there were noises outside the door, and she hissed to Nikalon: "Slide down quickly! Someone's coming!"

The Crown Prince had barely managed to slither back to the top of the diminished chain-piles when the door was unbarred. Boblen the Quartermaster appeared, holding a lantern, and behind him was the Goblin Kinglet carrying another.

Ledavardis pushed ahead of the seaman and came into the chain-locker. He had with him a large sack that bulged oddly. "Wait outside and close the door, Boblen. I would speak privily with these unfortunate children."

"Now look here, young Sire! It's bad enough that you take advantage of my good nature by sneaking down here — "

"Silence, man! Do you truly believe these infants could do me hurt? Wait outside, I say!"

Grumbling, Boblen withdrew. When the door was closed, Ledavardis hung his lantern on a nail, then swiftly emptied the contents of the sack onto the rough boards underfoot. There was a cork life-ring, a knife in a sheath, a small hatchet, a flat canvas packet, an oilskin bag half-filled with something lumpy, a water-gourd, and a little crock with a cloth cover tied on.

"By the Flower!" Prince Niki exclaimed softly. "What is this?"

"You must try to escape tonight," Ledavardis said without preamble. "The wizard has spent the entire day working on some prodigious spell with which he intends to salvage a drowned magic sword from these waters. Everyone on the ship will be watching as he and his three flunkies do the final incantations a half hour or so from now, when the Third Moon rises. This is when you must make your escape. Once the sword is retrieved, we will weigh anchor and head immediately for Raktum."

"I don't want to escape!" Tolo had begun to blubber again. "I can hardly swim at all."

"The life-ring will assist you," King Ledavardis said. "All three of you could cling to it if need be, and by kicking your feet underwater make your way silently to shore. This waterproof bag has food, and will also serve to carry some of your clothes, so you will have dry things when you land. The canvas packet has fishline and hooks and a fireshell kit. With these and the knife and hatchet, you will have a chance of feeding and sheltering yourselves until your own people rescue you."

"Mama would surely find us quickly with her talisman," Jan said eagerly.

"But is there no way we can rescue our father the King?" Niki asked.

"It is hopeless," Ledavardis said. "He is chained to a galleybench, surrounded by the slaves and the crewmen on watch. You must save yourselves. I overheard my grandmother arguing with Portolanus. Somehow, she has forced him to agree that if he retrieves the talisman sunk in the water, then *she* will take the second talisman from Queen Anigel as ransom for you and King Antar."

"Mama will never give up her talisman!" Niki declared stoutly. "And she and her knights are doubtless in close pursuit of this vessel, and will soon rescue us all."

"That is as may be," the King replied. "What I know to be true is that Ganondri intends to force your mother to hand over her talisman. Portolanus attempted without success to compel Queen Anigel by mild torture of your father —"

"Ohh!" Jan cried in horror.

Ledavardis continued: " — but my grandmother is made of sterner stuff. She intends to secure the second talisman promptly ... by torturing you, Nikalon, and you, Janeel, before the very eyes of your father and mother."

"Not me?" Tolivar inquired, his face bright with relief.

"Tolo!" his sister cried indignantly. "You should be ashamed!"

"Enough, Jan," the Crown Prince said. "There is no time for childish folly." Nikalon then said to Ledavardis: "We will be forever in your debt, King, if we do manage to escape. Will you tell us why you are doing this?"

"I do not know myself," Ledavardis admitted wretchedly. "I only know that I must. I fear your Royal Father is doomed, and I can do nothing to help him. But I can help you." He plucked the lantern from its nail. "Now I must go before I am missed. They will expect me to be present when the sorcerer performs. Begin your escape when the Third Moon rises. In that small jar is boot-blacking, which you should smear upon your exposed skin so that its paleness will not betray you as you swim away. And now, farewell."

Ledavardis slipped out of the door, closing it softly, and a moment later the three royal children heard the bar being replaced. Niki dropped to his knees and examined the contents of the waterproof sack.

"There is ship's biscuit here, and nut candy, and sausages. If we can catch fish and find fruit, it should be enough. We will put our shoes and cloaks also in the bag. It should float a little, and we can tow it behind us by its strings. I will knot the knife inside my shirt, and Jan, you tie the small axe to the girdle of your gown. Now let us make haste so that we will be ready when the time comes."

Tolo backed up against the damp wood of the hull. "I won't go!"

"You will!" Nikalon said fiercely. "I am the Crown Prince as well as your brother, and I command it!"

"Pooh to you and your stupid commands, Niki! There are things in the water. Dangerous things! Ralabun says—"

Both Niki and Jan groaned in unison.

"Ralabun! He is full of tall tales and Oddling superstitions," Niki scoffed.

"Ralabun says there are great fishes three times the length of a man," the little boy persisted, "with mouths as big as open doors, having three rows of teeth like butcher knives. And there are great blobs of swimming jelly that can sting you to death. And the sea-monster Heldo lives here in the South, and his eyes are as big as dinner-plates and his arms are like strong cables with claws at the ends. They twine about you and squeeze you until the blood pours forth from your ears and mouth—"

"No, no!" Jan said, going to Tolo and taking his hands. "There are no such things! The great danger is here on this ship, with the Pirate Queen and the evil sorcerer."

"The Goblin Kinglet said that Queen Ganondri was only going to torture you and Niki," Tolo said, "not me." His face was both sullen and calculating.

"That kind of talk is wicked," Jan reproved him. "Now stop arguing and take off your shoes."

"No! I won't go! The sea-monsters will eat me!"

"Curse that Ralabun," Niki muttered. He opened the jar of blacking and began to smear it on his face. "Look, Tolo. Don't I look awful? Wouldn't you like to blacken your face, too? We'll all look so grisly that the sea-creatures will flee from the sight of us!"

"No!" the eight-year-old shrieked. "No, no, no!"

Jan cocked her head, listening. "Hark! The chanting on deck — is it not becoming louder?"

"It is," Niki agreed. He caught her eye. "Come, Jan. Prepare yourself. If this stubborn baby insists upon playing the fathead, we shall simply leave him behind."

"Very well," she said, pretending to agree.

The two older children removed their shoes and stowed them in the bag. Jan drew her skirt forward through her legs and tied it to her girdle, along with the hatchet, and they darkened their faces and hands and bare feet. Fortunately none of the torn and soiled finery they had worn to the Zinoran coronation was light in color. Then Niki ascended one anchor chain, pulling the sack and the life-ring after and perching them on the winch-gears, while Jan again tried to coax Tolo. But he darted away from her behind the twin piles of chain.

"The Third Moon is about to rise!" Niki called softly. "Hurry!"

"I can't catch him!" Jan was frantic.

"I won't go with you!" Tolo cried. "Get away from me!"

"I'll come down and we will force him," Niki decided.

"If you do," Tolo warned, "I'll kick and scream and bite as you carry me off, and the pirates will catch you and torture you!"

"Crazy little devil!" Niki was already very frightened, although he had been careful to hide it. His small brother's recalcitrance was now fast robbing him of what courage he had left. "It would serve you right if we *did* leave you here!"

"Yes! Leave me! The pirates won't hurt me. The Goblin Kinglet said so. You two escape. Don't worry about me. I'm only a second prince. You said I wasn't worth much ransom."

"We cannot abandon him," Jan moaned.

Niki's response was somber. "And it seems that we cannot take him along. Shall we all stay, then, and sacrifice ourselves for his sake? Ledavardis did say that the Queen Regent would spare him, though heaven knows why. I may as well tell you, Jan: I have thought for some time that none of us would leave this ship alive, whether or not Mama gave up her talisman as ransom. It would be a great boon for Raktum if both Papa and the true heirs to the Two Thrones of Laboruwenda were slain."

"Do — do you think, then, that it is our duty to try to escape?" The Princess was trembling now, her wide eyes making two little white-rimmed circles in her darkened face.

"I do," Niki said.

"Me too!" Tolo squeaked. "Go on. Go!"

Jan held out her hands to her little brother. "Kiss me good-bye, then, sweeting."

"No," said he, "for you would only grab me!"

Jan's eyes filled with tears. "Farewell, then," she said, and began to climb the chain.

Tolo watched until both of them had gone out the hawsepipe. Then he scrambled up himself with some difficulty and peeped out. The Third Moon was just rising above the horizon and there was a good deal of noise coming from the afterdeck — loud chanting, and a peculiar loud sizzling noise that sounded like fireworks, and the creak of a winch or some other nautical apparatus. The boy looked down the curve of the right anchor chain and saw two indistinct masses gliding lower and lower along the huge metal links. Finally they reached the water. Triple moonlight sparkled on the gentle waves and this made it hard to see the blobs that were Niki and Jan's heads. They moved off slowly in the direction of the island shore and soon they were completely lost to view.

"Good," Prince Tolivar said to himself, well satisfied. "Good riddance! I know what they think of me — that I am only a brat, and a pest, and useless. But one day I'll show them."

Cautiously, he went back down the chain. At the bottom of the locker, he piled all three pallets into a thicker, more comfortable bed. Jan had left some of the food for him, and he lay down and chewed on a sausage and listened to the eerie music reverberating through the ship's hull.

"I thought I would be a pirate," the little boy said to himself. "But I have changed my mind. Pirates are rich and powerful, but they must be at sea all the time, puking up their dinners when there are storms and fighting battles with other ships. I would like to be something even better than a pirate when I grow up."

He smiled in the darkness. "When the guard comes, I will tell him to give a message to the sorcerer. Surely Portolanus would be eager to have a real prince for an apprentice."

Holding tight to the life-ring, Jan and Niki kicked and kicked, but it seemed that the shore never came any nearer, even though the trireme dwindled in size behind them. After a time they were completely exhausted and could only cling to the ring, listening to the noise of the ritual echoing over the water. The monotonous chanting went on without letup. It was impossible to see what was happening on the pirate ship, but occasionally red or blue flares arced into the sky and then fell back into the water.

"Have you rested enough?" Niki asked his sister.

"Yes," she said. "Let us go on."

They began to kick again, always being careful not to let their feet break water and cause a splash. As time went by, the muscles in their thighs turned to fire and their fingers grew numb with clinging to the ropes bound about the life-ring. But they kept going, ever more slowly. Kick . . . kick . . . kick. They could hear their own raspy breathing now and the thudding of their overworked hearts.

No longer did they even bother to look where they were going. They lay their cheeks against the scratchy canvas cover of the life-ring and moved their legs now only with the utmost difficulty. Jan lost her grip, went under, took in a noseful of water, and began to choke. She could not help but splash and struggle and gasp for breath. When she had recovered, Niki comforted her, saying that they were too far now from the pirate ship for anyone to have heard. But she was sobbing with exhaustion.

"I can swim no longer. I am going to die, Niki. Go on without me."

Carefully, he drew himself up, took a firm hold on the ring with one hand, and slapped her face with the other.

"Aaah, you horrid qubar!" she shrieked.

"Kick!" he shouted at her. "Kick, Jan! And hold tight to the ring! If you do not, I will strike you again!"

Still sobbing, she did as she was told.

And suddenly the water was no longer flat, crinkled with small wavelets, but rising. Up and down they went, and finally they soared, carried higher and higher on a great wave. Jan began to shriek again, but Niki cried: "Hold on to the ring! Only hold on!"

The breaker was rushing toward the shore and they were drawn to its crest. Ahead was a periodic roaring sound, and all around them a hiss that became deafening as the wave gained speed and height. Jan felt her fingers torn from the life-ring. She tried to cry out but was overwhelmed by the flood. Her mouth filled with salt water and she felt herself tossed head over heels in the loud darkness. She managed to hold her breath, to paddle with both her arms and legs, even though they had been useless things a scant moment before.

Up! Back up to the surface! She swept her arms strongly to her sides and kicked. Glowing bubbles. Her head breaking the surface. Foaming surf all around her. The slow rhythmic pounding of waves breaking on the shore . . .

Her feet touched bottom.

A great wave broke over her, slamming her underwater again, but it also thrust her ahead. Her knees scraped in the sand. She forced her head up and took a deep breath, then crawled. The sea was very warm, and now only small waves lapped about her in the shallows, encouraging her as she struggled up out of the water at last and collapsed on the sand.

It was a long time before she thought of Niki. Then a stab of guilt energized her. He had saved her life by slapping her. She had been a coward, willing to give up, and he had forced her to survive. Jan sat up with her feet still washed by the sea, scanning the shore first in one direction, then in another. The triple moonlight was deceptive, and there were dark rocks as well as mounds of seaweed lying on the strand above the thundering surf that she mistook for her brother's body. But finally she saw the distinctive white shape of the life-ring lying a dozen ells away, and she crawled to it. Niki lay just beyond. He was breathing, but did not open his eyes when she shook his shoulder. The life-ring had the oilskin sack still tied to it, and she fumbled inside Niki's shirt for his knife, cut the sack open, and took out a dry cloak. Then she lay close beside him and covered the two of them, and surrendered to overwhelming blackness.

Until the pain woke her.

"Stop hurting my sister!"

It was Niki's voice. Jan groaned, then cried out more strongly as a second blow smote her aching ribs. Niki was shouting furiously and she heard harsh laughter. Numbly, she opened her eyes — only to close them tightly again to shut out the terrible vision.

Nightmare! She had to be dreaming . . . but when the third blow struck, she knew what she saw was terrible reality:

A flaming torch, its light revealing three tall beings with glowing yellow eyes and hideous muzzled faces, grinning at her through discolored tusks. Aborigines. They had something of the appearance of the savage Glismak, but were even uglier and more ferocious looking. Two of them wore short kilts with gleaming pearls sewn on them, and were decked out with many strings of shells. They held stout wooden clubs studded with some kind of triangular animal teeth and one of them carried a torch. The third, who was much taller and more grandly attired, had a finely made sword of human style at his side and a huge pearl suspended around his neck. He stood looking down at the two bedraggled children with folded arms.

The warrior who had kicked Jan awake with his stubby-clawed webbed feet pointed to her and Niki, uttering a satisfied phrase in his native tongue. He pointed out to sea, where the Raktumian trireme was anchored, lit up like a festival float with skyrockets soaring up from it.

The impressive aborigine glowered and barked a question.

"I do not understand you," Niki said, calm now. "Do you speak the human language?"

"Yes," the being croaked. "I am the High Chief Har-Chissa of the Aliansa. Who are you and what are you doing here? Humans have been forbidden to come to these islands. And yet two of your ships have dared to anchor just off our sacred Council Isle, while numbers of others are slowly approaching. Did you come from that ship?"

"Yes." Niki brushed some of the sand from his face and tried to speak in a way befitting his station. "I am Crown Prince Nikalon of Laboruwenda and this is my sister, Princess Janeel. We were held prisoner by our enemies, and we escaped."

"Whose great ship is that?" Har-Chissa demanded.

"It belongs to the Raktumian pirate nation. It is heavily armed, and also carries a powerful sorcerer on board."

The Chief spoke urgently to the warriors in the native language, then turned again to Niki. "And the second ship — the smaller one anchored beyond that point of land. Who does it belong to?"

A tingling sensation made Jan's scalp stir. Who, indeed! Could it be the long-awaited rescuers? Could it be their mother?

"I do not know what ship that is," Niki said. "It may belong to our own people, come to save us from the pirates. If the ship is from Laboruwenda, you will gain a rich reward by taking my sister and me to it."

The High Chief roared with laughter, spoke to his followers, and they laughed with him. Then Har-Chissa reached down with one monstrous three-clawed hand, seized the Prince by his wet hair, and pulled him painfully upright. The children saw the Sea Oddling's slavering teeth gleaming in the moonlight.

"Take you to them? Insolent cub! Before morning both ships will be sunk by our warriors and their crews will be dinner-guests of the fishes. Thus do the Aliansa deal with saucy invaders! As for you two, we have a special treat."

"And what is that?" Niki inquired, still trying to maintain his dignity.

"We have a custom," Chief Har-Chissa said. "Those who dare to set foot on our islands unbidden must join the drums."

"The — the drums?" Jan faltered.

Har-Chissa let go of Niki, so that he almost fell on top of Jan. Then the Chief gave an order, and the two warriors began binding the Prince and Princess with shaggy ropes.

"What do you mean — join the drums?" Niki cried. "What are you going to do with us?"

"Relieve you of your skins," the Aliansa leader said. "You two will make rather small drums, but perhaps their tone will be interesting."

13

Queen Anigel woke late in the evening with a throbbing headache. The Three Moons were up and the *Lyath* was very quiet. She went below to find something to eat and seek out her sister, but Kadi was not in the noga's tiny saloon, nor did she answer when Anigel called out.

With a chill knot forming in the pit of her stomach, Anigel went to the forecastle and questioned Jagun. Her worst suspicions were confirmed when the little Nyssomu reluctantly admitted that Kadiya had gone off over an hour ago, leaving the ship in the company of Lummomu-Ko and two other Wyvilo, Mok-La and Huri-Kamo.

Anigel raced up on deck, crying out frantically to her talisman: "Show me Kadiya!"

Her mind saw threefold moonlight dappling the surface of the now calmed sea. One of *Lyath*'s rescue rafts floated there, little more than a platform of thick bamboo two ells square, covered all over with heaped and trailing fronds of wet seaweed, so that it looked a mere mass of flotsam. At first it seemed as if there were no living thing about the raft. But then amidst the weed Anigel spied a gleam of yellow eyes, and she realized that the three Wyvilo were clinging to the raft's edge with only the tops of their heads above water, and these disguised with the trailing plants. The raft seemed to be drifting briskly, in spite of the lack of wind. Doubtless the Wyvilo were propelling it with their partially webbed feet.

Kadiya was not visible, but she was surely among them.

"But what can she hope to accomplish?" Anigel exclaimed furiously.

"Great Queen, the Lady Farseer hopes to sink the pirate flagship," Jagun said, "and by marooning Portolanus on this hostile shore, gain time to retrieve her talisman."

The voice of the Nyssomu distracted Anigel and her vision dissolved. "Lords of the Air! Doesn't Kadi realize that the sorcerer must be safeguarding himself with his damned magical machines? She and the Wyvilo will be discovered and killed!"

"My Lady Farseer and her warriors intend to approach the Raktumian ship with the disguised raft and then swim underwater. I begged her not to go, but she was adamant."

"If I had only wakened in time! . . . "

Jagun hung his head. "Great Queen, it pains me to tell you this, but the fruit drink I gave you in the afternoon contained a few drops of tylo extract, sufficient to bring about a brief, deep sleep. My Lady ordered this, and knowing that it would not harm you, I obeyed."

"You may have thereby brought about Kadiya's death," said the Queen starkly.

"Yes," said the little man, his voice breaking. "But she bade me to do it if I loved her, saying it was her only chance to recover her talisman, and without it she would rather be dead . . ."

"The fool!" cried Anigel. "If she sinks the pirate ship, what will happen to Antar and the children, confined below? They could be forgotten in the confusion!"

Jagun's great eyes bulged in distress. "I fear the Lady Farseer did not think — "

"No," the Queen retorted grimly. "She wouldn't. Her talisman is all that matters to her." Anigel considered for a moment. "Jagun, bespeak my sister's Wyvilo companions and tell them to remind Kadiya of the danger to my loved ones. Say also that if she does not call off this rash scheme, I will be forced to warn Portolanus of her coming."

"Oh, Great Queen — you could not do that!"

"I do not know whether I could or not! Let us pray that the mere threat will be enough to bring that idiotic Kadi to her senses! . . . Now bespeak her, while I descry what is happening on the Raktumian ship."

Anigel asked her talisman to show her the forepeak locker where the children were confined. The vision vouchsafed was very dim, and she saw little Tolivar clinging to a chain, looking out of the wide-open hawsehole. On the floor was an indistinct lump of bedding, and she thought that Niki and Jan must have gone to sleep. She then called up a Sight of Antar, and found him in a cramped chamber belowdecks lit by a single guttering candle-lantern, conversing amiably with a group of galley slaves about the possibility that he would have to join them in rowing the trireme back to Raktum. One of the King's ankles was chained and he had been stripped of his royal garments, so that he now looked much like the other oarsmen, except that his body was clean and not yet scarred from the lash.

Satisfied that her family was still safe, Anigel asked the talisman to show her Portolanus.

He was at the very stern of the trireme, in the after part of the high deck called the poop royal, and perfectly visible to Anigel's farseeing eye. Either he did not care whether she watched him, or else the incantations he was performing left him with no occult energy to spare in masking his form. His eyes were once again starry and blazing as he chanted in a strange language. The three acolytes were in their repulsive trance, kneeling frozen side by side like man-sized dolls dressed in yellow, purple, and black. Resting atop a cloth-of-platinum cushion at the sorcerer's feet was the star-box.

Two sailors, seeming nearly frightened out of their wits, stood by a small derrick-crane, grotesquely out of place on the gilded and bedizened royal lounge deck. The crane's long arm was thrust over the stern, and from it hung a rope with a hook at the end. From this, only an ell or two above the water, dangled an even more prosaic object — a wide-bladed shovel. Most of the ship's crew and officers, as well as Queen Regent Ganondri, the boy-King Ledavardis, and their mob of courtiers, were gathered on the main deck below watching the magical proceedings as well as they could.

Jagun diffidently tapped Anigel's arm.

She emerged from her vision and asked him: "Does my sister agree to forbear?"

"Great Queen, she was full of remorse when reminded of the great peril attending the King and the children. She now swears by the Flower that she will do nothing to endanger them. She has given up her plan to sink the pirate ship."

"Thank God! And is she on her way back here, then?"

Jagun hesitated, then shook his head. "She says she will watch, and if there is any way to frustrate the sorcerer's theft of her talisman without causing hurt to your royal family, then she must try it. I had the Wyvilo remonstrate with her, but she would yield no further."

Anigel bit her lip. That would have to suffice—but damn Kadi's stubbornness!

Jagun flinched at the anger in her eyes, and she felt pity for him, torn between loyalty to his mistress and a sure knowledge that what she had done was not only futile but possibly even disastrous. It was not his fault, poor old soul, that Kadiya was a self-centered firebrand.

"Jagun—would you like to share my vision of the pirate ship?"

"Oh, yes, Great Queen!"

"Then take my hand," Anigel said, "and we will watch what happens."

The trireme in its deep-water anchorage loomed up against the night sky like a floating castle adorned for a gala ball. Lamplight shone from many of the portholes, and there were innumerable lights on the many-leveled decks and even up in the rigging of the three masts. The gold leaf and the bright enamels on the flagship's woodwork glimmered splendidly, and the gaudily dressed Raktumians gathered on deck were clearly visible to those watching secretly from the water.

"They will be dazzled by all that light," Lummomu-Ko whispered to Kadiya, "and will not see us if we are cautious in venturing closer."

Slowly the three big aborigines and the human woman paddled with their feet, clinging to the raft with only their hands and heads out of water, and those well-camouflaged with seaweed strands. They were approaching the trireme from the bow, and the attention of those on board was fixed on the stern, where Portolanus's chanting had reached a frenzied pitch. He was shrieking a single word over and over, but his voice was by now so overused and ragged that the infiltrators could not tell what he was saying.

"The children are in the forepeak, in the chain-locker," Kadiya said softly. "With all that ruckus at the stern, it should be an easy matter to creep up the anchor chains and rescue them. King Antar poses a knottier problem. If the pirates did not move him, then he is still confined in the lowest of the three oarsmen's compartments on the shoreward side of the ship. But I do not see how we can get to him. The holes in the hull for the oars are too small to admit us."

"There must be accommodation-doors in the side of the ship for the on-loading of supplies and the off-loading of refuse and ordure," Lummomu said. "Surely such things would not be trucked through the body of a grand vessel like this."

"Any doors in the hull would be tightly fastened and too high above the water for us to reach," said Mok-La. He was a shrewd Wyvilo logger who was nearly the equal of Lummomu in strength. "But we could probably gain access to the galley compartments by entering through the anchor hawseholes and breaking out of the chain-locker into the forward holds."

"The battle-axes we brought will likely enable us to do the job if we are careful," said Huri-Kamo, the third Wyvilo, who was known for his ingenuity and mechanical acumen. It was he whom Kadiya had consulted as to the practicality of sinking the pirate ship, and he had speedily come up with a good plan — which now was perforce abandoned.

Mok-La said: "Most of the crew will be up on deck, watching the sorcerer raise the sunken talisman. With luck, we can break into the compartment where the King is held without too much commotion, subdue whatever guards are about, and free him."

"It could work," Lummomu said. "Shall we take a chance, Lady of the Eyes?"

Kadiya's words were almost inaudible. "I was unforgivably selfish not to think of the danger to Anigel's family when we set forth on this mission. The only way I can atone is to attempt to rescue them. If I succeed with your help, my friends, my sister's heart will be eased and her talisman saved from the foul sorcerer. If we fail . . . we may lose our lives, but Anigel will be no worse off than before."

"We are at your service, Lady, even if it should lead us to pass beyond," the leader of the Wyvilo tribe said. The other two warriors also grunted their assent.

"Very well," she said. "This is what we will do: We will take the raft apart. Its ropes will be useful for those who must escape with the King, and we can all easily swim to shore from here. After we ascend the chain, Lummomu and Huri will take the ropes and attempt to find and free King Antar. Let us hope that they can leave the ship through one of the accommodation-doors, sliding down a rope. Meanwhile, I will carry little Tolo down one anchor chain while Mok brings Niki and Jan down the other. We will swim as quickly as we can with the children to the shore of Council Isle. If Lummomu and Huri succeed in liberating Antar, they will swim ashore with him. If the King cannot be found, or if the worst happens, those of us on the island will hide until daybreak, then try to make our way through the forest to the place where *Lyath* lies at anchor. We can attract Anigel's attention there and with luck be off and away before the Raktumian trireme can catch us. Is this agreed?"

The Wyvilo grunted.

And so they brought the raft cautiously up under the stem of the gigantic ship, where it would no longer be visible from above. The lashings of the bamboo raft were carefully undone and the many small ropes knotted into one long one. After this the rescuers swam to the chains and began to swarm stealthily up the huge links.

From the deck above came a tremendous shout. Kadiya and the Wyvilo feared for a moment that they were discovered; but then there was a great splash astern and more screaming and yelling, and they realized that the tumult was a reaction to whatever wizardry Portolanus was engaged in. The rescuers abandoned all wariness at that point, and climbed as fast as they could. In a few minutes more Kadiya reached the hawsehole on her side and found herself face-to-face with little Prince Tolivar.

"Aunt Kadiya!" the child squeaked. But his face wore an aspect of consternation, not delight.

"We have come to rescue you," said she. "This will be easiest if you go back down inside and wait with Niki and Jan. Hurry!"

"But I don't want to go —"

"Don't be ridiculous!" Kadiya snapped. "Be quick, now! There is no time to waste. My Wyvilo friends, here, must find King Antar and save him before the sorcerer discovers what we are about."

With a panicked expression, Tolo disappeared from the opening. Kadiya climbed easily inside and Mok-La followed at her heels, cursing under his breath at the tightness of the hole's fit about his powerful body. Lummomu and Huri were already inside the other hawsehole and sliding down.

"By the Holy Moons!" Lummomu's voiced boomed up from below. "The other two younglings are gone!"

Kadiya tumbled to the planks, then made a dash to take hold of Tolo, who was trying to hide behind a great pile of chain. "Where are your sister and brother?" she demanded.

Tolo burst into terrified wails. "Th-they escaped and swam ashore . . . I didn't go . . . b-because I wanted to be the sorcerer's apprentice instead of a rotten old second prince."

For a moment Kadiya was rendered speechless. Then she said to the Wyvilo: "All three of you go to seek out the King. I will take care of this silly little vart-scat. May the Lords of the Air go with you." And she said to Tolivar: "No more nonsense! Climb on my back and hold tight to my neck. We are going to swim ashore."

The weeping little Prince cried: "I won't!"

Huri-Kamo had already broken through the locker door with the broadax that was the traditional Wyvilo weapon. The hold beyond was black and untenanted. The other two aborigines, their luminous eyes aglow, drew their own axes from the back-sheaths and slipped away.

Kadiya untied the sodden seaman's neckerchief she wore and brandished it at the balky child. "If need be, I shall stuff this into your mouth, and tie you to my back with my belt. But first, I shall wallop your royal bottom so that you will eat your meals standing for a month! Now . . . are you ready to come quietly?"

"Yes," said Tolo forlornly, rubbing the tears from his eyes with his grubby fists. Then a malefic little smile touched his lips. "But it will be your fault if the Sea Oddlings get us as well as the others."

"The — *what?*"

"Sea Oddlings. I saw their torches on the beach."

It was only when she had swum well away from the trireme that
Kadiya saw how Portolanus planned to retrieve her talisman from the
depths. She had traveled a hundred or so ells shoreward with Prince
Tolivar, finally gaining a clear view of the area around the stern, and
from there she saw that the water aft of the ship was fearfully roiled,
all full of white foam and an uproar of choppy waves. The sorcerer
was leaning over the rail shaking his fist and shouting. His eyes shone
like white beacons, and the shovel suspended at the end of the crane-
hook swung wildly in their light. The people on the main deck had
fled as far forward as they could get, howling and cursing.

As Kadiya and the child clinging to her neck watched astounded,
the great trireme began to rock and shudder. Portolanus went into a
paroxysm of rage. He pulled some small thing from his robe and
tossed it into the air, and there was a great explosion accompanied by
an eye-searing white flash. Immediately the sea calmed and the ship
steadied. The frightened people on board were also stunned to silence, so that Kadiya could finally hear what the sorcerer was saying.

"Heldo! Damn you, Heldo — come up, I say! Cease this rebellious
thrashing! You are bound by my spell, and you must obey me. I will
not release you until you do as I command. Heldo, lord of the watery
abyss, attend me!"

About a dozen ells off the stern, the dark sea seemed to hump up.
Then Kadiya and Tolo saw the water broken by a formless gigantic
shape that gleamed in the light of the Three Moons. Higher and
higher it rose, taking on a smooth elongate form with a rounded top,
until it towered far above the poop deck, being nearly half as high as
the trireme's mizzenmast and more than seven ells wide. At first,
Kadiya thought it must be some undersea eruption of volcanic rock
thrust skyward — but then she saw two scarlet-glowing orbs down
near the water's broken surface and realized that they were eyes.

"It's the sea-monster," Tolo said with sour satisfaction, "just like
Ralabun said. He'll probably eat everybody on the pirate ship, then
come and eat us."

"Be silent, little squit," Kadiya said. "The sorcerer has summoned this thing to retrieve my talisman! O Lords of the Air, forfend!"

"Great Heldo!" Portolanus intoned. "Take this instrument"—he pointed to the shovel dangling from the crane—"and prepare to do my bidding."

The creature called Heldo tipped back, and from out of the water emerged four enormous tentacles that coiled and stretched. Tusklike appendages glistened at their tips and their undersides were strangely fringed, dripping myriad sparkling droplets. Heldo then uttered an eerie trumpeting cry unlike anything Kadiya had ever heard. The awful sound seemed to paralyze her, and she even forgot to tread water until Tolo cried out that they were sinking.

"Take the instrument!" Portolanus ordered once more. And finally, with great delicacy, one of the writhing tentacles gripped the wide shovel and removed it from the hook. Another tentacle hovered above Portolanus, and still another menaced the two pirates at the crane, who screeched at the sight of it and fled down the steps and onto the main deck, leaving the sorcerer and his three immobile Voices alone.

"Now attend me, Heldo! You will be freed from the spell that binds you as soon as you do me one small service. Directly beneath this ship is a magical device that looks like a dark pointless sword with a three-lobed pommel. It glows green in the depths. Find this thing, and lift it carefully to the surface with the instrument I have furnished you. Do not touch the magical sword with your own flesh, or it will kill you! Do you understand?"

Heldo trumpeted.

Portolanus now knelt and opened the star-box. "When you have secured the sword, put it into this box. After you have done this, I will release you. Now go!"

There was a tremendous splash that set the trireme lurching, and the monster disappeared.

Kadiya groaned. "O God, let it not happen! Haramis! Anigel! Hear me and help me! Beseech the Triune to return my Three-Lobed Burning Eye to me! Let it not fall into the sorcerer's hands—"

The sea surged again and luminescent foam was thrown in all directions as Heldo shot up again to the surface, one tentacle high against the sky. At its tip, balanced on the shovel's wide blade, something shone like a long and luminous emerald. The tentacle holding it swooped toward the ship and Kadiya wailed:

"No! No! Come to me, talisman! You belong to me!"

The star-eyed figure of the sorcerer stood waiting. A great stillness now filled the night as the waves subsided about the monster and Kadiya's anguished cry faded away. The green-glowing talisman seemed to detach itself from the tentacle-tip and fall as slowly as a feather drifting.

"Come to me," Kadiya whispered, tears streaming down her face. She lifted one hand out of the water in supplication.

At the stern of the pirate ship a brief golden spark flared. Kadiya heard the voice of Portolanus utter a surprised oath — and then there was a sharp clang signaling the fall of the Three-Lobed Burning Eye into the unbonding box of the Vanished Ones. Portolanus's voice changed to a crow of triumph.

But Kadiya held in her hand a piece of glowing amber, and in her mind she seemed to hear a familiar voice, an almost forgotten memory drawn from the remote past:

Years come and go with speed. That which is lofty may fall, that which is cherished may be lost, that which is hidden must, in time, be revealed. And yet I tell you that all will be well . . . But now you must flee, Petal of the Living Trillium, and gain the land before the sorcerer realizes what has happened and wreaks his vengeance upon you. Make haste! Swim for your life and beseech your amulet's aid!

Her amulet . . . she had worn it all her life until it had flown away from her to embed itself in her talisman. And now it had come back to her. But its magic was a puny thing compared with that of the Three-Lobed Burning Eye —

Swim!

The command in her mind jolted her back to the clear and present danger. Gripping the warm amber tightly, Kadiya struck out for the island shore. "Hang on, Tolo!" she cried.

Behind her, a tall form wavered behind the trireme. Kadiya thought at first that it was Heldo, but then she realized that the sea-monster had submerged, and this thing was much taller and thinner, a black silhouette outlined against the sky like a titanic, swaying snake. Clouds came racing from nowhere to shroud the Moons and the stars. A deep crimson bolt of lightning flashed briefly, followed by a mutter of thunder. Portolanus was once again commanding the storm, probably to drive Heldo away, and the trireme tossed like a toy on the suddenly troubled waters. She felt a gust of strong wind. Tolo began crying, and there was now also a keen buzzing sound in the air that grew rapidly in intensity. Kadiya finally realized what the sorcerer had done.

He had created another great waterspout, and by chance it was rushing directly toward them.

"Black Trillium, be thou my rescuer!" she cried, closing her eyes. She clutched one of Tolo's spindly wrists in one hand and the amulet in the other. In an instant she and the child were engulfed and flung helter-skelter, but the flood that enveloped them had no wetness and the dark did not snatch their life's breath. Over and over they tumbled, helpless as leaves in a torrent, until they came to rest with shocking suddenness. Tolo's arms loosed from Kadiya's neck, and he fell away softly moaning.

They sat on wet sand in the midst of a deluge.

On Council Isle.

Rain mixed with salt water poured down on them as if the sluice-gates of heaven had been opened. There were even a few unfortunate fishes falling from the sky in the aftermath of the watery tornado. It was impossible to see anything out to sea, where giant waves were leaping skyward and newborn surf crashed on the shore. Almost continuous lightning and thunder smote Kadiya's senses. She had wit enough left only to hold tight to the shivering little boy as they huddled together in the roaring downpour.

A sturdy dwarfish figure came hurrying toward them from a madly tossing grove of lown-trees. At first she thought that, by some miracle of the Flower, Jagun had been sent to help her. But when the aborigine approached, she saw that he belonged to a race of Folk unknown to her, with more humanoid features than the broad-faced, wide-mouthed Nyssomu possessed, and a more powerful body clad in the heavy garb of a northerner.

"Come quickly with me!" the little man shouted above the tempest. "There are cruel natives hereabouts who will surely capture you if you stay on the open beach."

Kadiya struggled to her feet, fighting against the muddle of fatigue and confusion clogging her brain. The aborigine swept up Tolo in strong arms and they all dashed for the shelter of the grove. Moments later the three of them plunged into the heavy undergrowth, and fell gasping beneath the huge leaves of a sprawling island shrub.

"There are two other human children in dire jeopardy near this place," the aborigine said, when he had caught his breath. "I saw them only a short time ago, staked out on the ground in preparation for some terrible torture. Being alone, and the natives many, I did not know how to save the poor young things. I hid away in here. But now that you have come, perhaps we can work out something together."

"Niki and Jan!" Kadiya exclaimed. "In the hands of the Aliansa! Merciful God, what are we to do? . . ." And for some time she could only sit motionless, trying to marshal her body's flagging resources. Finally, she said: "My friend, the captives are my niece and nephew, of the royal family of Laboruwenda. I bless you for offering to help save them . . . But how is it that you are here? I see from your dress that you are not native to the Windlorn Isles."

The little man's inhuman eyes shone faintly, and Kadiya's amber amulet also gave off a discreet golden light. Prince Tolivar was silent, his head resting on Kadiya's breast and his eyes wide open.

"So these are the Windlorn Isles, are they?" The aborigine shook his head. "And where might they be?"

"In the far Southern Sea, below Zinora," Kadiya said.

"Ah. That still tells me little, for I have heard neither of the Sea nor of this Zinora. I was whisked here in the blink of an eye through a magical viaduct. A strange voice said I would go where I was needed — and thus I came here!"

"Who are you, and what Folk are your kin?"

"My name is Shiki. I was once a simple mountain guide and hunter of the Dorok tribe of Tuzamen — but recently I entered the service of the Archimage Haramis."

"She is my sister! I am Kadiya, called by some the Lady of the

Eyes. The Archimage has truly sent you where you were needed, Shiki! . . ."

She looked down at little Tolivar, whose frail body was shivering from shock and the sudden chill caused by the magical storm. Without a word, Shiki took off his heavy fur-trimmed jacket and wrapped the boy in it. The rain was still pelting down, but not much of it penetrated the shelter of the overhanging leaves.

"Tolo, will you remain here and behave yourself while we go after your sister and brother?" Kadiya was stern. "There must be no more silliness, or you may endanger our lives. Do you understand?"

"Yes, Aunt," the boy whispered meekly.

"Good." Kadiya felt her strength returning. There was no time to waste. She plucked a wiry vine and began to strip off its foliage, and then she strung the amulet of trillium-amber upon it and tied it around her neck. She drew her small dagger and honed it briefly against the back of its sheath, and used her kerchief to tie back her dripping hair.

"Now I am ready," she said to Shiki. "Lead me to where the children are being held, and we will do our best to rescue them."

The aborigine beckoned, and the two of them crept off into the rain.

14

The waterspouts disappeared and the trireme rode steadily again, even though the storm continued unabated. The magical tempests of Portolanus were quick in the summoning but took rather longer to dissipate. The jubilant sorcerer revived his three Voices and led them to his large stateroom, taking along the star-box with the Three-Lobed Burning Eye safely enclosed.

After speaking a suitable incantation, the sorcerer opened the box and permitted the awestruck acolytes to gaze upon the great treasure, which still sparkled with drops of salt water and had a strand of seaweed draped over it.

"Is it safe to touch, Master?" the Yellow Voice asked.

"Not yet. I must perform a certain ritual, using those colored things inside the star-box's corner. Then the talisman will be bonded to me and I can safely wield it." Even as he spoke his fingers danced over the gemlike appurtenances. A series of gentle musical notes sounded and the jewels within the box gleamed brightly. Then all of the little gems darkened and Portolanus lifted the talisman.

"Ah!" cried the Voices.

"Now the Three-Lobed Burning Eye is cleaved to my body and soul," the sorcerer proclaimed. "No other beings may touch it without my permission, lest they perish in flame!"

"What magical deeds will the talisman do, Master?" inquired the Purple Voice eagerly.

"It will smite mine enemies, grant me Sight and clairaudience without my having to drain your long-suffering brains, and share with me arcane knowledge that will help me become ruler of the world . . . once I fully understand its secret operation."

The Voices once again exclaimed in wonderment.

"I grant you three Voices of mine permission to touch the talisman without harm to yourselves," Portolanus went on. "This permission lasts until I revoke it — or until you renounce your loyalty to me."

"We never will do that!" the Black Voice asserted, and the others were quick to concur.

"You understand, my Voices, that by yourselves you will be unable to command the talisman. But I, working through you, will be able to do so just as I can speak and hear through you from afar."

The Black Voice, now bending over to study the talisman more closely, pointed to a depression where the three dark lobes of the sword's pommel met. "Master, it seems that some object might have once been inset there. A jewel, perhaps?"

Portolanus cried out like a man stabbed. "The trillium amulet! It's gone! Now I know what caused the golden spark to soar away whilst Heldo still carried it! The amulet has returned to its owner!"

And he cursed Kadiya most foully and also cursed the Dark Powers, while the three acolytes fell back in confusion. Then, regaining his composure somewhat, he murmured: "Perhaps the loss of the trillium-amber will make no difference to the talisman's operation. Or *perhaps —*"

His face changed abruptly and now bore a look of great excitement. He lifted from out of his robes the battered and blackened star that always hung about his neck on a platinum chain. "Perhaps . . ." he repeated softly, and brought the talisman's pommel close to the pendant.

Each of the three dark lobes seemed to split open, revealing large and gleaming eyes. One was the golden-yellow eye of the Folk, one was brown and quite human, and the third was a peculiar silvery blue with a golden spark in its depths, like unto Portolanus's own eyes.

The talisman seemed to glare at the dangling, dingy, many-rayed star. Then there was a bright burst of light, and an instant later the pendant was nestled securely among the three lobes of the pommel, now as shiny and perfect as when it had been first given to its owner long years ago by an aged sorcerer named Bondanus of Tuzamen.

"Glory be to the Dark Powers!" Portolanus exulted. "Now, talisman, you are truly mine own!"

I am truly your own.

The sorcerer was laughing with full-throated glee as he gripped the talisman by its hilt and waved it about his head. His guise of age and decrepitude fell away completely and he stood tall and vigorous, with a face that was seamed by hardship but comely withal, and hair and beard shining white. He cried out: "Did you hear? Did you hear the talisman speak?"

"No, Master," the Voices admitted.

"It says that it belongs to me! To me! . . . Talisman! Show me that arrogant bitch, Kadiya."

Obediently, a vision filled his mind showing the Lady of the Eyes and an unknown aborigine creeping through a rain-lashed forest.

"Hah! She has gone ashore, and now doubtless seeks to incite the local savages against us . . . Yellow Voice! Hasten to Admiral Jorot and command him in my name to up anchor and rouse the oarsmen. We must be away from this hostile island immediately. Tell him that I will send later what course to follow in order to rendezvous with our other ships."

When the Yellow Voice had gone, Portolanus bade the talisman: "Now show me exactly where on the island Kadiya is."

He beheld a bird's-eye view of Council Isle, and upon it was a shining white dot near the main village of the Aliansa.

"It is as I thought. Now show me where Queen Anigel is, and then permit me to view her."

He saw again the Sight of the island, and this time the glowing dot was out in the small inlet just north of the larger bay where the Raktumian trireme lay at anchor. Then the vision changed to one of Anigel standing calmly in the bows of her little ship, her own talisman on her head and her eyes seeming to be fixed upon his own.

"Yes, I know you are watching me, Portolanus," said she, "for all that you cloud your form from my Sight. I saw how you stole Kadiya's talisman with the help of the sea-creature, and how you bonded the

Three-Lobed Burning Eye to yourself. But even in spite of this, you will not prevail."

"Ho! We will see how bravely you talk when your husband and your children are put to the torture before your eyes! Your own talisman is now forfeit, proud Queen, and if you do not set it adrift in a small boat at once, I will have the pirates begin their dainty work on your loved ones."

Anigel wore a peculiar smile. "Will you indeed!" And she vanished.

Puzzled by her seeming callousness, Portolanus tried to resummon the vision of her; but the bow of her small ship now appeared to be empty. No doubt her talisman was concealing her from his Sight, just as he was hidden from hers. Well, it did not matter what games she was playing.

"Purple Voice! Go to the pirate Quartermaster and have him bring the royal urchins to the grand saloon under guard. We will see how firm the Queen's resolution remains when her son's fingers are severed, one by one, and the tender toes of her daughter are dipped into a brazier of hot coals."

But before the Purple Voice could reach the cabin door, a loud banging upon it commenced. The Voice yanked the door open and there stood the First Mate, a tall, saturnine pirate named Kalardis.

"Your prisoners have escaped," he said brusquely. "While you were frolicking with the sea-monster, three Wyvilo aborigines invaded the quarters of the galley slaves, freed King Antar, and took him away through one of the slop-doors. Nearly fifty oarsmen of the third bank also absconded, and this cursed storm of your concoction has very likely drowned the lot of them!"

"The royal children are gone, too?" croaked Portolanus. He had immediately reassumed the cloak of old age as the mate appeared.

"Aye," said Kalardis. "My men checked the chain-locker immediately. Its doors were smashed from the inside, as were those of the locked holds hard by and those in the corridors leading to the slave compartments. The rascals must have come up the anchor chains."

The sorcerer spoke low, with an anxious urgency. "Have we enough oarsmen left to move the ship? We must get away from this place before hostile Sea Oddlings attack us. I do not think my storm will hold them off for long. There is also the possibility of Queen Anigel doing us some great mischief with her own talisman, now that her family has escaped the ship."

"I met your minion on my way here and he told me of your orders to get under way. The other two banks of oars are still manned. We will move — although not as swiftly as before. We would not be able to make any turn of speed under the best of circumstances, however. Your storm will hinder the lookouts, as does the darkness, and we will have to take constant soundings to keep from running aground or piling up on a reef."

"The storm will soon cease, and I will see us safe with my magical talisman — " Portolanus started to say, but the mate broke in.

"Not until you wait upon the Queen Regent's pleasure." Kalardis grinned, revealing stained and broken teeth. "Or, rather, her *displeasure*. She expects you at once in the royal saloon, and I would not be in your boots for all the plunder in Taloazin."

Queen Ganondri, attended by six heavily armed pirate-knights, sat at a gilded table with a chart of the islands spread upon it. No sooner had Portolanus stepped into the saloon than two of the big Raktumians seized his arms and held him fast. He had not had time to pull the Three-Lobed Burning Eye from his belt.

"Give me a reason," Ganondri said with venomous sweetness, "why I should not command my men to cut your scrawny throat, since you allowed the royal prisoners to escape."

The sorcerer took a deep breath. "Talisman! I command you to strike my captors dead!"

The two pirates uttered gasping curses. At once they unhanded Portolanus and drew their swords. The Queen Regent started up from her seat, her face livid.

Nothing happened.

Desperately, the sorcerer took hold of the talisman and waved it in a sweeping arc. "Talisman, smite all mine enemies in this room with your vengeful fire!"

Again, nothing happened.

Ganondri fell back, laughing in relief. All six of the enraged knights converged upon Portolanus. One of them ripped the talisman from the sorcerer's fingers, taking hold of it by the dull-edged blade.

At once the three orbs of the pommel opened and the living eyes stared for a moment at the hapless Raktumian. Then from the human eye shot a golden beam, and from the Folk eye a green, and from the strange silver-blue eye a ray of searing white.

The armored pirate was instantly bathed from helmet to heel in pulsating radiance. His gauntleted fingers let the talisman fall, but the magical flames only waxed brighter, wrapping him in a tricolored shroud of light. He uttered no sound, but those around him cried out in horror and revulsion, for his face had gone black and charred below its uplifted visor, and thick smoke leaked from every joint in his armor. There was a dreadful crackling sound and a subdued roar like a fire up a flue. The burning knight crashed to the carpet. Two of the other pirates hauled down a tapestry and flung it over their doomed comrade, but none dared touch him. Portolanus, who had backed against one wall, regarded the scene with as much amazement and fear as did the Queen and her men.

Abruptly, the awful muffled sounds beneath the tapestry ceased. The smoke and stench vanished, leaving the air in the saloon clear and sweet. Portolanus squared his shoulders, assumed a solemn mien, and marched forward to lift the heavy cloth.

The leather straps joining the victim's armor had burnt away, and scorched plates lay helter-skelter. There was no sign of a body, or even bones. In the midst of the heat-warped pieces of armor was the talisman, quite unharmed, once again seeming to be nothing more than a Sword of Mercy made of dark metal, lacking a point and having unsharpened edges.

Portolanus picked it up and thrust it into his belt, then let the tapestry fall again. He said to the knights: "You men, leave us."

"No!" Ganondri cried. "Wizard, take care! Have you forgotten my warning? Even if all on this ship should perish, in the end you would find your ambitions confounded without the aid of great Raktum. Only with my help can you achieve your goal!"

The sorcerer came forward and leaned upon the table with both palms flat. His face was now drawn and tired, and his voice harsh.

"You are quite right: I need your help more than ever now that Anigel's talisman is out of reach. But unless you would have these louts witness talk that should remain privy between us, dismiss them."

He pulled up a gilded chair, dropped down into it, and smiled wryly. "You are safe enough with me, Great Queen. You have seen that my mastery of the talisman is imperfect. It kills only the person who tries to take it from me—worst luck! I swear by the Dark Powers I serve, and by the talisman itself, that I will not harm you."

The Queen's hand was shaking as she finally gestured for the knights to gather up the blackened armor of their incinerated companion and leave. She then took a decanter, poured brandy into a large goblet, and was barely able to lift it to her lips. After she had gulped the whole thing, she seemed steadied, although her eyes still smoldered with hate, together with a profound terror barely suppressed by her great power of will. She said:

"This situation is unacceptable, wizard. We must renegotiate our alliance once again. You have your talisman, but *mine* is now beyond reach."

"Not necessarily! Let us see if this balky magical sword can do more than roast the unwary pilferer." Before the Queen could protest, he drew it and held it upright by the blade. "Talisman! Show the two of us King Antar."

Ganondri gave an exclamation as the vision formed. She saw a dark and choppy sea pocked with a few raindrops. Appearing and disappearing amidst the waves were the silhouettes of three grotesque muzzled heads clustered about a smaller human one. Antar and the Wyvilo were paddling slowly toward the luminous surf-line of the island shore.

"Ah," said Portolanus. "So they did make their escape in spite of the storm and Heldo. It should not be too difficult to resnare our regal guest! . . . Now, talisman, show us Prince Nikalon, Princess Janeel, and Prince Tolivar."

In their mind's eye the sorcerer and the Queen Regent saw Niki and Jan lying supine in the wet mud of a native village compound. Their limbs were tied to stakes and they seemed to be unconscious.

With the rain dwindling to occasional drops, a few Aliansa were peering from the doors of their huts and calling out to each other.

"Well, well! It seems the two elder waifs are being honored with some local demonstration of hospitality. I don't think their fate need concern us. Now what about the third royal child?"

Obediently, the vision shifted to Tolivar. He was moving purposefully through the jungle undergrowth, muttering to himself. Portolanus and the Queen could distinguish only a few phrases:

". . . Aunt Kadiya can't make me . . . don't care if the pirates find me . . . rather be a wizard than a rotten second prince . . . I'll miss Ralabun, but none of *them* . . ."

Portolanus banished the vision and sat frowning thoughtfully. Finally he commanded: "Talisman, show me precisely where King Antar and his three children are situated now — and also Kadiya."

In his mind a picture of Council Isle materialized, together with glowing points of white light. He knew immediately what each light signified. King Antar was still nearly half a league offshore, swept some distance to the south by the storm winds. Little Tolivar was at the forest edge approaching the open beach, opposite the anchorage of the Raktumian flagship. The two captive children were at the large Aliansa village a league or so inland and further north. Kadiya was near them, apparently not having moved from her previous position.

"Now show me Prince Tolivar again," Portolanus commanded.

Through the open ports of the saloon came a sound of shouted commands and running feet. A vibration spread through the trireme as the twin capstans in the bow were manned and the two great anchors were raised.

The Queen surged to her feet. "Who ordered that we get under way? We must send armed parties ashore at once! If we regain even one of the escaped prisoners, we will have sufficient leverage to force Anigel to give up her talisman to me." She rushed toward the door, flung it open, and began to shout for Admiral Jorot.

Portolanus was still engrossed in his vision of Prince Tolivar, speaking to himself. "The little devil! So he would, would he? The audacity! . . . But he did seem quite taken with me, did he not? And I thought I detected about him the faintest aura of magical potential! I suppose that's why I hadn't the heart to consider torturing him. One very well might be able to make a sorcerer of him . . . I wonder if he is old enough yet to understand matters of state? Might he be of direct assistance to us in the overthrow of the Two Thrones?"

Ganondri reentered the stateroom. "I have ordered that the flag-ship remain hove to with the anchors up while six boats full of armed men go after King Antar and the little Prince. We can forget about the two children held captive by the Sea Oddlings. No doubt Queen Anigel has already spied them out. She will pay scant attention to us while her precious brats are menaced by savages. Now you must — "

"I will not go ashore!" the sorcerer declared.

"Surely the Sea Oddlings would not endanger a mighty enchanter such as yourself," the Queen said archly. And then her tone sharp-ened. "You must guide the landing party directly to Antar and Prince Tolivar through your talisman. There is no time to waste!"

"My Black Voice will accompany the party going after the King, and my Purple Voice will guide those who seek Prince Tolivar. I will communicate to the Voices the exact places where the King and the little Prince are to be found. There is no reason for me to leave the flagship."

"You will go because I command it!"

"No! It is unnecessary."

Portolanus and Queen Regent Ganondri glared at one another in silence for a moment. Then he said softly: "You will *not* maroon me on this Oddling island, Pirate Queen. Get that notion out of your head. We will remain allies, for better or worse, and I will see that at least one royal hostage is retaken so that you may barter with Queen Anigel for her talisman. However, I strongly suggest that you do not attempt the exchange here. Anigel will be in no mood to be reasonable once the Aliansa have tormented and slain two of her children. We should set sail just as soon as we have either Antar or the little Prince."

"And then?" the Queen snapped.

"You will deliver me and my people safely to my Tuzameni vessel. Through my talisman's Sight, I can ensure a speedy rendezvous with it and with the three other ships of your flotilla. They cannot be more than a few days' sail away from us. After that, if you wish our alliance to continue, we can undertake our journey home in convoy. You may carry the royal prisoners as before — "

"And the star-box," Ganondri said firmly. "You will give it to me now, or your alliance with great Raktum is at an end — and so are your ambitions to conquer Laboruwenda!"

Portolanus drew the talisman from his belt and slowly brought the pointless dark blade toward the Queen Regent's throat. She stiffened, but neither flinched nor cried out as the metal touched her flesh harmlessly. If the sorcerer was commanding her destruction in his mind, the talisman declined to obey.

Ganondri's mouth curved in a small, wintry smile. "The star-box," she repeated. "Now. And you will show me how to use it."

Portolanus withdrew the talisman, stood up from the table, and bowed. "It seems we have reached a stalemate, Great Queen. Let us both attempt to dismiss the rancor that divides us at this moment. Let us try to think instead upon the considerations that originally brought us together. We need not love one another to work toward a common goal. You know very well that my ambition is not so petty as the conquest of Laboruwenda. That proud Land of the Two Thrones shall be yours."

"And so will Queen Anigel's talisman." The Queen's smile tightened to the ferocity of a lothok's grimace and she tapped the fingers of one hand upon the table before her, so that her many rings flashed in the lamplight. "Let me tell you what the new terms of our agreement are to be, magician. Great Raktum will be your loyal ally for as long as you forswear treachery against her and her Queen Regent. But I will retain Anigel's talisman until the day I die, and you will instruct me in its operation."

Portolanus flung up his hands in frustration. "I do not yet know how to use my *own* talisman properly!"

"I have no doubt that you will learn."

The sorcerer sighed. "Very well . . . I swear by the Dark Powers and by this talisman — may it destroy me if I violate this oath — that I will faithfully adhere to the conditions you have set. I will send my Yellow Voice to you with the star-box immediately, and then undertake the recovery of the royal prisoners."

Ganondri nodded imperiously. Portolanus then went out of the royal stateroom, closing the door softly behind him. When he had gone, the Queen Regent began to laugh, and her mirth and exultant triumph so overwhelmed her that she could not stop until she drank another full goblet of brandy.

When the Yellow Voice came anon with the star-box, she snatched it rudely from him and pushed him out the door. Then she began to laugh again.

15

Haramis did not hurry along the Way of Light. She walked over the cold deep waters of the sea deliberately, as though the sparkling insubstantiality beneath her feet were a stone pavement. The arctic breeze bore the peculiar scent of sea-ice, and the aurora flamed over the entire sky, veiling the stars and the Three Moons and illuminating the gigantic drifting icebergs with pale rays of blue and red.

The largest of the floating ice-mountains, toward which the Way of Light led, shone also with an interior glow of its own. This had not been evident to Haramis when she started out from the shore; but as she drew closer the iceberg seemed to become more and more luminous, until it finally took on the appearance of a titanic beryl gemstone, blue green in a hundred different tints, embedded in the black glass of the northern ocean. Its radiance continued underwater, dimming with depth, and Haramis realized that the great mass of ice towering above the water was only a small proportion of the incredible bulk that lay hidden beneath.

She walked for over two leagues before she reached it. The Way of Light took her into an overarching grotto that pierced one side of the iceberg, a corridor having a floor of water that was no longer black but midnight blue, still skinned with the stardust sparkle that rendered it firm for her feet. The walls had a gleaming irregular surface and were cupped and faceted and carved so that the light within seemed to shine through fantastic shapes of pale emerald and aquamarine, shadowed with sapphire blue.

Without thinking, she reached out and touched the nearest wall.

"By the Flower! It is not ice after all!"

The surface was smooth and wet, but only moderately cold to the touch and certainly warmer than the sea. Could it be glass? She rapped it with her fingernails. It seemed more yielding than crystal, unlike any substance she had ever known. It was magical stuff, undoubtedly made by the Archimage of the Sea. A simulation of an iceberg.

And then Haramis realized that inside the transparent walls fishes and other marine animals were swimming toward her. They rushed in countless numbers to swarm in on both sides of the cleft, as high as her eye could see into blue dimness. The artificial iceberg was hollow and crowded with life.

She stared, and the creatures looked her over as well, their eyes seeming to be wide with astonishment. They were mostly colored silver, grayish blue, or white, and some were transparent save for the pulsing organs within. There were huge fish with glittering mirror-scales and mouths full of jagged teeth, resembling the deadly milingals of the rivers in the Mazy Mire. Schools of smaller fish with electric-blue eyes whisked about with a unified precision that made them seem directed by a single brain. There were languidly flowing fish like wide white ribbons stitched with silver foil, and fish shaped like swords, and fish so grotesque that they were scarcely recognizable as such, all studded with knobs and spikes and appendages like flexible lances with silver banners waving at the tips. There were great passive hydrozoans like fringed ovoids of rainbow-tinted jelly, and smaller ones that resembled lovely floating blossoms with questing pastel petals. Snowy tentacled creatures with droll faces zipped about among the slower swimmers, and shoals of translucent shellfish traveled in stately splendor, harried by some kind of shapeless silver predator that occasionally engulfed a heedless victim and then dropped out of sight. Glassy, angular little crustaceans were everywhere, hovering like crystal bees about the flower-animals, moving fearlessly in and out of the gaping maws of the silvery milingals and even hitching rides on the less fierce-looking creatures.

Haramis could not help uttering an exclamation of delight.

I am glad that you enjoy my pets.

Startled, she looked about her. But the aquariumlike cleft was empty of other humans. "Is it the Archimage of the Sea?" she whispered.

Of course! Do hurry along, child. I'm so impatient to meet you. You may study the denizens of my home later if you wish. But our supper is getting cold and I'm so very hungry!

Haramis suppressed a smile. Evidently this Archimage was not one to stand upon ceremony, nor did her mental voice sound in the least pompous or condescending. Haramis had tried to avoid speculating about what kind of personage she was about to meet. Officially, they were equals; actually, they would be student and tutor. She prayed only that this fellow-Archimage would be straightforward, and not as feeble and enigmatic as Binah had been. She needed help of a practical sort, not exposure to more mystery. Kadiya's talisman was almost surely lost to Portolanus, and Anigel's would very likely be given to the sorcerer in ransom before long. If she herself did not master her own talisman soon, there was no doubt in her mind that Portolanus would achieve his goal of mastering the world.

Denby thinks that is a foregone conclusion. But you and I will show him a thing or two! As to being practical . . . that, my dear, is entirely your affair. I'm certainly not one to let myself be starstruck by a charming enchanter — but I'm not at all sure about you!

Haramis uttered a low cry of outrage, then drew herself up and grimly resumed her journey into the heart of the sham iceberg. She spoke to thin air:

"It is evident, Lady of the Sea, that you can perceive my thoughts. But I doubt very much if you can read my conscience. I come to you as a supplicant, it's true, and if your teaching can only be done through the shattering of my dignity, then so be it. But I had hoped for a warmer and more friendly relationship. I know I am young in comparison to you, but I am not a child, nor am I a fool. I have ever carried out my duties as Archimage to the best of my ability, not letting myself be distracted by any person or thing —"

— yet! But you will be, proud one! Just as you once were twelve years ago, before you assumed your cloak of office. Not only distracted from duty, but strongly tempted to evil. Admit it!

Haramis stopped short. "I will not try to justify myself. It is true that I once loved the sorcerer Orogastus and was briefly led astray by his vision of power. But I repudiated him. If he is still alive, as I suspect, I will try with all my heart and soul to reject him again and foil his evil design . . . But I need your help desperately. Will you give it?"

I would not have summoned you through the viaduct otherwise. But you proved your resolution by going to the Kimilon, so I decided you were a fit subject for special treatment — never mind what Denby thinks. Not only the balance of the world, but even its very existence is endangered by the resurgence of the abominable Star! Drastic measures are called for in desperate situations! Denby thought Binah was a lunatic to risk setting the Threefold Sceptre of Power free to countermand the threat, and he got all in a swivet when she arranged for you three to be born. Nevertheless, even he admitted that the Star Man would have got hold of the Sceptre sooner or later, even without the mistakes you three Trillium Petals have made. Binah gambled that given time, you'd be able to resolve the menace once and for all in spite of your silly fumbling. Fresh young blood, fresh young minds tackling the ancient problem. You see?

"No! I have no idea what you're talking about." Haramis suddenly felt freezing cold, even though the air within the artificial iceberg was quite warm. She drew her white furs more closely around her and spoke sharply. "Explain yourself, Archimage! Tell me just what kind of danger threatens the world and what role my sisters and I are to play in thwarting it. I warn you that I have no intention of being fobbed off with mystical flummery or evasions any longer."

Ha-ha! Full of spirit! I like that. Come ahead, Haramis-who-will-brook-no-nonsense! We're going to get along splendidly.

The Way of Light ended when the tiny arm of the sea pinched off in the narrowing corridor, leaving Haramis standing upon a glowing platform. Three tunnels branched out from it, but only one was illuminated. She followed it for a considerable distance more, growing light-headed from the illusion of being suspended in ice-choked bright water. The hordes of creatures had deserted her, evidently having seen enough; and now the water behind the transparent walls

showed only an occasional indistinct shape finning by. As she continued on, the illumination slowly dimmed, as if she were getting farther
and farther from its source. The aqueous colors shifted to deeper
hues — ultramarine blue and jade green, shadowed with violet.

And then there was a door, opaque white, with a great ring-latch of
silver that resisted her pull. She touched it with her talisman and once
again the bell-chime sounded that had signaled the mysterious viaduct. The door swung open to darkness.

Resolutely, Haramis went in. She stood frozen as the door closed,
leaving her with only the pale yellow glow of the trillium-amber
embedded in the talisman to reassure her that she had not gone blind.

A low chuckle sounded. "Give yourself a moment to adjust. Then
you'll see well enough. My old eyes aren't what they used to be, and
this situation is most comfortable for me. Give me your hand . . ."

Tentatively, Haramis lifted her arm. She felt her hand grasped by
fingers that were damp but not unpleasant, and she was drawn
forward for a dozen steps. There was a salty tang in the air, and a
lingering reverberation from the chime that seemed to call forth other
subdued musical notes from somewhere in the darkness.

"Here we are. Do you feel the chair? Be seated while I fetch our
supper."

Groping about, Haramis managed to slide onto an oddly shaped
wide stool without a back. Its sides and legs seemed to be studded all
over with irregular smooth knobs, and the seat-cushion was warm
and yielding, beyond doubt filled with liquid. It was very comfortable.

Sitting in the dark, waiting, she discovered that her vision was
returning. She was in a large chamber filled with faintly luminescent
furnishings. The table with its two chairs was made of cemented
shells, each one of which was pricked out in a spiral of tiny green dots.
On the table were dishes and goblets, also fashioned from shells, that
glowed dimly rose and topaz. Flecks of azure and crimson formed
flowing patterns on the floor. Here and there about the room were
great urns, also made of the green-dotted shells, in which feathery
plants like giant ferns grew, having a dim orange luster beneath their
leaves.

to take the second from my sister Anigel. I would also like you to tell me whatever you know of the Vanished Ones, and their Sceptre of Power that the three talismans compose. I also hope that you will explain to me the difference between true magic and the high science that activates certain of the marvelous ancient contrivances — and how magic and science intermingle in the conflict between Portolanus and the Three Petals of the Living Trillium."

Iriane sighed and set down her spoon. She sipped some of her own drink, then said: "Some of your questions I cannot answer, Haramis. Others demand lengthy responses, and I must postpone them until later. Let me answer your easiest question first . . . by telling you the story of the Vanished Ones."

Twelve times ten hundreds ago [Iriane said], the World of the Three Moons was home to a large population of human beings. They came here from elsewhere, from another place far beyond the firmament, and used their great knowledge to transform certain aspects of this world, so that it would be more suited to their life-needs.

In the course of time, a faction of selfish power-seekers arose, calling itself the Guild of the Star. They were skilled in science, and also skilled in the magical arts that have their source in the human mind and the inmost nature of the universe. The Star Men and their adherents brought about a devastating war that lasted for over two hundreds. In the course of it, their weapons and evil magic not only killed nearly half the populace, but also changed the very climate of the world, bringing about an Age of Conquering Ice.

As you know, the world-continent even today is sheathed with a vast Sempiternal Icecap. Only at its fringes and in the south is there glacier-free land. But in the time before the Ice Age only the highest mountains had glaciers upon them. The world-continent then had a gentle climate overall, and there were many huge lakes dotted with beautiful islands where the most elaborate cities were built. When the endless snowstorms began, all of these inland cities were perforce abandoned, and only those along the shore or under the sea or in the lower firmament remained inhabited.

The Guild of the Star fought more fiercely than ever when it lost the support of the common people and even the most sanguine members realized that the cause was lost. When it seemed that the Star Men would destroy the world utterly rather than capitulate, the magical device called the Sceptre of Power was created by the Archimagical College to turn the Star Men's own terrible sorcery against them. But there was a tremendous danger involved in utilizing the Sceptre, and in the end those who had made it were afraid to use it.

The headquarters of the Star Men was finally destroyed by one of the world's greatest heroes, the Archimage Varcour, and those villains who remained alive scattered to the four winds, ending the war. But the World of the Three Moons was ruined. No amount of science or benevolent magic exerted by the Archimages could restore the temperate climate of what had once been a beautiful and happy land. The world-continent could no longer support large numbers of human beings, and neither could the ice-choked sea or the more precarious habitations of the inner firmament.

Most of the survivors made preparations to go away to another home far beyond the outer firmament. But a group of thirty brilliant and altruistic souls of the Archimagical College, including the great Varcour, decided to remain and do what they could to repair the terrible damage that humanity had caused. One of their principal good works was the engendering of a new race, more hardy than humanity, that might multiply and repopulate the devastated World of the Three Moons after thousands of years had passed and the ice finally began to melt.

When human beings first came to this world, the most highly developed aborigines they found were the primitive and unrelentingly savage Skritek. These warm-blooded, scaly monsters were minimally self-aware and of low intellect, but they did possess the power to communicate both with and without words. They knew nothing of love, had no art or culture, and lived a predatory existence. In their revolting manner of reproduction, the mother was more often than not devoured by her ravenous young at their birth.

Using both science and magic, the savants of the Archimagical College merged the blood of these unpromising creatures with that of humankind, creating the handsome and intelligent people that you know as the Vispi. At the same time, a companionate race of tele-pathic giant birds called lammergeiers was also created to assist the Vispi in their survival. Colonies of newly engendered Vispi and lam-mergeiers were planted all around the diminished margin of the world-continent before the bulk of the human population went away, becoming the Vanished Ones.

At the last minute before departure, a few thousand ordinary people elected to remain behind also, to assist the Archimages and eke out whatever life they could amidst the Conquering Ice. These formed the nucleus of the human population living on the World of the Three Moons today.

As hundred after hundred passed by, the raging snowstorms came to an end and the climate slowly warmed again, melting the inland glacial cap little by little and freeing dry land for habitation once more. Guided with subtle discretion by the Archimages, the Vispi multiplied — but so did the surviving Skritek. From time to time miscegenation occurred and many other aboriginal races came into being, more or less human in appearance. Humans also occasionally mated with the Vispi, so that traces of aboriginal blood now exist in virtually all of us.

Since human beings are inherently more fertile than the aborigines, our race increased at a more rapid pace. After thousands and thou-sands of years, the most fertile and salubrious lands were entirely occupied by humanity, while the aborigines lived in the marginal areas — the high mountains, the swamps, the deep forest, and the remote islands. The members of the Archimagical College retired from the secret Place of Knowledge built by Varcour to individual retreats, where we continued to foster and guide both humans and aborigines. Using our ancient science, we are able to live to a great age. Often, a dying Archimage is able to train a replacement; but this did not always prove possible, and over the succeeding tens of hun-dreds our numbers slowly diminished, as did the need for our services to humans.

And now, my dear, we Archimages are only three: you, I myself, and Denby. As Archimage of the Land, your work is the most urgent and strenuous. My own is much less so, and Denby has the least of all to do, and so he has grown crotchety and self-indulgent and reclusive, largely ignoring both humanity and Folk and spending his time in the study of arcane celestial trivia — much good may it do him!

Your predecessor, Binah, elected to live in the Peninsula, since the greatest concentration of intelligent aborigines now resides there. The other enclaves of Folk scattered about the world-continent either fended adequately enough for themselves without an Archimagical guardian, or were superintended by me. Most of my own clients live on the myriad scattered islands in the far northwest of the world, where few humans go.

In the immediate past the principal tasks of the Archimages have included shielding aborigines who were in danger of being exterminated by hostile humans, and collecting and disposing of dangerous or inappropriate artifacts of the Vanished Ones that turned up in the ancient ruined cities. It is only in the most recent times that an entirely new problem manifested itself — once again endangering the balance of the World of the Three Moons.

I refer to the reappearance of the Star Men.

Unknown to the Archimagical College, the evil Guild did not die out when its last members fled. Somehow, they lived on and passed their knowledge of the Dark Powers from generation to generation. There were never very many of them, for they are jealous and secretive. Their strongholds tended to be in places where the human strain was least diluted by the blood of the Folk, and numbers of them possessed the robust physique, platinum hair, and silvery-blue eyes of the original criminal elite faction of the Vanished Ones . . .

Ah! I see that strikes a chord in you. Yes, child, the remote and inhospitable land of Tuzamen was one such outpost of the Star Men, and the sorcerer you know as both Orogastus and Portolanus is the first of his kind to attempt to reclaim the ancient heritage of the Guild — the domination of the world.

Yes . . . Orogastus is alive. It was Denby, the Archimage of the Sky, who long ago foresaw his coming; but *he* elected to do nothing beyond calling the dire future event to the attention of Binah and me. She and I worked together for nearly nine hundreds to nurture the human bloodline that culminated in you and your triplet sisters, the

Three Petals of the Living Trillium, hoping that you would have the vigor to counteract this most dangerous of Star Men.

The flower emblem, which is symbolic of the Triune God and also of the physical, mental, and magical nature of the universe, dates back to the Vanished Ones — as does the many-rayed star of their wicked antagonists. The Black Trillium, however, is a living thing — for all that it nearly became extinct — while the Star is as lifeless and consuming as death, even though it is beautiful.

You three sisters, empowered by the magical amulets Binah fashioned for you, were permitted to reclaim the talismans that make up the dread ancient Threefold Sceptre. Once again, it was the ineffable Denby who determined that this magical implement offered the only way to save the world from the Star, even though its use posed great peril. Then, contradicting his own discovery, Denby counseled *against* letting you girls reassemble the three talismans. He judged that the world was better off ruled by the wicked Star Guild rather than possibly destroyed by the Threefold Sceptre of Power.

Binah and I did not agree.

And so you young princesses went on your quests, and were successful in retrieving the three talismans. And at your great moment of testing, the Lords of the Air guided you in the right way to utilize the Sceptre of Power.

Orogastus was taken from you, banished to a place where a certain occult device called the Cynosure of the Star Guild had been placed for safekeeping by an Archimage long forgotten. The star pendant hanging around his neck was the sorcerer's salvation — for without it, he would have been consumed as a feather is consumed in an inferno once the Sceptre turned his own magic upon him. As it was, the protective Cynosure drew him and the pendant to it, saving his life. This was a terrible surprise to me, for I had never suspected that the Star Men had managed to fashion any sort of countermeasure against the Sceptre.

While Orogastus still lay senseless I hastened to the Kimilon through the viaduct and took away the Cynosure. I feared that it might have other unknown functions that might allow the exiled sorcerer to escape. The Cynosure lies on my worktable in the corner at this minute. I have studied it for years, and found no other use for it than the one it first demonstrated.

Orogastus did not understand how or why he had survived. He still does not. During the twelve years of his exile in the Inaccessible Kimilon, he pored over the ancient repositories of forbidden knowledge that had been hidden away there, seeking a way to escape the Land of Fire and Ice and resume his interrupted mission of conquest.

By a continual exertion of magic, I was able to conceal the viaduct from him. But I could not prevent him from learning how to use a certain other machine, a mechanical communicator of the speech without words, to summon rescuers. The decrepit bespeaker device worked only once. But that was sufficient to bring the sorcerer's minions to the land of the Dorok, where the one called Shiki was compelled to help Orogastus escape. The sorcerer took with him from the Kimilon many ancient weapons and other devices that later helped him to subdue Tuzamen. After further study, he also obtained the star-box, another countermeasure of the Star Men that Binah and I never knew existed. Denby may have known of it, but he never said a word to us.

I do not know whether we two Archimages would have dared to resurrect the Sceptre, had we known that its parts might be taken away from the Three Petals and bonded to Orogastus. But what was done is done.

Now the sorcerer has already made one part of the Sceptre of Power his own. He does not yet know how to use it, but he will learn, through happenstance and experimentation and the talisman's own subtle teaching, just as you three sisters have.

Full knowledge of the Threefold Sceptre's use, and the use of the talismans that are its parts, comes only from the assembled Sceptre itself. No one now living knows its entire potential. You three young princesses were not permitted to obtain this dangerous knowledge. Denby and I impelled you to break the Sceptre apart, immediately after Orogastus was banished, so that the peril to the world would be minimized. You girls were very immature then and your wills were susceptible to our coercion. This is no longer true. For better or worse, you now control your own destinies, and the fate of the world is in your hands.

If Orogastus should obtain all three talismans — or perhaps even two of them — you and I would probably be unable to prevent him from discovering most of their secrets. He is a mature sorcerer, hardened by long years of deprivation, and his will is extremely strong. Even the merged magic of all three Archimages would be hard-pressed to break the Star Man's volition, so powerfully attuned has he become to his abominable goal. The Archimage of the Sky is quite afraid of Orogastus. I fear that Denby would not have the courage to stand up to him. It matters little to the Dark Man of the Sky after all, that the world falls out of balance and its human population and Folk become subjected to the malign rule of the Star. His own comfortable circumstances would be little affected . . .

But let us not dwell upon such horrid contingencies. You are here at last — and while I cannot advise you on the working of the entire Sceptre, I can and will help you learn to use your own talisman as best I can. Yours is the key talisman, after all. The Triune willing, you will use it to find a way to defeat Orogastus once and for all. Three tennights should see the task of education accomplished. The lessons will be difficult, for they involve self-discipline even more than the accumulation of knowledge. But I have confidence in you, Haramis-who-will-brook-no-nonsense. You will win through . . .

Now. Let me bring in the special dessert I prepared in your honor — a delicious fish-egg custard!

16

Kadiya and Shiki hid in a thicket that hedged a stream along one margin of the Aliansa village. The stormy sky was beginning to clear and the small creatures of the island forest seemed to be tuning up to resume their interrupted nocturnal songs. Swollen by the rain, the creek brawled over rocks in the darkness, and Kadiya and Shiki had forded it with extreme care. In the village, where scores of tall torches had been set out around the compound, more than three hundred Sea Folk were engaged in a ceremonial dance around the two child-victims pegged out in the mud, singing in their deep voices and playing upon simple instruments.

Prominent in the native orchestra were a great many drums.

The primitive music, the splashing stream, and the animal sounds masked any noise Kadiya and Shiki made as they crept through the last bit of cover and prepared to make their move. He was armed with the stout hand-catapult traditional to the Dorok Folk and a broad blade nearly the length of a short-sword. Kadiya's only weapon was a small belt-knife.

"I will stride out boldly among them when the ceremony of sacrifice begins," she said. "The Aliansa will remember me from our earlier conference and think that I still have the Three-Lobed Burning Eye to defend me. If my bluff works, I will free the children and take them up into my arms and return to you here. You must guard us from any pursuit as we flee . . . If the ruse fails, I will attempt to kill enough of the brutes so that you may take advantage of the confusion and rescue the children yourself while the Aliansa are dealing with me."

"But then you will surely perish!" Shiki said.

Kadiya made an impatient gesture. "If I do, you must take the children away from here and hide with them. My sister Anigel will find you through her magic and eventually come to your aid... Look! There is something going on in the big council house. We will not have to wait much longer."

"Lady, at least take my knife," Shiki pleaded, holding out the blade.

"No. It is too large to conceal in my garments. I must walk out boldly into their midst." Her hand clasped the warm amulet hanging around her neck, a drop of honey-amber in which was embedded the fossil blossom of a small flower. A wry smile played over her lips. "Perhaps this charm will protect me, just as it seemed to bring me and the boy safe to shore."

"Do you think the amulet might fend off your attackers — or perhaps even kill them?" Shiki's face now lost some of its grim hopelessness. The rescue plan of the Lady of the Eyes had seemed to him clumsy and unlikely of success, but he had not dared to voice his doubts to her. However, if this amulet of hers was truly magical...

Kadiya let the amber drop onto her bosom with a sigh. "It certainly will not kill. As for helping me in other ways, its magic was ever capricious. One had to believe in it firmly if it was to work. In truth, I do not know whether I can now do that — now that I must act cold-bloodedly, as an adult, rather than in a panic or as a trusting child. In times past, when I was but a simpleminded girl, this trillium-amber shielded me from the evil sorcerer's Sight, and carried me safe through the air when I jumped from a great height, and guided me through a fearful swampy wilderness. Tonight, it again appeared to carry me through the air, away from the waterspout. But I was beside myself when I asked its help, not commanding it deliberately. And — and I may have only imagined that a miracle took place. Tolo and I could have been flung ashore by a great wave, rather than by magic."

"There was so much of a commotion on the beach that I could not tell the manner of your arriving," Shiki admitted.

"When the boy and I were out in the sea, I thought also that I heard the voice of a woman long dead — she who gave me the amulet and sent me on my life-quest. But this also I might have imagined."

"I know little of magic," Shiki said slowly. "But in most difficult endeavors, one must have confidence in order to succeed. May I dare to suggest that you should muster confidence in this amulet of yours so that it will grant success in our rescue attempt?"

"Your advice is good," Kadiya said. "Whether I can follow it, another matter. I am accustomed to relying on myself — and upon a certain precious object that was lately stolen from me. Without this object — this talisman — I am not the woman I once was."

She related briefly how she had lost her talisman, and how Portolanus had retrieved the Three-Lobed Burning Eye from the depths, and what the loss of one part of the great Sceptre of Power meant to her and her sisters and perhaps to the entire world. Then she concluded: "You must see, Friend Shiki, what a poor substitute this drop of amber is for that which I have lost."

Shiki placed his three-fingered hand gently upon her shoulder. "The amber surely retains its magic. Did it not fly back to its mistress when the wicked sorcerer would have seized it?"

"That is true . . . From the time of my birth, when the Archimage Binah gave it to me, the amulet and I were never separated. It embedded itself in the talisman when the Three-Lobed Burning Eye became my own. And when I lost that talisman, it was as if the heart had been torn from my body!"

"And yet it is the amber, not the talisman, that has been truly yours since your birth. Have you considered, Lady, that your greatest loss might not have been the talisman at all — but the amber?"

Kadiya stared at him, speechless.

Shiki smiled encouragement. "And now you have it back. There is no good reason not to trust in its magic. And in yourself."

"If you could be right . . ." Her mind worked furiously as she stared at the leaping Aliansa out in the torchlit clearing. Their dance was becoming more frenzied and the drumbeats so rapid that they blended into an unending roar, obliterating the singing and the sound of the other instruments.

"Lady Kadiya, it is *good* to question one's self, and not to trust too firmly in one's own ability to recognize truth. That way lies arrogance. What is not good is surrendering to doubt — using it as an excuse for bad actions, or no action at all. This is a kind of pride, and evil. Can you understand? Certain gifts are vouchsafed to each person at birth and we must use them as best we can. If you were born to lead, then do it. If the role of leader is taken away, be accepting. If it is your role to be a conduit for magic, accept that as well — but not proudly, as if you deserved power. Know your limitations, Lady, but dare to exceed them when a greater good than yourself impels you to act. Yes, you may fail. But therein is no disgrace, but rather transcendence."

The drums stopped.

Kadiya embraced Shiki, kissing him on the forehead. "Thank God you were sent." She took a deep breath. "Once my sister Anigel escaped unseen from her captors with the aid of her own amulet of trillium-amber. On another occasion she was able to disable enemy sentries by approaching them invisible. I never could stomach such a stratagem myself, for my style of action has ever been straightforward and bold rather than artful. But now I am going to accept your advice . . . and *open* myself. If I can indeed be a simple conduit for magic, then I beseech the Lords of the Air to use me as they will. My own doubts and impatience are unimportant. The only thing that matters is saving poor little Nikalon and Janeel. Shiki — are you ready?"

"Yes," he said.

"Forget my earlier plan." Her eyes glittered in the firelight. "Only be alert, and when the moment seems right, carry off the captive children."

She vanished.

There were now about fifty armed Aliansa warriors gathered about the two mud-splattered little forms staked out in the middle of the compound. The other natives were massed further back, among the emplanted torches. Nikalon and Janeel had lain motionless, as though unconscious, from the time Kadiya and Shiki had first approached the clearing; but now, with the cessation of the barbaric music, they stirred.

The Crown Prince turned his head toward his sister and spoke to her. She managed a tremulous smile. Then the two children lay utterly still. their eyes fixed on the starry sky. Ten-year-old Janeel wore nothing but a soiled shift, while the Prince was clad only in his loincloth.

From out of the largest hut came the Aliansa leader Har-Chissa, closely followed by another native bearing a large package. The High Chief's inhuman body was magnificently decked in a pearl-studded cloth-of-gold kilt and a stomacher and upstanding collar of gold mesh inset with pearls and precious coral. Ropes of pearls twined about his furry limbs. Every skin-scale of his back, chest, upper arms, and thighs was adorned with a design done in gold or crimson paint. His protuberant yellow eyes were painted round with scarlet, and strapped to his forehead was a gem-encrusted frontlet bearing a great curved horn of pearl set in a golden socket.

Har-Chissa intoned a questioning phrase in the tongue of the Aliansa. The mob of warriors and other Sea Folk chanted an enthusiastic reply. Then the drums began to beat again in a slow, intricate rhythm — deep booming notes and thunderous rolls from the largest drums, many-pitched tunking, harsh taps, and ominous rattling tattoos from the drums of medium size, and strident insectlike sounds from the smallest drums.

Har-Chissa stalked into the middle of the open space. He bent over Princess Janeel, and with a single sweep of one great hand, ripped the flimsy shift from her body. She could not help uttering a shocked cry, but then she was silent, as was Crown Prince Nikalon beside her, who continued to gaze steadily at the sky while his eyes filled with tears.

As the drumming accelerated slightly and intensified in volume, Har-Chissa beckoned to the attendant who had stood some distance back. She was an elderly female, dressed almost as grandly as the Chief, and she knelt now before him and unrolled the package she had carried.

It was full of knives.

The watching throng gave an encouraging shout.

Har-Chissa gestured for them to be still. Then, with the drumming lending drama to his deliberation, he studied the neat rows of shining blades, which were arranged according to size. Finally he drew out a very small pearl-handled scalpel that glittered in the torchlight. Moving with the complex tempo of the drums, he began to brandish the knife above the little Princess, miming the actions that would strip the skin from her living body. With each ritual gesture, the Sea Folk howled approval.

Then the drumming stopped.

Har-Chissa lifted one of Janeel's slender arms and bent down with the scalpel poised.

Shiki lifted his slingshot and prepared to shoot one of the leaden balls that served the Dorok as missiles. Unfortunately, the scaly head of the Aliansa leader with its horned frontlet was a distant, uncertain target.

But wait —

Abruptly, Har-Chissa's long neck arched and his head flew back. His muzzle gaped, his black tongue protruded from between his tusks, and he screamed in surprise. The skinning knife flew from his hand and arced oddly through the air, reflecting the torches, so that it seemed like a small flame itself. The scalpel slowed, then hovered in an uncanny fashion immediately behind the Chief. Frantically, Har-Chissa sought to tear the great pearl-horned headpiece from his brow. To the stunned spectators, the ceremonial frontlet seemed to have come to malignant life, forcing the leader's head back farther, farther, until his unscaled throat with its tawny fur was fully exposed. The fiery little scalpel flashed like a meteor as it came swiftly forward.

Across the throat of the Aliansa High Chief a crimson line appeared. It widened and began to gush darkly, and Har-Chissa's despairing scream bubbled and dwindled to a horrible hissing moan. He began to topple. Hot blood flooded over Princess Janeel's body, covering her nakedness. She closed her eyes but made no sound.

Har-Chissa had fallen in the midst of a spreading pool of red. Bloody footprints sprang into being about the two supine children. At the same time Shiki slithered through the undergrowth to get even closer, confident that none of the shouting, horrified Sea Folk would be watching the trees.

The mob remained frozen with confusion while the floating pearl-handled blade slashed at the bonds holding the little Princess. But the female attendant with the pack of knives proved to be more quick-witted than the others. She plucked forth a terrible weapon like a serrated cleaver and lunged purposefully toward Prince Nikalon.

Shiki took aim with his catapult, using as his target one of the monster's glaring yellow eyes. The ball of lead went home and she fell, stone dead with a missile in her brain. An instant later both children were cut free.

Then the bloody footprints raced away from the captives, through the ring of armed warriors, who were still mute with shock, to the edge of the crowd where the torches flamed. Two of the tall brands were hauled out of the muddy ground and began to whirl and thrust at the warriors, driving them back from the children. The Aliansa fell about screaming, and many who delayed their retreat were burnt. Some of the warriors slashed impotently with their swords at the invisible demon or flung spears every which way. But they struck nothing save each other. Finally the two whirling torches were flung full at the bolder Aliansa. The demon pulled more of the flaming staves from the ground and tossed them one by one among the armed aborigines. From the edge of the clearing, Shiki sent ball after leaden ball hurtling into the throng with a force that shattered bone.

Most of the unarmed Aliansa and many of the warriors now turned and began to flee through the lines of huts into the dark forest beyond. Those who stayed and attempted to fight fell prey to Shiki's catapult, or were belabored by the demon-controlled torches and their fur and garments set afire. Shrieking in pain and bewildered fury, they stumbled about and slashed at thin air like creatures gone mad. None noticed when a small figure darted from the woods, swept up the Prince and Princess in strong arms, and made away with them.

Finally all of the torches had been uprooted and flung, and their flames sputtered out. The only light now came fitfully from the open doorways of the deserted huts and from the wanly radiant Three Moons riding high in the sky. No more bloody footprints appeared. The groans of the wounded Sea Folk made a melancholy contrast to the renewed chorus of forest creatures.

When it became evident that the invisible demon was gone, taking the young human prisoners with it, the surviving Aliansa warriors crawled and staggered into the council house to exclaim over the dire happening and bewail the murder of their High Chief. Those whose minds were not hopelessly befuddled sent forth messages via the speech without words, alerting the other Aliansa villages of Council Isle and the adjacent islands to the presence of the hated foreigners and their invisible demon. It was some comfort to know that fellow-warriors were setting out at once, by both land and sea, to attack the two ships belonging to the invaders.

But then another awful deed was discovered by those villagers returning fearfully from the forest, and this was a sacrilege so appalling that it renewed the courage of the defeated Sea Folk and inspired them to take up arms again. Every warrior who could move charged off down the trail to the shore, their earlier terrors forgotten, vowing that no human should escape the Windlorn Isles alive.

For every one of the Aliansa nation's precious ceremonial drums was found to have its skin head slashed by the humans' invisible demon. They would never sound again.

Q ueen Anigel, Jagun the Nyssomu, and the thirteen Wyvilo warriors who had remained
aboard *Lyath* set off for the island shore in two
small boats just as soon as the Queen concluded her brief farspoken
dialogue with the sorcerer Portolanus. The plight of Niki and Jan
demanded immediate action, and Anigel was convinced that Kadiya
would need help to rescue the children. As the storm ended, the
Queen's well-armed party landed on the shore of the small cove
adjacent to Council Bay and began to hurry down a trail toward Har-
Chissa's village.

"It is only two leagues away," Jagun said. "Take my hand, Great
Queen, and I will lead you while you continue to survey the captive
children through your talisman Sight."

Anigel stumbled along, growing increasingly agitated as she
watched the resumption of the deadly Aliansa drum ceremony. "They
have relit the torches and started dancing again! . . . We cannot possibly get there in time! . . . Oh, if only my sister could *do* something!"

When Har-Chissa seemed about to flay poor Janeel, and Kadiya
finally became invisible and slew him, the Queen was so shattered by
emotion that she stopped short on the trail, her eyes staring at nothing, all but paralyzed and unable to utter a sound.

Jagun and the Wyvilo gathered about her motionless form. They
were stricken with dread themselves, for up until that last awful
moment Anigel had given them a running commentary upon events
taking place in the village. Now none of them dared speak, for they
feared that little Princess Janeel had been killed — or that a fate even

worse had befallen her. Jagun, still holding Anigel's icy hand, knelt beside her with head bowed. The tall Wyvilo raised their arms in supplication toward the Three Moons, praying silently in the manner of the Forest Folk.

At length Queen Anigel shuddered, and gave a great sighing exhalation. "Friends," she whispered. "Kadiya has saved the children."

Jagun and the Wyvilo all cried out their relief. Anigel bade them gather closely about her so that she might share the amazing scene with them through her coronet's magic. They beheld Har-Chissa lying dead, and the terrorized Aliansa belabored by a torch-wielding invisible presence. They watched as an unknown little man of the Folk took up the gore-smeared children and carried them safely into the shadows.

"Thanks be to the Lords of the Air and my Lady Farseer!" Jagun exclaimed. "But who was that stranger assisting her?"

"Kadiya called him Shiki," Anigel replied. "But there is no more time for us to use the Sight. We must hurry and meet Kadi and the others before the natives recover."

They plunged through the dark forest with creatures hooting and whistling and calling on every hand. Now and again there was a loud crashing in the brush; but the night-vision of the Wyvilo determined that only animals were abroad in this part of the island, not hostile natives. Then Anigel used her talisman to descry that Kadiya and Shiki and the children were fleeing along a side-trail nearly parallel to the one they themselves traveled. The Wyvilo took out their axes and began to hew a direct route to it through the jungle undergrowth. Jagun uttered a penetrating warbling cry that he said his mistress would recognize, and when the rescuers finally broke through to the side-trail the others were waiting.

The Queen clasped Nikalon and Janeel to her bosom, weeping for joy. Both of the children seemed benumbed, having no memory of what had happened. Janeel was wearing Shiki's embroidered blouse, and the Crown Prince had on the Dorok's zuch-wool undershirt, leaving the little aborigine clad only in his heavy leather trews and boots. Wiping the tears from her eyes, Anigel also embraced and kissed her sister, saying:

"The blessings of the Triune be upon you, dear Kadi — and upon your brave friend Shiki as well — for saving my little ones. But we cannot linger here. Antar is swimming ashore in Council Bay with Lummomu and the two other Wyvilo, and Tolo is also hiding in the trees down there. We must go and collect them. Part of our group will have to carry Niki and Jan back to the *Lyath* while the others go on to Council Bay."

"Let Jagun and Shiki and two of the Wyvilo warriors take the children to the ship," said Kadiya. "I will accompany you in the rescue of Antar and Tolo." She lifted the trillium-amber on its vine-string and smiled, her bloodstained face alight with grim triumph. "My talisman may be lost to the sorcerer, but I still have my amulet's magic — and it is formidable enough to have dealt justice to the villainous Aliansa. Sister, the two of us together will yet be a match for Portolanus!"

"May it be so," Anigel responded in a low voice, but her eyes were somber and unconvinced. She spoke soothingly to Niki and Jan and kissed them good-bye, and in moments the children were on their way to the *Lyath* with their escort. Then the Queen touched her coronet, commanding it to show her the scene at Council Bay.

When she had Sight of it, she cried out in fresh consternation: "The sorcerer is sending boats after Antar and Tolo!"

Kadiya cried to the Wyvilo: "Quickly, my friends — lead us to the shore of Council Bay as fast as you can!"

They all set off at a run, the noise made by their pounding feet drowning out the faint sounds of inhuman shouting now coming from Har-Chissa's village.

"There they are!" exclaimed the Black Voice.

He stood in the bow of the leading boat, with four other craft following close astern. From his eyes shone twin white beams, and he spoke with the tongue of Portolanus, who had spied out the position of the fugitives with his talisman and guided the searchers to them. Rowing at triple time, the pirates had managed to overtake King Antar and his Wyvilo companions when they were less than fifty ells from shore.

Suddenly the four heads moving through the quiet waters disappeared.

"They are diving, Lord!" one of the Raktumians warned.

"The King is too weak to stay submerged for long . . . Quickly, you and you!" The Voice indicated two of the boats. "Move toward the shore with all speed to cut off any attempt of theirs to escape by land. The rest of you — ready the small lines with the grapples, and keep a sharp watch!"

A number of pirates in the remaining three boats took up coiled cords, at the end of which were small but fiendishly sharp gang-hooks with three points. For some minutes the only sound came from the creaking oars of the two boats that had been ordered toward the land. The sea was dead calm, reflecting the tiny Moons. A quarter of a league away to the north, the sixth pirate boat commanded by the Purple Voice neared the shore, its occupants prepared to begin searching for Prince Tolivar.

Suddenly there was a splash, and a sound of pained gasping.

"The King! There!" The eye-beams of the Black Voice picked out Antar's sodden fair hair and half-submerged face not six ells away. One of the pirates in the Voice's boat whirled his grapple and let it fly. The King screamed as the hooks narrowly missed his head and bit into his naked shoulder. Three more grapples struck his body, the barbs sinking into flesh. Antar's anguished writhing only served to entangle him in the cords and bring him to the point of drowning. Soon enough he ceased his struggles and floated unmoving with his head under water. The Black Voice gave urgent commands that the King should be drawn quickly into the boat, lest he perish.

But no sooner was Antar aboard than the boat carrying him and the Black Voice began to rock violently. The pirates bellowed imprecations and one screamed: "Oddlings in the water! They will sink us!"

Lummomu-Ko, leader of the Wyvilo, rose dripping over the transom of the Voice's boat with his fierce eyes alight and his jaws gaping. He took hold of a shrieking pirate in each hand and pulled the men overboard, rending them with his teeth as they fell into the water. The other two Wyvilo, Huri-Kamo and Mok-La, continued their attempt to capsize the leading craft while the pirates aboard beat at them with oars.

"Swords, you imbeciles!" cried the Black Voice. "Use your swords!" He crouched over the unconscious King, shielding him from the would-be rescuers with his own body.

Again Lummomu shot up with a tremendous splash, and dragged two more pirates headlong into the black sea. Mok-La seized another. A fourth man lost his balance in the wallowing craft and fell in while trying to strike a blow with his sword. The Voice, Antar, and the two Raktumians left in the boat now tumbled helplessly about in a welter of flailing limbs and flying weaponry, and the three Wyvilo uttered howls of triumph.

But the two accompanying boats now drew near, as did the other pair that had headed ashore but turned back when the commotion began. The Raktumians in them fell to with grim efficiency, using both spears and longswords on the Wyvilo in the water. There was a howl of agony as a blade hewed off one of Huri-Kamo's clawed hands, and he sank beneath the sea. Lummomu-Ko and Mok-La were stabbed and slashed mercilessly until they, too, disappeared. Six men from the Voice's boat had been pulled overboard to their doom, and of the two remaining, one groaned from a wound inflicted by his own mates.

"Tow us back to the flagship," croaked the Black Voice. "Make haste!"

The single uninjured pirate in the Voice's boat tossed a line to the nearest craft, then settled back gingerly. "Do y'think the scaly devils are drownded, Lord?"

The sorcerer's minion was silent, the beams from his eyes shone out over the water as his head swiveled to and fro. "They are gone, at any rate." And to the men in the other boats: "Row faster! I must get the King to the flagship in order to tend to his injuries. If he should die, all your lives will be forfeit."

In the other boats, the men were murmuring among themselves as they bent to the oars, and one addressed the Voice anxiously. "Lord, Yokil here thinks he sees lights out to sea. Just beyond that southern promontory."

"Yokil has a keen eye," the Voice said in a level tone. "It is the Aliansa, the Sea Oddlings from nearby islands, on their way to attack us. They will be upon us in less than half an hour. Now save your breath, damn you, and *row*."

With that, Portolanus withdrew from his Black acolyte, whose bright eyes abruptly went dull, and turned his attention to the recapture of Prince Tolivar.

"My talisman shows that the child is hiding in this grove of trees," said the Purple Voice to the eight pirates following him across the sand. "Spread out and listen carefully for any movement."

The Raktumians uttered surprised obscenities as two bright stars blazed suddenly beneath the acolyte's hood, piercing the darkness of the undergrowth. He began to speak with the unmistakable accents of the sorcerer himself.

"There is no reason for you men to be alarmed. It is I, Portolanus, acting through my Purple Voice. Keep your throw-nets handy as we go into the trees. On no account is the little Prince to be harmed — "

But before the Voice could finish, a faint sound of chanting swelled on the warm night breeze, and myriad pinpoints of dancing yellow light appeared suddenly down on the beach to the south. The Aliansa were swarming from the woods, having come from the inland settlements.

"Sea Oddlings!" cried one of the pirates, pointing. "Coming right at us."

"And look there!" Another man pointed out to sea. "More of the ugly bastards! Lord Purple, we gotta get back to the flagship! It's no time to be huntin' royal brats. The Admiral will be streakin' for the high seas before those savages turn the trireme's hull into a sieve!"

The rest of the Raktumians muttered agreement.

"There is yet time to find the child," the Purple Voice of Portolanus insisted. "I am going to conjure up another storm to delay the war-canoes of the lowborn wretches."

"Plague take the canoes," a ruffian growled. "What about that bunch comin' up the shore? They can't be half a league distant! I'm for gettin' outta here!"

The other men shouted their assent, and before the Purple Voice could stop them they all turned tail and went rushing back toward the boat. The furious acolyte followed, trying in vain to rally them.

Suddenly a shrill cry came from back among the trees. The Raktumians kept running but the Purple Voice halted and whirled about. The bright beacons of his eyes illuminated a small figure that had emerged from the tangled vegetation and now dashed toward him across the moonlit sand, wailing piteously.

"They're coming from the village, too! I hear them! Don't let the Sea Oddlings get me! Take me with you!"

"By the Bones of Bondanus — it's the Prince!" the Purple Voice exclaimed. "Hurry, then, lad!"

"Tolo — no!" came a faraway shout. "Don't!"

The Prince slowed and looked back over his shoulder toward the dark forest.

"Quick, or I must leave you behind," warned the Voice.

Tolivar put on a burst of speed and flung himself into the acolyte's waiting arms. He clung to the man's neck as he sprinted toward the waiting boat.

"Hold on tight, boy!"

"You talk like the wizard," Tolo said.

"I *am* the wizard," Purple gasped. "For now." He clambered over the gunwale, the child nearly throttling him. The boat immediately shoved off.

"You mean, you're hiding inside this man's body?" The Prince was fascinated.

"In a manner of speaking . . . but I must leave him now to see to other business."

"Did you catch my Royal Father again?" Tolivar asked.

"Yes. And this time neither one of you will escape until your ransom is paid. But do not be afraid, Tolo. I have a feeling that you and I will become good friends."

"Wizard? . . . Do I have to go home if I don't want to?" the Prince asked softly.

But the Voice's starry eyes were dimming, and as their radiance winked out the acolyte sighed gustily. "Sit there in the bow, Prince, and stay out of the way of the oarsmen." His voice now had a completely different timbre.

"You're not the wizard anymore, are you?"

"Be silent," said the Purple Voice coldly. "You will meet my Master soon enough."

The pirates were rowing fit to burst their hearts, and the boat seemed to fly over the glassy water. The native force downshore was fast approaching, and there were now so many torch-bearing canoes out on the water around the southern promontory that their number could not be counted. Above the noise of the chanting natives, a human voice was calling:

"Tolo! Tolo!"

Prince Tolivar stood up in the boat, straining to look back inland. The Purple Voice took hold of him with an oath.

"It sounds like my mother," the boy said calmly. "Look — that must be her coming out of the forest. She can see me with her magic talisman."

"Tolo!" came the despairing cry.

The boy waved. He said to the Purple Voice: "She can hear me, too . . . Good-bye, Mother!"

Then he sat down again, and watched the sails being raised on the great Raktumian trireme. Fresh-gathering stormclouds smothered the light of the Three Moons.

"Tolo! My poor son, what have you done? . . . Oh, dear God, no! Now Portolanus has recaptured both of them! Talisman! I command you to bring my husband and my son back to me! Smite their abductors! Kill them all, I say! Do it, talisman! Do it . . ."

Anigel's brokenhearted screams brought no response whatsoever from her talisman. She flew into a demented rage, and would have run all the way to the water's edge if Kadiya had not restrained her. The sisters and their cohort of Wyvilo warriors remained at the edge of the grove of lown-trees, watching helplessly as the pirate boats raced back to the trireme. The wind was rising, rattling the long, stiff leaves, and the torch-bearing Aliansa mob was now so near that the individual warriors could be distinguished, waving their weapons. Plainly, the human women and the Wyvilo had already been spotted.

Kadiya tried to restore her distraught sister. "Ani, that way will not work. Calm yourself. Think of some — some *positive* command for your talisman."

Her beauty disfigured by grief, the Queen struggled half-crazed in Kadiya's grip. "Positive command?" she shrieked. "You talk like an idiot! How can I think of anything, save that my darlings are again in the hands of that fiend? He will torture them to death! And this useless talisman of mine can do nothing to save them. Nothing — "

Kadiya slapped her face.

Anigel's mouth made an O of affronted dignity and pain. And then her heartstricken expression changed to one of sudden determination. "Nay, I am the fool! Thank you for that blow, Kadi. It has restored my poor scattered wits. Of course the talisman can save them!"

And the Queen lifted her face skyward and shouted: "Portolanus! Hear me!"

I hear you, Queen Anigel.

"My talisman is yours!" She tore the Three-Headed Monster coronet from her hair and held it high. "Only give me Antar and Tolo, and I will do with it whatever you say."

"Ani — no!" Kadiya shouted, and again took hold of her.

But Anigel's tear-reddened eyes now shone with fevered resolve. "Beware, Sister! Remember that if you touch this talisman without my permission, you will die as surely as the basest Raktumian pirate would! . . . Are you listening to me, Portolanus? I will give you the talisman now!"

Alas, Queen. I cannot accept your ransom.

Anigel faltered. "You — you cannot accept it?"

No.

"But why not?"

The clairaudient speech was tinged with irony. *Now is not a propitious time. No, indeed. If you value your own life and those of your companions, you will flee back to your own ship before you provide the Aliansa crafters with materials for a fine new set of ritual drums. There are more natives coming from the village, as well as the mob on the shore.*

"We can make the exchange at sea," Anigel pleaded. "Anywhere, anytime. Portolanus, give me my husband and my child!"

No. King Antar and Prince Tolivar must now remain my guests for a certain span of time before we can reopen negotiations for their release. I am taking them to the Raktumian capital, Frangine. Fear not for their welfare. They will be well treated if you forbear from rash action.

"No! No! Take the talisman now, I beg of you!"

In time I will bespeak you concerning their ransom. I will not communicate with you again until then. Farewell, Queen.

Dazed, Anigel whispered to her sister: "You heard?"

"Yes." Kadiya's voice was glacial. "I heard you attempt to make a craven bargain! Ani, you are a hopeless weakling and a silly fool. Thank God the sorcerer did not accept your offer! With two talismans in his hands, who can tell what evil he would wreak upon the world?"

"Lady of the Eyes, we must flee this place," one of the Wyvilo said urgently. "Come away! There is no time left. Even now the Aliansa warriors may already have reached the *Lyath* ahead of us and destroyed it."

Kadiya turned her back on her sister. "You are right, Wummika. Let us be off." And she led the Wyvilo into the trees at a run.

After hesitating only a moment, Anigel followed, all feeling gone dead within her and the coronet cold and forgotten in her hand.

It was only much later that she discovered that the Flower within the amber inset at the front of the talisman had turned from black to blood red.

18

The work was desperately hard. And the more that Haramis learned — the more she realized how incompetent an Archimage she had actually been — the more she despaired at ever being able to master herself and her talisman.

She now knew the dispassionate, utterly objective frame of mind necessary to command the highest magic; but knowing it and *living* it were very different things. The mental exercises that Iriane drilled her in, that were intended to strengthen and lend discipline to her immature thought processes, were exhausting and boring. Even worse, they seemed beside the point. She could not understand why she must spend endless hours doing meditational gymnastics rather than actually practicing magic with the talisman itself. The Blue Lady's stern insistence that mental schooling must precede the actual working of magic at first vexed Haramis, then drove her to the brink of despondency, then finally vouchsafed a glimmer of hope that she might actually be *getting* it!

After studying for fifteen days, she had laid the groundwork for the commanding of high magic. Like a beginning flute-player who has finally learned to read music and create pure-toned notes but has not yet been able to play a flawless tune, she knew the form of the mental impulses that would call forth magic, yet lacked the expertise to be certain that her technique would produce the desired result. Iriane strictly forbade her to attempt high magic yet, warning her that she risked injury or even death if the new knowledge were applied wrongly.

It sometimes seemed to Haramis that she would never be able to compel her flighty brain to think invariably in the precise and harmonious manner that Iriane insisted upon. Her attempts at deep concentration and free-floating objectivity were always being shattered by stray niggling worries or sudden brainstorms of rebellion or downheartedness. Haramis was also greatly concerned about her two sisters, since the Blue Lady forbade her to use her Sight during the first half of her instruction period. But the most maddening episodes of distraction involved insidious memories of Orogastus. Now that she knew for a fact that he was alive, recollections of his face and voice intruded upon her persistently, and she dreamed almost entirely of him during the brief hours Iriane allowed her to sleep.

At one point, sunk in a morass of discouragement, Haramis begged the Archimage of the Sea to determine whether the sorcerer himself was somehow responsible for her torment and incompetence. The Blue Lady coldly declared that no uninvited intelligence could possibly penetrate her sanctuary. The reassurance served only to depress Haramis more than ever. If Orogastus was not to blame for her distraction, then the fault was entirely her own.

Haramis spent nearly every waking hour laboring over the mental exercises. At first, she worked under Iriane's merciless tutelage. Then more and more she was isolated in a "meditation chamber" with featureless black walls and floor, her stinging eyes fixed upon the glowing amber embedded within the Three-Winged Circle and her beleaguered mind striving not to give in to fatigue or distraction but only to be at one with the talisman.

I must master it, she told herself again and again. Only one Petal of the Trillium can be the keystone of restored balance, the initiator of world-healing. I am that one!

I initiate. Kadiya gives impetus and endurance. And Anigel provides the human insight and unselfish love necessary for the mission's fulfillment . . .

The ancient chant of the Uisgu Folk of the Golden Mire affirmed the roles of the three talismans and their appointed wielders:

One, two, three: three in one.
One the Crown of the Misbegotten, wisdom-gift, thought-magnifier.

Two the Sword of the Eyes, dealing justice and mercy.
Three the Wand of the Wings, key and unifier.
Three, two, one: one in three.
Come, Trillium. Come, Almighty.

I *can* put it all right again! Haramis thought. If only I can truly use this talisman of mine that is the key and unifier of the others. Lords of the Air, help me! Help me! . . .

"They will," Iriane's voice said. "Never lose confidence that they will."

The featureless dark of the meditation chamber became richly blue, and the ample figure of the Archimage of the Sea materialized. She was smiling, and she carried a covered basket woven of flexible sea-pen stalks on one arm and the creature named Grigri on the other.

"It is time for a respite, child. You have dwelt in my world over-long, and a brief change will refresh you. Follow my little friend, here, and he will lead you to the top of my dwelling. Rest there in the open air, under the sunny sky. Eat and drink of the things packed in this basket. Use your talisman to descry your sisters and your captive brother-in-law, and reassure them of your loving concern. Using such low magic, you can come to no harm. Take Sight even of *him*, if you feel you must . . . and then return to me. I know you are dejected, but I somehow sense that you are very close now to opening the ultimate mental door that has thus far defied you. We will lay siege to it together from now on, you and I. And we will prevail."

Painfully, Haramis arose from the kneeling posture prescribed for her mental exercise. She took the basket without a word. The seg-mented many-legged Grigri, who resembled a worram except for his scanty white pelt and red eyes, uttered a brief hiss and wriggled off, looking back once to be sure that she followed.

They went out of the Blue Lady's apartment into the transparent part of the artificial iceberg, where curious fish and other creatures once again came swimming to peer at her through the glassy, irregular walls. A corridor with shallow steps spiraled upward, upward, while the light grew gradually brighter. Haramis realized finally that true sunshine was illuminating the magical aquarium, not some subtle enchantment, and her spirits rose. She found herself almost running after Grigri, who also seemed energized by the daylight. As they emerged into the brilliant open air the animal gave a purring trill and reared up on his hindmost set of legs, exposing his bare underbelly and closing his eyes in ecstasy.

"Poor Grigri! So you miss the sun, too."

The creature seemed to sigh in contentment. As Haramis watched, his body darkened, the fur becoming richly green and the twelve legs turning from ghostly white to black. When he opened his eyes, they were no longer red but deep blue, like those of the common worrams of the Misty Mire.

"So life in this enchanted iceberg is unnatural for you, too," Haramis mused, stroking Grigri's back. "I wonder why your mistress does not take pity on you and set you free?"

The creature turned on her and hissed indignantly. He slithered out from under her caress and pattered off in a comical huff, resuming his sunning some distance away.

"I beg your pardon, Grigri. I should have known that your love for the Archimage is stronger than the demands of nature."

The animal ignored her; but he did begin to purr again.

The view from the summit of the gigantic artificial iceberg was one of exquisite beauty. The sea was purest cobalt blue, dotted with genuine bergs and intricate mosaics of floating ice. The far horizon, punctuated by tall islands with ice-clad summits, met a cloudless sky. The mainland a few leagues away had a gently rolling, dun-colored surface with no trees; but much of it fell off precipitously at the water's edge in dramatic cliffs, and the exposed strata revealed gorgeous layers of pink and orange and even wine-purple rock, with equally gaudy sea-stacks lying offshore. White birds reeled and dived in all directions. If there was a disturbance in the balance of the world, it did not extend to these tranquil northern waters.

Haramis sat down on the dry, irregular surface. Its transparency was somewhat unnerving, as were the occasional fish that swam obliviously beneath her. She opened the basket — and was touched to find that the Archimage had filled it with foods familiar to her from her childhood in Ruwenda, rather than the peculiar marine delicacies that Haramis had bravely eaten for politeness' sake since the beginning of her visit. Smiling, she took up a rosy ladu-fruit and bit into its crisp skin.

But, what am I thinking of? . . .

Ashamed, she put the fruit back in the basket, swallowed the morsel, and put her hand to the talisman hanging about her neck.

"Anigel! Sister, respond to me!"

The vision came — and Haramis exclaimed in astonishment.

This was no mere depiction within the talisman's silvery circle, nor even a Sight that blinded her to events around her, while her mind's eye took in a faraway scene. Instead, she *stood* beside Anigel on the canopied fantail of the Laboruwendian flagship as it raced along with all sails set, on an easterly course a few leagues from land. She smelled salt air, felt the wind of passage and the planks of the deck beneath her feet. Lady Ellinis and the Lords Penapat, Owanon, and Lampiar were seated with the Queen at a table spread with maps and documents. And on the carpeted deck nearby, playing at a hop-square board, were Prince Nikalon and Princess Janeel.

"Hara!" Anigel cried, leaping to her feet with a face gone white. "You're here?"

The others were similarly overcome with surprise at the apparition, and Haramis made swift to tell them that her appearance was only a Sending. "I did not even do it consciously," she said, with a small laugh of embarrassment. "It seems that the lessons I am learning at the feet of the Archimage of the Sea are more effective than I heretofore supposed."

Still exclaiming, the Queen and her officials bade Haramis to be seated. Young Princess Janeel crept up and made as if to touch her gown, but then cried out in disappointment when her hand encountered no substance.

"Aunt Hara, you are not truly here at all!" the girl said. "Is it your ghost that we see?"

"Something like unto it, sweeting," Haramis said. "And I am sorry for it. But let me kiss you and Niki and hug you — and your mother as well. Even if you cannot feel me, I can touch you! My dear ones, I am so relieved that you are safe."

And relieved to see the talisman called the Three-Headed Monster resting safe on the table, half-covered by the Queen's papers.

"We are not all safe," the Queen said, her eyes looking away and her lips tightening after she had accepted Haramis's spectral embrace. She took a deep breath and addressed the courtiers. "I must speak to my sister alone. Would you and the children withdraw, and return when I summon you?"

The four arose, bowed, and retired, Lady Ellinis shepherding the Crown Prince and the Princess.

When they two were alone, Anigel seated herself again at the table with the illusionary form of her sister. The Queen's face was reproachful.

"I tried so many times to bespeak you of the events that had transpired, Hara — tried to seek your advice and comfort — but you never responded to me!"

"It was not possible for me to communicate with you. I will explain it all. But first, tell me everything that has happened since Orogastus took Kadi's talisman."

"Orogastus!" Anigel was wide-eyed with dismay. "Then he *did* disguise himself as the mountebank Portolanus?"

"Yes. For what purpose, I do not know. He was not killed by the Sceptre twelve years ago, but transported instead to a remote place of exile deep within the Sempiternal Icecap. He escaped and became Master of Tuzamen. I am relieved beyond measure that you did not have to give up your talisman to him in ransom — "

"I would have. I offered it to him! But he refused to take it. Antar and little Tolo are still his prisoners in the great flagship of the Queen Regent of Raktum. By now they must be nearing the Raktumian capital of Frangine, propelled by winds of sorcery."

"He would not *accept* the talisman as ransom? But why?"

"I do not know." The Queen's voice was dull, and she would not meet her sister's eyes. "He said the time was not propitious, and that he would communicate with me later. When he does, I will give him the coronet freely — and nothing you or Kadi can say will dissuade me."

The Archimage bit back the horrified protest that rose to her lips. If

Antar and the boy were still prisoners, any pleading on behalf of a greater good would have to wait until Anigel truly understood the situation.

"Tell me," Haramis said quietly, "exactly what befell."

Anigel did, describing how Kadiya had rescued the Crown Prince and Janeel, and how Antar was recaptured, and how Tolo had gone willingly with the sorcerer's minion. The Queen, Kadiya, and their friends had scarcely made it back to the little ship *Lyath* before canoes full of enraged Aliansa came racing after them. Only another great storm, which the sorcerer undoubtedly called up to aid his own escape, saved them. The Wyvilo warrior Huri-Kamo had been killed in the attempt to rescue King Antar; but Speaker Lummomu-Ko and his companion Mok-La managed to swim back to the *Lyath*, even though they were wounded.

"We met with our own flotilla once the storm blew itself out," Anigel said. "The doughty captain of the little Okamisi ship was tendered a handsome bonus for having helped us and sent on his way. Our four Laboruwendian ships then sailed north in pursuit of the five enemy vessels. We caught up with the Tuzameni galley of Portolanus, which was much slower than the pirate ships. We engaged it in battle and sank it with all hands aboard. The sorcerer was unfortunately still on the Raktumian flagship, so he is quite safe. He made no attempt to aid his doomed compatriots. As we chased him northward the distance between the Raktumian ships and ours steadily increased. They reprovisioned in Zinora and were gone two days before we arrived.

"King Yondrimel refused my request to send fast cutters in pursuit of the pirates. His excuse was original: that his entire fleet was on a special mission to Galanar, escorting a royal envoy who was requesting the hand of one of Queen Jiri's daughters on Yondrimel's behalf. But when we arrived in Mutavari a sixnight later, we learned that it was far more likely that the Zinoran fleet was out on war games, preparing for an invasion of Var. The capital of Var was in an uproar, and poor King Fiomadek and Queen Ila were petrified at the dire rumors, which had Zinora allying with the Raktumian pirates.

"Of course, you know that our Peninsular Concord requires us to come to Var's aid. Kadiya, Jagun, and the contingent of Wyvilo set off northward at once up the Great Mutar River to alert the garrisons in Ruwenda. With luck, our knights and men-at-arms will arrive in time to defend Mutavari and foil the invasion. But Lord Marshal Owanon and my other military leaders fear that sending the Ruwendian forces south will leave Labornok wide open to a massed assault from the north. The invasion of Var may actually be only a feint, disguising the real intent of Queen Regent Ganondri and Portolanus — an attack upon *us*. Raktum has so many ships that it can easily spare a small fleet for the assault on Var and have ample numbers left to attack Triola and Lakana and our other northern ports, and even Derorguila itself. Raktum's scheme may well succeed, especially if Lord Osorkon has turned traitor — which seems probable, given his sister's involvement in the abduction of the children. And if Labornok falls, so will Ruwenda.

"You must understand, Hara, that without Antar, the union of the Two Thrones will surely falter. I myself cannot hope to rally the loyalist nobles of Labornok against the combined might of Osorkon's faction, Raktum, and Tuzamen. This is one more reason why I am determined to give up my talisman, if I can ensure the return of my husband and the defense of our nation by doing so."

Haramis had listened to this recital with increasing misgiving. Now, with Anigel having fallen silent, she asked: "What does Kadiya intend to do? Lead the Ruwendian troops in the defense of Var?"

"Nay. She . . . she and I had a fearful quarrel over the matter of the ransom. I think she would have killed me, had she dared, to prevent my handing the coronet over to the sorcerer. She said she would rally the Ruwendians and send them south. But then she plans to travel to the Place of Knowledge and ask of its sindona Teacher a way to stop me from exchanging my talisman for Antar. She will not succeed. Not while I live."

The vivid blue eyes of the Queen brimmed with tears, but her jaw was set and hard. Haramis knew that now was not the time to remonstrate with her sister. Instead, with great gentleness, she told Anigel of her own adventures in the Kimilon and at the strange home of the Archimage of the Sea. She expressed her joy that Shiki had helped in the rescue of Niki and Jan, and urged Anigel to take the loyal Dorok into her service until it was possible for him to rejoin Haramis.

"And soon," Haramis added, "God and the Lords of the Air willing, I shall complete my studies with the Archimage of the Sea. If you can only hold off giving up your talisman until I gain full mastery of my own—"

Slowly, Anigel removed the Three-Headed Monster coronet from its place among the papers. She held it over the table, between herself and Haramis's phantom presence, and spoke in a voice unyielding as stone. "I will give this coronet to the sorcerer whenever he asks for it, if he certainly ensures that my Antar is returned to me safely. And the Triune God witnesseth this."

Haramis sat frozen, staring at her sister's talisman in shocked disbelief. The tiny fossil trillium flower embedded in the amber at the coronet's front was no longer black, but as red as blood. Mutely, she pointed this out to Anigel.

"Yes," said the Queen, unperturbed. "And Kadi's is red also. The flowers were transformed at our angry parting. But it does not matter. Nothing matters, save that I have my dear husband safe again, and his country has its King."

"Kadiya! It is I, Haramis."

"Great God!" cried the Lady of the Eyes, for her sister seemed to be standing on the storm-tossed waters of the Mutar River, directly in front of the bow of the huge Wyvilo canoe that bore her. Two of the craft were speeding upstream, and sheets of rain lashed their occupants, even though the Dry Time was well advanced.

The amazed Wyvilo slowed their paddling, and the two boats bearing Kadiya and her party hovered in the midst of the turbulent waterway.

"Hara, have you learned to walk upon water?" Kadiya exclaimed.

"It is only that I have become more proficient in the use of my talisman," the Archimage replied. "It is an image of me that you see, having no true substance. You note that I can now bespeak you directly, even though you have no talisman of your own. I can now communicate across the leagues with any being."

"Good," said Kadiya tartly. "Bespeak that royal numskull, Ani, and convince her not to give up her talisman to the sorcerer!"

"I have tried, and I will try again. But what concerns me now is the antagonism between you two. I see that Ani was correct in saying that the trillium in your amulet has turned blood red. But tell me she was wrong in believing that you would have killed her to prevent the ransom of Antar."

Kadiya's brow was as stormy as the Tassaleyo Forest sky. "You and I know what it would mean if Portolanus had two talismans in his possession." She gestured at the unseasonable tempest. "He is the reason that the balance of the world is upset! Do you know there have been earthquakes in the northern Tassaleyo? Lummomu's people have bespoken him the news! And Jagun's Folk say a terrible restlessness afflicts the abominable Skritek, and they have been rampaging all over the Blackmire, violating my truce. In the north, there is an epidemic of the fainting sickness among the Uisgu. All over the land, disasters are multiplying — and it is entirely the fault of Portolanus! If Anigel gives him her talisman in ransom, things will grow even worse. Only some caprice of the sorcerer himself stopped our sister from handing the coronet over earlier, like a meek togar bending its neck over the chopping block! Ani puts her love for her husband and her duty to her Two Thrones above the welfare of the world. Her folly is criminal —"

"But even more so is your threat against her . . . Kadiya, think! Does not the blood red color of your trillium give you pause? We are intended to be Three, working together in sisterly love. It is the sacred Flower that unites us, not the Sceptre of Power."

For an instant, doubt softened Kadiya's adamant, dripping features. "So said Shiki the Dorok, whom you sent to aid me in my rescue of Niki and Jan . . . Nevertheless, if Portolanus gains two talismans, he will surely not rest until he has the third. And even with two, he can subdue the entire Peninsula, if not the known world."

"Perhaps." Haramis held her sister's gaze. "But I am laboring to prevent him, and my own talisman is the key to the full operation of the other two. I have learned this, and many other important secrets, from a kindly mentor who is instructing me in the magical arts."

Haramis briefly related her discovery that she was not the only Archimage, and her studies with Iriane, the Blue Lady. "The Archimage of the Sea has stood aloof from our mainland affairs thus far, but she intends to do so no longer. She will be a powerful friend to us in our struggle against Orogastus."

"Orogastus!"

Haramis nodded slowly. "He lives, calling himself Portolanus. We did not kill him after all with the Sceptre. He is one of the Star Men, the descendant of a powerful society that fought against the Vanished Ones in ages long past."

"And a man you still love," Kadiya declared, her voice sharp with anger. "Lords of the Air, defend us! I doubt that even the Teacher in the Place of Knowledge can help me to save the world now!"

Haramis reached out a spectral hand through the pelting rain. "It does not all depend on you, Sister. Certainly, you should consult the sindona. But do not be hasty in condemning Anigel or me. I know that the Teacher will admonish you to be more understanding—"

"I will not see my beloved Folk made slaves to an evil sorcerer!" Kadiya flared. "Not for Anigel and Antar's sake, and not for yours. Find a way to destroy Orogastus once and for all! Find it before Anigel pays the ransom! Then talk to me of love and understanding."

Haramis bowed her head. "I will try. And I will bespeak you again when my studies are complete. Farewell."

As Kadiya's stubborn face faded away Haramis again felt despondency take hold of her and drag her down like quickmire. Perhaps the worst aspect of what her fiery sister had said was its pitiless truth: Anigel *must* be prevented from giving up her talisman.

If Anigel refused to listen to reason, was there perhaps another way to persuade her? Would the Queen listen to her husband, when she had refused to listen to her sisters?

"Talisman, I would have Sight of King Antar, and bespeak him secretly, with no vision of me appearing."

Immediately she saw the King—and the vision was a dire one, for he was imprisoned in a kind of wheeled cage, being drawn along a cobblestoned city street by a team of volumnials. The place was mobbed by a taunting throng of tatterdemalion humanity, and four grinning Raktumian knights with naked swords kept the bolder ones from approaching too near the captive monarch.

It was evident that the Raktumian flotilla had finally arrived in Frangine, the capital of the pirate kingdom, and an impromptu triumphal procession was moving from the docks to the palace, accompanied by the cheers of the rascally citizenry. Files of heavily armed men formed the vanguard of the parade. More knights hedged about Queen Regent Ganondri, who was dressed in a bejeweled green and gold riding habit and mounted upon a spirited fronial with gilded antlers and emerald silk caparisons.

Behind her, the boy-King Ledavardis sat a fine black charger. In the saddle his deformities were less obvious, and he looked older and more majestic in a suit of shining parade armor and a plumed helmet with an open visor. Ledavardis never turned his head or altered his stolid features to acknowledge those who hailed him, but the affection of the people was nonetheless clearly with the young uncrowned monarch. Few voices were lifted in praise of the Queen Regent. She, with a fixed proud smile upon her face, appeared unconcerned.

The royal pair were followed by Admiral Jorot and the captains of the other three galleys. Then came the cage with the captive King of Laboruwenda and a colorful throng of mounted nobles and knights. Banished to the rear of the procession and flanked by marching men-at-arms was a rickety open coach carrying the outlandish Master of Tuzamen, Portolanus. He seemed unaware that the crowd was covertly sneering and laughing at him, and he waved and winked and chortled at the onlookers and occasionally conjured up a bouquet of flowers for some comely wench or a handful of comfits to toss to the children. The three Voices of the sorcerer rode sorry nags behind his carriage; but little Prince Tolivar was seated beside Portolanus in the coach, dressed in a fine brocade suit and smiling happily.

Haramis spoke low: "Antar, can you hear me? It is I, Haramis."

The King's head lifted and his lips parted in astonishment. He had been reclothed in the rich garments in which he had been abducted, but he sat incongruously on straw.

"Do not speak out loud or give any sign, dear Brother-in-Law, but simply respond to me in thoughts. My powers have been augmented in recent weeks, and I hear you and see you plainly. First: Are you in good health?"

Yes — save that my heart is darkened with melancholy. I was torn by barbed hooks when the scoundrels recaptured me, but Portolanus used some magical unguents upon the wounds and they healed cleanly and without scars. I was not locked up with the slaves on the return journey but treated quite decently. I had good food and a comfortable bed in a guarded stateroom . . . Tolo, as you can see, is not only healthy but also a keen chum of the damned wizard! I can't imagine what's come over the silly little sprog. Mayhap he is a victim of some evil spell —

"I am quite sure that he is not bewitched, so put your heart at ease. Do you know what plans the Queen Regent and Portolanus have for the two of you?"

No, save that I am to be held in the palace here . . . Haramis, something very odd is going on between Ganondri and Portolanus. There may have been a falling-out between that precious pair of villains! The Queen Regent came to me from time to time while I was recovering on shipboard, showing an unwonted concern for my welfare and comfort. Apparently she wished to be sure that my medical treatment by the wizard was indeed restoring me to health, and not harming me. She was very solicitous, and you may imagine how amazed I was by her change in attitude. I declared to her that my Royal Spouse was no more likely to be swayed into paying the ransom by my cosseting as by my torture. At this Ganondri only laughed. Later, I heard her warn the guards to stay close to me whenever Portolanus entered my locked cabin. They would die hideous deaths, she said, if any harm came to me through the sorcerer.

"How very strange! Antar, you do know, don't you, that Anigel offered the talisman for your release? But Portolanus refused to accept it."

By the Flower! No, I did not know . . . Haramis, you must not allow Ani to give up the coronet. Beseech her to think of the calamities such a course might wreak upon the people of the world! Tell her that I forbid it — that I would gladly die, rather than have her relinquish her talisman for my sake.

"I will tell her. But so must you."

How? I cannot bespeak her, nor has she the ability to communicate with me by the speech without words, as you now do.

"Frame the message in your heart and deliver it to me as though I were Anigel herself. I will implant your image and your words in her dreams so that each night she sees you and hears you speak."

Great God — you can do such a thing?

"I am being trained in the highest magic by another Archimage. I have discovered that I am not alone in this office. There are two others besides myself who serve as guardians and guides to the world through the wielding of benevolent magic. The Archimage who is teaching me to use my talisman is named Iriane, and she lives in the far north, in the Aurora Sea. In another two weeks, if I manage to complete my studies satisfactorily, I will make an attempt to rescue you and little Tolo. I also hope to find a way to counter the schemes of the sorcerer and Queen Ganondri."

Pray God you do! From the rumors I heard on shipboard, Raktum and Tuzamen are planning to attack the Two Thrones — possibly with the collusion of Lord Osorkon and his faction of malcontents.

"Anigel believes this also. I will do my best to defend your nation, just as soon as I have mastered my talisman."

But what of Portolanus and Kadi's stolen Burning Eye? Will he not be an antagonist impossible to counter?

"I do not know. My only hope is that he does not yet know how to use the talisman properly, and through some stratagem I can get it away from him. Pray for me! And now, Antar, bespeak your message to Anigel. Urge her to be steadfast in refusing the ransom, for if the sorcerer obtains a second talisman, the entire world may fall under his thrall."

When Haramis had enfolded Antar's loving message in her heart and the caged King's image had vanished, she found herself back on the summit of the artificial iceberg. She first sent the dream winging to Anigel's mind, then uttered a deep sigh and let her talisman fall to the end of its chain. So confidently she had spoken to the others of mastering the Three-Winged Circle! But what if her hope was only rash presumption?

Grigri came wriggling to her, having forgiven her earlier lack of sensitivity, and after fondling her limp hand, he began rooting in the picnic basket.

"Ah, little one. How fortunate you are to have such simple problems!" She took out a portion of roasted fowl, broke it, and fed it to the creature. "I could not let Ani and Kadi and Antar know of my concern that I may not be able to utilize the talisman effectively, even after my studies with Iriane. It is true that my bespeaking is greatly enhanced — but this is the most modest of the Three-Winged Circle's powers. Will I actually be able to gain victory over Orogastus and the pirates of Raktum through magic? What if one part of the Sceptre is quite unable to contend against another part? . . . If that should be true, then Orogastus and I will face each other virtually unarmed, as we did when we first met — only a man and a woman, mortal antagonists at the same time that we are lovers, with only our own souls' resources to fall back on . . . Oh, Grigri. Would I be able to do him harm, even to save the world?"

The creature gobbled the meat rapturously, ignoring her.

Haramis lifted her talisman. "I know I should not look upon him, for this would weaken my resolve to reject him. And yet I long so to see him once again! I know that he would be unable to hide himself from me now. I would see no blurred uncertainty this time, but his true face. His face . . ."

The talisman was warm in her hand, waiting for her to command it. The drop of honey-amber inset among the three silvery wings held a tiny black fossil flower.

Even as she watched, it turned vivid crimson.

"Oh, God," she whispered, closing her eyes against the sight of it. "Is that the price I must pay? Will even a loving glimpse of him jeopardize my soul? Surely not! . . . Or is this another one of Iriane's wretched tests of my resolution? Giving me leave to look upon him, then revealing to me the consequence of leading myself into temptation? . . . Very well! I will not command a view of him this time, since my desire is merely a personal indulgence! I will *not* feed my love, but starve it instead! Talisman — are you satisfied? Give me back my Black Trillium! And thou, O Flower — strengthen me as I do my bounden duty, always seeking the greatest good rather than my own selfish desires."

She reopened her eyes.

The flower was black.

Haramis arose. She gathered the scraps Grigri had left and wrapped them tidily in a napkin. "Come along, little friend. You have eaten well, and the ladu-fruit shall be my meal as we return. I have taken enough time away from my work."

With the animal leading the way, she started back into the depths of the iceberg. In the distance, thick clouds were building up over the land and a chill wind began to blow.

19

Every other day, Prince Tolivar was permitted to visit his Royal Father's comfortable cell in the midlevel of the West Tower of Frangine Palace. Tolo's friend the sorcerer always provided some tidbit of food for the boy to bring, and sometimes a book of tales to help the King while away his hours of captivity.

Today the little Prince brought along a tempting dish of candied fruit and a book of pirate adventures. The genial prison warden, Edruk, fetched the ring of keys when Tolo presented himself in the guards' anteroom.

"How fares my Royal Father?" the boy asked politely. He and Edruk walked down the torchlit corridor toward the chamber where the King was held. There were locked iron doors on both sides, and behind them dwelt certain enemies of the Queen Regent whom she did not dare to put to death.

"The King seems to grow ever more cheerful as the days pass, young Lord." Edruk opened the door to Antar's cell. "And this is a great contrast to my experience with most prisoners . . . Enter. I will return to let you out in half an hour."

Tolo thanked the warden gravely and went in. The door clanged shut behind him and the well-oiled click of the lock followed. Antar looked up from a letter he was writing and smiled at his youngest son. He wore simple clothing and his hair and beard had been trimmed since Tolo saw him last. He did look quite content. Through the narrow glazed embrasure of the cell the boy could see falling snow, but the chamber was warm and snug.

When the Prince spoke his greeting and placed the gifts on the table, Antar gathered his son to his bosom and kissed him.

"Well—and are you still working as hard as ever at becoming the sorcerer's apprentice?"

The boy pulled away. "I wish you would not make fun of me, Papa. Master Portolanus never does. He says I possess the natural aura of a born thoo—thaumaturgist!"

"I apologize." Antar's blue eyes were twinkling. "Still, I trust that you are not getting so fond of that mountebank's amusements that you would prefer them . . . to going home."

The boy's face fell. "Home? Is Mama sending her talisman as ransom for us after all? The sorcerer said she had refused! I thought you would stay locked up here for a while. Portolanus has sent to Tuzamen for his collection of magical machines, and he says they will arrive soon. But if we are ransomed now, I will not be able to see them!"

The King's jocular manner abruptly changed to one of stern disappointment. He took hold of Tolo's shoulders. "My son, do you realize what you are saying? No—of course you don't. I know you have become fond of this sorcerer. But he is not a kindly worker of marvels as you might think. He is a wicked man whose ambition is to destroy the Two Thrones."

The Prince turned away, his brow setting in an obstinate scowl. "That's what the Pirate Queen says. But it's not true. *She's* the one who wants to conquer our country, not Portolanus."

"That may be what he told you." Antar spoke more gently. "But it is Portolanus who has lied to you, Tolo. If he should obtain your mother's talisman, he would be in a position to conquer the world. He and his Raktumian allies would invade Labornok and Ruwenda and kill our people and steal our riches. In time, all of the other peaceful nations would fall before him as well."

"But he doesn't want Mama's talisman!" the boy cried. "He has Aunt Kadi's, and he says that's enough. She didn't know how to use it to do great things. But Portolanus is finding out its secrets! He told me so! He is going to use it to turn his poor little country into a great one. The talisman will make the sun shine on Tuzamen, and turn the soil rich instead of barren, and make the farm animals multiply and grow fat, and bring jewels and gold and platinum pouring out of the mountains!"

"Dear God. Is that what he told you?"

But the Prince rushed on. "Portolanus doesn't have to conquer other countries. The talisman will give him anything he wants! That's why he told Mama he didn't want her talisman when she offered it to him. He *did* have us all kidnapped to get her talisman. But when he got Aunt Kadi's instead, he didn't really need Mama's anymore."

"He lies, Tolo. I know that he turned down the chance to get your mother's talisman in the Windlorn Isles, refusing when she offered it as ransom. Why he did that is a mystery. But consider carefully, lad! If Portolanus does not still covet the talisman, why are you and I still held prisoner?"

"It's the Pirate Queen's fault," Tolo whispered. "Portolanus promised me he'd help get you away from her."

"Lies . . . lies." Antar shook his head. "You are so very young. But you are old enough to know that grown-ups think very differently from children, and they do not always say what they mean. Portolanus does not want riches, my son — he wants power. He wants to command kings and queens and entire nations, not live peacefully in Castle Tenebrose, playing magical games with you and showering gold and diamonds on his people."

"He says I can be Master of Tuzamen someday."

"*What?*"

"He says he'll make me his heir," the boy declared. "He's taken a great fancy to me. I won't just be a useless old second prince anymore. I'll learn to be a wizard like him, and when he retires to do nothing but study old-timey magic, I'll rule his country! He hasn't got any children of his own. He says really great sorcerers can't have any. They have to adopt an heir . . . and he wants to adopt me!"

"You would renounce your own family in favor of this villainous trickster?" the King cried, his fingers tightening on the boy's arms. But Tolo twisted about like a frenzied animal, pulling away, and ran defiantly to the cell door.

"You don't know what you're doing!" Antar exclaimed. "You're only a baby! A silly baby!"

The cell door opened.

"It is time for the Prince to go," Edruk said. His usually amiable face had gone grim.

"I *want* to go!" Tolo shrieked, darting out into the corridor. Tears had begun to stream down his cheeks. "Papa, I don't want to see you anymore!"

"My son, come back! I should not have spoken so unkindly." The King strode toward the door, but Edruk barred the way, and a moment later the lock was turned.

"Tolo!" Antar's voice was muffled by the iron and the stone walls. "Tolo, don't go!"

The boy wiped his face on his sleeve, then followed the prison warden out into the anteroom. Two cruel-faced men wearing the livery of the Queen's personal service waited there.

"Here he is," Edruk said, with a sigh. "Both Zillak and I overheard his conversation with his father. It was as the Great Queen suspected."

Powerful hands seized each of Tolivar's upper arms. "You'll come with us," one of the servitors growled. At Tolo's frightened squeal the man laughed. "And step lively. Her Majesty doesn't like to be kept waiting."

There were loud voices coming from behind the closed door of Ganondri's private sitting room. Two armored noblemen stood outside with crossed swords and prevented Tolo's escort from knocking.

"But the Queen Regent would want this royal whelp to be brought to her immediately!" one of the burly servants protested. "He has information of great importance!"

"She is with our most gracious Lord, King Ledavardis," one of the pirate-nobles said brusquely. He and his companion both wore the King's badge. "And you will wait."

The two pairs of retainers glowered at one another while the shouting continued within, and Tolo's fear turned to fascination. Clearly the Pirate Queen and her grandson, the Goblin Kinglet, were having a flaming row! It was impossible to understand what they said.

After a few minutes the door was yanked open and Ledavardis, white-faced with rage, stalked out.

"No — you shall not turn your back on me!" Ganondri screamed after him. "Come back, you arrogant ingrate!"

Ignoring her shouts, the sturdy young hunchback beckoned for his two men to follow and tramped off down the hallway.

Ganondri now came to the door, her features twisted by fury and her elaborately dressed auburn hair pulled awry. She wore a purple gown and a matching light cloak trimmed with gold lacework. At the sight of Tolo and the servants she reclaimed her dignity with some effort and motioned for the men to bring the boy inside. At a table a bottle of ink had been upset over a sheaf of official papers and black liquid dripped slowly onto the priceless carpet beneath. Another document, ripped into fragments, lay scattered on the floor together with a quill-pen that had been snapped in half.

Paying no attention to the disarray, the Queen Regent went to a serving tabouret and poured herself a crystal tumbler of brandy. After she had drunk, she whirled about and fixed her glittering green eyes on Prince Tolivar.

"Is it true," she asked in a quiet, harsh voice, "that your mother, Queen Anigel, offered to give her talisman to Portolanus while we were yet in the Windlorn Isles?"

"Yes," the boy mumbled, staring at his shoes. "I think so."

"Speak up!"

"My — my Royal Father said so. He never lies."

"And Portolanus told *you* that he did not want Anigel's talisman. Is that correct?"

"He — no. He never said that."

She darted forward suddenly and took hold of his ear, tweaking it sharply so that he bawled with pain. "Tell the truth!"

The Prince sobbed: "I am! Owww . . . that hurts!"

"Did Portolanus say that he had no need of your mother's talisman? Tell me, you cringing little slime-dawdler! Or I shall have my men slice off your nose and throw you into the deepest dungeon!"

Weeping and trembling, Tolo sagged to the floor. "Don't hurt me any more! Yes! He did say it! He did."

Ganondri turned him loose and looked down at him with distaste. "That's better . . . What a craven, contemptible piece of work you are! You have no more loyalty to that conjuring rogue, your benefactor, than to your own father. Faugh! You disgust me. Even my misbegotten grandson is made of better stuff than you."

"Don't hurt me." The Prince sniffled, shielding his head with his arms. The two servitors hauled him upright.

"Take the little wretch away," Ganondri told the men, "lock him in his room, and guard him well."

The men bowed and dragged Prince Tolivar out. He was weeping again.

When they were gone, Ganondri said to herself: "It is worse than I thought. But I may yet salvage the situation by bold action — provided that Portolanus has not gained sudden expertise in the use of that damned Burning Eye."

Pulling on a bell-cord, she had her lady-in-waiting summon the Captain of the Palace Guard and twenty men. Then she set off for the apartment that she had assigned to Portolanus.

"Great Queen, what an unexpected honor!" Rubbing his gnarled hands nervously, the decrepit sorcerer arose from a table piled high with books to greet the royal visitor and the small army accompanying her. The Black, Yellow, and Purple Voices peered forth from an inner chamber, displaying ill-disguised alarm.

"Take his henchmen in hand," Ganondri commanded. The Captain of the Guard gestured, and six heavily armed men seized the acolytes, while Portolanus first squeaked in consternation, then galloped across the room, slippers flapping, toward a great carved chest of polished wood.

"Stop him!" the Queen Regent cried. "He is after the talisman!"

The Captain and four men with drawn swords sprang after Portolanus and grabbed hold of his tatty robe. He howled, slipping out of it, and dived at the chest wearing nothing but a breechclout about his scrawny loins. But one of the guardsmen gave the box a mighty kick with his mailed foot and sent it sliding out of the sorcerer's reach.

"Well done!" Ganondri exclaimed, a thin smile brushing her lips. Three of the guardsmen restrained the squirming old man, and he suddenly slumped, breathing heavily, and gasped:

"Great Queen, this is a most regrettable misunderstanding. I would be happy — "

"Silence, conjurer!"

She seated herself on a cushioned bench while Portolanus was made to stand before her. "Let us begin our discussion with Ledavardis. You assured me that you would cast a spell of docility upon my unruly grandson. And yet, when I presented him with certain important documents to sign this evening, he not only refused flatly, but also insulted me to my face and declared that my reign would shortly come to an end."

"I cannot understand it!" the sorcerer whined. "My Voices have administered the required potion to the young King every day since our return to Frangine. He should by now be as meek as a newborn woth!"

Ganondri uttered a disdainful snort. But then her expression grew more ominously thoughtful. "Incompetent! . . . Or have you decided to disavow our alliance in spite of my warning? Is that it? Do you think that, now that we are back on dry land, you will be able to set some new scheme in motion against me? Are you fool enough to think that you can use my witling grandson as your tool?"

"Never! You are mistaken, Great Queen!"

"Am I also mistaken in my belief that Anigel of Laboruwenda offered you her talisman as ransom weeks ago, while we were still in the Windlorn Isles? And you refused to accept it?"

"No, I do not deny that. I feared that if I made Anigel's offer known to you, you in your eagerness to have that all-but-worthless trinket would release the King forthwith. And this would have been a fatal blow to our design for conquest. We *need* King Antar captive, if our plan to subdue Laboruwenda is to succeed! Only he would be able to rally the divided loyalties of the Labornoki nobility. His countrymen will never fight wholeheartedly under the banner of the Two Thrones unless Antar himself leads them. If Antar remains a prisoner, the invasion will allow Lord Osorkon, our creature, to seize control of Labornok. The conquest of Ruwenda will follow the capitulation of Labornok as day follows night, given that the bulk of the Ruwendian forces have gone away to the south, to defend Var."

"How very plausible," Ganondri said archly. "And this is the true reason why you declined to accept *my talisman?*" She screeched the last two words in a towering rage.

"I swear it! What good would the thing do you, woman? Are you a sorceress? Claiming it would be a fruitless gesture."

"The decision was mine to make, not yours!" she said. "And yet you dared to keep it from me! You feared what would happen if we were to become equals in magic!"

"Nonsense. You are being quite ridiculous."

"How dare you!" Ganondri shrieked. "You—you—"

Beside herself, the Queen surged up from her seat. Drawing the jeweled dagger from the sheath at her belt, she flung herself at Portolanus.

The sorcerer said: "Enough of this comedy."

As the Queen Regent faltered before him, not believing what her eyes showed her was happening, Portolanus assumed his normal physical appearance. His nearly naked body became tall and stalwart, his beard and hair shining white, and his silver-blue eyes incandescent. Held high in his right hand was the Three-Lobed Burning Eye.

Queen Ganondri seemed to become a statue, poised on one foot, with the dagger lifted to strike.

The men of the Palace Guard likewise froze, unable to move except for their wildly rolling eyes.

The acolytes wriggled free of their petrified captors and hastened to bring their master a fresh white robe. The Black Voice opened the wooden chest, reverently lifted out the silver leather belt and scabbard that had been newly made for the Three-Lobed Burning Eye, and fastened it about the sorcerer's narrow waist. The Yellow Voice and the Purple scrambled about, disarming the guardsmen and relieving Ganondri of her deadly little poniard. Then they stepped back. Portolanus sheathed his talisman and released Ganondri from her paralysis with an offhand gesture.

"Of course you were right about my deception," he said to the Queen in silken tones. "It would never have done for Anigel to give her talisman to you! While we remained on shipboard, your prudent precautions stayed my hand. But now the time for dissembling is over . . . Ledo! Come forth!"

Young King Ledavardis stepped out of an inner chamber, approached his grandmother, and stared impassively at her. He held a small object carefully in both hands.

"You were very clever, Queen Regent," the sorcerer went on, "and thought you had maneuvered me into a trap from which I could not escape without losing the Raktumian alliance. You adjudged yourself safe from any machinations of mine because you rule Raktum, and any move against you by me — a foreigner of most dubious repute! — would seem to your people to be a threat to Raktum itself. As you correctly pointed out, I need Raktum's good will! But, Lady, I do not need yours . . . only *his*." Portolanus pointed to Ledavardis. "And he hates you, for good and sufficient reasons."

The Queen's green eyes darted from her grandson's pitiless face to that of the smiling sorcerer and then back again. "You do not dare to kill me!"

Portolanus nodded. "That is true. Nor do I dare to exile you or lock you away. Fortunately, the customs of your own pirate kingdom provide me with a solution to the dilemma. These witnesses" — the sorcerer gestured to the paralyzed guardsmen — "retain full command of their wits. I enjoin them to observe and remember what next befalls."

The sorcerer nodded to the boy-King, who approached his grandmother and showed to her a small golden box. Using the greatest care, he removed its close-fitting lid. A wide-meshed screen of fine gold wire stretched across the box's opening. Ganondri glanced down, and gave a thin mewling cry. Her face went gray. Turning away from her, King Ledavardis displayed the contents of the box to all of the frozen guardsmen.

Inside, something small and dark and glistening with slime reared up. A tiny appendage thrust momentarily through the mesh, a kind of tentacle with two needlelike stings at the end. Twin drops of venom, glistening like crystal beads, hung from their tips.

"You men know what this is," the hunchbacked young monarch said. "In the ancient days, when a corsair of our nation was accused of betraying his comrades, he had the choice of pleading guilty and taking his own life, or undergoing the ordeal of the shareek. Sometimes, the shareek adjudged the accused innocent."

"No!" whispered Ganondri. "You . . . you cannot do this to one of your own flesh and blood!"

"Queen Regent," said the youth, "I accuse you of depriving me of my rightful throne. I accuse you of conspiring to have me declared incompetent so that you might rule Raktum in my place. I accuse you of the murder, torture, and imprisonment of over three hundred souls who were my loyal adherents . . . And now you will be judged."

He seized the Queen's right wrist and inverted the box, placing the gold-mesh opening upon the back of her hand. "Let the shareek decide your fate according to the ancient law of Raktum as I count to three. One . . ."

There was silence.

"Two . . ."

The pupils of Ganondri's eyes were so wide in her livid face that the emerald irises were obliterated by black. She made no attempt to struggle.

"Three."

Ganondri uttered a hideous, inhuman cry, like that of a beast consigned living to the flames. As Ledavardis withdrew the golden box those watching saw that the back of her hand had two tiny pricks upon it. Immediately, the skin around the wounds turned purple, then black. The contusion spread into her fingers, up her wrist. She began to quake, to crumple. As she sank to the floor, the folds of her silken gown and cloak falling around her, her eyes rolled slowly up into her head and the creased lids quivered and closed. Her uninjured hand took on the same blackish, bruised appearance as the stung member, and the hideous discoloration crept up her neck and finally suffused her entire face. But by then Queen Regent Ganondri breathed no more.

Strangled exclamations came from several of the palace guardsmen. King Ledavardis replaced the lid of the golden box tightly and put the shareek into his belt-wallet. He nodded to Portolanus.

"Men of Raktum," the sorcerer intoned, "I release the magical bonds holding fast your bodies."

The captain and his twenty men groaned and staggered and stretched.

"Remember what you have seen!" Ledavardis said. "Now, Captain, have a litter brought, and notify the late Queen's women to prepare her body. There will be a very modest funeral — and an even more modest coronation."

"Yes, Great King." He and his men filed out.

Ledavardis looked upon the dreadful thing that had been his grandmother for a few moments more, then lifted his clumsy head to gaze speculatively at the transformed sorcerer.

"You have shifted your own erstwhile ugly shape to one more pleasing to the eye, Portolanus. Dare I hope that you might change my miserable body also?"

"This is my natural form," the sorcerer said. "The other was an illusion, worn to dupe my enemies into underestimating me. I regret to say that my knowledge of the magical arts is not yet advanced enough to restore you, Great King. But you are sturdy and strong enough, and if you wish, I can clothe you with an illusion of manly beauty."

Ledavardis made a dismissive gesture. "No. I will wear no mask. My people will continue to accept me as I am."

"And will you honor the original pact made between Tuzamen and Raktum?" the sorcerer asked softly. "Ganondri attempted to repudiate that alliance, which I made in good faith. I offer it again to you: All the nations of the Peninsula and the Southern Seas shall be yours to rule, if only you allow me primacy in matters relating to magic."

"Including Queen Anigel's talisman?"

"Yes. And, in time, the talisman of the Archimage Haramis as well. In return, I swear by the Dark Powers I serve never to harm you through magic, but rather to aid and abet you in all of your ambitions that I deem legitimate."

"But you will be supreme," the boy-King said in a level tone.

"Yes. But only I and these three loyal Voices of mine shall know it. It is a small price to pay. My concerns are with matters as remote from royal governance and commerce as the Three Moons are remote from the surface of the world. I will be to you a guide and a benefactor — not an oppressor."

Ledavardis nodded. "Very well. I accept your pact."

The sorcerer drew and held up the Three-Lobed Burning Eye. "And by this talisman let it be sealed . . . I give you leave to touch it, only once, to confirm your oath."

Perspiration dotted the young King's coarse brow. But he stretched forth his hand and laid it briefly upon the cold, dark lobes.

"There! I have done it." He smiled with relief. "I suppose that if I should betray you, the talisman would smite me dead."

The handsome sorcerer laughed. "Let me put it this way: There would be no need for the shareek! But let us busy ourselves with more pleasant matters now. Where do you suppose Ganondri might have hidden your late father's crown? You will want to wear it at your first official meeting with a fellow reigning sovereign."

"And who might that sovereign be?" Ledavardis inquired.

"Anigel of Laboruwenda," the sorcerer replied. "If I whistle up my magical winds, we can blow her tardy flotilla into the roads of Frangine within three days. You may condescend to welcome her, and give her her husband back in exchange for her talisman . . . Then you and I shall make ready to take their country away from them."

20

The first one to disembark from the Laboruwendian flagship was Shiki the Dorok, bearing the blue, gold, and red banner of the Two Thrones. Queen Anigel marched after him down the carpeted gangplank, heedless of the gently falling snow that was transforming the Raktumian capital of Frangine into a scene of exotic beauty. She was dressed in the royal robes she had worn at the Zinoran coronation and had the magnificent State Crown of Ruwenda upon her golden hair. Owanon the Lord Marshal and Penapat the Lord Chamberlain followed her closely, together with a noble bodyguard wearing full armor and holding great two-handed swords before their faces. Lampiar the Lord Chancellor and Lady Ellinis the Domestic Minister came then, clad entirely in black. All of the other nobles and knights who had accompanied the Queen on her ill-fated journey to the Zinoran coronation marched in a gloomy procession behind, wearing sable plumes in their helmets and black cloaks.

The day itself was memorably mournful in aspect, with leaden clouds and an icy breeze keen as a knife that blew in off the heaving waters of the harbor and made the snowflakes dance. The seasons were truly topsy-turvy, but none of the citizens of Frangine seemed to care. They crowded every alley and byway, ogling the somber procession in silence.

King Ledavardis and his courtiers waited at a cobblestoned square just uphill from the docks. Anigel had refused to come to Frangine Palace. What must be done would be done under the open sky.

A canopied dais had been set up for the youthful King's throne. He waited, entirely surrounded by a bodyguard of grinning pirate-knights with drawn swords, and warriors having bristling spears or halberds held at the ready. Ledavardis wore warm and sumptuous robes and a crown inset with hundreds of large diamonds. At the head of his sceptre was the so-called Heart of Zoto, a diamond the size of a man's closed fist, which had been stolen from the Royal House of Labornok five hundreds agone.

The Master of Tuzamen, clad in a white fur-lined cloak with a hood drawn far forward so that his face was entirely shadowed, stood at the monarch's right hand; Admiral Jorot, now wearing the sash and emblem of the Prime Minister, was at his left. The square was mobbed with scruffy Raktumian citizens and hung about with gaudy banners that snapped in the wind. No one uttered a sound while the Laboruwendians ascended the steep and slippery street and arrayed themselves in front of the dais.

A flourish of trumpets played as Shiki stood aside with the flag and Queen Anigel approached the throne. Ledavardis arose and nodded to her courteously and she inclined her head to him.

"I have come to ransom my husband and child," she said simply.

"Your talisman!" the hooded sorcerer demanded.

She did not deign to look at him, but kept her eyes upon the pale face of Ledavardis, which was sweat-bedewed despite the icy wind. "The ransom will be produced and duly handed to you, Royal Brother, when I see my loved ones safe here with me."

"Certainly."

The King made a curt gesture and the throng of armed men at the right-hand side of the dais parted. Anigel could not help but utter a piteous cry as she beheld an elaborate painted and gilded cage. The Captain of the Palace Guard unlocked it and bowed respectfully as Antar walked out of it, followed by little Tolivar. Both were splendidly attired and draped in magnificent cloaks of golden worram fur, with gleaming manacles and chains of solid platinum imprisoning their gloved wrists.

Antar's face wore an expression of resigned sorrow. Tolo scowled. Father and son were escorted by the Captain to the foot of the throne, and a platinum key was turned over to Ledavardis.

He proffered it to Anigel. "Madam, you may release the prisoners."

"The talisman!" barked the sorcerer.

Ledavardis seemed not to hear. Since Anigel only stood staring at her husband, a look of mingled defiance and grief upon her face, the young King himself unlocked first Antar's manacles, then those of the boy. "Go. You are free."

The King of Laboruwenda lifted his wife's bare, waxen hand and kissed it tenderly, then went to stand beside his old friend the Lord Marshal.

Anigel took up a gold-brocaded reticule that hung at her waist and opened it. She removed the slender, silvery coronet called the Three-Headed Monster and held it out in a trembling hand. Before Ledavardis could touch it, the sorcerer took three long steps forward.

"Ledo! Beware! She may have commanded it to kill you!"

Anigel shook her head wearily. "It would not harm him."

The little Black Voice popped out from behind the throne carrying the star-box. Smirking, he placed the thing at Anigel's feet and opened it. The sorcerer said: "Madam, place the talisman inside."

Anigel knelt in the trampled snow and did so. There was a dazzling flash of light, whereupon the young King flinched while his guards cried out and brandished their weapons, and the ragtag rabble of Raktumian citizens screeched and howled and uttered many a vile oath. Anigel only stepped back, now seeming to be indifferent.

"Have no fear!" The wizard quickly reached into the box and made finger play. A moment later he arose, threw back his hood, placed the talismanic coronet upon his own brow, and drew the Three-Lobed Burning Eye from his belt. He was beardless now and his long white hair streamed in the wind. His face was weathered by hardship but very handsome. Crowned with Anigel's talisman and holding Kadiya's high amid the falling snow, he let his aura of power enfold him. At that, the Queen finally recognized him as the old antagonist who had so nearly vanquished her and her two sisters in their youth.

"Orogastus!" she cried. "So it *is* you. Oh, you base scoundrel — may the Lords of the Air requite you as you deserve for having stolen the two talismans!"

He smiled condescendingly at the stricken Queen. The coronet now had a many-rayed star at its front, where the trillium-amber of its former owner had once been inset.

"Stolen? Nay, you do me an injustice, Madam. The one talisman is mine by right of finding and salvage, the other freely given in ransom, according to the laws of great Raktum. And in the latter case, you have been amply recompensed. Open your hand! It is not only your husband and King that has been returned to you."

Anigel stared wordlessly at the glowing amulet resting in her palm. A tiny scarlet flower shone in the amber's heart.

"Tell your sister Haramis that I will be expecting her," Orogastus said, still smiling. "And now, it would be best if you and your party set sail for Derorguila. This snowstorm will shortly turn into a north-westerly blizzard that will blow you handily home . . . Come, Tolo."

He turned on his heel. Little Prince Tolivar, who had stood by with a glum face, now brightened. "May I, Master? You will let me stay with you?"

"If you wish to," said the sorcerer, looking over his shoulder.

"I do!"

"Tolo, no!" the Queen exclaimed.

"Would you like to carry the star-box for me?" Orogastus asked the boy. He ignored the sudden look of dismay on the face of the Black Voice.

"Oh, yes!" The little Prince snatched the box from the glowering acolyte and held it up like a trophy for all the crowd to see.

"Tolo!" Anigel was openly weeping now. "You may not go with that terrible man! How can you think of such a thing? Come to me, my poor boy!"

Prince Tolivar, standing at the side of the tall sorcerer, only stared silently at her through the thickening fall of snowflakes.

"The child may do as he wishes," King Ledavardis declared. "It is his choice to make."

"Antar!" the Queen cried helplessly. "Speak to your son!"

"I have." The Laboruwendian King's face was without hope. He took one of his wife's arms as she realized the truth and began to wilt, and Owanon took the other. "Come, my dear. There is nothing more we can do now."

Queen Anigel said no other word as they led her back to the ship, dazed and with tears pouring from her eyes, followed by all their grieving company.

Inside of half an hour the lines were cast off, and the free galleymen of Laboruwenda dug in their oars and began to row the four ships toward the open sea and home.

21

A pattern of prismatic light-rays filled the mind of Haramis like an auroral tapestry. It seemed that she had been commanding those beams of radiance for day after day, willing them to form concrete images as the Archimage of the Sea prompted her. She ordered a tiny crystalline castle and it appeared — then seemed to become solid and real before her eyes. She banished it, then commanded the light-rays to form a saddled steed. A fronial materialized there before her, a creature sparkling with rainbow facets. It turned to warm flesh and seemed to regard her in comic puzzlement, tossing its antlers, until she dismissed it into the void from whence it had come. Thing after thing Haramis created — and place after place as well, for when properly enjoined, the Three-Winged Circle was itself a magical viaduct that could transport its owner anywhere in the blink of an eye. But Iriane permitted her student to travel only to drab, uninhabited parts of the world that she herself designated. These were difficult lessons Haramis was learning, and she must not be distracted by the sight of people or even by familiar places.

At the beginning of this part of her training, the sparkling things she "created" and the places she willed to visit were often called up ineptly, and the crystal visions would not translate into reality. But with Iriane's guidance Haramis learned at last to control the creative power most of the time. Now she was doing very well: if only she could avoid the pitfalls of overconfidence, she might yet master this talisman of hers!

"You are far from mastering it," Iriane's voice remarked tartly.

"But you are no longer the virtual ignoramus who first presented herself at my iceberg! . . . Take care lest you become arrogant or foolhardy, and you may yet fulfill your duty with honor."

"I pray so," said Haramis, with as much humility as she could muster.

The wondrous palette of malleable colored light began to dull and dwindle to darkness. Haramis found herself back in the meditation chamber on her knees, which sore pained her. The Archimage of the Sea arose from the stool she had sat upon, stretched, and yawned.

"Ah, how weary I am, child — and starving. Come, let us go to supper. I have a fine sucbri stew for us tonight, fresh from the Greenmire of your native land, and fogberry tarts that you will also find familiar and delicious."

Haramis climbed haltingly to her feet, arranging her white Archimage's cloak about her. "I fear I will not be able to eat much. I am too tired. All I can think of is sleep! If only you were not such a hard tutor and would let me stay longer abed — "

"You may sleep as long as you like tonight. Your instruction is at an end."

Haramis gave an exclamation of misgiving. "But I have not truly learned to command high magic."

Iriane waved a dismissive hand and led her pupil into one of the aquarium-corridors. "The three tennights of your sojourn are over. There is now nothing more I can teach you. You already command far more magic than I have ever known, with and without your talisman. The rest will come to you in time."

"But how can that be? . . ."

"Believe it." Iriane's round, kindly face with its faintly blue pallor had a sweet, enigmatic smile. The two women walked down the glowing, transparent hallway and came into the comfortable dimness of the room with the living marine mural.

"Since the time of the Vanished Ones," Iriane continued, "no other Archimage save you has ever possessed a part of the Sceptre of Power, or known so much about its use. The Vanished Ones were afraid of it, but you cannot afford to be. You have a vast responsibility now, to wield your magical power in a way that will restore the lost balance of the world, and to ensure that the other two parts of the Sceptre are not used in the service of evil."

Haramis tried to conceal her profound uneasiness. She seated herself at the dining table while Iriane went to fetch the food, which was prepared in some mysterious fashion that Haramis had never thought to question. When the Archimage of the Sea returned with the savory dishes, Haramis only picked at them.

"It is not only that I am tired," she said, when Iriane admonished her. "I am also filled with a terrible sense of foreboding . . . May I have your permission to bespeak my sisters?"

"You do not require my permission for anything anymore, Archimage of the Land." Iriane spoke solemnly. "But I will answer the one question that gnaws at your heart: Yes, the talisman called the Three-Headed Monster has been given in ransom for King Antar. It is now in the possession of the sorcerer Orogastus, and he has bonded it to himself."

"Dear God — I feared as much! Why did you not tell me what was happening? I might have stopped her!"

Iriane was serene as she nibbled at a berry tart. "You would *not* have stopped her. And interrupting you at a critical point in your magical training would have disrupted your concentration beyond repair, just when you were finally getting the hang of it."

Haramis was on her feet, flushed with agitation. "If Orogastus has two talismans and I only have the one, will he not have the advantage over me?"

"Only if he gains as much knowledge of his talismans as you have of yours. Even then, yours is the key to the Sceptre, as I have told you."

"Both of my sisters were able to use their talismans to kill, but I think this was done accidentally, and without their true volition. I presume that Orogastus might also inadvertently cause death. But would he be able to kill me deliberately?"

Iriane shook her head. "Thus far, he lacks the occult knowledge to wreak intentional mortal harm upon you with his talismans."

"But I . . . do I have the power to kill *him*?"

"No Archimage may deliberately bring about the death of another thinking creature. I do not know whether you would be able to kill him through indirect means. That information was not in my reference books. The Vanished Ones would have been very circumspect about such things. Denby claims not to know, either, but he may be lying. There is probably only one place where you might find out — the ancient Place of Knowledge where the Vanished Ones had their greatest university. The Star Men attempted to destroy it with a terrible weapon shortly before the hero Varcour managed to vanquish and scatter them. The buildings aboveground were obliterated, but there still exists a labyrinth of underground structures, guarded by inhuman beings called sindona."

"I know of them and the Place of Knowledge. My sister Kadiya received her talisman there — and she was on her way back to the place when last I bespoke her. There is a certain sindona in the place called the Teacher — "

Iriane nodded. "Go to her. She may be able to tell you more about the Sceptre. It was the sindona who were charged with breaking it and concealing its three parts twelve times ten hundreds ago. Since they are not flesh and blood, it was known that they would not be tempted to keep the talismans for their own use, nor impart knowledge of them to the unworthy."

Haramis suppressed a shiver, drawing her white cloak about her. "Iriane, would you mind very much if I went away to the Place of Knowledge at once?"

The Archimage of the Sea touched her lips with a blue napkin and arose. "Of course not. But there is something you had better take with you." She went to her workbench in the corner of the room. "Do you remember my telling you the way that Orogastus escaped death and was sent to the Inaccessible Kimilon?"

"Through some device you called a Cynosure."

"Exactly! And here it is."

The Archimage had been rummaging among the clutter of strange objects on the bench, and she now held up a hexagon less than half an ell wide, made of some dark metal. At its center was emblazoned a small many-rayed star.

"I secretly retrieved it from the Kimilon immediately after Orogastus arrived there unconscious. He does not even know that it exists. I have kept the Cynosure ever since, to ensure that it was not used to a mischievous end."

Haramis stared at her blankly. "You mean, so that Orogastus would not use it somehow to escape the Kimilon?"

"No, no . . . never mind!" Iriane was strangely flustered. "Recall how it works: If one of the Star Men is in danger of having his own soul's magic turned against him by the Sceptre of Power (and this is the way the Sceptre kills), this Cynosure will draw the intended victim to it ahead of the consuming magic fire, saving his life."

The Archimage of the Sea handed the thin hexagon to Haramis.

"But what am I to do with this?" Haramis inquired, mystified.

"Keep it safe from *him*, for a start," said Iriane incisively. "If he ever gets hold of it and learns its purpose, he will be all but invulnerable! Perhaps the Teacher will know a safe hiding place. At any rate, the Cynosure is properly your responsibility now, and you must take charge of it."

"But would it not be easiest to simply destroy it?"

"Try," the Blue Lady invited. "I did, and it resisted my every attempt! Perhaps you, with your talismanic powers, will have better luck."

Haramis commanded the Cynosure to suspend itself in the air before her. It complied. Then she told it to dissolve, visualizing its crystal simulacrum turning to bright dust.

It continued to float in the blue twilight, unchanged. Haramis tried again to demolish it, but the thing remained obstinately whole, with the star twinkling at its center.

"You see?" Iriane shrugged. "That star emblem on it perfuses it with resistant magic. You will have to find some other way to safely dispose of it."

Haramis plucked the hexagon out of the air. "Perhaps the Teacher at the Place of Knowledge will have a suggestion . . . But now I must go."

The two women, one tall and black-haired and robed in white, the other rotund and swathed in sparkling azure draperies, eyed each other in sudden silence. Then Iriane took both of Haramis's hands in hers, drew her down, and planted a moist kiss on her forehead.

"Do not forget me, dear Haramis, Archimage of the Land. I am ever your good friend and sister in duty. If you ever find yourself in a dire extremity, call upon me and I will do what I can."

"Thank you for what you have already done." Haramis returned the embrace. "I hope we will meet again on a more happy day."

She stepped away, holding the Cynosure tucked under her left arm. With her right hand she clasped the talisman. Nodding one final time, she vanished.

Iriane sighed and shook her head. Then she called to Grigri, went back to the table, and shared the rest of the plate of tarts with him.

The musical tone connoting travel through space sounded in Haramis's mind. She saw for a fleeting instant a scene seeming to be carven from glittering diamonds — and then it became real. She stood in a large brightly lit chamber, striking in its silence. Turning, she saw a pool of deep water surrounded by a low wall of white marble. The pavement beneath her feet was of metallic blue mosaic tiles. Opposite the pool was a marble stairway leading upward into the source of the light. On either side of the stairs, stationed on each broad step, were ranks of what appeared to be statues.

The sindona.

Haramis approached the nearest pair. They were a full head taller than she, but otherwise had the appearance of human male and female images, fashioned by a master sculptor. Their bodies had no trace of hair, pore, fleshly crease, or blemish. They were perfectly smooth, universally of an ivory tint, and resembled polished bone. The dark eyes of the sindona were like inset stones, and within the pupils lurked that glint of gold that Haramis had come to associate with the Vanished Ones. Their pale, serene faces were shadowed by elaborate crown-helms with the visors lifted. These and three belts — two crossed over the breast and one about the waist — were all they wore. The belts and helms were inset with small shining scales having many different tints of blue and aqua and green. Scales of gold edged the habiliments and formed elegant designs.

Haramis touched one of the statues with her talisman, and at once its carven lips parted and it spoke in resonant tones that were more like the sounding of a musical instrument than human speech.

"Welcome to the Place of Knowledge, Archimage. What is your desire?"

"To consult the Teacher," Haramis replied.

The sindona nodded and lifted one hand to point up the stairway. Even though it moved, it still appeared to remain hard as stone, and Haramis marveled at the ingenuity of those who had created it.

"The Teacher awaits you in the garden above, Archimage. Please ascend."

"Thank you," she said, and slowly went up the deep steps, studying the inhuman beings as she went. Each one had features subtly different from the others. They were not merely machines, nor were they creatures of flesh, but something utterly different.

"Why were you made?" she asked.

"For service," scores of gentle voices replied, and the sound of them was as breathtaking as a sweet chord from a great orchestra. "We are the sentinels, the messengers, and the bearers. Some of us also teach, some are consolers, and some take away life according to the Mortal Dictum."

"You *kill*?"

"Some sentinels have that ability."

"Great God!" Haramis murmured, climbing more energetically. Startling new thoughts flew about her mind like bright papillons. Might these strange sindona be allies against the evil of Orogastus?

"We were created to oppose the Star." The sindona seemed to read her thoughts. "Most of us perished in bringing about its first downfall in ages past. Those sindona who remain defend the Place of Knowledge."

Haramis stood stock-still, a great notion blooming within her. "And would you follow me, if I ordered you to once again defend the world against a threat by a latter-day Star Man?"

"Only the entire Archimagical College may issue to us a new duty," sighed the motionless sentinels.

Haramis saw her idea die stillborn, along with the hope it had engendered. The entire College? But they were long dead! . . . Well, it had only been a thought.

Eventually she came out into an open area flooded with radiance, where white pathways twined among lavish plantings of flowers, blossoming shrubs, and graceful ornamental trees. Here and there were ponds set like jewels in the midst of neat areas of short grass, and from them flowed small streams crossed by exquisite bridges of marble. Dotted amongst the greenery were benches, also of white stone, flower-banked grottoes, open garden houses, and arbors supporting fruit-laden vines. One particular path seemed to beckon Haramis, and she followed it to a graceful belvedere having a domed roof supported by slender columns. All about it grew bushes laden with purple and white and vivid pink blooms that filled the air with fragrance.

But there were no insects probing for nectar, no birds singing in the trees, no small animals frisking about and making off with the fruit. The landscape was uncannily silent except for the purling of the little brooks and the faint rustle of leaves in the breeze. Haramis looked up into the dazzling sky and saw no clouds — and no sun. She remembered suddenly that Iriane had said that the Place of Knowledge was located underground . . .

"Can it really be true?" she asked herself. She knelt to examine a bed of mixed flowers, riotously colorful, and recognized not a single one. The silhouettes of the trees were also unfamiliar, and the very greensward had grass that was exotic in appearance, unusually fine and as dense and springy as a carpet. Each individual blade was smooth-edged rather than finely serrated, as were all the grasses she knew —

"Greetings, Daughter of the Threefold."

Haramis started at the sound of the voice, which was human in its intonation. She looked up from her inspection of the grass to discover that a woman was coming toward her from the garden house.

A woman? No, not really. For all that she was of normal stature and clothed in flowing pastel gauze. Her bare arms and face gleamed an inhuman ivory white, and on her head was a close-fitting cap of metallic gold, carved into the semblance of a short, curled coiffure. She, like the noble sentinels, was a sindona.

"I am the Teacher," she said, her features impossibly smiling while at the same time remaining hard as stone. "I am at your service, Archimage Haramis. If you would, accompany me to the belvedere yonder, where we may sit in the cool shade and you may question me at your leisure."

Haramis followed her along the path. Inside the little domed structure was a white marble table and two wicker chairs with russet velvet cushions. A crystal pitcher of some rosy drink and a single tumbler half-filled with balls of ice waited. The Teacher gestured for her guest to be seated, poured the beverage over the ice, and handed the tinkling glass to Haramis.

"You may find this way of serving fruit-juice to be strange, but our former rulers, the Vanished Ones, were very fond of it."

"Thank you for your courtesy, Teacher."

Haramis sipped. The unusual sensation of the ice touching her lips at the same time as the chilled juice was delightfully refreshing. Unbidden, the inane thought came to her that she must search for an icemaker among the ancient machines of the Cavern of Black Ice when she finally returned home to Mount Brom . . .

Recalling the seriousness of the situation, Haramis looked into the Teacher's calm face and began her interrogation. "Is it true that you and your kind were created by the Vanished Ones, and that you are not truly alive?"

"We were made by the members of the original Archimagical College. We live, but our lives are not the same as those of ensouled ones such as humans and Folk. We do not give birth; and when we die, our spirits merge with those of us who still live. I am the only Teacher now living, but within me reside the spirits of two hundred Teachers of lesser longevity. When I die, I must pass into a sentinel or a bearer or a messenger or a consoler, and share its duty. Thus it shall be until only a single sindona remains, and at that one's death we shall be extinguished at last, like the last ember of a great fire finally fading to ash."

"How — how many sentinels remain?" Haramis inquired.

"Three hundred and twenty-one. And there are seventeen servers, and twelve bearers, and five messengers, and two consolers. But these latter reside with the Archimage of the Sky and are unable to minister to those of land or sea without his permission."

"This Archimage of the Sky!" Haramis's interest was intense.

"What can you tell me of him? My friend the Archimage of the Sea gave his name as Denby, and would say only that he was a remote personage, having little to do with worldly affairs. Yet it seems to me that if he is a true Archimage, then it is his duty to guard and counsel humanity. If I besought him, would he lend me aid?"

"I do not know. I can tell you nothing of him without his express permission . . . and this he does not grant. Nor is he disposed, at the present time, to become involved in affairs of the land and sea. Or so he says."

Haramis eyed the Teacher sharply. "You have just now consulted him on this?"

"Yes."

Haramis fumed inwardly. Another hope dashed! Was there no one who would join her in actively opposing Orogastus?

"There are," the Teacher responded unexpectedly. "Humans and Folk, sindona and Archimagi, the plants and animals of the world, the very air and water and rock and the bolides of the firmament — all may respond to your request for help if it is made in the proper fashion, at an appropriate time."

"Can you teach me how to summon this help?"

"I am sorry. This is knowledge that you alone can discover. Your talisman must enlighten you."

"I see." Haramis was becoming not a little exasperated, but she plunged ahead with her other questions. "Tell me, please: Does Orogastus have the advantage over me, since he has possession of two talismans of the Sceptre of Power, while I have only one?"

"Orogastus does not have the advantage — except in his natural gifts."

Taken aback, Haramis exclaimed: "Do you mean he is more clever than I?"

"Not more clever. He is wiser and more experienced, and his mind's working is colder and more logical because of his devotion to the Dark Powers. But you, O Archimage of the Land, have a greater potential in that you are a Daughter of the Threefold."

"My sisters . . . but their flowers have turned blood red."

"When their amulets again hold the Black Trillium in their hearts, they will be capable of great and selfless deeds once again. And able to rejoin you as Daughters of the Threefold — Petals of the Living Trillium. Until then, they are relegated to the mass of unadept."

Haramis nodded. "And so Orogastus and I are essentially equal in magical power?"

"This is not strictly true. But with the parts of the Threefold Sceptre cleaving two to the Star and one to the Flower, the world will ever stay unbalanced, to its peril . . . until the talismans in Orogastus's unlawful possession are taken from him, and the Three Petals of the Living Trillium combine to turn his Dark Powers against him."

"But how is this to be done?"

"I am unable advise you on that. The way depends too much upon mere happenstance. I suspect, however, that its fulfillment will not involve high magic, but rather some more human action."

"Can you give me no help at all in discovering how best to overcome Orogastus?" Haramis pleaded. "Can I not . . . somehow convert him from his Dark Powers?"

"Love is permissible," the Teacher said mysteriously. "Devotion is not. As to conversion, I have no information. He is of the Star, and his predecessors were steadfast in their evil beliefs unto death. The heart of Orogastus is unknown to me."

"And to me," Haramis murmured. "But then, so is my own heart, God help me!" Abruptly, she cast aside the dangerous pall of self-pity that threatened to deflect her from her goal and became once again calm and to the point. "Teacher, when I leave here, I know my sister Anigel will ask my aid in defending her country against villainous invaders. I have already determined that a great fleet of warships will shortly set forth from Raktum. Orogastus and King Ledavardis plan to lay siege to the northern capital city of Laboruwenda. I have notified my sister Queen Anigel of her danger, and she has begged me to lend her magical assistance. Is it wise for me to go at once to help her, or should I concentrate entirely on the problem of Orogastus and the talismans?"

"Your most immediate concern," the sindona woman said, "is not Anigel but your other sister, Kadiya, who came here some days ago to consult me about a way to prevent Queen Anigel from giving up her talisman. When I told Kadiya that the ransom for Antar was surely destined to be paid, she was beside herself with rage. I advised her to reconcile with Anigel and put herself at your service. This counsel Kadiya rejected forthwith. She is now on her way to an aboriginal village on the Upper Mutar River. When she arrives, she will attempt to rally the stouthearted little Uisgu of the Thorny Hell and the Goldenmire around her. She also plans to have the Uisgu send out a Call to the Nyssomu, the Wyvilo, and the Glismak — and even hopes to entreat the abominable Skritek to join her cause. When a great horde of Folk has been assembled, Kadiya, the Lady of the Eyes, hopes to seize all of Ruwenda as an inviolate homeland for aborigines."

"She would make war against the human dwellers therein?" Haramis was aghast. "Oh, no! Not when the Two Thrones must succor Var on the one hand and defend themselves against Raktum and Tuzamen on the other — "

"Kadiya calculates that this unstable situation will enhance her likelihood of victory."

"Oh, the hotheaded fool! . . . I suppose I shall have to talk some sense into her. And then see what I can do to aid Anigel and Antar. After that there will be time for me to deal with Orogastus — "

"Archimage, you still do not understand! You can do *nothing* to vanquish the Star Man without both Kadiya and Anigel standing wholeheartedly at your side."

"By the Flower, I might have known it!" Haramis clenched her fists and lowered her head so that the hood of her cloak of office hid the anguish of frustration that engulfed her.

They were inescapably Three. They were forever One. Neither her talisman nor her newly obtained Archimagical powers would conquer the Star . . . but only the Living Black Trillium.

She thrust her emotions aside and again met the Teacher's patient, inhuman gaze. "Thank you. Now I know what must be done. I will go to Kadiya at once."

She rose from the stone chair, and as she did, the hexagonal plate called the Cynosure clattered to the marble floor of the belvedere. She had completely forgotten it. Taking it up, Haramis said: "You surely know what this is. Can you tell me if it is possible to destroy it?"

"*You* could not do so. Neither could the sindona. Only the Star Council can do it, or the entire Archimagical College."

Balked again! Haramis pursed her lips grimly. "Then tell me how best to dispose of the Cynosure so that Orogastus may not use it again to escape punishment for his crimes."

For the first time the Teacher hesitated before answering. "If you placed it at the bottom of the sea, or threw it into an active volcano, or dropped it into the midst of a glacial crevasse, then one who was drawn to it by the backlash of magic would die, rather than find himself spared."

Haramis felt her throat tighten. "I had hoped . . . you knew of a place where I might put the Cynosure in order to safely imprison Orogastus alive. Perhaps here, in this stronghold of powerful magic, where the sentinels could guard him from possible rescue by his acolytes."

Again the Teacher hesitated. Then she said: "There is one place only that might serve. Follow me."

She set off at a rapid pace along one of the paths. Haramis followed, almost at a run, with the Cynosure tight under one arm. The two of them came to a grove of weeping trees with pale green leaves, and beneath them was a large rock garden bedecked with shade-loving exotic plants. Their flowers were bizarre in shape and the colors unwholesomely vivid, almost luminous in the green gloaming.

On the other side of the rockery was a dark hole in the ground, surrounded by a circle of large white stones.

The Teacher pointed into it. "This is the Chasm of Durance. Its only entry is through a subterranean shaft with steep sides as slick as glass, permeated with the most powerful magic of the Place of Knowledge. During the wars between the Star Men and our Vanished rulers, certain captives were confined by the Archimagical College in a cavern at the base of the shaft, until they were judged and vouchsafed either clemency or death at the hands of the Sentinels of the Mortal Dictum."

"It sounds like the very place!" Haramis breathed. "Would it hold Orogastus?"

"If he were deprived of the potent talismans, yes. He might survive indefinitely in the Chasm of Durance under our guard."

"I will inspect the place," Haramis said, "and if it is as suitable as you say, I will place the Cynosure there."

The Teacher nodded. "Are there any other questions you have for me, Archimage?"

Haramis's smile was rueful. "Only one, and I have begun to despair of ever getting an answer: Is it true magic or some arcane science that empowers the Black Trillium and the Threefold Sceptre?"

"It is magic."

"Ah! . . . And what *is* magic?"

"That which gives truth and beauty to reality, and binds the physical and mental universes into one."

"I — I will think upon that," Haramis said. She lay her hand upon her breast so that it touched the wand of the Three-Winged Circle hanging from the platinum chain about her neck. Among the tiny silvery wings, the amber amulet with the black Flower in its heart glowed brightly. "I have no more questions for you at this time, Teacher. Thank you for helping me."

The sindona woman bowed formally, then turned and walked away into the trees without another word.

Haramis addressed her talisman: *Take me to the bottom of the Chasm of Durance.*

The chime sounded. The now-familiar crystalline image existed for a moment, then translated to full reality. She stood in a place like a vast cave, overly warm and humid. Part of the roof was solid rock, dripping with stalactites like translucent stone icicles and pillars; the rest of the area overhead was a black void, at the center of which an infinitesimal star seemed to twinkle feebly. Haramis knew at once that this was the steep shaft leading to the surface, and the pinpoint of light marked the faraway upper opening to the Chasm.

A flickering deep crimson glow lit the place, pouring out of obscure nooks and crannies. Haramis strode to one radiant crevice and peered within. She saw an adjacent cavern, much smaller and deeper, and its floor was a river of incandescent magma. She withdrew, and made a further brief exploration of the Chasm itself, finding dark pools of water and many curious rock formations. There were also crumbling remnants of human occupation: blackened rings of stone that had held cooking fires, broken clay jars, plates, grease-lamps, moldering pallets, and a decaying volume that fell to dust when she ventured to touch it.

And on one wall rather smoother than the rest, inscribed defiantly with a sooty stick, was a many-rayed Star.

No other traces remained of those prisoners of twelve thousand years ago. Had any of them ended their lives here? Haramis let her Sight roam afar. She saw that the prison chamber was huge, with many alcoves bearing evidence that they had been some individual's private space. But there were no bones and no marked graves. Nevertheless, Haramis found herself offering a prayer for those who had lived and suffered in this terrible penitentiary, for all that they had deserved their fate. And as she contemplated their ancient misery she could not help but recall her own troubles. She stood alone in the lurid Chasm, praying also for herself.

"Dear God, give me the strength and wit I need to overcome Orogastus! I nearly succumbed to that man once before: let me resist him now! I cannot help but love him, and yet I must find a way to thwart his evil ambition. Help me!"

But the prayer seemed a futile thing, and gave her no solace. Deep within her heart, she knew there were only two ways the sorcerer might be thwarted — by death, or by permanent exile from the world. Haramis realized that, as an Archimage, she would not be able to kill him.

Could she then banish him to this awful place, compared with which the Inaccessible Kimilon was a paradise? . . .

Two scenes from her youth were reborn in memory: the vision of her mother, Queen Kalanthe, pierced by a sword, her life's blood spilled at the sorcerer's feet; and the vision of her father, King Kreyn, torn to pieces in his own throne room at the behest of that same sorcerer.

Could I banish Orogastus here?

"Yes," she said aloud. Stooping, she lay the Cynosure on the floor of the cavern.

She then clasped her talisman, and bade it carry her to Kadiya.

The magical Nut-Wars game had reached a frenzied climax. Prince Tolivar's army of red-painted blok-nuts had suffered heavy casualties in the last battle, but he urged them recklessly to make a final push for the treasure. The defending blue kifer-nut battalions came galloping on their tiny legs, lances outthrust and little faces grimacing with silent howls. Tolo made his charging red troops form a wedge and aimed the point right at the treasure. A desperate maneuver was called for if the red nuts were not to be defeated once again.

"Forward, my men!" the Prince urged, pounding one fist upon the carpet. He lay flat on his stomach so that his eyes would be almost at skirmish-level.

The blok-nuts hit the line of kifers. Soundless tiny pops of light signaled clashes between the individual soldiers. Red-coated warriors, struck by the lances of the blue foe, fell vanquished. Their legs retracted, their faces disappeared, and their little bodies rolled as helplessly as beads when their magical "lives" ended. Blue kifer soldiers fell, too, but the greatest carnage was among the blok-nuts.

"Don't stop!" Tolo admonished his dwindling forces. "Don't turn back! You must seize the treasure now or all is lost!"

The brave remnant of his army tried.

The blunted red wedge re-formed, even though it was now entirely surrounded by massed blue kifer-nuts. It pressed ahead, growing smaller and smaller in numbers as nuts at the outer edges were slain. Slowly, the wedge approached the citadel of the three-legged footstool near the hearth, where the treasure gleamed in the shadows. There were fewer than twenty blok-nuts left alive! Those heading the assault thrust their lances faster and faster at Tolo's command. Blue nuts fell! A tiny space opened.

"Now!" the Prince shouted.

His decimated troops swarmed forward, their legs twinkling. They scattered the foe, slaying those who dared hinder. The poor red-coats in the rear lost their lives, but still the diminishing little arrow of fighters thrust courageously onward. Now there were only five valiant blok-nuts left out of the original force of one hundred. The treasure lay less than a double handspan away.

"You've almost got it!" cried Tolo. "Go! Go!"

Two more reds fell. The surviving trio plied their lances madly and Tolo was dazzled by the death-flashes of the enemy. Then — oh, *no*! First one blok fell, then a second. The last hero pressed on . . .

. . . and its lance touched the treasure.

Instantly all of the blue-coated kifer-nuts gave up their lives in a mad fusillade of sparks, rolling impotently legless about the carpet. The winning blok warrior momentarily glowed like a hot coal as it nestled against the ovoid rusa-nut treasure. The big golden rusa was almost instantly roasted, its tough shell cracked, and the sweet meats fell out ready for Tolo to eat. The tiny face on the last living blok-nut grinned at its human commander. Then it, too, expired.

"We won!" Tolo caroled, scooping up the edible treasure. "We finally won!" He stuffed the rusa meats into his mouth and chewed them with gusto. "What do you think of that, Yellow? And you said I'd never get the hang of it!"

The Yellow Voice did not answer. He was mending one of Orogastus's heavy white boots, and also reluctantly baby-sitting the Prince. The Master had ordered that Tolivar was never to be left alone, in case the insidious Raktumians took it into their heads to make away with the lad and use him in some ploy. The three Voices had also been warned to see to their own safety, going armed and testing all food for poison while yet they stayed in Frangine Palace. Treachery was only a remote possibility; but none of them, not even the Master himself, would be entirely safe until the Tuzameni army and the supply of magical weapons arrived and the war against Laboruwenda began.

Young King Ledavardis had proved less pliable than the Master had hoped. He was by no means the tongue-tied nincompoop he had seemed while under the malign influence of his late grandmother. Instead, he had grown increasingly troublesome, most lately insisting upon full control of the pirate forces in the upcoming conflict, rather than placing them under the command of the Tuzameni General Zokumonus as the Master had urged. Some fresh stratagem would have to be worked out in order to keep Ledavardis in his place.

What a relief it would be when they were all quit of this decadent hive of jumped-up cutpurses —

"It *was* a good game, wasn't it, Yellow?" Prince Tolivar demanded.

"Had it been a real war, rather than one among silly nuts," the Voice said, his lip curling, "the outcome would have been a total disaster. All of your men save the single winner died."

The Prince gathered up the magical red and blue nuts into their pouch, then tossed the nut shells into the fire. "Pooh! What do you know about it? The Master made the Nut-Wars game for me. Winning battles is a job for a prince, not a —" Tolo fell prudently silent, glowering at the stocky, shaven-headed acolyte in the wrinkled saffron robe.

"If you can call that sorry performance winning," the Voice said snidely, pulling a great needle threaded with sinew through the vamp of the boot.

Tolo eyed the acolyte with a sly little smile on his face. "You're jealous. That's why you and the others always make fun of me."

"Don't be silly." The Yellow Voice clamped his lips shut and studied his handiwork with a scowl.

"You are! All three of you are jealous! You can't bear that the Master wants me to be his heir and not one of you!" The boy climbed to his feet, dusted the knees of his trews, and straightened his tunic. "Take me to Portolanus right now."

"He's busy in the library. The last thing he needs is a spoiled child whining about."

Tolo spoke very quietly: "Take me."

Uttering a martyred sigh, the Yellow Voice set his work aside. He took the little Prince by the hand and led him out of the spacious chamber they two shared. The library was at the other end of sprawling Frangine Palace, and the acolyte and the boy had to walk for what seemed like half a league through corridor after ornate corridor, hall after echoing hall. At every turn they encountered haughty pirates and their strident women in flamboyant court dress — some loafing about, some trading gossip, some nervously awaiting an audience with some royal official, a few conducting actual business. Supercilious lackeys dusted the gilt furnishings and picture frames, swept gorgeous carpets looted from the Isles of Engi, stoked the fires, refilled the silver wall-sconces with scented oil against the coming of evening, and scuttled hither and yon on various errands. Stalwart guards kept an eye on the other palace inmates, frowning and gripping their halberds more tightly as the Yellow Voice and Tolo went by.

At last, after the two passed through an untenanted salon full of Varonian sculpture and pearl-studded tapestries from Zinora, they entered a passage of simple dressed stone that dead-ended at a pair of tall gonda-wood doors banded with iron. Standing without was a Raktumian man-at-arms. Beside him upon a folding stool, perusing a decaying volume, sat the runty Black Voice.

Black lifted an inquiring eyebrow.

The Yellow Voice said formally: "Prince Tolivar would speak with the Master."

"Lord Osorkon is due to meet him here very shortly," Black said. "The boy will have to be quick about it."

Tolo looked the man straight in the eye. "My business will not take long." He turned to the Yellow Voice. "You may wait out here."

Yellow genuflected with mock servility and pulled open the heavy doors so that the Prince could slip inside.

The library was a cold, spooky, vaulted chamber with grimy leaded skylights high in the ceiling. Rickety open stairways festooned with dusty lingit-webs gave access to three galleries encircling it. Crowded bookshelves filled these upper levels, and more freestanding shelves occupied the central area of the main floor. Round about the perimeter stood stout tables and benches, all except one gray with the dust of years. The single clean table bore one of the sorcerer's magical lamps that shone with its full strength, for the library was dim except where a few wan, mote-laden beams of afternoon sunlight came through narrow windows on the west side. The great snowstorm had finally ended.

Orogastus was carrying three big tomes bound in crumbling leather back to their shelf. He smiled as Tolo appeared and slipped the books into their places.

"Well, lad! Have you come to help me glean this vart's-nest of its few nuggets of useful magical lore? One can tell from the filth and neglect that the pirates care little for scholarship. Still, they might possibly have stolen something useful when they still bothered to carry off books, so I felt obliged to examine the palace library while we were here in Frangine. Thus far I have discovered only seven volumes worth taking back to Castle Tenebrose, and none of them are especially valuable. Would you like to see how I search? I use the Three-Lobed Burning Eye as a dowsing rod. Do you know what dowsing is?"

"The finding of water or rare minerals through magic," Tolo replied politely.

"Correct — as far as it goes." The sorcerer's once-white robe was blackened by grime and his platinum hair had strands of lingit-web and mold-crumbs in it. He beckoned to the boy to follow him to the next standing shelf, then took the talisman from its scabbard and pointed it at the row of decrepit books. "I have instructed the Burning Eye to point out to me any book containing magical writings . . . thus!"

He swept the dark pointless sword along the shelf. A very small book covered with ruined scarlet leather and a huge one bound about with tarnished brass bands promptly glowed green in the dusk.

"Hah! You see?" He resheathed the talisman and took the monstrous tome in his arms. "You carry that red one to the table and I'll carry this, and we'll see what the Dark Powers vouchsafe."

Dutifully, Tolo followed Orogastus bearing the little red book. The sorcerer wiped both volumes with a grubby rag, then took out the talisman once more. He opened the great book, lay the dull-edged sword-blade upon the opening page, and closed his eyes. "O talisman, reveal to me in a terse summary the contents of this tome."

Tolo could not help but give a start of astonishment as a strange voice intoned:

Herein are contained the incantations of the Sobranian witch Acha Tulume, taken in booty from a vessel of that nation eighty-seven years agone. The book's contents, set down in the Sobranian tongue, are largely shamanistic trivia. The most important spells are useful in controlling zach infestations in feather cloaks, curing armpit itch, bringing about successful bird-hunts, and dissuading jilted lovers and cast-off spouses from doing mischief to their former partners.

Orogastus snorted and slammed the cover shut. "Worthless — unless one intends to set up shop in the Land of the Feathered Barbarians! Now let us try your book, Tolo. Perhaps it will be a prize, for all its slenderness ... Do you know the saying 'The smallest package oft hides the most precious gift'?"

"Yes, Master."

Orogastus opened the tattered cover, upon which much-faded gilt lettering could be seen. "The language is that which most of humanity speaks, but the spelling is archaic. That means it is very old indeed ... Hmm! *A History of the War.* Which war, I wonder?"

He gently laid the talisman across the title page and besought knowledge of the book's contents as before.

Herein is contained a history of the great magical conflict between the Vanished Ones and the Star Men, written some ninety hundreds after the fact by a descendant of a family of data-organizers who survived the Conquering Ice and dwelt in the Smoky Isles —

"Enough!" cried the sorcerer. His silver-gray eyes were wide with excitement as he took up the little book and turned the fragile pages with the greatest care. "Yes! Oh, yes! And rarity among rarities, it is a book written in the land of Raktum itself — before its wretched people embarked upon their career of piracy. This is a treasure indeed, Tolo. I shall have to study it most carefully."

The little Prince, who had worked hard to conceal his boredom, now spoke eagerly. "I, too, won a treasure today, Master! In the Nut-Wars game you made for me. It was a great triumph!"

Orogastus laughed indulgently while examining the red book's dimly scribed table of contents. "Such a game would have been impossible for me to fashion before, with my limited powers. But the two talismans taught me how to make it in the blink of an eye! . . . Of course, it is but a child's toy."

"The Yellow Voice mocked my victory," Tolo said dolefully. "Master, he and the other Voices are jealous of me. When you aren't about, they speak to me rudely, like a person of base blood, rather than treating me like a prince. They are sorry that you made me your heir. I am sure they thought that one of them would be the next Master of Tuzamen."

Orogastus burst out laughing and closed the *History*. "Oh, they did, did they? And have they done any real harm to you, lad? Aside from denying you the deference due to one of your royal birth?"

Tolo looked away, his feigned hurt feelings abruptly changed to sullenness. "No, but — "

"And how do you treat my acolytes?" The sorcerer's voice was now serious. "Are you gracious, as a true prince must always be to his inferiors, or are you toplofty and boorish? Do you realize that my three Voices are my most loyal friends? They rescued me from my exile on the Sempiternal Icecap because their minds were sensitive enough to hear my magical call, and they have served me unselfishly ever since. Much of my success would have been impossible without their help."

The Prince peeped up at the sorcerer with innocent blue eyes. "But now that you have the talismans, you will not need their help so much. I have heard them speak of it among themselves, when they did not know I was listening."

Orogastus frowned for a moment. But then his face cleared and again he laughed. "You do not understand the ways of grown-ups. If you would please me, treat the Voices as loving older brothers. Be polite and kind to them and act modestly. Then you will see that their manners will improve."

"If you say so, Master." Tolo sighed. "But I still think — "

"Obey me!" The sorcerer's affability fell away like a discarded cloak. "And now you must go. I wish you to play a new game. Request of my Yellow Voice a goodly map of the Western World, and study it for the rest of the afternoon and all of this evening. Look especially upon Raktum and the neighboring Labornok coast, and decide how you would invade the land of the Two Thrones if you commanded a pirate armada. Work hard. I will summon you tomorrow, and we will play the game together."

The Prince brightened. "An invasion! That sounds like great fun!"

Orogastus waved a hand in dismissal. The boy bowed his head and trotted obediently away. The sorcerer opened the door for Tolo, using a simple bit of magic, then sat brooding when he was once again alone.

Permitting the little Prince to stay with him had been a decision without logic — one that Orogastus realized was certainly rash and possibly even dangerous. But Tolivar had seemed such a forlorn waif on the ship, frail of body, sharp of wit, so at odds with his robust older brother and sister and seeming not to care that he was separated from his royal parents. The hint of a magical aura about him, and the child's frank hero worship of Orogastus, even in the latter's guise of a repulsive old man, had touched some odd vulnerability in the sorcerer. Not since his first meeting with Haramis had he felt so touched, so . . . ruled by unreason.

In the lonely, discontented little Prince, Orogastus recognized long-buried reflections of another misfit child — a naked foundling taken grudgingly into the household of the venerable Bondanus, who was the greatest sorcerer in the known world and the Star Master of Castle Tenebrose in the seaside city of Merika. That wretched baby, nursed by a drunken slut and begrudged the filthy rags that had clothed him, had nevertheless grown into a strapping lad who earned his precarious keep as a togar-herd and a scullion. He was always maltreated and half starved — until the unforgettable day that his intelligence and his unformed but powerful psychic aura caught the attention of the Star Master of Tuzamen.

The child Orogastus had also been eight years of age when he was nominated as the sorcerer's apprentice.

Bondanus was a harsh mentor but a fair one. He had never shown love for his young protégé nor even fondness; nevertheless he made it clear that Orogastus would inherit all of his magical secrets, and succeed him as Master of the desolate little northern nation. Orogastus became both the pupil and the personal servant of the aging wizard, laboring and studying with naïve enthusiasm, never noticing that the Master isolated himself more and more from the affairs of the country, relegating its rule to a gaggle of predatory and homicidal warlords who carved Tuzamen into a patchwork of tiny, hostile fiefs unified by nothing save their mutual antagonism.

While the Tuzameni peasantry lived in dreary hopelessness and its merchants fled to more prosperous lands, the Master spent his final years meditating upon the ancient Star philosophy of which he had been a lone proponent. When Bondanus finally lay dying, he bequeathed to his apprentice Castle Tenebrose (by then a nearly uninhabited ruin), a small trove of ancient magical apparatus which the old wizard considered to be of only minor importance, and the most precious possession he owned — a platinum medallion in the shape of a multirayed star. This emblem, hung about the neck of Orogastus at the culmination of a frightful initiation ceremony, had given the young man full membership in the ancient Society of the Star.

At that time Orogastus was eight-and-twenty years of age. The ordeal of initiation turned his hair pure white.

Orogastus discovered soon enough that the villainous warlords of Tuzamen would not accept him as their sovereign. The dead Bondanus had ignored them for too long. Orogastus attempted to cow the people with magic, especially with the command of the storm that was his special area of expertise. But the stubborn barons only barricaded themselves in their rustic fortresses when he would have compelled them to serve him, and the commoners were too dull-witted, too ground down by hardship, and too poor to be of any value to an ambitious sorcerer.

For three years he studied the collection of antiquated machines that Bondanus had always dismissed as trivial. Orogastus decided they were nothing of the sort, and in time he found his loyalty shifting from the esoteric, unsettling (and often capricious) magic of the Star Society to the more practical Dark Powers named Aysee Lyne, Inturnal Bataree, and Bahkup. These three deities ruled the Vanished Ones' miraculous devices; and if they were properly invoked, they gave their single worshiper the grace to wreak marvels more immediately useful than the secrets of the Star.

The most important of the machines contained information that eventually led Orogastus to discover another cache of the Vanished Ones in a remote ruined city near the headwaters of the White River, far to the west in Dorok country. There he found magical weapons, as well as many contraptions that would impress and intimidate the simpleminded. Bringing this booty back to Castle Tenebrose, he began once again his thwarted campaign to make himself the true Master of Tuzamen. He might have succeeded if Crown Prince Voltrik of Labornok had not come visiting just then — and changed the direction of Orogastus's life.

Voltrik was a kindred restless soul, a man frustrated by having to wait overlong for his senile uncle to die and relinquish the throne. The Crown Prince suggested that Orogastus extend his vision beyond the miserable wilderness of Tuzamen into the rich Peninsula lying to the south. Together, they might found an empire through conquest!

And besides, the savants of Labornok knew of many other ruined cities, where the sorcerer might find more of the magical gadgets he so coveted . . .

So Orogastus abandoned the land of his birth. Seventeen years later, as the newly crowned King Voltrik's Grand Minister of State, he participated in the invasion and conquest of Ruwenda — only to have all his glorious schemes come to naught because of the interference of Ruwenda's three young Princesses. Protected by a magical Black Trillium even more ancient than the Star, the triplet girls each embarked upon a quest that led to the finding of a mysterious talisman. The three talismans, when assembled into a single dread Sceptre of Power, had turned Orogastus's own sorcery against him. In some incomprehensible manner he had been cast into exile in the Land of Fire and Ice rather than killed by the Sceptre.

"How?" he mused, idly turning the brittle pages of the little red book. "How was it done? The Princesses wanted to destroy me. I know that was their intent! And yet I did not die . . ."

Absently, he fingered the silvery coronet clamped to his brow, the talisman adorned with three grotesque faces that was named the Three-Headed Monster.

"What unknown god took pity upon me and spared me so that I might return to the world and take up again the reins of the ambition denied me so long ago? . . . Master of Tuzamen! I am that now, and the nation that was a barbarous laughingstock now enjoys a modest measure of prosperity and prestige. I am at the threshold of my greatest scheme of all, which will climax in the conquest of the world. I have two magical talismans, and one day I may have all three, and the limitless power they promise! . . . But what is the answer to the mystery of my survival in the Kimilon?"

Look in the book.

Orogastus gave a great start and he clapped one hand to the hilt of the Three-Lobed Burning Eye hanging at his waist. But it was not that talisman that had spoken. The voice in his mind was a new one, no doubt emanating from Queen Anigel's coronet.

With fingers that shook slightly, he riffled the crumbling parchment pages until he caught sight of a portion of text that glowed, even in the bright lamplight.

"Cynosure? . . . "

The strange word leapt out at him, and he read, engrossed, for many minutes. When he understood at last, he lifted his eyes and touched the coronet.

"Talisman! Show me this wondrous Cynosure that preserved my life and drew me to the Kimilon!"

A vision of a black hexagon came into his mind.

This is the Great Cynosure, created by the Star Men twelve times ten hundreds ago to counteract the Threefold Sceptre of Power.

He shouted with excitement. "Ah! I remember! I remember now! The world seemed to explode when the Sceptre of Power smote me, and I thought I was dead. But before my senses left me, I perceived that thing! And it preserved my life, did it? I never saw it when I awakened. Where was it hidden? . . . Would it draw me safe again to the Land of Fire and Ice if the Archimage Haramis used the power of her talisman against me?"

No. The Great Cynosure was taken from the Kimilon by the Archimage

Iriane, who gave it to the Archimage Haramis, who placed it in the Chasm of Durance at the suggestion of the sindona Teacher.

Orogastus was staggered. What was this? Another Archimage? And the sindona . . . All reference books he had read said that the prodigious living statues of the Vanished Ones had been destroyed in the war of the Conquering Ice.

Read on, sighed the voice inside his head.

He lowered his eyes to the glowing pages of the little red book — and it was all there: the survival of certain members of the Archimagical College, the subterranean Place of Knowledge with its guardian sindona, situated in remote Lamarilu, north of the Thorny Hell of Ruwenda . . . and even the Chasm.

His vitals turned to ice as he read of the terrible place where the ancient Star Men had been imprisoned. And Haramis had put the Cynosure there.

"Can I get hold of it?" he asked the talisman. "Can I remove it from the Chasm and hide it in some place of safety?"

Only an Archimage may enter the Place of Knowledge without invitation. It is so pervaded with ancient magic that even the power of two talismans may not countermand it.

Orogastus swore a foul oath blaspheming the Dark Powers. "Can the Cynosure be destroyed in some other way?"

The Archimagical College can destroy it, working in concert. The Star Council, who made it, can also destroy it. But the Star Council no longer exists. You are the only Star Man, and since you are but one, you do not possess the power.

"If — if I could initiate more into the Society of the Star, how many of us would there have to be to destroy the Cynosure?"

At least three.

"Three . . ." Orogastus took a vast breath. He slumped like a creature relaxing from pursuit and wiped his streaming brow with one sleeve of his dirty gown. "Three," he repeated softly.

The red book had lost its preternatural glow. For a long time he stared at it unseeing, while memories swirled chaotically in his brain. Even now, Orogastus could scarcely think about his initiation into the Star without quailing. But the old books and regalia for the ceremony still existed. Orogastus had not bothered to take them along when he had abandoned Castle Tenebrose and accompanied Voltrik. For seven-and-twenty years they lay hidden in an old secret cubbyhole in the castle, and when Orogastus returned from the Kimilon he had found them still safe.

He could create more Star Men! Initiate the Voices! It would take intensive preparation, for the ceremony was so horrendous that unfit novices might be driven insane or even frightened to death. But these Voices were strong and intelligent, much more worthy than his first trio of acolytes, who had perished at the hands of the Princesses. How long might it take to get the Voices ready? A tennight? Two? . . . But the damned war would demand his attention before that! There was not enough time to go back to Castle Tenebrose —

He realized that someone was knocking upon the library doors with increasing vigor. Almighty Bahkup! He had forgotten about the meeting with the turncoat Labornoki nobleman, Osorkon.

Orogastus gestured and the great portals swung open. A man entered, wearing a full suit of black-enameled armor and a heavy raffin-skin cape. His open helm was surmounted by the image of a fierce looru with wings widespread, and the same device, embroidered in gold and crimson, adorned his black silken surcoat. He held in his mailed fist a sword nearly as long as he was tall.

"Are you so uneasy in my presence, Lord Osorkon?" the sorcerer remarked, smiling. "True, we have not seen each other in twelve years, and we were not close comrades then. But the times have changed. We both need one another very much these days." He closed the little red book and motioned for the Labornoki to be seated.

Osorkon sheathed his sword with a singing hiss, then hauled off his helmet and set it on the table.

"It's these pirates I do not trust, wizard! Every step of the way from the docks to the palace, my men and I were harried by gangs of foulmouthed churls who jeered at us and flung snowballs — and worse — without once being deterred by our so-called escort of pirate-knights! Did we not come here at your express invitation? And yet, when we entered this tarted-up den of thieves, we were received without courtesy, forced to hang about in a frigid anteroom for hours, and offered neither refreshment nor so much as an invitation to make use of the garderobe!"

Orogastus wagged his head in sympathy and pointed. "The small door, right between the two pillars."

"Never mind! . . . That surly bastard Jorot finally condescended to receive our delegation. My comrades Soratik, Vitar, Pomizel, and Nunkaleyn of Wum are conferring with Jorot and his admirals now, making certain that our assault by land will coordinate with the sea invasion. And I, as you requested, am here to meet with you."

The sorcerer snapped his fingers and a steaming crock of potent ilisso liquor appeared on the table, accompanied by two large mugs. There was also a loaf of hot bread, a platter of sausages smoking from the grill, a firkin of pickles, and a salver of sliced nutcake spread with cream cheese.

"Let me make small amends for the failure of Raktumian hospitality," Orogastus said. "I fear that the pirates are feckless amateurs at diplomacy. The very notion of alliances is foreign to their culture."

"They're a pack of snotty bandits, you mean." Osorkon stripped off his metal gauntlets, dropped them to the flagstone floor with twin clunks, and blew on his hands. They were blue with cold. He quaffed a warming draft of the liquor, then helped himself to the buffet. "I don't understand why we had to bring Raktum into this scheme anyhow. With my three thousand men and your army — plus some supernatural fireworks, like the kind you had going for us back when we invaded Ruwenda — we can whip the Two-Throne loyalists of Derorguila handily. No need to involve these foppish buccaneers."

Orogastus sniffed a pickle and crunched it up with strong white teeth. In no way was he about to admit that his Tuzameni "army" consisted of only about sixteen hundred men, commanded by nine warlords whose military experience consisted mainly of the ambush of unwary peddlers, livestock rustling, and smash-and-grab raids on each other's villages.

"We need the pirate navy for the swift transport of my men and my magical weapons," the sorcerer explained earnestly to his guest. "The Raktumian warships will ensure that no reinforcements reach Derorguila by way of the sea. The Raktumian flame catapults will neutralize the forts at the entrance to the enemy harbor, and the eight thousand pirate warriors will ensure the swift capitulation of the Two Thrones. It is vital that Derorguila fall as quickly as possible. If the fighting is prolonged, there is a chance that the Archimage Haramis will find some way to come to the aid of her sister."

Osorkon's eyes narrowed. "You mean to say that the Archimage could counter the magic of your two talismans?"

"My powers are now far beyond hers," the sorcerer declared loftily. "But she could wreak great havoc on our plans by spiriting away the royal family or by some other unexpected action. We must strike with irresistible force while Antar and Anigel still have some hope of repelling our invasion, before the Archimage can convince her sister to flee."

"That makes sense," Osorkon admitted grudgingly.

"With their Ruwenda-based force having been diverted to Var, the Two Thrones are left with only about four thousand loyal fighting men . . . plus your own provincial army of three thousand. The total is sufficient to lure them into believing they have a chance against us."

Osorkon burst into raucous laughter. "Until they discover that my followers have turned against them! The Var diversion was a brilliant piece of work, sorcerer—provided that the fun and games down south don't end too soon." His mirth subsided and he scowled. "As it is, we'll likely have to invade Ruwenda all over again to tidy up."

Orogastus smiled over the rim of his cup. "The returning Ruwendian loyalists will discover that another problem awaits them in the Misty Mire. The redoubtable Lady of the Eyes has taken it into her head to incite the Oddlings of Ruwenda to rebellion. All of them! Their objective will be to expel humanity from the country so the Oddlings can rule it themselves."

The old soldier whistled. "Well, well! You *have* set the stewpot a-boiling, haven't you? I suppose you intend to let the Oddlings and the Ruwendian loyalists slaughter each other."

"The humans will certainly be disposed of quickly enough if this unseasonable weather continues. The aborigines have an overwhelming advantage in the Misty Mire during the Rains."

Osorkon tipped the sorcerer a wink. "I suppose you're responsible for the tempests and the earthquakes and all the rest of it, eh?"

Orogastus made a mendaciously modest gesture and refilled the Labornoki lord's mug. "It is all part of my great plan."

"How do we retake Ruwenda after the Oddlings win?" Osorkon asked. "We still need its natural resources — the ship timbers and minerals, especially."

"It's quite simple. All we need do is kill the Oddling leader — the Lady of the Eyes. Without her, the aboriginal host will disintegrate."

"Haw! That's right! You've thought of everything, wizard." Osorkon paused long enough to devour several sausages. "You know, your proposal for an alliance came at a very opportune time. We lords of the western provinces of Labornok have chafed overlong under the insipid rule of the Two Thrones. Some kind of crisis was inevitable. All of my old comrades agreed that your scheme to kidnap Antar and the royal children at the Zinoran coronation was brilliant."

"I am sorry about the death of your sister, Sharice."

Osorkon shrugged. "She agreed to do her part readily enough. She was sick to death of that big blubbergut, Penapat, but afraid to divorce him for fear of losing the favor of the King and Queen. My first duty on assuming the kingship of Laboruwenda was to be the removal of my dear brother-in-law's fat head."

The sorcerer laughed. "You will still have that chance seven days from now, if all goes well. Tuzameni ships should be arriving in Frangine tomorrow with my magical equipment and my army. We will coordinate the invasion forces, then go south in the faster, more heavily armed pirate ships with my magical gale speeding us on. We will put you and your four friends secretly ashore at the port of Lakana, then hide until the appointed day in a great fogbank I will conjure up. You and your force will attack Derorguila by land, and we will invade simultaneously from the sea — "

"And crush Antar like a lingit between two bricks!"

The sorcerer lifted his mug of steaming ilisso in a satiric salute. "I foresee a quick and decisive victory."

"It must be a fine thing to be able to read the future," Osorkon remarked sardonically. Then a look of regret crossed his rough-hewn features. "A pity that Anigel caved in so soon and paid the ransom, though. With King Antar leading the loyalist troops, we'll have a rougher go of it than without him. Even though the defenders are outnumbered, they'll fight like fiends if Antar urges them on."

"I tried to hold off his release, but there were problems. I had a nasty confrontation with Queen Regent Ganondri, and after her timely demise the Goblin Kinglet became unexpectedly stubborn about keeping Antar imprisoned. Ledo is a good friend of mine, but he is a very chivalrous youth, and I could not dissuade him from accepting the ransom immediately when Anigel offered it the second time. However, my having her talisman as well as Kadiya's should more than balance the scale in our favor. We will confront Antar's defenders with magic as well as armed might. His force will be outnumbered more than three to one when we attack Derorguila. With luck, we will win out in a single day."

Lord Osorkon was lost in thought as he licked the sweet cheese off a slice of nutcake. "Queen Ganondri . . . that she-devil! A good thing we won't have her to contend with anymore. Her meeting with the fatal shareek was the talk of the waterfront when we arrived. I trust that the Goblin Kinglet otherwise dances as you pull the strings?"

"I can deal with Ledo," Orogastus asserted.

"I certainly hope so." The Labornoki lord used his tongue to clean his sticky fingers. "It would be a calamity if his pirates got out of control after the victory and began rampaging among the other port cities where my own supporters live. Let the Raktumians loot Derorguila and then return home, and my people will be content. Just remember, wizard: Our bargain does not include turning my future kingdom into a ravaged, burnt-over wasteland!"

"That will never happen," the sorcerer declared. "I swear it by the Dark Powers and by the sacred Star that empowers my two talismans."

Orogastus now rose, waved his hand, and made the food and drink disappear. As an afterthought, he eradicated the dirt from his white robe, and then tucked the precious little red book into its pocket. "I have finished my work here. My magic shows me that Prime Minister Jorot, his admirals, and your stouthearted friends are engaged in a nasty wrangle over who is to have looting rights to Derorguila Palace. Rearm yourself and we will go together to negotiate a cease-fire. Then perhaps we can begin our real council of war."

23

Haramis found her sister Kadiya paddling down the flood-swollen Upper Mutar, accompanied by her faithful companions Jagun and Lummomu-Ko and a second canoe full of Wyvilo. When the Archimage materialized in the boat between the Lady of the Eyes and Jagun and calmly erected a magical umbrella against the pouring rain, Kadiya stared at her sister in speechless chagrin.

"I know what you plan to do," Haramis said, "and I have come to dissuade you."

"What do you mean?" Kadiya's gaze faltered.

"The Teacher at the Place of Knowledge has told me about your new scheme. It is a piece of incredible folly — to say nothing of showing a base disloyalty to our sister, Anigel. You must abandon it."

"My plan is not folly," Kadiya exclaimed. "What do you know of the relations between humanity and the Folk? You have hidden away studying sorcery while disaster after disaster has afflicted our poor Peninsula! You did nothing to help me save my talisman from Orogastus. You did nothing to prevent that idiot Anigel from paying her ransom to him! And now you presume to meddle in my affairs!"

"I come to you out of loving concern — "

"Go away! Nothing you can say will prevent me from doing what I must do. The only way you will stop me is by killing me!"

Little Jagun, who knew nothing of Kadiya's scheme, cried out to her: "Farseer, do not speak so to the White Lady!"

She turned on him like a gradolik deprived of its prey. "Be silent! This is a matter between my sister and me!"

"But it is not," the Archimage said, a great sadness suffusing her face. "It affects Jagun's people, and Lummomu's, and all of the other Folk as well. I am their protector and guardian — "

"They have elected me their leader, not you!" Kadiya said. "Have I not the right to put my proposal to them so that they may judge it — and me — and make a free decision?"

Taken aback, Haramis was silent.

"You know I have the right!" Kadiya cried in triumph. "And you have no way of forcing your will upon the Folk, for they are free souls and not your chattels. So leave us!"

"Only let me explain to you — "

"Archimage, go away," Kadiya said, in a voice low and dangerous, "unless you are prepared to use violence to compel my attention."

Haramis bowed her head. "Very well. I can see it is impossible to reason with you now. But I shall return."

She vanished, and the rain pelted down upon the two canoes more intensely than before.

"Farseer, what have you done?" Jagun moaned. "You should have at least listened to what the White Lady had to say."

"Aye," Lummomu said, and his dismayed Wyvilo companions murmured their agreement.

"I *know* what she would say," Kadiya retorted. "But her speaking would gain her nothing. There was no point in my listening to her."

"But she is the White Lady . . ." Jagun protested.

"And I am the Lady of the Eyes!" Kadiya smote the trefoil upon her breast. Above it dangled her amber amulet with its blood red trillium. "Unless you would all abandon me and go your own way, do not vex me further! Only paddle so that we may reach our goal by nightfall."

The time had finally come.

The Archimage sat alone in her study, in the Tower on Mount Brom that had once been his home and now was her own. A snowstorm of unspeakable violence roared outside, but she never noticed. She went to her favorite chair by the fireplace (that hearth where the two of them had sat together and first come to know one another) and lifted her talisman, gazing into the empty circle. The drop of trillium-amber held in the midst of the three wings at its top shone with a steady golden light, and the three-petaled tiny Flower within was black . . . black.

Now, she thought, I have a true need to look upon him and listen to him. I must determine what his plans are and what danger he poses to my sister Anigel's Kingdom of the Two Thrones and to the rest of the world. Talisman, will you permit me to scry him without loss of my soul? My love for him remains. I cannot help it. I know there is danger in the very Sight of him, but I would be derelict in my duty if I did not look. And so I will.

She said: "Show me Orogastus."

And he was there, striding with heedless confidence along the surging deck of a great Raktumian warship that raced headlong through mountainous seas. His white hair streamed in the wind and his wet robes were plastered to his tall, magnificently muscled body. His face had changed little, except for being more deeply lined, from the way she remembered it. His lips were thin but finely cut, his cheekbones high, his eyes a pale glacial blue beneath snowy brows. He was clean-shaven and wore an expression of exhilaration, as if he partook of the energy of the gale. He had neither of the purloined talismans about him.

Pausing outside the entrance to the trireme's towering sterncastle, he gripped the ship's rail and looked out over the heaving waters. He smiled . . .

Haramis caught her breath. In some way — a way that had nothing to do with the Black Trillium or the Three-Winged Circle — she knew what he was thinking. Not of the conquest of the world or the triumph of the Society of the Star. Not of the Dark Powers or even of the Sceptre of Power that he coveted.

He was thinking of her.

Her heart turned over within her breast and she felt a near-uncontrollable desire to burst into tears. And then to call out to him across the leagues, to bespeak his name and thrill to his answer, to go to him, to touch him . . .

Within the wings of her talisman, the tiny Flower seemed to throb like a beating heart. It was still the color of velvet night, but in another moment it would change —

"No! No no *no*!" She sobbed aloud and flung the talisman from her. It swung on its platinum chain, the vision within the circle extinguished.

She sat for a long time, only praying. Then, charged with fresh resolution, she took a deep breath and said again:

"Show me Orogastus."

He was in a sumptuous stateroom, his clothing completely dry and his hair well groomed, engaged in earnest conversation with his three acolytes. The little minion dressed in black held the curiously wrought coronet called the Three-Headed Monster. The henchman in yellow carried the dark, dull-edged sword lacking a point that was named the Three-Lobed Burning Eye.

" — must keep the King and Queen under close surveillance night and day," the sorcerer was saying. "And you, my Yellow Voice, must oversee the machinations of the Lady of the Eyes. As for you, my Purple Voice — "

Coldly, Haramis settled down to listen.

Kadiya had chosen the Uisgu settlement of Dezaras, deep in the Thorny Hell, as the place to reveal her plan to make all of Ruwenda an aboriginal homeland. Her old friend Nessak, whose life she had saved at the time of the talisman-quest, was still First of the House and Speaker of the Law there; and it was from Dezaras that the original Call had gone out twelve years earlier, rallying the Uisgu and Nyssomu Folk to Kadiya's side for the great battle against King Voltrik that had accomplished the liberation of Ruwenda.

On most of the trip downriver from the Place of Knowledge, Kadiya had been silent and pensive, saying nothing to Jagun or the others of her conversation with the Teacher or the terrible news about Anigel's talisman. In spite of the unsettling visit of the Archimage, the unveiling of Kadiya's new and drastic intention when they reached Dezaras was as much a surprise to her escort party as it was to Nessak and the Uisgu villagers.

Kadiya set forth her war-plan with fervid eloquence, citing the many injustices of the past and emphasizing that conditions for an easy victory were at hand, most especially if the Skritek joined their cause. Her strategy called for attacks only upon the human armed forces. Human civilians were to remain unharmed. Laboruwendian troops returning from Var would be confronted at the natural barrier of Tass Falls and driven back down the river. In Ruwenda itself, the Citadel and the other centers of human habitation would be surrounded and besieged. Cut off from supplies, isolated by the unnatural Rains, the trapped humans would have no choice but to surrender without bloodshed. When they had all been expelled from Ruwenda, the Queen's Mireway leading from the Citadel to the Labornok border would be destroyed utterly, and the isolated plateau of the Misty Mire would become a haven for the Folk alone, a nation that they themselves would rule.

She, the Lady of the Eyes, vowed that she would negotiate a treaty to that effect. And if it was the will of the aborigines, she would also represent the interests of the Folk in all future dealings with humanity.

As a climax, Kadiya told them the amazing statement made secretly to her by the sorcerer Orogastus. He had promised with formidable oaths that the Misty Mire would belong to the Folk for all time once the human settlers had been driven away.

The aborigines did not react to Kadiya's plan with the enthusiasm she had expected. Instead, they listened with faces that were either stunned or frankly horrified. The call to arms by the Lady of the Eyes shocked them deeply, for peace had been almost universal in the Misty Mire since the accession of Antar and Anigel and their Union of the Two Thrones. Only the fractious Glismak of the Tassaleyo Forest and the Skritek, whose bloodthirstiness not even the Archimage or Kadiya could wholly inhibit, had broken the peace during the past twelve years. But now the Lady of the Eyes herself was calling for a war against humanity!

Nessak of Dezaras listened to Kadiya's long, impassioned discourse with unreadable features. When it was finished, the Speaker of the Law agreed to send out the proposal in a telepathic Call to all Uisgu. And because her people were much more powerful bespeakers than Jagun or Lummomu-Ko, Nessak also agreed that certain elders of the village would Call the leaders of the Nyssomu and Wyvilo tribes and solicit their decisions. She promised to contact the Glismak also. However, no matter how much Kadiya urged her, Nessak refused to transmit the war-proposal to the Skritek. If the Lady of the Eyes wished to involve the savage Drowners in her plan, she would have to deal with them herself, at a later time.

Kadiya bowed to the aboriginal leader's resolve, whereupon Nessak, Jagun, Lummomu, and the others withdrew. Kadiya was left to wait alone in the austere guest hut where the meeting had taken place.

She waited for five days.

The rain was incessant and heavy, and the hut a damp and cheerless place for a human. With the Upper Mutar running over its banks in the Thorny Hell because of the unseasonal weather, there was no dry land at all in the village of Dezaras. Its fifty or so small grass houses on stilts were islands in a swollen brown lake. Wicker canoes with empty harnesses for the rimorik pullers were moored to each Uisgu dwelling save for the hut where Kadiya waited. The two big dugouts belonging to her Wyvilo escort were tied up at the house belonging to Nessak and her family.

From time to time food was brought to Kadiya, but the person bringing it would give no news of what the Folk had decided. Finally night fell on the fifth day, and with the darkness a thick mist settled in. As she had done on the previous nights, Kadiya went to the open door from time to time to see if anyone was coming. But she saw only fuzzy lights marking the nearest huts, and heard only the unending patter of the raindrops, together with subdued insect and animal noises.

"They *must* agree to fight for a land of their own!" Kadiya said to herself. "They must!" And she closed her eyes and offered a silent and desperate prayer . . . only at the end of it, she found her right hand straying willy-nilly to the scabbard hanging at her belt, seeking the magical affirmation of the talisman that had once hung there.

But it was gone. Her scabbard now carried only an ordinary sword. "They must fight beside me," she groaned, "or *everything* is lost!"

"It is not," said a soft voice.

Kadiya opened wide her eyes, and uttered a cry of anger as she beheld Haramis, just materializing on the uncovered porch of the guest hut.

"You again!" Kadiya exclaimed. Her sister stood regarding her somberly, her white cloak of office remaining quite dry in spite of the deluge. "I will not let you interfere! You have no right to hinder the free choice of my Folk!"

"I am not here to interfere, nor have I yet spoken to your Folk. I simply wish to have a brief conversation with you. May I come in?"

Kadiya regarded Haramis with seething hostility and made no answer. The Archimage entered and approached the stingy little fire at the hut's center, which burned within a ceramic tray full of sand. Smoke rose sluggishly in the dank air and collected under the rafters, some of it seeping out through the crevices in the sooty thatch and the rest swirling about the interior, helping to drive off the bloodsucking insects of the Thorny Hell at the same time that it made humans wretchedly uncomfortable.

The evening was already becoming chilly, but Kadiya was sweating in her ceremonial corselet of hard golden fish-scales. Her amulet hung from a cord at her neck and her auburn braids were bound tightly to her head. She sat down stiffly on one of several wicker stools beside the fire-pan. When Haramis calmly joined her, Kadiya began to make a great business of pulling dry fern stalks from a nearby basket. She broke them up for fuel and fed them into the small blaze, which she blew upon to keep it from smoldering too badly.

Haramis waited.

Kadiya stayed stubbornly mute for some time, then finally asked: "Did the Teacher send you again? Or was it Anigel this time?"

"The Teacher only told me what you intended to do. I have not bespoken Ani of your terrible plan, but I have warned her that Orogastus and the pirates are sailing down upon Derorguila."

"I knew it would happen. I am sorry for Ani and Antar, but the Folk and I will do what must be done. With two talismans in the hands of Orogastus, humanity is doomed to fall under his power, no matter how hard you may try to prevent it. But the Folk are of no interest to him. If they and I live here peacefully in the Misty Mire,

Orogastus will let us be — no matter what horrors he wreaks upon the human nations."

"How do you know this?" Haramis asked dubiously.

"Orogastus appeared to me in a Sending and told me so."

"And you believed him? Have you lost your mind?"

The trace of a grim smile touched Kadiya's lips as she fed the reviving fire. Flames painted her features with a crimson sheen and the red Flower shone on her breast. "Our old enemy is as handsome and debonair as ever! He, too, can now bespeak anyone in the world through his talismans. But no doubt you two have already had many a cozy chat, disposing of the fate of the world between you."

"No, I have not spoken to him at all," Haramis replied stiffly. "Nor will I, until I am ready to requite him as he deserves. I have commanded my talisman to shield me from both his oversight and his importuning voice."

"You still love him. Deny it if you can!"

"I do not deny it. But I will do my utmost not to let my emotions sway my actions."

"I will believe that when you seek justice for the Folk with the same zeal that you apply to human affairs!"

"My duty is to be a guardian and guide to all persons living on the land, be they Skritek, human, or Folk. This is why I have come to warn you not to make this terrible mistake —"

Kadiya lifted a defiant chin. "It is I, not you, whom the Folk deem their leader! While you remained aloof in your Tower, I have lived and worked with them for twelve years, and sought justice for them in their dealings with our own race. You say that you love them — but what have you done to prove it?"

Haramis remained calm. "The Folk were brought into being by the Archimagical College. Long before there ever was a Lady of the Eyes, there was an Archimage of the Land watching over the aborigines who dwelt there. It is unfortunately true that up until now, I have not been as effective as I might have been." She touched the Three-Winged Circle, and its trillium-amber displayed a sudden surge of golden light. "But things will be different now."

"You intend to supplant me — is that it?" Kadiya exclaimed.

"No. Only to persuade you."

"Then do your damnedest!" Kadiya leapt to her feet. "Show me how you will smite me if I defy you!"

Haramis only shook her head, pityingly.

"Surely you would not let an emotion such as sisterly affection deflect you from your duty!" Kadiya's face wore a mocking grin. "Or is it something else that compels you to a more gentle way of dealing? . . . Tell me, almighty Archimage: Are you truly here this time, or am I once again confronted with a mere ghost?"

"I am here truly. I can travel anywhere now with the help of my talisman, and I can take you with me — "

Kadiya's sword was suddenly in her hand. "Touch me at your peril, Hara. If you attempt to carry me off by force, by all the Lords of the Air and the Three Moons, I will slay you."

"Kadi, Kadi!" Haramis remained seated, keeping her hands folded in her lap, and inclined her head so that her sister would not see the grief that made her eyes glisten. "I would never harm you, never coerce you. Oh, my dear Sister! Why can't you understand? We triplets are Three and we are One! Only if the Petals of the Living Trillium work together can Orogastus and his evil schemes be vanquished. The Teacher tried to tell you this. I have just seen and spoken to her, and she has given me valuable advice that may lead to a solution of all our troubles . . . Put up your weapon and listen to me."

"Leave this place! Only thus will you convince me that your real purpose in coming here is not to traduce me to my Folk. I will not permit you to sway their decision — "

"Kadi, it is too late." The Archimage lifted her head and pointed to the open doorway. "Look."

Kadiya strode out onto the open porch, ignoring the pelting raindrops. A constellation of small blurred lights was approaching through the mist: four canoes with torch-bearers.

"They are coming." Kadiya threw a bitter glance at her sister, back inside the hut. "Will you stay and harangue them? Or bedazzle them with witchcraft if they refuse to obey you?"

"I will do nothing of the kind . . . but you can be sure that I will be watching and listening."

With that, the Archimage vanished.

Still trembling with fury, the Lady of the Eyes sheathed her sword and went down the ladder to the floating landing platform. She took the lines handed to her and made the boats fast. Speaker Nessak and her council of village elders occupied the first three craft; the last one carried Jagun, Lummomu, and several other senior Wyvilo.

Kadiya waited until all of them had ascended, then she followed them into the guest hut.

None of the Uisgu was taller than a human child eight years of age. They somewhat resembled Jagun the Nyssomu, but were shorter and more fragile in appearance, with wider, more upstanding ears, larger golden eyes, and sharper teeth in their broad mouths. Their facial and body fur was oily and their palms slick with protective slime. All except Nessak wore simple grass kilts and had variously colored rings of paint around their eyes. The Speaker was more richly attired in a skirt of blue trade-cloth, a little bejeweled golden collar, two thin gold bracelets, and triple white rings of eye-paint.

Nessak lifted both her taloned hands in salute to Kadiya, speaking in the Uisgu dialect.

"Lady of the Eyes, this one has spent many hours bespeaking our kindred of the Mire. Honebb, here, has bespoken the Discerner Frolotu of the Nyssomu. Kramassak has bespoken Sasstu-Cha of the Wyvilo, and Gurebb has done the best he could with the Glismak. To all of these Folk we sent your Call. Now let us hear the replies . . . Gurebb!"

A venerable little Uisgu male came to Kadiya and saluted her. "This one had a hard time making sense of the forest-creepers' rantings. But it seems, Lady, that they are very willing to join you in war against the humans."

Kadiya's eyes shone and she stood taller. "Thank you, Gurebb."

"Kramassak!" intoned the Speaker.

A Uisgu woman spoke up clearly. "The Elder Sasstu-Cha, polling his people in the absence of the Designated Speaker Lummomu-Ko, states that the Wyvilo will follow the Lady of the Eyes in battle . . . provided that any other race of Folk besides the Glismak does like-wise."

Kadiya beamed at Lummomu and his warriors. But the Wyvilo

chief did not return her smile, but only stared impassively into the fire.

"Honebb — it is your turn," Nessak said. "What of the Nyssomu?"

"The Discerner Frolotu," stated another male, "having consulted with others of her kind, makes it known that the Nyssomu Folk will remain at peace with humanity."

Kadiya's features froze into granite. She turned to Nessak. "And what of the Uisgu, my old friend? What of the Folk who were the first to stand by me in the conquest of the wicked invaders of Labornok? You who first hailed me as Lady of the Eyes, as Light Bearer and Hope Carrier?"

"This one must tell you the truth." Nessak spoke with kind firmness. "We know that the Glismak have quarreled with humans, and we also know that some Nyssomu have from time to time been treated unfairly by human traders. We know that the Wyvilo would prefer to sell some of their precious forest products to the people of Var in the South who promise higher prices, rather than sell all of it to the Two Thrones as they are now compelled to do. But these wrongs can be righted in peaceful ways . . . and so we will not go to war. The Uisgu themselves have no grievance with the human race. Our homes are in the most remote parts of the Misty Mire and our only enemies are the abominable Skritek — and even these monsters harry us only rarely nowadays."

The other Uisgu present nodded and murmured.

"But wicked humans would come!" Kadiya cried. "The Two Thrones are doomed to fall before the armies of Raktum and Tuzamen. There will be a new king in Labornok — and he is Osorkon, one of those vile men who burnt your villages and slew your children twelve years ago. He will make slaves of all living in Ruwenda — unless you follow me and fight to turn this place into a nation of Folk. I have the solemn word of the sorcerer Orogastus that we will then be left in peace — "

"We do not believe Orogastus," Nessak said gently. "Nor do we believe you, when you say that war is the only course open to us."

"My way is the best way!" cried Kadiya desperately. "I would never lie to you! I have dedicated my life to you! I love you — "

Nessak came close to the Lady of the Eyes and looked up at her with sorrow. "I do not think you would deliberately tell us an untruth. And we will always love you. But we can no longer permit you to lead us. May the Flower grant you wisdom!" She pointed to the glowing red trillium within Kadiya's amulet. "I do not speak of *that* flower of blood, but of the other, which you have forsworn."

She turned and walked out into the storm, followed by all of the other Uisgu.

Kadiya looked wildly about at those who remained. "And what about you, Lummomu-Ko?"

The tall Wyvilo leader came and knelt on one scaly knee. "Lady, we have followed you faithfully while the Three Moons thrice waxed and waned. Now we ask you to discharge us, since the other Folk have made their decision and, in doing so, forced our own."

"I—I—" The words caught in Kadiya's throat. But she would not weep or otherwise relinquish control of herself. "Go," she managed to say at last, and Lummomu-Ko rose and bowed, then led his warriors away.

Kadiya watched them go, still disbelieving. Then she shook her head and slumped down onto one of the wicker stools. She began once again to feed pieces of fern-stalk into the fire. "And you, Jagun? Will you also abandon me?" Her voice was dull now.

The little old Nyssomu hunter came out of the shadows where he had stood throughout the drama and climbed onto a stool beside her. He opened his belt pouch and rummaged in it while she waited for him to answer.

"Nothing left to eat but dried adop roots," he complained. "What a day it's been!" Using his knife, he cut a chunk from one of the tough, gnarled things and offered it to Kadiya.

She accepted the piece and chewed it reflectively. "When I was a tiny child and you first took me into the swamp, you taught me to eat these rations. And how many times, as we fled King Voltrik's soldiers, did we sup frugally upon them?"

Jagun nodded. "We have been friends for long years, Farseer. How could I leave you now?" He smiled and held out another bit of root.

Kadiya took it, then turned quickly away as the tears came at last. "Thank you, Jagun."

For a while they ate in silence. Jagun also shared with her his flagon of water.

She said: "Was I wrong, then, as my sister Haramis says? Tell me the truth, old friend."

Jagun ruminated for a time, then replied: "Yes. You were wrong. This war of yours, this plan, was not well thought. If you look deeply into your heart, you will discover that there was a dark motive for it that you refused to recognize."

"What are you saying? Tell me plainly what you think this motive is!"

"Farseer, I cannot. You will believe it only if you find it for yourself . . . but I think the trouble began with the loss of your talisman."

She nodded in agreement. "Yes. Without it, I am no longer the leader I was."

"Nonsense!" said the Nyssomu harshly.

Kadiya blinked in astonishment. He had never dared to speak to her without respect. "But you yourself said that the talisman's loss was the source of my trouble!"

"You mistake my meaning. In your talisman was great power: magical power! But that was not part of *you*. In it was neither your true strength, nor your life, nor that which gives meaning to life. Shiki the Dorok tried to tell you this, and I say it also."

"You are both wrong!"

He shook his head, cutting off another piece of root and popping it into his mouth. It was several minutes before he spoke again. "Power is a thing that few of us are vouchsafed by the Triune. It is neither good nor evil — but it may become one or the other, according to how it is wielded. One may renounce it for good reason and still retain one's integrity. The *loss* of power is harder to bear and may bring humiliation, but it need not dishonor one."

"Anigel's giving of her talisman to the sorcerer was an act of despicable cowardice!"

"No," the old hunter said. "It was done for love, and there is no greater motive. The Queen is neither shamed nor diminished by the renunciation alone."

"But I am both! And this debacle, this rejection of my leadership by the Folk, proves it." She lifted the lurid amulet. "*This* proves it!"

"No, it does not. I think it was not your loss but the way you fought against that loss that darkened your soul. The talisman was not truly an essential part of you until you made it so."

"I don't understand what you are trying to say. All I know is that I am severed from my life's work, a rootless and useless person, and I think my heart will break from the pain of it. What am I to do, Jagun? I do not know what will become of me now —"

"Queen Anigel needs your help most sorely," the old hunter said. "She is threatened by rebellion within and invaders from without, and her own trillium is a sorry blood red because her love for you has soured to hatred. Can you not forget your quarrel and stand by her?"

"Would Ani accept my help after the awful things I said to her? I doubt it . . . But you are right, Jagun. I did judge my sister too harshly — perhaps because I know so little of the love between men and women. She believed sincerely that ransoming Antar was best for her country as well as a solace for her heart, since it restored the King to his people in the hour of great need. She simply did not understand that the three talismans are more important to the safety of the world than her family and her nation. Her decision was a foolish and sentimental one, but I was wrong to berate her so cruelly."

Jagun nodded. "And this war you would foment among the Folk. Can you not see the wrongness in it as well?"

She stared at him, and after a long pause she spoke in a voice both hesitant and incredulous. "Did I — did I wish war so that I might reassert my own lost power? Oh, Jagun! Can I have been so mean-spirited?"

"Only you can say if you did such a thing deliberately."

"I did not!" Her cry was full of misery. "I swear from the bottom of my heart, I did not have such a motive . . . knowingly." She looked away from him, her expression changing to one of incredulous horror. "But one does not always recognize the impulses of the secret heart. And it is possible — oh, God, it is possible that I did it unawares, carried away by the strength of my emotions. You know how impetuous I have always been, how my temperament flames as readily as a pinch of tinder sparked by a fire-shell. Lords of the Air, pity me! I see now . . . but what am I to *do*?"

Jagun said: "You can make amends. This is always possible, as long as you are willing to forsake your wounded pride and continue loving. Loving the Folk who turned from you! Loving your sisters!"

"I *do* love the Folk without reservation! You know that." Kadiya was nearly beside herself with desperation. "And — yes! — I would willingly go now to Anigel, to help her if I could and to atone for my misesteem and failure of love. But it is impossible for me to reach her. It would take me nearly two tennights to reach Derorguila by the overland route in this terrible weather."

"No, it would not," said the Archimage, suddenly reappearing.

"Hara! You said you would listen . . ." Kadiya was torn between her old resentment and her fresh mood of repentance. "Then you know everything. Tell me: Have I judged myself rightly?"

"Answer your own question, dear Sister."

Kadiya clasped her amulet tightly in one hand. "I have wronged both Anigel and the Folk — and I have wronged you, too. For this I am sorry, and as the Triune wills, I will do my best to make it up to all of you."

All agitation fled from her countenance as she let the amber swing free.

"Farseer!" Jagun cried, pointing. "Look!"

Kadiya gazed down at her breast, bereft of speech. Within the gold-glowing pendant was a tiny three-petaled Flower the color of night.

Haramis lifted her cloak. Beckoning Kadiya and Jagun to stand close, she swept out the wings of white fabric to enclose them. "Two Petals of the Living Trillium are reunited," the Archimage said. "Now it is time to seek out the third."

She bade her talisman carry them to Derorguila, and the world around them turned to iridescent crystal.

24

The Black Voice emerged from his trance, his face gone ashen. As soon as the Archimage reappeared in Dezaras he had lost his Sight of Kadiya. But he had seen and heard enough.

He removed the Three-Headed Monster coronet cautiously from his brow, secreted it in an inner pocket of his salt-stained robe, and left his cabin. The Master would have to be informed at once about the collapse of his hopes for a war involving the Lady of the Eyes and the Oddlings of Ruwenda.

Orogastus was in the grand saloon of the Raktumian flagship, playing his new Invasion game with little Prince Tolivar on a large table at the center of the chamber. The table was mounted upon gimbals, so that it remained level even though the big galley was heeled over to take advantage of the powerful storm winds driving the fleet southward. Orogastus and Tolo appeared to be sitting upon thin air, floating neatly in place no matter what gyrations the ship made. As the Voice staggered in through the tilted door, bringing a gust of spume with him, the sorcerer read the thoughts that Black's mind virtually shouted. He then restrained the minion from blurting out his bad news in front of the boy.

"I know what has happened," Orogastus said, accepting the talisman that the chief of the Voices now handed to him. "It is a setback, but by no means a fatal one. Say nothing of this to our noble allies. Go and relieve the Yellow Voice in his surveillance of our port of destination, taking charge of my Three-Lobed Burning Eye. Pay very special attention to any new players who may come upon the scene — if it is indeed possible to view them. See that the Burning Eye never leaves your possession for an instant. Tell Yellow to join the Purple Voice, instructing our men in the use of the magical devices."

"Master, I obey." The wiry little Black Voice bowed and withdrew.

Orogastus put the talisman on the table next to the map, and Prince Tolivar stared at the silvery coronet with keen interest. "My mother never let another person touch that while she owned it. She warned us all that the talisman was bonded to her alone, and if another even laid a finger on it, he would surely die."

"My Voices have permission from me to use the talismans in descrying and overhearing certain events taking place around the world. I do not have the time nor the inclination to spend all my time on watch."

The boy reached out a tentative hand toward the talisman. "Would you give *me* such permission, Master? It would be a great honor."

"Perhaps, someday." Orogastus moved the coronet out of Tolo's reach. "But not now. Do not even think of touching the talismans, lad. They are very powerful and very dangerous. Your mother, the Queen, never knew how dangerous! A half-formed wish, absent-mindedly directed through a talisman, can have terrible consequences. The magic may even turn upon the talisman user if improper commands are given."

"You — you cannot simply order it to do something magical?"

"No. The command must be delivered very precisely, in exactly the proper fashion. To do otherwise is to risk disaster. I allow my Voices only to use the talismans in simple matters, such as the Sight. They know very well not to exceed my orders."

"They do not *always* follow orders," the boy said, with studied casualness. "The Black Voice has been reading the little red book, even though you forbade anyone to open it."

Orogastus frowned. "Indeed?"

"He takes it when you are asleep. I've seen him do it more than once while we've been on shipboard. He takes it to the cabin he and the Purple Voice share. Maybe they read it together."

"That is very naughty of them." The sorcerer spoke lightly. "Perhaps I shall have to put a spell on the book to protect its secrets. It is a very special book, as I have told you."

The Prince's face shone with virtue. "*I* would never read it without your permission, Master."

"Good." The sorcerer made a curt gesture, indicating the map spread before them. "Let us finish the game. Soon I will have to take care of other matters."

Prince Tolivar hitched closer to the table on his invisible seat, shook the bones, and read them. He moved the red-stained ivory marker representing one of his warship fleets closer to Lakana, the large port city nearest to Derorguila on the Labornoki coast.

"I know what you are thinking," Orogastus said with a smile. "You want to keep busy any Lakana reinforcements that might come to the aid of the beleaguered capital."

"Yes. Lakana has fast ships. If it knew Derorguila was under siege by my warships, it would hasten to help."

Orogastus nodded slowly. "I see. But while this move of yours would be good *tactics*, it would not be good *strategy*. Do you know the difference between those two things?"

"No, Master."

"Tactics are the maneuvers you use to win battles. They have short-range goals. Strategy concerns long-range goals —"

"You mean, winning the war?"

"Exactly! Now, I warned you at the beginning of the Invasion game that your turncoat Laboruwendian allies are not sincere friends of your Raktumian invaders. If the pirates attack Lakana, some — or even all — of the rebels may very well change sides again, because many of them have families in Lakana."

"But maybe they wouldn't!" Tolo had a reckless glint in his eye.

Orogastus shook the bones and spilled them. "Let us see. I have as much control of the rebels as you . . . aha! Got you!"

Prompted by the throw of bones, Tolo's entire rebel force turned away from Derorguila to defend Lakana, leaving the sorcerer's loyalists free to repel the dismayed Prince's divided navy. In five more moves, Tolo found his Raktumian invaders defeated. The capital city of Derorguila, which Orogastus had defended, was safe.

"Next time I'll win!" Tolo predicted. "When it's my turn to defend Derorguila. It's my home, after all. I mean . . . it's my home until I move to Tuzamen."

Orogastus laughed. "And you would try much harder when you were defending your home . . . Yes. That is one of the unpredictable things about a war. The bravery and fighting spirit of both sides. Even an outnumbered and poorly armed force may win if its heart is greater than that of its foe."

Tolo eyed the sorcerer shrewdly. "If you *really* wanted to win — more than anything — how would you do it?"

"Not an easy question to answer, lad. I'm no general. But if you simply want my opinion, I'd say that the most valuable weapon of war is surprise. If I were determined to win a real war at all costs, I would choose to do something unexpected."

"Do you mean that you would cheat?" Tolo asked, hesitantly.

"By no means. In a real war, the rules are not as restrictive as in a game. Sometimes, there are no rules at all." Orogastus swept the bones and the red and blue markers into a box of carved horik-ivory. The map that had been their playing board was left in place. "Now you must leave me. Go into the sterncastle lounge for a time. Read some of the books I gave you. I must attend to important business. We are nearly at the end of our voyage, and the great surprise I promised you will soon be revealed."

"Oh, please tell me where we are going!" the Prince pleaded. "No one but the navigator knows where we are — and he won't say anything to me. Are we going to Castle Tenebrose in Tuzamen? I do hope so! I want to see all the magical things! Or are we heading back to the Windlorn Isles to punish the wicked natives and take their treasure?"

"Patience! You will find out in good time. Now be off with you."

The boy dropped out of the air onto the canted, carpeted deck and cautiously made his way through the door leading to the smaller parlor-cabin aft, that had been turned into a temporary library and workroom for the sorcerer.

Orogastus locked the door with a snap of his fingers and sat for a time in silence. Then he placed the Three-Headed Monster talisman on his brow. "Show me the Archimage Haramis," he whispered.

In his mind a swirling mass of light, a rainbow maelstrom, sprang into being, obliterating his sight of the ship's saloon. As always, he exerted his willpower to the utmost, commanding the talisman to reveal the Archimage to him, reaching out to *her* and imploring her to meet him at last, mind to mind. But when the talisman spoke to him, it used the same discouraging formula as before:

The Archimage Haramis will not permit you to descry or bespeak her.

"Let her bespeak me, then!" The sorcerer demanded. "Tell her there is still time to prevent the terrible bloodshed that will begin on the day after tomorrow in Derorguila. She can be the instrument of peace if she will only listen to what I have to say — "

She knows what you would say and rejects any concord between you.

"Damn the woman! . . . She cannot read my mind! What I would propose is new! Talisman, beseech her at least to hear what I have to say. Then if she must reject me, let her do it face-to-face!"

The Archimage Haramis will not permit you to descry her, nor will she bespeak you or meet with you face-to-face until a time of her own choosing.

Orogastus groaned and cursed, tearing the talisman from his brow. The spinning colors vanished, and he saw again the gilt and painted paneling of the Raktumian flagship's saloon. He sighed.

The Queen Regent's portrait, which had hung above the sideboard in the place of honor in the ship's largest chamber, had been replaced by a simple seascape. King Ledavardis did not want his unlovely features adorning public places. Orogastus frowned as he recalled how the young man had refused to cede command of his pirates to the Tuzameni warlord Zokumonus. He intended to lead his eight brigades himself during the attack on Derorguila.

The Goblin Kinglet would have to be carefully watched throughout the upcoming assault — and not only for signs of weakness or treachery. If he should die or be seriously wounded, the Raktumians would probably fly completely out of control. Between the volatile buccaneers and the slippery turncoats, this invasion was going to be touch and go. Orogastus knew he was as yet unable to command great magical prodigies with the two talismans. He could use them to defend his troops and spy out the movements of the enemy; but he was less confident of their offensive potential. He would not win this war with the Three-Headed Monster or the Three-Lobed Burning Eye.

Nevertheless, of the ultimate outcome the sorcerer had no doubt. The defenders were too greatly outnumbered to prevail — and he had the magical weaponry of the Vanished Ones on his side, while the Two Thrones had only Haramis.

Damn her! Why could he not thrust her out of his mind once and for all? His great design had no need of her. *He* had no need of her! . . .

"If she refuses to join me, then she will have to die with all the rest," he told himself aloud.

He sat for some minutes marshaling his composure. Then he asked the coronet to show him the position of the Ruwendian forces who had gone to the relief of Var, helping to drive off Zinora and its pirate allies. That conflict was over now, and the successful warriors of Ruwenda were on their way home.

On the map before him, a scatter of glowing dots materialized along the Great Mutar River, down south in the vast Tassaleyo Forest that formed the indeterminate border between Ruwenda and Var.

Good enough. There was no possible chance that they could come to the defense of Derorguila.

He next oversaw Lord Osorkon and his rebels, and was satisfied to find them hidden in a spindly woodland some sixteen leagues west of the Labornoki capital city. Their presence was kept secret only by murdering the poor charcoal-burners who inhabited the place, together with a few luckless travelers who had chanced to pass along the byway that was the forest's only thoroughfare. The presence of the lurking army would not remain undetected much longer, however. Even if Haramis did not discover them, it was only a matter of time before King Antar would think to question the absence of Osorkon and his provincial lords from the mobs of armed men and knights streaming in to defend Derorguila.

Ah, well. It looked as though matters were progressing as satisfactorily as possible. The Raktumians would have to be alerted to the possibility of loyalist ships coming upon their flank from Lakana, but that was easily done. Orogastus laughed out loud. Another useful piece of intelligence gleaned from innocent Tolo! The boy had also let slip some valuable details of the fortifications around the palace. Haramis would no doubt try to defend her sister with magic, but in the end Queen Anigel, Crown Prince Nikalon, and Princess Janeel would either be captured or die, and so would Kadiya if she chose to make a stand with her sister.

With the lot of them executed, Antar slain in battle, and the loathsome Lord Osorkon dealt with as he deserved (one could never let turncoats live), little Prince Tolivar would be the only living heir to Laboruwenda. It would become a docile vassal-state to Raktum . . . for so long as it pleased Orogastus to humor the Goblin Kinglet.

Everything was going to work out so beautifully. And it would even be legal.

Orogastus nodded with satisfaction as these thoughts and others passed through his mind. The world had never been more ripe for his domination. Boy-Kings in Raktum and Zinora, and soon in Laboruwenda as well. Senile monarchs in the Isles of Engi, and a dithering twit on the throne of Var. Imlit and Okamis were republics governed by feckless merchants, while the rich southern nation of Galanar was ruled by an aging woman whose only heirs were silly daughters. Sobrania, with its hard-nosed barbarians, would take a bit more muscle to subdue, but in time it would also fall . . . and the known world would finally be at his feet.

Then there would be no magic he might not accomplish! If the third talisman did not come to him at once, it would eventually. The Society of the Star would finally rule, after twelve thousand years of waiting.

The Star . . .

Its new members would have to be completely loyal to their Master.

Orogastus now frowned as he recalled what Tolo had said about the Black Voice's surreptitious reading of the little red book. Although he made light of the matter to the little Prince, the sorcerer had been deeply troubled at this hint of insubordination on the part of his chief acolyte. Black, for all of his puny stature, was the most able of the Voices, the one most suited for near-immediate induction into the Society of the Star. But was his submission to the Master truly wholehearted? And what of the loyalty of the Yellow and Purple Voices?

Brooding, Orogastus came to a reluctant conclusion.

It was no longer possible for him to postpone what had to be done. Before the turmoil of the war began, he would have to determine once and for all whether the three Voices were truly faithful to him — or whether they had allowed discontent and jealousy to poison their convictions.

He put the coronet back on his head and called the acolytes to him.

The Black Voice, the Yellow Voice, and the Purple Voice came hurrying into the saloon. The wind had diminished and the great ship now rode on an even keel. Black, who had been using the Three-Lobed Burning Eye to survey Dezaras as well as Derorguila, was quick to tell his Master that the Uisgu villagers were agog at the mysterious disappearance of Kadiya and Jagun.

"Some fear that the two have been abducted by you, Master," the Black Voice said to the sorcerer. "We know this is impossible — and the inescapable conclusion is that the Archimage has somehow spirited them away."

Orogastus rose from the table and began to pace to and fro, considering this unwelcome possibility. Might Haramis have learned such an impressive trick? He knew nothing at all of what she had been up to for the past twelve years. But if she could transport people magically, why had she not rescued Antar or the children earlier? Why had she not transported Ruwendian soldiers to assist in the defense of Derorguila? Orogastus knew better than to ask his talismans for the answers to these questions. They were adamantly silent concerning every aspect of the Archimage and her affairs.

The Black Voice was continuing his report. "I saw no trace of Lady Kadiya in Derorguila. But, of course, if she is under the magical protection of the Archimage, she would be as invisible to my Sight as the White Lady herself. Master, this incident could be of the gravest import. If the Archimage can spirit people away, might she not take the Queen and the two older royal children from Derorguila during our attack? That would frustrate your scheme to have Prince Tolivar become the heir to the Two Thrones and surrender Labornok and

Ruwenda to you after the deaths of the other members of the royal family."

"I think not," the sorcer replied, after some thought. "Even if Anigel did escape death, she would be helpless to prevent our victory. She is no warrior like her sister Kadiya. We can always give out news that she and her children have perished, and Laboruwenda would have capitulated long before the Queen could issue a denial or scrape up a new army to oppose us."

"You are undoubtedly right, Master," said the Purple Voice. "Not even the Archimage can turn away a force of thirteen thousand men."

"If she could," the sorcerer said with a smile, "she would have done so long before now. Within another hour this fleet will be in position off the coast of Labornok. Lord Osorkon's men are already poised to strike. All that remains is the final coaching of our Tuzameni warriors, who will use the weapons of the Vanished Ones. We will proceed with the original plan to attack Derorguila on the day after tomorrow . . . And that brings us to my reason for summoning you, my beloved Voices."

He held out his hand for the Three-Lobed Burning Eye, and the Black Voice surrendered it with a servile bow. The three acolytes stood expectantly in a row. The sorcerer held the talisman by its dull-edged blade so that the three lobes were upright. On his brow rested the Three-Headed Monster.

"My Voices, in recent times I have learned disquieting things: that some of you were jealous of little Prince Tolivar, resenting my plans for him; that some of you feared I would no longer need you, now that I have two talismans to augment my magical powers; that some of you have disobeyed my injunction not to touch the small red book entitled *History of the War.* Even worse, there have been two occasions when I sought out the star-box and could not locate it until I asked the help of the talismans. And then I found the box where someone had left it . . . apparently to examine in secret."

The three Voices broke out in a babble of fervent denials and declarations of fealty. Orogastus lifted his hand to command silence. "There is no need to speak. Not when this talisman"—and he lifted the pointless sword—"provides a sure way of ascertaining the truth."

The three acolytes stared at the dark triple pommel with dawning comprehension. Beads of moisture broke out upon the brows and shaven skulls of the Yellow and Purple Voices. The Black Voice turned waxen as a corpse in his funereal garments.

"Now, there are some sins that are venial," Orogastus went on. "Sins such as imprudent curiosity, or pettishness, or spiteful murmurings that are not heartfelt — these may be easily repented and easily forgiven. But there are other sins that so stain the soul that no forgiveness is possible short of the life beyond — and these sins heaven may forgive, but I will not! They include the kind of malicious jealousy that would do the envied person harm, and disloyalty to one's master, and coveting of the master's power."

Orogastus held the talisman before the Purple Voice. "Place your hand upon the pommel and swear that you harbor in your soul none of the mortal sins I have just cataloged."

With trembling lips and eyes that had begun to leak tears of fear, the Voice touched the three lobes. "I — I swear," he whispered.

The triple lobes split open and three Eyes gazed briefly upon the Purple Voice. Then they closed and the man seemed to collapse like a pricked balloon. "They did not kill me!" he cried shrilly, then burst into sobs, hiding his face in his hands.

Not without pity, Orogastus said: "Compose yourself, my Purple Voice. You have passed the test, and one day soon you shall be inducted into the mighty Society of the Star."

The Purple Voice gulped, and his weeping ceased like a tap shut off.

"And now you, my Yellow Voice," Orogastus said.

The burly minion in the saffron robes was braver or more righteous than his brother. He did not falter as he touched the lobes. The eyes of the Folk, of humanity, and of the Vanished Ones opened wide, studied him, and then closed. The Yellow Voice breathed a heavy sigh.

"You too, my Voice, are proven," Orogastus said. "And now the final test."

He held the talisman before the Black Voice.

For an instant the chief of the acolytes hesitated, looking deep into

Orogastus's own eyes. The merest hint of regret creased his parchment-pale face, and he spoke without emotion:

"We submerged our lives — our very identities — in you, Master. We served you with all our strength. And yet when the time came to choose your heir, you did not choose one of us. You would have given all to that wretched brat . . . but not to us, who had so loved you."

He slapped his hand down upon the triple lobes defiantly, and when the talisman's eyes opened, they glared. A blast of blue-white light burst forth from them, striking the Black Voice full in the forehead. Without a sound he fell to the carpeted deck, his black garments untouched while the body within was burnt to a cinder.

Orogastus turned away so that the other two would not see his face. "Remove the cadaver and consign it to the sea. Then you, Yellow Voice, may return here for the Three-Lobed Burning Eye. Continue your careful surveillance of Derorguila while the Purple Voice completes the instruction of the troops."

"Master, we obey." Numb with shock, the two acolytes bent to pick up the remains of their former brother.

On the other side of the inner saloon door, Prince Tolivar moved trembling away from the keyhole and crouched in the darkest corner of the cabin with his thumb in his mouth. He was frightened almost to insensibility. Had not he himself coveted the power of the talismans? Had he not committed a sin that was even worse? Oh, why had he given in to temptation?

If the Master should ever think to test *him,* he would be blasted to death as surely as the Black Voice had been.

And the game of Invasion, that Orogastus and he had played so happily, was not a game after all! The sorcerer was sailing to Derorguila, and he and the pirates would *really* invade the city. And kill Mother, and Father, and Niki, and Jan . . . and use *him* as their puppet, the way the horrid Pirate Queen had used the Goblin.

"I have been a silly baby," Tolo said to himself, "just as Father said." He would have started blubbering, except something told him that if he made any noise — or indeed indicated in any way that he had heard what had happened in the next chamber — he would die as quickly as the Black Voice had.

And so Prince Tolivar climbed up on a settee, opened one of the port-lights, and took deep breaths of the cold, salty fog outside. When his funk had somewhat abated, he sat down with one of the books the sorcerer had given him and forced himself to read, moving his lips as he silently sounded out each word.

Orogastus unlocked the door over an hour later and said it was time for supper. "And did you learn much from your studies?"

Tolo giggled sheepishly. "Not so much as I might have, Master. I'm sorry — but for most of the time, I was asleep. Reading these big words is so very hard, and I was tired after our exciting game."

"Never mind," said the sorcerer kindly. "There will be plenty of time for you to read later."

He took the little boy by the hand, and they went together to the royal mess where King Ledavardis and General Zokumonus and the nobles of Raktum and Tuzamen waited.

T here! Did you feel it that time?"
Queen Anigel's voice was shrill and
strained, and her hand went involuntarily to
the bosom of her gown, where the trillium amulet was hidden within
the folds of heavy woolen cloth. She stood with King Antar at the
window of their withdrawing room on the uppermost level of the
great Zotopanion Keep of Derorguila Palace. They had finished
supper and had been looking down at the diminishing activity in the
courtyards below when the new tremor occurred. This time the earth
movement was strong enough to make the glassware on the supper
table tinkle faintly and the hanging gilt lamps began to sway.

The King took hold of his wife's chill hand. Even with a great fire
roaring in the hearth, the room was frigid. "Yes, I felt it. It was
certainly a small earthquake. But there is nothing especially sinister
about it, beloved. When I was a lad, there were minor disturbances of
the land from time to time, but never any harm resulting."

"This is different," the Queen insisted, her sapphire eyes shadowed with dread. "Something deep within me senses a terrible
catastrophe poised to come upon us. And not only Orogastus and his
wretched fleet of pirates! Something worse. The earthquakes are
another symptom of the growing imbalance of the world for which I
am responsible —"

"Hush, my love. It is no wonder that you are overwrought, with the
Raktumians ready to attack us."

Antar pressed a gentle finger to her bloodless lips and took her in
his arms. He had on the heavily padded leather undergarments that

are worn beneath armor, for he planned to tour the fortifications that evening. His face was drawn and there were dark circles about his eyes from lack of sleep. Both of them had worked long hours during the past six days, ever since the Archimage had told them of the invasion plan of Orogastus; but mere fatigue could not account for the Queen's state of near hysteria, and Antar worried as much about her as he did about defending his capital.

"Nearly ten thousand pirates!" Anigel whispered, clinging more tightly to her husband. "They could be approaching the city at this very moment under the cover of the storm!"

"But your sister the Archimage assured me once again this morning that their invasion would not begin until day after tomorrow. And she has promised to help us counter the evil magic of Orogastus so that the fighting will be man against man, insofar as is possible."

"Haramis promises to help, but she does not say how! Why has she been so evasive about the nature of her new powers? When I begged her to destroy the pirate fleet with her talisman, she said she could not! I told her that only four thousand trained warriors responded to our call to arms, and yet she says it is impossible for her to transport the returning Ruwendian troops to Derorguila by magic —"

"If Lord Osorkon and his army remain loyal, as I still have reason to hope, we will have enough reinforcements to turn away the foe even though we be still outnumbered. Derorguila's defenses are strong. Raktum has attacked us five times without success during the past hundred. Even if our blockade of Dera Strait fails, the bombards on the fortified heights on either side of the harbor entrance will surely repel any attempt by the invaders to come ashore. As to the nature of the help that the White Lady may give us, we can only wait upon her pleasure. She said she would come to us when she could. Until then, I can only make the most prudent preparations possible and pray for the protection of the Triune and the Lords of the Air." He took Anigel's face in his hands. "And you must do so as well, my love. Pray also that my strength and courage will not falter."

"I'm sorry," Anigel whispered, holding tight to him. "What a fool I am, making things more difficult for you with my morbid fancies."

He kissed her. "I love you. Remember that."

It was still raining heavily, and now and again bits of sleet ticked against the windowpanes. Sleet — in a place as far south as Derorguila, and in the Dry Time to boot! The King repressed a shudder. Anigel's queer premonition of worldwide disaster might well have truth in it after all . . .

Although it was barely sundown, the city was nearly as dark as night, enveloped in icy mist. The streetlamps and the watchfires along the palace ramparts were already burning, adding smoke to the miasma that hung over the sprawling capital. Derorguila, the largest and richest city of the Peninsula, was in the final stages of preparing to repel the Raktumian invasion.

The inner precincts of the palace grounds were filled with troops of newly arrived soldiers, knights mounted upon war-fronials, and squads of guardsmen. Outside, a few late-coming carts loaded with food, firewood, and ammunition for the catapults came up the royal promenade. Officers waving torches kept the teamsters moving and preserved order among the thinning streams of carriages and pedestrians. Most of the noncombatants who had been ordered to leave the city were already gone. Those mansions near the palace that had not been abandoned by their panicked owners were having their lower windows boarded up by servants.

The sky in the direction of the waterfront glowed crimson from the bonfires kindled along the docks. The larger ships of the Laboruwendian fleet had long since put out to sea in order to engage the pirate armada when it finally approached the shore; and now the smaller vessels that would chain themselves together and block the harbor entrance were taking on men and supplies and preparing to move into position.

A gust of wind wailed and more sleet smote the window like a flung handful of coarse sand.

"This ungodly weather!" Anigel drew her heavy shawl more closely about her shoulders. "Our warriors are not properly equipped to fight in such cold, and the civilians who have fled into the countryside will suffer terribly if the siege of the city is much prolonged."

"If Osorkon and the other provincial lords remain loyal, we may hope to prevail. They can muster at least three thousand men, and in a defensive situation their reinforcements should suffice. The foul weather is more of a disadvantage to the foe than to us."

"But will Osorkon come?" The Queen was dubious. "He has continued to profess loyalty, I know, and denies that he colluded in the plot of his sister Sharice. But he and his followers have always resented the presence of Ruwendians in the government of the Two Thrones."

"Osorkon will come," the King insisted. "Only a few hours ago a messenger from Kritama arrived with word that his troops are on their way. They would have taken to the road sooner had the storms had not made the highways in the western provinces nearly impassable."

"If I only had my talisman!" Anigel sighed. "With it I would be able to spy Osorkon out and determine whether he has really cast his lot with our enemies, as Owanon and Lampiar believed he would . . . The talisman would also let me confirm or disprove a certain dire rumor that Lady Ellinis heard today from one of the carters."

"And what is that?"

Anigel hesitated, and her reply was heavy with foreboding. "Oddlings are said to have come down from remote mountain valleys in the far west, driven from their accustomed haunts by the great cold. They told the peasants that the Conquering Ice was once again on the move and would engulf the world if its imbalance were not put right — "

"Nonsense!" scoffed the King. "The tempests are surely the work of the abominable sorcerer. He is using the weather as a weapon. Even in the old days he boasted of how he ruled the storm. But he dare not continue his meddling for much longer, lest his own people be endangered — *Great Zoto!*"

Again the massive stone walls of the keep shook. This time the temblor was so vigorous that a cloud of black soot rolled forth from the chimney, half smothering the fire. Two small panes of the window cracked, and the King's armor that had been laid ready on a trussing coffer fell clanging to the stone floor. Anigel buried her head in her husband's chest, but made no outcry while the building continued to tremble.

Then all was still.

"It is over," Antar said. "We had better go on a quick tour of inspection —"

Someone began to pound upon the door.

"Enter!" called the King.

Lord Penapat the Chamberlain stood at the threshold, his round face pale. Close behind him were three caped and hooded figures.

"My — my Liege, these great ladies and their companion have just arrived and request an audience with you and the Queen."

A woman in a white cloak pushed past the Chamberlain and came into the room. "We did not expect to be welcomed by an earthquake, however."

"Hara!" Queen Anigel cried joyfully, recognizing her elder sister and rushing to her. "Thank God! And you're really here, not merely Sending your image! How wonderful!" The two embraced. "Did you fly here on lammergeier back?"

"No. My talisman will now take me anywhere in the world — together with those whom I touch." Kadiya and Jagun the Nyssomu also entered from the corridor, and Anigel stared at the two in blank astonishment.

"You can transport *them* by magic — but you cannot bring the reinforcements from Ruwenda?"

"I cannot bring enough men in time to do you any good," the Archimage said. "And the Ruwendian warriors are worn-out, and many recovering from wounds suffered in Var. It is better if I use my magical energies more productively."

"Tell us how — *oh!* God help us! It is happening again!"

The palace shivered once more in a minor earthquake.

Haramis lifted her talisman and murmured words none could hear, then said: "I have surveyed the earth beneath Derorguila. There is at the present time no danger of a severe quake."

"We must tell our people not to worry," the King decided. "Penapat, go at once and spread the news that the Archimage is here and will protect —"

"No!" Haramis exclaimed. "No persons save those here must know of my presence. And you must all take care not to betray me. Orogastus spies upon you constantly through his talismans. My assistance to you will be most valuable if the sorcerer has no inkling of where I am, or what I plan to do."

"But the people will be terrified of further temblors," the King said. "Can we not reassure them?"

Haramis considered, then her face brightened. "Lord Penapat, go to the savant Lampiar. Have him announce that his geomancers have determined that the earthquakes are over and there is nothing more to fear. But remember! Say nothing of my presence here, nor of the Lady Kadiya or Jagun."

The Chamberlain bowed and withdrew, closing the door.

Now Kadiya approached the Queen, holding out her hands with a tentative smile. Anigel's expression at once lost its warmth. She only nodded at the Lady of the Eyes, then turned from her and spoke to the Archimage.

"Tell us what news you have of Orogastus and the pirates. Is it still their plan to attack Derorguila two days from now?"

"The Raktumian fleet could be here in less than three hours," Haramis said. "They are hove to in the open sea just off Dera Strait, concealed in a bank of fog. They are only awaiting the sorcerer's command to strike. However, from what I have overheard through my occasional descrying, they still plan to invade on the day after tomorrow. There is a matter of training the warriors in the use of certain unusual weapons that Orogastus has provided."

"What of Lord Osorkon and his sympathizers?" the King asked urgently. "Are they on their way to help defend Derorguila, as they promised, or do they plot treachery?"

"I can find these people for you," the Archimage said, frowning, "but I cannot read their hearts. Still, they may betray their intentions as I observe them. Give me a moment to determine their whereabouts . . ."

With Antar and Anigel anxiously waiting, Haramis again took hold of her talisman and her expression became remote. She stood frozen for many minutes, and as the time of her trance lengthened Kadiya ventured to speak:

"I understand your reluctance to welcome me, Anigel. I acted toward you in a despicable fashion. I had no right to upbraid you for giving your talisman in ransom for your husband and children. The decision was your own to make. I — I regret my hateful behavior from the bottom of my heart, and I beg your pardon."

"I forgive you," Anigel said coldly. But she made no move toward her sister.

"I will gladly help in whatever way I can in the defense of your country," Kadiya added.

"One more warrior," the Queen replied, "can hardly make a difference when Raktum and Orogastus attack our outnumbered force. But if my husband would have you join his fighters, I can hardly object." She turned away again and busied herself picking up the fallen pieces of the King's armor. Little Jagun, effacing himself, had crept away to the fireplace, where he began to sweep up the soot and ashes and add fresh fuel to the faltering flames.

"I am sorry that my apology seems unable to heal the breach between us." Kadiya spoke low and fervently. "If my presence affronts you, I can ask Hara to transport me elsewhere. But I swear that I would give my life in the defense of you and your children."

"Thank you, but that will not be necessary. Since you long ago cast your lot with the aborigines rather than with humankind, it would probably be best if you rejoined them . . . If certain rumors are true, the Folk may soon require all the help you can muster."

"What do you mean?" Kadiya exclaimed.

Anigel whirled about, a single steel gauntlet in her hands. Tears were starting from her eyes. "We are doomed — that is what I mean! Humankind and aborigines alike. I do not speak only of the invasion of this city and the fall of the Two Thrones, but of the very destruction of the world! And it is *my* fault, and yours also, for letting our talismans fall into the hands of that devil Orogastus!"

"Has she gone mad?" Kadiya inquired of Antar, appalled. "Surely what she says cannot be true!" She held up the amber amulet that she wore around her neck. "Ani — dearest Sister — look! My Flower has turned again to its proper black. Surely this is an omen of good fortune and not a signal of impending doom."

Tears continuing to course down her cheeks, the Queen put down the metal glove and drew her own amulet out of her clothing. The scarlet of the trillium embedded within was like a splash of blood on her bosom.

"Perhaps I was wrong then about the fate of the Oddlings, and it is only humanity that will perish as the Conquering Ice reclaims our poor world!" Anigel gestured at the window. "Do you hear the frozen rain and the howl of the biting wind? Such weather may be commonplace in the high mountains and in the northern wilderness of Tuzamen — but it is unheard of on the temperate shores of Labornok. The world is turned upside down because of those damned talismans of ours! You and I never knew how to control them, and I am convinced that Orogastus does not know how to, either. He is loosing God knows what upon us, and the earthquakes and the awful weather are only hints of the great cataclysm to come! Let our sister, Haramis, deny the danger if she can!"

Antar and Kadiya looked to the Archimage, but she was still in her trance.

"What does she mean about the Conquering Ice?" Kadiya asked the King.

"It is a rumor — only a rumor of Oddlings fleeing their inland valleys." He threw up his hands. "But who can say if it is not true? Lampiar, who is the greatest savant among us, avers that this land has never known such a calamitous stretch of weather within historical times. During the last sixnight nearly a third of the Labornoki grain crop has been destroyed. What has not frozen has been spoiled by flooding, and the crops remaining are greatly endangered. What does it matter whether the disasters be supernatural in origin or not? Even if we did not face an invasion, our country totters on the brink of ruin."

"I have found Lord Osorkon," said the Archimage suddenly. Antar and Kadiya turned to her with renewed hope and even the Queen's woeful face lifted. "He and an army of some twenty-nine hundred men are encamped in the Thicket of Atakum sixteen leagues southwest of this city."

"Wonderful!" the King exclaimed. "Why, they can be here tomorrow easily!"

"I fear not," said the Archimage. "They have been in the Thicket

for at least two days, and they show no sign of being ready to move
out. In my quick oversight of the camp I was unable to glean any
concrete information about Osorkon's plans . . . nothing except the
certainty that his army will not move until the Raktumian invaders
land in Derorguila and the fighting is well advanced. Only then will
Osorkon march into the city."

"Zoto's Teeth!" groaned the King. "Then he is indeed a traitor!
And not only to the Two Thrones, but very likely to his filthy pirate
allies as well. Beyond a doubt his scheme is to hold back until our
defenders and the Raktumians are both decimated. Then he will
attempt to seize control of the city himself."

"The treacherous qubar-spawn!" Kadiya cried.

King Antar turned to the Archimage. "White Lady, it seems now
that you and your magic are our only hope. With only four thousand
warriors, we cannot possibly defend Derorguila against attacks from
both land and sea."

"I am one woman and my expertise is but new-fledged," Haramis
said. "I will certainly try my utmost to help you, but Orogastus may
very well be able to counter my magic with his own powers . . . And I
can in no way seek deliberately to bring about the death of these
invaders. Such would be contrary to the archimagical principles that I
live by. I am charged to be the protector and guardian of all persons
who live in this land, no matter what their nation or their race."

"You — you would not use your magic to slay these unjust aggres-
sors?" Queen Anigel cried, full of indignation.

"No," the Archimage replied. "Not even to save your Two
Thrones."

Kadiya spoke calmly. "But, Hara, what if Ani is right and the very
world is endangered? Would you not kill Orogastus to save it?"

Haramis lowered her gaze. "The point is moot. If I can overcome
his magic, it will not be necessary to kill him. There is . . . a place
where he can be safely imprisoned."

"*If* he does not destroy you first!" Anigel cried. "*If* he does not
destroy the world!"

Haramis said: "Orogastus does not understand the mortal danger
inherent in the Sceptre of Power, nor do I understand it fully. I shall

have to consult with my friend the Archimage of the Sea to determine how best to counter the disturbances of the natural order."

"You had best do it quickly," Anigel cried out, "before the pirates burn Derorguila to the ground, and Orogastus brings the Three Moons themselves tumbling down about our ears!"

"Ani—how can you speak like that?" Kadiya said, stunned by the Queen's bitterness.

"Peace, wife, peace!" urged the scandalized King. "Your sisters have come here seeking to help us. Can you not show them gratitude rather than this undeserved reproach?"

Anigel looked wildly from Haramis to Kadiya, then exploded into a storm of weeping, her entire body shaking with anguish.

Once again Haramis opened her arms to the Queen. She cradled her and murmured comforting words as she had done long years ago when the three of them were young triplet princesses, with Haramis the sensible eldest and Anigel the youngest, timid and shy. Kadiya pulled up a chair and Anigel subsided into it and then began to recover.

"I am behaving like an idiot," the Queen whispered. "Like a child rather than a monarch of the Two Thrones. Ever since my trillium turned to scarlet, I have been beset with horrid nightmares and feelings of dire foreboding. My courage has deserted me and I see only darkness ahead."

"If you could restore your Flower," Kadiya said, "your soul would also heal."

"I have no doubt of it." Anigel now spoke listlessly. "Since your own Black Trillium returned to you, perhaps you should tell me how you managed it."

"I only know that when I repented of my hating and despising you, and accepted that my Folk had rightly rejected my call to war, the Blood Trillium was transformed."

"I have already told you that I accept your apology," the Queen said. "As you have seen, it made no difference to my amulet."

"I saw," said Kadiya, "and the sight froze my heart. But what the remedy is, only you can say, little Sister." And the Lady of the Eyes looked away from Anigel and addressed herself to the King.

"Would you have me leave, Brother-in-Law, or can I be of service to you?"

Antar had stood mute, impotent in the face of his wife's pain. But now his countenance furrowed with thought and a fresh light of resolution came into his eyes.

"Rather than answer that, let me tell you of an idea that has just occurred to me. A way that might possibly serve to neutralize Osorkon's treachery. The plan is audacious and dangerous, and perhaps it is even futile. You three will have to help me decide."

Haramis and Kadiya nodded gravely. The Queen seemed to shrink into her chair, seized with fresh apprehension. But she said nothing.

"I do not believe that the provincial lords following Osorkon are irrevocably committed to him," said the King. "If I were to sally forth this very night to the Thicket of Atakum with a small troop of my most valiant knights, and if I challenged Osorkon to single combat and vanquished him, then I am virtually certain that his followers would adhere again to the Two Thrones if I pledged them amnesty. There are nearly three thousand of them. With those additional men fighting on our side, we would at least have a chance of turning away the pirate invaders from our country . . . whatever the subsequent fate of the world."

"No!" cried Anigel. "Osorkon is an unchivalrous scoundrel! You would be slain before you could ever announce your challenge."

Antar inclined his head to the Archimage. "Not if the White Lady were to use her magic to help me penetrate the camp of the traitors without being discovered. If she could render me and my men invisible, or perhaps disguise us in some other way so that we would not be stopped until I called out Osorkon, my plan would work. He could not refuse me without disgracing himself in front of his army."

"It is a splendid idea, Antar!" Kadiya said. "Let me go with you."

Haramis nodded judiciously. "Your idea does seem feasible. I can keep Osorkon's force under surveillance, advising you of his movements and his intentions as you approach his camp. I can also screen you from the oversight of Orogastus. He would certainly warn Lord Osorkon if he descried you and your knights on the move."

"He would do more than that!" Queen Anigel cried. "He would begin his invasion at once! And you, my husband, would be caught away from Derorguila. Our troops would once again be lacking their King, and what could I tell them? That you had gone away seeking reinforcements?"

Kadiya said: "But Hara would still be here to help defend the city—"

"No," the Archimage stated bleakly. "In order to ensure that Antar is undetected, I would have to accompany him. I could not screen him from the oversight of Orogastus's talismans except through the presence of my own Three-Winged Circle."

The King groaned. "So much for that idea! Marshal Owanon would probably be able to keep the troops under control in my absence—but I cannot leave Anigel and the children menaced by Orogastus."

The Queen sprang up from her chair, her eyes suddenly alight and color flooding into her pale face. "There is a solution to the dilemma. Niki and Jan and I will go with you!"

"Great God, no!" cried the King. "I cannot risk your lives!"

"Our lives are already at risk," the Queen declared. "Without more troops, we cannot hope to hold Derorguila. Do not waste time agonizing over us, my dearest! The Thicket is only two hours' ride from the city. We must leave at once, and arrive at Osorkon's camp before his men retire for the night. All of them must see you challenge the traitor and vanquish him. The alternative is to wait until both Orogastus and the turncoats fall upon us, crushing us as in a nutcracker. In such a situation—with magic as well as armed might arrayed against us—the children and I would surely be taken."

"Let your sister transport you to a safe place while I challenge Osorkon!" Antar exclaimed.

"The only way I will leave this city," Anigel stated, "is at your side. We are the co-monarchs. *We* are the Two Thrones."

"She is right," Kadiya put in sternly. "You may not think of your Queen as an ordinary wife, nor the Crown Prince and Princess as ordinary children."

"No," said Antar. "But if Osorkon should win our duel—"

"He will not!" Anigel flew to her husband and threw her arms about his neck.

The Archimage said: "I must accompany you and your knights.

That is inarguable. If Anigel and the children go along as well —
and Kadiya, too, of course! — I can protect you all. Furthermore,
the sorcerer will be unable to discover what we are up to until
Osorkon is slain and his army begins its march toward the city. But
make no mistake: Orogastus will certainly strike at once when that
happens."

"And then?" the King asked.

The pale blue eyes of the Archimage of the Land became as cold
as the Conquering Ice. She drew the shimmering white cloak of her
office closely about her, and the others shrank away from the uncanny aura that blazed forth momentarily from her body. But an
instant later she was Haramis again, smiling ruefully as she said:

"I will counter Orogastus as best I can. But I cannot perform more
than one magical act at a time, and I am no expert in military matters.
We will all be in dire peril — I myself as much as the rest of you. If a
stray arrow or an unexpected sword-thrust strikes me unawares, I
may be wounded and unable to control my magic. Or I might even
die."

"And your talisman . . ." Kadiya began.

"You could none of you take it up and use it without the rebonding
action," the Archimage said. "It would fall to Orogastus and his star-
box by default."

The King, white-faced, declared: "I did not realize what I was
proposing. We must forget my plan. Give us what help you can to
save Derorguila, Archimage — but never to the point of endangering
yourself."

"I have already decided what I will do," Haramis said.

"Then let us be off," said Queen Anigel briskly. "We can be ready
to go within the hour. Antar, you must collect our knightly escort. We
will also take Shiki the Dorok with us, since he is experienced in cold
weather, while we are not."

"Jagun will also be a help to us," Kadiya said to Anigel. "And I will
assist you in readying the children."

The Queen stiffened and the ardor drained from her features.
"That will not be necessary."

Antar said to his wife: "How I would rejoice if you and your sister

Kadiya could be truly reconciled before we fare forth on this fateful mission."

But the Queen replied: "I said that I forgive her! What else do you expect of me?"

"Ani." The Archimage spoke urgently. "Will you let me see your trillium-amber?"

Anigel's lips tightened. She drew the amulet on its golden chain out of the bosom of her gown. "There! Are you satisfied?"

The Flower was like a tiny splash of blood within the Queen's hand.

As the others stared at her without speaking Anigel thrust the amulet back into her clothing. "I will see to the children after I find Shiki. Antar, you must take Hara, Kadiya, and Jagun with you in order to shield your conversation with the knights and our leavetaking preparations from the sorcerer and his spies. I will join you within half an hour."

She hurried briskly from the room, all trace of her earlier malaise having vanished.

"Perhaps you should send me away after all," Kadiya said. "It is clear that Ani continues to resent me."

Haramis walked to the window and looked out at the dreary scene. "No. We must face this crisis together. I am certain of that, as I am certain of nothing else."

"White Lady." The King was hesitant. "Is my wife's fear of world catastrophe fanciful, or is it real?"

"It is real," the Archimage admitted.

"I was afraid of that." The King squared his shoulders. "Ah well. I shall concentrate on saving my little country. The salvation of the world must be your responsibility! . . . Ladies, Jagun, let us go together to the council chamber."

The four of them went into the corridor. Outside Derorguila Palace, the cold wind blew ever stronger, tearing the mist apart, and the sleet began to change to fat flakes of snow.

26

They rode off through the palace's postern gate into a night of stinging whiteness, through a city with cobblestone streets already muffled by snow three finger-widths in depth. The ornamental trees and shrubs of the squares and boulevards were pathetic things in the unseasonable weather, with leaves and flowers blasted and branches bending sadly beneath their sparkling new covering. All of the defenders had by now taken their positions in the fortifications and the supply trains were gone. Derorguila seemed nearly deserted in the blizzard, the buildings dark and shuttered, with only the occasional smoking chimney pot giving evidence that a stubborn householder was still in residence.

They rode two by two on tall, antlered fronials with quilted caparisons. First were the Archimage and King Antar. He held the reins of her steed so that she would be unencumbered in working her magic. Then came the three stalwart sons of Lady Ellinis: Marin, Blordo, and Kulbrandis, together with Kadiya. Next was Queen Anigel, and beside her on a single mount were Prince Nikalon and his sister, Janeel, muffled to the eyes in furs. Close behind them, perched awkwardly on their huge beasts, which also bore bundles of supplies, came Jagun and Shiki the Dorok. The rearguard of six doughty knights was headed by two noblemen of unimpeachable loyalty: Gultreyn, Count of Prok in Ruwenda, and Lord Balanikar of Rokmiluna, Antar's beloved cousin.

The King, Kadiya, and the eleven human males were armored only with helmets, cuirasses, and scale-mail sleeves because of the need to wear warm clothing. They carried both longswords and lances. Both of the aborigines had crossbows and knives, and even the two children had daggers to defend themselves.

As the party rode along the abandoned streets the animals left no hoofprints, nor were there any shadows cast when they passed guttering streetlamps. The Archimage had extended her protective aura about them with little difficulty; ordinarily, the space within arm's length of her was inviolate to Sight with no effort on her part at all. She had reassured Antar and Anigel at the start of their journey that she possessed an ample magical reserve to oversee Osorkon or the sorcerer. When she was not descrying, she would be able to perform certain other actions from time to time that might aid them in their mission.

Unfortunately, sheltering them all from the cold and the driving snow was impossible under the circumstances. The talisman kept Haramis warm, but she was unable to lend similar comfort to the others, who huddled stoically in their saddles without a word of complaint.

They reached the Great South Gate of the city, which was barred and its towers fully manned. Watchfires burned at the guardhouse and along the massive wall, their flames blowing almost horizontal in the gale.

"I shall go ahead and order the gate opened," Antar said to Haramis.

But she shook her head. "Even such an action might be observed by Orogastus. If he or his Voices saw the gate unbarred and no one passed in or out, he would suspect at once that magic was at work. No, I can do better than that."

As the oblivious sentries went about their business the riders halted. Haramis rode alone to the massive barricade and touched it with her talisman. At once the stout timbers and the iron hardware seemed to turn to glass. Antar and the others could not help but cry out in wonder as they saw past the eerie transparency to the dark highroad beyond.

"Ride on," Haramis commanded, and she and her fronial moved through the closed gate as a knife slices through water. Awed, the others followed. When they were all outside the walls the Great South Gate was restored to its former solidity.

"White Lady, we knew that you were an enchantress of great power," exclaimed the venerable Count Gultreyn, "but never have I heard of such a thing as this!"

"Nor have I," Haramis replied calmly. "I did not know for certain that it would work until the moment it happened. I have only recently acquired a new proficiency in the use of magic, Count Gultreyn, and I suspect we are all in for some surprises as time goes on. Only pray that they will be welcome ones."

They rode on.

Now the night was unrelieved dark. Only the sky overhead retained a faint gray luminescence, useless to storm-lashed travelers. Shiki the Dorok brought out long ropes he had advised them to pack, and these were used to link the two lines of fronials together so none would stray. The animals moved at a brisk pace at first; but they slowed as the snow deepened, and it became evident that the trip would take longer than they had first thought.

They met no one on the highroad. The inhabitants of the villages just outside the city seemed to have fled. After traversing some three leagues, the party turned off onto a lesser route that led through scattered small farmsteads, whose lights were barely visible in the blowing snow, although they were only a stone's throw from the road.

The Archimage led the way with confidence. Even when she sat rapt in a trance, her mount plodded on steadily under her guidance, apparently unperturbed by the blizzard, puffing great clouds of steam from its nostrils and tossing its head to shake the snow from its eyelashes.

When they had been on their way for more than an hour, Princess Janeel fell asleep in spite of the storm and nearly slipped from her place behind the equally drowsy Crown Prince. Fortunately, Shiki saw what was happening and urged his mount up, managing to catch her before she fell to the frozen ground. After that, Queen Anigel had both children tied to the saddle.

When they started on their way again, Antar said to Haramis: "The storm worsens by the minute. How can Osorkon and I possibly fight a duel in such a pother of snow? We will scarce be able to see one another!"

"Osorkon is encamped among trees that greatly temper the force of the wind," Haramis said. "Have no fear on that score."

"It was only a minor concern," the King admitted. "I have another more critical, which I will admit to you now that Anigel cannot overhear us. My physical condition is far from what it should be. The magical sleep that Orogastus cast over me, and my subsequent imprisonment, were poor preparation for hand-to-hand combat. If I enjoyed my usual health, I could lick Osorkon handily. As it is, it will be a near thing, even though he is twenty years older than I. He is a sturdy old brute, famed for his prowess with a long blade."

"I could help—" the Archimage began.

"No! That is what I must warn you against, even though my wife will surely entreat you to do so. There can be no unfair advantage of magic on my part if we hope to win over Osorkon's followers. They must not even know of your presence! I must beat Osorkon fairly, by my own efforts alone . . . or accept defeat."

"Even death?" Haramis asked, her voice barely audible above the boisterous tempest.

"You must exert your powers to the utmost to save Anigel and the others if I fall vanquished, but you dare not attempt to save me. Surely you understand!"

"Yes." Haramis sighed. "I will do as you ask."

They rode on unspeaking then for a long time, over ground that rose steadily in elevation. The road became nothing more than two frozen ruts clogged by blowing, drifting snow. There were no more fenceposts, nor were there bridges over the ice-clogged streams. Scrubby little trees and bushes crusted with snow appeared on either side of the narrowing track. The travelers were entering the Thicket of Atakum at last, and before long the spindly forest was dense enough to mitigate the force of the storm.

Haramis called a halt when they reached a small and shabby hut, the former abode of charcoal-burners who had been murdered by Osorkon's troops. The party dismounted and the fronials were tied to saplings near the crude rock kiln, after which the people all took shelter within the hut, crowding closely. The trillium-amber in the Archimage's talisman glowed like a golden lamp as half-frozen containers of food and drink were unpacked by Jagun and Shiki. When the Archimage tapped the victuals and spiced wine with her talisman, they turned instantly hot and the travelers ate and drank eagerly. Those suffering from frostbite found relief at the touch of Haramis's hand, and Jagun kindled a small fire in the hearth of the cramped hovel that soon moderated the terrible cold.

"We are now nearly arrived at the encampment," Haramis said. "I have descried the provincial army and Lord Osorkon, and they suspect nothing. Thus far, we have avoided detection."

"And the sorcerer?" Anigel asked. She crouched near the fire, holding the two children close to her.

"The Yellow Voice of Orogastus uses the Three-Lobed Burning Eye to oversee Derorguila. The sorcerer himself wears the coronet, and earlier in the evening he did communicate with Osorkon, admonishing him to be ready for the upcoming attack on the city. Now Orogastus is exerting himself without success in an attempt to bring certain objects from his castle in Tuzamen to his ship. He seems completely engrossed in his task, and we are probably safe from his scrutiny for the time being."

"Then we are ready to advance?" King Antar spoke somberly.

"Yes," said the Archimage. "We will leave the animals here and go on foot through the woods. Osorkon's camp is less than a third of a league distant. Bring only your swords. I will lead the way."

A general murmur of assent came from those present. A large jug of steaming wine was being passed from man to man, and many of them were eating hot rolls or small meat pies. Crown Prince Nikalon swallowed a mouthful of bread and spoke up in a clear voice:

"And what of my sister and me, Father? Will we accompany you?"

"No," the Archimage made answer. "You and your mother, the Queen, will remain here. Count Gultreyn and the three sons of Lady Ellinis will guard you, as will Jagun and Shiki."

"No!" Anigel cried desperately. "Antar — let me go with you!"

The King pushed through the crowd of armored, fur-cloaked bodies and took hold of her hands. "My love, you must stay. You and the children would distract me by your presence. I know it will be hard for you, not knowing what happens, but it is for the best. You are in no great danger here. And if the worst should happen, the Archimage will see you and the others to a place of safety."

"My place is at your side! We agreed!"

"And what if Antar should take a fatal blow," Kadiya put in, in a voice without mercy, "from having you divert his attention from his foe?"

"Oh, damn you, Kadi!" Anigel wailed. "I would never — "

"You would not do so intentionally," the King said. "But this fight will be the most difficult of my life. Dear one, I beg you to stay. I would fight with a lighter heart."

Anigel looked up at him with eyes brimming, her face framed in golden worram fur to which droplets of melting snow still clung. "Antar . . . oh, my darling! Here I am again, hindering you in your duty for the sake of my selfish needs. Forgive me. Of course I will stay." Their lips met, then she slipped away from his arms and beckoned Niki and Jan. "Kiss your father good-bye, my little ones."

The children came gravely to the King, and he bent to embrace them.

"We will pray for you," Anigel said. "Remember that I love you with all my heart and soul."

The King said nothing more, only donning his helmet again and checking his sword to see that it slipped easily from its scabbard. The knights who were to accompany him did likewise, then came one by one to make their duty to the Queen and receive the blessing of her hand before following the Archimage outside.

Kadiya was the last to leave. "Sister," she said to Anigel in a tentative voice, "would you have me stay with you?"

But Anigel shook her head and turned away in silent misery, forgetting to offer the blessing.

"Then I will be the one standing closest to the King during his ordeal," Kadiya said, "and either the first to congratulate him on his victory, or the first to give my life to avenge him. Farewell."

"Kadi — " The Queen lifted her head slowly.

But the Lady of the Eyes had gone.

Little Shiki, his inhuman eyes filled with grief, exclaimed impetuously: "Oh, Great Queen! Can you not forgive your sister?"

"I have," Anigel insisted, staring into the flames. But the blood red trillium dangling from its golden chain gave her the lie.

What does he seek with such urgency? Haramis asked her talisman. Earlier, she had been too distracted to consider the implications of the sorcerer's peculiar magical activity; but now as she hurried through the darkness, the others following, the question assumed a dire importance.

The Three-Winged Circle replied: *Orogastus seeks to transport to himself the paraphernalia for initiation into the Society of the Star.*

Good God! And what persons would he initiate — his Voices?

Yes.

But why?

His motives are hidden from me by the Seal of the Star.

Haramis uttered a brief cry of irritation. But then, as she continued to lead the men and Kadiya single file through the snowbound woodland, the answer came to her. Of course! The Cynosure! What had the sindona Teacher said? . . . Only the Star Council or the entire Archimagical College could destroy the black hexagon that was the key to the permanent exile of Orogastus!

Already knowing the answer, she again questioned the talisman: *How many persons are needed to make an effective Star Council?*

Three or more.

And that explained it.

Drawing to a halt, she took hold of the talisman to again descry the sorcerer on his ship — and drew a sharp inhalation at the Sight.

Orogastus was no longer dressed in his usual white garments, but had donned the awesome vestments that he had worn long ago in honor of his Dark Powers. He was clad in a long robe of silver mesh with panels of gleaming, supple black leather. His cloak was also black, lined in silver, with an ornate clasp and a great multirayed star emblazoned on the back. On his hands were silver leather gauntlets. His features were nearly hidden by an extraordinary silver mask that covered all but the lower part of his face, haloing his head with tall,

sharp-pointed starry rays. On the brow of the mask shone the talisman called the Three-Headed Monster. The eyes of the sorcerer were
twin points of brilliant white light.

Kneeling side by side at their master's feet were the Purple and
Yellow Voices, their hoods drawn back from their shaven heads and
their eye-sockets seeming to be empty black holes. One of the sorcerer's hands hovered above the motionless acolytes; the other held
high the unpointed sword of the Three-Lobed Burning Eye.

"I command you, talismans!" he intoned. "I adjure you in the name
of the Star! Transport to me here the ancient coffer sealed with the
Star that rests in my inner sanctum at Castle Tenebrose in Tuzamen.
Carry it through the air to me on swift winds of magic! Obey me!"

No! Haramis said. *I order thee, my Three-Winged Circle, to debar the
coffer's coming.*

But in her vision, a decayed old trunk was already materializing in
midair before Orogastus — a thing bound about with blackened silver
straps, having upon its lid a dark, corroded Star.

Haramis fixed her mind upon it, visualized it turned to iridescent
crystal, and with all her might willed it to return to where it had been.

And it did.

The two Voices convulsed in a sudden paroxysm and slumped
senseless at the sorcerer's feet. He faltered, regarding them with
dismay, and then gave a roar of rage.

"Haramis! *You* have done this!"

Yes, she said.

Slowly, Orogastus lowered the Burning Eye, swallowing the
curses he would have uttered, seeking desperately to control himself.

"Haramis, show yourself," he pleaded in a broken voice. "Where
are you? Why have you not responded to my calls? Speak to me!
Come to me! We can yet prevent the destruction of your sister's
nation and the deaths of thousands. My dearest love — only hear what
I have to say! Let me see your dear face. You must!"

Pierced to the heart, Haramis hesitated. Then, with a cry of pain,
she banished the Sight of him and stood shuddering amidst the falling
snow, gripping the wand of her glowing talisman with bare hands.
Her face was drawn with horror. Kadiya, Antar, and the knights

regarded her in numb astonishment, knowing that something frightful had happened, but unable to comprehend.

"Without thinking, I almost went to him," she whispered.

"Sister, what is it?" Kadiya said, full of anxiety. "Has aught gone wrong in the camp of Lord Osorkon?"

The Archimage gave a great start, then pulled herself together. "No. It is nothing . . . nothing that need concern us now. Follow me."

They went on.

At length, with the snowfall diminishing, they saw the orange glow of firelight through the trees ahead. Then they spied the first of the sentries glumly pacing his rounds. They passed within six ells of the provincial warrior without his seeing them. Continuing, they encountered many other guards who remained equally blind to their presence.

Finally they came into the encampment itself and walked through rows of small tents. There were still many junior knights and men-at-arms wandering about or huddled around fires, but none paid heed to the Archimage and her companions. Unimpeded, they made their way toward an ornate pavilion fronted by a broad area of trampled snow. A bonfire blazed before the great tent, and lances bearing the pennons of Lord Osorkon and the four provincial lords who were his confederates stood upright on either side of the doorway.

King Antar marched to the center of the open space and halted. He drew back his fur-lined hood so that the crown-helm of Labornok, with its visor like the open jaws of a fierce Skritek monster, gleamed in the firelight. Kadiya and Balanikar stood on either side of him and the six other loyal Laboruwendians ranged themselves behind.

Haramis had rendered herself invisible and now bespoke the King:

Now it is up to you, dear Brother-in-Law. I will remain unseen so that Osorkon will have eyes for you alone, but I will keep careful watch in case any base person attempts to interfere with this affair of honor.

"Thank you," whispered Antar. "When will Osorkon and the others become aware of our presence?"

As soon as you call him out.

Antar took off his cloak, passing it to Kadiya, and drew his sword. The others followed suit, holding their blades at the ready.

"General Osorkon!" Antar cried. "Osorkon, come forth and answer to your King!"

At once the inhabitants of the camp became aware of the intruders. They came running toward the great tent of the noblemen, grabbing up their weapons on the way. But when they arrived, they found themselves mysteriously unable to enter the open space. Gawking and shouting their alarm and amazement at the sight of King Antar and his companions, they gathered in a huge mob round about and waited to see what would happen.

"Osorkon, come forth!" the King repeated. "I declare you to be a traitor and a wicked violator of your oath of fealty. I declare that you have conspired with the pirate nation of Raktum and the vile Master of Tuzamen, who even now are poised to invade Derorguila. Perfidious rogue! Betrayer of your country! Come out and meet the justice you deserve."

There followed a long silence. Only a few snowflakes sifted down now and the wind had fallen away. At the King's side, Kadiya felt her heart pounding. She was suddenly stifling in her fur cloak and felt drops of sweat trickle down her neck beneath the scaled neck-guard of her golden helmet. She dared to look down, and saw the Black Trillium within the drop of amber that glowed brilliantly on her breastplate.

Flower of the Threefold, she prayed, give him strength! Grant him victory! Save my dear sister's husband!

The tent-flap opened and Osorkon strode forth. He had managed to put on only the upper-body pieces of his black armor. He carried his winged helmet under one arm and his gigantic two-handed sword was naked in his other hand. Kadiya drew in her breath at the sight of him. She had forgotten what a huge man he was. He was nearly bald and his beard was streaked with gray. He wore a thunderous glower as he strode toward the King, stopping some four ells distant. He was followed by his henchmen, Soratik, Vitar, Pomizel, and Nunkaleyn — plus a stumbling gaggle of squires bearing shields and assorted weapons, who frantically assisted their masters in adjusting their armor.

"So!" Osorkon bellowed. "I am a turncoat, am I?"

"I solemnly affirm that you are," Antar replied. "You and your late sister Sharice conspired in the abduction of me and my children. And now you have led these good men" — and the King gestured to the surrounding throng — "astray with lies and traitorous utterances, preventing them from doing their duty. Them I offer amnesty if they will repudiate you and reaffirm their loyalty to the Two Thrones. But you, Osorkon, must die unless you fall to your knees before me and disavow all that you have done, then submit to my just punishment."

"Never!"

Antar lifted his sword. "Then I challenge you to single combat before these witnesses, in defense of the honor of the Two Thrones."

Uttering a bark of defiant laughter, Osorkon clapped on his helmet and closed the visor. Kadiya and the others fell back, leaving the King standing alone to await the customary ceremonial preliminaries to the duel.

But Osorkon was in no mind to observe the rules of chivalry. With an agility that amazed the onlookers, the old general leapt forward, raised his great sword above his head, and swept it down with stunning speed. It was a blow that might have parted the King's body from crown to crotch — but it clanged instead into the frozen ground as the monarch dodged to one side.

Antar swung around with his own blade, landing a heavy blow on the side of Osorkon's head. He reeled, falling back beyond the King's reach. But the heavy steel of his helmet had saved him, and an instant later he recovered and lunged forward. The two men rained blow after parried blow on one another then, striking sparks as their swords met. Pressing an advantage, Osorkon forced the King into a defensive posture, flailing without respite, pursuing Antar halfway around the circle of spectators while Kadiya and her companions watched helplessly from the center.

"Oh, God, do not let him give way!" Kadiya prayed softly. She had let the King's cloak fall to the ground and now her right hand clutched the pommel of her own sword while her left held tight to her trillium-amber.

Antar's foot struck a stone embedded in the frozen mud. He pitched backward and the partisans of Osorkon gave a great shout. But in falling, the King kept a firm grip on his sword and swung it well. It caught Osorkon a glancing blow at the place where the steel gorget protecting his neck was weakest. The black-enameled steel gave way and the King's blade sliced deeply into his foe's left collarbone. Osorkon gave a hoarse cry. His uplifted sword, which he had been about to swing down in a death-blow, wavered, then fell aside as his left hand lost its grip on the hilt. With a mighty effort, he saved himself from pitching forward onto the downed King and rolled aside in the snow.

Antar sprang to his feet. Blood was streaming from Osorkon's wound and the King did the honorable thing, granting his opponent a moment's respite in hope that he might surrender. But the big man on the ground only took a firmer hold of his sword with his good hand and thrust ignominiously at the King's unarmored legs, narrowly missing him. A shout of disapproval and cries of "Shame!" rose from the crowd.

Osorkon paid them no heed. He pulled himself upright and stood in an expectant crouch, poising his sword low for a second foul blow. But when it came, the King turned it aside, and they two smote and chopped at one another in a fury, again moving some distance. But this time Antar had the advantage and forced his opponent to retreat.

Osorkon's men now seemed to be cheering equally for him and for the King. When Antar's sword sliced the upper part of the crest from his foe's helm, coarse laughter as well as groans of dismay arose from Osorkon's men. The remaining dangling wings of the ruined heraldic device half blinded the general and he broke away from the combat to rip the helmet from his head and fling it aside. When Antar similarly bared his head, a murmur of appreciation arose even from the four lords who were Osorkon's confederates.

Trading swift short blows like frenzied blacksmiths, the two now fought near to the great bonfire. Again Osorkon thrust foul, opening a wound on the King's unarmored thigh. But Antar did not falter in the rhythm of his sword-strokes. The old general's face wore a tortured grimace now, compounded of fury and fear. He was weakening as the blood continued to flow from his shoulder. His eyes rolled wildly when the two combatants momentarily separated. He flung back his arm, then brought it forward in a terrible scything swoop at the level of the King's groin. But Antar leapt back safely, whirling his own blade overhead before pressing Osorkon backward toward the fire. The traitor staggered. One unarmored foot came down among the hot coals. He shrieked, attempted a cut at Antar's head, and missed.

The King's sword was a gory blur. With both hands he swept it from right to left, severing Lord Osorkon's head.

"Antar!" screamed Kadiya in joyous triumph. "Antar! Antar!"

A dark fountain of blood poured forth as the general's body tumbled into the mass of flames. The onlooking army groaned. Balanikar and the other loyalist knights joined Kadiya's continuing chant of the King's name. And then, one by one, the erstwhile traitors joined in. Soon they were almost all cheering at the top of their lungs, shouting the two syllables over and over until the air rang.

Antar stood still, his blade lowered to the scarlet, trampled mud. Then he turned his back on the newly fueled bonfire and walked slowly to where the four friends of the dead general stood gaping. The King sheathed his sword and lifted his hand.

The encircling army fell stone silent.

Antar looked upon the quartet with a face that was stern but without rancor. "Soratik, Vitar, Pomizel, Nunkaleyn . . . I offer you amnesty if you will follow me faithfully now and fight in the defense of Derorguila and the Two Thrones."

The four of them dropped to their knees. Soratik, the eldest, said: "Great King, I pledge to follow you faithfully till death."

"And I," said the three others as one man. Once again, a thunderous cheer went up from the onlooking knights and men-at-arms.

Kadiya found herself grinning, and she took hold of her amulet and whispered: "Hara! Tell Anigel the good news!"

I have already done so, and she is on her way here with the children and the others.

Kadiya strode forward then, followed by the other loyal knights, to deliver her felicitations to the victorious King. Antar was already giving the command to break camp and march to Derorguila, and the reprieved traitor-lords hastened to call their officers and obey.

In a small grove of trees behind the late Osorkon's pavilion, the Archimage let herself become visible once more. Her work here was done, and she had already told Queen Anigel that she must go elsewhere for a time. Taking hold of her talisman, she saw what she knew she must see: an armada of more than sixty Raktumian warships, led by fourteen huge triremes, streaking down the Strait of Dera toward the entrance to Derorguila harbor. They had undoubtedly broken from cover the moment that King Antar began his contest with Osorkon.

"Show me Orogastus," she said.

This time he was waiting for her, and she gasped at the realization that his mind's eye saw her as well as she descried him.

"My talismans are reluctant teachers, for some reason," he said to her, smiling. "But I am an extremely able student! No longer will you be able to have Sight of me without my knowing it, my dear Haramis. Now when you spy upon me, I will also be able to observe you! Soon I hope to be able to neutralize your protective aura as well so that you will nevermore be hidden from me. What a pleasure it will be then to communicate with you and see your beloved countenance again without hindrance."

"You have launched your assault upon the city," she stated baldly.

"I would halt it in an instant if you would come to me and engage in a quiet discussion. I know you now have the power to travel anywhere through magic."

"When I come to you," she said slowly, "it will be for our final confrontation, and a combat as mortal as that of King Antar and the late traitor, Osorkon."

"Fought with talismans instead of longswords?" The sorcerer laughed, shaking his head in fond condescension. "Ah, Haramis. Why do you trouble yourself with the petty conflicts of the lowly? You and I are not such as they! We are destined to live for thousands of years and see kingdom after kingdom arise, prosper for its tiny moment, then give way to another. Do you understand what that means? Can you even conceive of the life you will lead as Archimage? It will be desperately lonely, in spite of the great power that you will wield. But you do not have to be all alone — nor does the governance of the World of the Three Moons have to be your solitary burden. Come to me, beloved! Let me tell you of the amazing things these two talismans have revealed to me, things your poor earthbound sisters never dreamt of! And we can — "

"No!" She cut him off with the sick realization that once again she was on the verge of being mesmerized. "You are as smooth and beguiling a liar as ever, Orogastus. But you betray your own ignorance even as you tempt me. I will foil your invasion of Derorguila. And then we will see whose magic is the stronger."

She abolished the vision of him and stood trembling, bracing herself against the trunk of a slender young gonda-tree. In the encampment, tents were being struck and the sharp voices of sergeants giving orders rose above the racket of an army preparing to march.

As Haramis recovered her equanimity she chanced to look up at the tree branches, sagging and splintered from the unaccustomed weight of snow. Leaves that had been lush and green a sennight ago creaked gently in the newly risen wind, frozen stiff and enveloped in a pall of ice.

Did Orogastus even realize what was happening?

Did he have any notion that the world was out of balance and teetering toward catastrophe?

No, she told herself. He could not know. Very likely he dismisses the earthquakes and volcanic eruptions as natural, and considers the calamitous weather to be his own doing. Commander of the Storm! He had so styled himself twelve years ago and doubtless did it still.

Oh yes, certain of the ship-propelling gales were undoubtedly of his conjuring, and so were the waterspouts and the smaller tempests that had furthered his crimes down south. But he could never have commanded the deadly frost that had descended upon Labornok, nor the fresh advance of the Conquering Ice.

"Talisman," she whispered, "can I stop it?"

The answer seemed forever in coming. The branches of the little trees were in full motion now, and the snow that had clung to them was fast dislodged by the wind, forming a whirling white cloud like a blizzard low to the ground. Haramis shivered in spite of the magic that warmed her. Would the talisman even deign to answer? Did it even know if it were possible to stop the Conquering Ice?

The Three in One may stop it . . . if they act in time. But the time is fast running out.

27

In the dream, Prince Tolivar was home again in Derorguila. The King and Queen took him on an informal visit to the royal menagerie in Guila River Park, and for once, Niki and Jan weren't along to spoil things. It was a gorgeous Dry Time day with little white clouds frolicking in the blue sky, and Tolo had his mother and father all to himself.

At first, he had a very jolly time at the zoo in his dream. Instead of scolding him for running about and making noise, and telling him how princes had to set a good example, his parents were especially kind and attentive. They laughed when he tossed sweet biscuits to the big shaggy raffins to encourage them to beg. Their smiles were indulgent when he teased the horiks so they would bellow and gnash their long ivory teeth. He had great fun frightening the graceful shangars, causing them to leap about their enclosure in a very entertaining manner.

And then Tolo decided it would be even more amusing to wake up the evil-tempered looru, who came from deep in the swamps of Ruwenda and were said to drink people's blood. (In the zoo they had to make do with qubar soup.) He picked up a handy stick and ran to rattle the bars of their big cage.

What a noise the stick made! There were twenty or so of the ugly looru in captivity, the largest with a wingspread of over two ells. Tolo's sudden commotion caused the sleepers to fall from their perches and flap about, screeching insanely. The mass of infuriated creatures flung themselves again and again at the cage front, making a terrible din and trying to seize him with their clawed limbs. He darted back, laughing, and picked up a stone to throw.

And then the bars broke.

First one dark-bodied flier and then another escaped, until the whole swarm was at large, their eyes blazing red and their cruel long-toothed beaks open wide, seeking prey. Tolo flung himself beneath a handy bush, covering his ears from the sound of their awful whistling cries, hoping they wouldn't find him.

The looru paid no attention to him at all. Instead, the swarm dived on the helpless King and Queen, burying them in a mass of claw-edged leathery wings and foul-smelling furry bodies. The sky turned black in an instant. Lightning flashed and deafening peals of thunder made the ground shake. Tolo heard screams — who was screaming? — and suddenly his bushy refuge was whisked away from him, torn up by the roots! He cowered, waiting for the looru to rend his flesh from his bones. When nothing happened, he dared to look up.

His aunt the Archimage towered above him. She seemed to be at least ten ells high. Her face was lit by lightnings and she wore a terrible expression of anger. "Your poor parents have perished through your fault! Now you will pay the price for your villainy!"

"No!" Tolo wailed. "I didn't mean to do it!"

"Wicked!" the Archimage thundered. "Evil!" She reached down for him with one enormous hand.

"I didn't mean to do it!" Tolo was up and running for his life.

"Stop!" Her voice was a stunning drumbeat. "Stop!"

Fleeing, he looked over his shoulder. She was coming — taller than the trees! — each footstep making the earth shake. She lifted her magical talisman, staring at him through the silvery circle. He saw one enormous magnified Eye, and it got bigger and bigger until it was the only thing in the world, and he was going to fall into it and die.

"Stop! Stop!"

"No! I didn't mean it! Noooo—"

He awoke with his own howls echoing in his ears.

But no looru. No mother and father torn to pieces. No gigantic angry Archimage. He was safe in his little cabin on the flagship of King Ledavardis of Raktum. It had only been a dream.

Nevertheless the incessant loud crashes of thunder continued, and so did the bloodcurdling, many-throated scream of the flying predators. He even heard the rattling noise his stick had made —

Stop! Stop!

— and the monstrously amplified voice of the Archimage.

The little Prince jumped from his bunk, ran to the cabin port-light, opened it, and pulled up a stool so he could see outside.

The fog was gone. It was still nighttime. Continuous explosions of brilliant multicolored light filled the sky and reflected on a black sea crowded with ships. Some of them were pirate galleys, and they were firing the magical weapons of Orogastus, soaring globes of white and green and scarlet and gold that detonated like ball-lightning when they struck one or another of the defending ships, which carried on their sails the Black Trillium and Three Golden Swords of Laboruwenda. The defenders used catapults to fling fiery bombards at the invaders, and these made huge orange arcs as they sailed through the air.

From both antagonists came continual flights of iron crossbow-darts. The darts had small whistles attached and as they flew they made the eerie screaming noise he had mistaken for looru cries. As Tolo watched, openmouthed, a volley of darts struck the Raktumian flagship's hull with a sound like rattling hailstones.

Stop! Stop this conflict! Sailors of Raktum, beware! Turn back, or your fate will be a terrible one!

The thundering words of Aunt Haramis rang out across the water . . . and another supernatural voice replied — that of the Master, Orogastus!

Are you tiring of your futile actions, Archimage? Yes, I can see that you are. The constant use of magical powers drains the soul of the practitioner, and now you resort to lies in a foolish attempt to turn away our brave warriors. But we will not be deterred!

Prince Tolivar thought he might still be dreaming, so fantastic was the scene out on the water. Not a single one of the flaming missiles from the defenders struck the pirate ships. Sorcery stopped the gobs of fiery pitch a hundred ells short of their targets, and they bounced as if hitting an invisible wall before falling harmlessly into the sea.

Crossbow bolts did hit the flagship and the other Raktumian vessels, and so did rocks lobbed by the defender's catapults. Evidently the magic that fended off the burning pitch was ineffective against iron or stone, or perhaps the Master could concentrate only on one danger at a time.

The effect of the weapons of the Vanished Ones on the Laboruwendian ships was much more devastating. Tolo clearly saw a globe of shimmering green fire waft from a pirate craft toward a target, only to veer away from its intended victim as though deflected at the last minute by the Archimage. But moments later the same Laboruwendian vessel was hit by a cloud of searing white sparks coming from another direction, racing through the air like a flock of close-flying griss-birds. The sparks set a hundred fires in the luckless warship's rigging, and soon it, like many of its fellows, was a mass of flames.

Tolo realized that Aunt Haramis was trying to shield the Laboruwendians, but she was not doing a very successful job of it.

The ships from Derorguila were greatly outnumbered and mostly propelled by sails alone. With the winds light and erratic (were the Archimage and Orogastus fighting each other for control of them?) the Laboruwendian navy was at the mercy of the oar-driven pirate galleys. Ship after ship of the defenders was rammed broadside by the Raktumians and sunk, or struck by the meteoric weaponry of the Vanished Ones and consumed in fire. Some vessels managed to escape destruction thanks to the intervention of the Archimage, but she seemed unable to weave a spell powerful enough to continuously shield them all.

The titanic laughter of Orogastus sounded among the constant thud of explosions. The outside air coming through Tolo's port was icy cold and he hugged himself to keep from shivering too badly. But he never for a moment considered going back to bed, or even leaving his post long enough to get a blanket to wrap himself in.

For a time that seemed endless to the little Prince, the sea-battle continued. In the east, the sky began to brighten. And then, beyond a doubt prompted by some magical command of Orogastus, the pirates abruptly changed their tactics. The galleys disengaged from their limping opponents and their oars began to churn. Tolo's sharp ears picked up the increasing rhythm of the flagship's oar-drums. Lashed by their overseers, the Raktumian galley slaves now put forth a great effort that sent the seventy-four ships of the armada racing away at top speed from the battle scene in the coastal waters, heading for the entrance to Derorguila harbor.

The heavy triremes leading the way used their armored bows to smash through the inadequate blockade of enchained small boats that had been strung across the harbor entrance. Magical weapons made short work of any counteraction from the outer harbor defenses. Tolo saw no sign of any opposing magic from the Archimage Haramis. With oars splashing and banners flying, the invasion force advanced upon the capital of Laboruwenda without a single enemy ship to stop it.

The sun was beginning to rise. The fortified palace, with bulky Zotopanion Keep at its heart and tiny dots of fire on its battlements, was silhouetted against a sky colored purple and crimson. The docks, the streets leading down to them, and the city buildings were mantled in snow tinged pink by the dawn. Thin filaments of smoke rose vertically in the morning calm from some of the wharf structures. In the inner basin, surrounded on three sides by land, the frigid air's meeting with the warmer sea had enshrouded the surface of the water in a thick blanket of mist. It looked as though the Raktumian fleet plowed through cloud as it moved landward. When the triremes got within range of the catapults set up along the shore, they shot off a torrential bombardment of yellow, blue, and scarlet ball-lightning from the weapons of the Vanished Ones.

But this time the deadly meteors never reached their targets. As the watching Prince cried out in wonderment, hovering mist gathered itself together to form a huge hand. Glowing faintly from the reflection of the blazing missiles, it swept away the fireballs like a weary person dispersing a pesky cloud of insects. More balls of colored light flew, and the protective hand lashed out again, flinging them high into the air, where they eventually winked out.

Now the mist around the advancing Raktumian fleet surged and billowed as though other ghostly hands would arise from it at any moment. The voice of the Archimage boomed out:

Go back, Raktumians! Leave the harbor before it is too late!

Orogastus's reply was condescending: *What kind of a silly spectacle is this, Archimage? Do you think to repel us with child's play? We know you have just subjected us to an illusion! Our missiles landed on shore and did great damage. Your gigantic hand is only a phantom. You cannot harm us at all!* And he laughed.

The voice of Haramis now seemed tinged with desperation. *If you do not turn back, sorcerer, you and all your followers will meet an unspeakable doom!*

Really? Orogastus inquired with arch skepticism. *Tell me this, Archimage: If you are so powerful, why do you not turn our own missiles back upon us? Why do you not burn our ships with astral fire, or raise up rocks to tear holes in our hulls, or conjure a tidal wave to drown us all? . . . I know why! It is because you are unable deliberately to inflict death or even injury upon a living person! A little red book told me this, together with many other secrets.*

Again his laughter rolled over the water. Then he said in harsher tones:

We will waste no more time chaffing with you! Our valiant troops are impatient to come ashore —

Tolo gasped. Suddenly, the entire league-long expanse of the city waterfront seemed to burst into a wall of flame taller than the tallest building.

Orogastus spoke in a chiding tone:

Poor Archimage! Do you think the men of Tuzamen and Raktum are frightened by this pathetic trick? Are we Oddlings who cringe before will-o'-the-wisps? No! We know full well that your pretty display cannot harm us. Nor will we falter should you conjure up slavering Skritek hordes, or barriers of thorn-fern, or imaginary avalanches. We will forge ahead to the palace, killing all who stand in our way . . . but you dare not kill us! You dare not! Admit it!

There was no reply. The flames winked out. For the time being, at least, it appeared that the Archimage had withdrawn in defeat.

Now the Raktumian flagship moved majestically toward the main anchorage, escorted by the other triremes. Tolo was trying vainly to see whether any soldiers were waiting onshore when the door to his cabin was flung open.

The burly Yellow Voice stood there. His eyes shone like stars and he spoke in the commanding tones of Orogastus himself: "Prince Tolivar! I have need of you. Dress in the royal attire that my Yellow Voice brings you, and then join me at once on the flagship quarter-deck."

"Y-yes, Master." Almost fainting with shock, the boy came down from the stool. He had not seen this particular manifestation of the sorcerer's power since that day long ago (or was it so long ago?) in the Windlorn Isles when he had chosen to go with the Black Voice rather than with Mother. What a stupid blockhead he had been! Mother . . . Father . . . they were going to be killed. And this time it would not be a dream.

The magical light in the Voice's eyes winked out. When Tolo made no move to doff his nightshirt, the minion spoke in his customary peevish accents: "Well, don't stand there like a besotted night-caroler getting ready to serenade the Three Moons! Come here. Must I clothe you like an infant?"

"No," Tolo said. But aside from his shivering he was as inert as a doll, lifting one arm and then the other, one leg and then the other, while the sorcerer's grumbling assistant put a golden suit upon him and then a rich sky-blue velvet robe. A jeweled baldric went over one shoulder, and from it hung an equally gem-studded scabbard in which was a small royal sword having a ruby hilt. How Tolo had once coveted such a sword! But now that he had it, he would have traded it in a trice to be free, back with his parents and his brother and sister.

Around the Prince's neck the Yellow Voice placed a miniature replica of the King's Chain of Labornok, links of gold having what seemed to be great diamonds inset within, and hanging from it a pendant of black-enameled gold in the shape of a trillium. Finally the Voice opened a wash-leather bag and took from it a crown. It was a duplicate, except for being smaller in size, of his mother's magnificent Queen's Crown of Ruwenda. Seeing it closely, Tolo noticed that the drop of amber forming the finial had no fossil Black Trillium within, and the sparkle of the gems was dull. Were they false?

"Put it on, boy!" the Voice snapped. "The Master awaits us."

"But I cannot masquerade as a king!"

"You shall," the Voice growled, "for as long as it pleases the

Master. You are to be the King of Laboruwenda as well as the future Master of Tuzamen!"

"I don't know how —"

The boy's protests were cut off rudely by the Voice. "Put on the crown or face the anger of Orogastus, you impudent whelp! Are you so silly as to think you will actually rule, or be called upon to exercise the powers of a sovereign? You are a showpiece — a puppet, and nothing more."

The Voice clapped the crown onto Tolo's head. It was heavy and uncomfortable. A white fur cape lined in gold tissue was fastened about the Prince's neck and its hood pulled up to cover the crown. At last the boy was ready, and the Yellow Voice hustled him out of the cabin. They almost ran up the companionway steps.

As the little Prince stepped out onto the trireme's deck, a command went out to let go the anchors. A tremendous rumble and two great splashes followed. Seamen swarmed about the shrouds overhead and manned the winches, lowering the ornate sails of the flagship. The beat of the oars ceased. They drifted, snubbed up to the anchors, then finally came to rest in the middle of the harbor basin while the other warships of the armada continued ominously on toward the docks. A few of them had splintered masts, broken woodwork, or other signs of damage; but most seemed unscathed after their bout with the defenders.

Tolo and the Voice ascended to the quarterdeck. King Ledavardis, Prime Minister Jorot, and General Zokumonus of Tuzamen were there, clad in splendid armor and heavy furs. The Purple Voice stood diffidently behind Orogastus, who wore his awesome silver-and-black vestments with the star-mask. Poor Tolo was struck dumb at the sight of him.

The sorcerer handed the Three-Headed Monster coronet to the Yellow Voice. He was wearing the other talisman at his waist. "Take this, my Voice, and accompany the King, Minister Jorot, and Lord Zokumonus as they prepare for the land assault. Be diligent in searching out the enemy and reporting its intentions so that the warriors of Tuzamen and Raktum will speedily take possession of Derorguila. But I caution you not to use the coronet for any other magical chore save scrying, lest its mysteries harm you or our good allies."

"I will obey, Master." Bowing, the Voice took the talisman and fitted it to his shaven skull.

"One thing more," Orogastus said. "You know that you will be unable to descry the Archimage, since she hides behind a screen of magic. But there is a remote chance that you might catch sight of her with your mortal eyes. If this should happen, be calm. Remember that she cannot harm you while you wear my talisman, but under no circumstances should you confront her! Command the coronet to render you invisible and then bespeak me at once, telling me of her location."

"I understand," said the Voice. He turned to young Ledavardis. "I am ready, Great King."

The hunchback eyed Orogastus. "So you will not accompany us on the assault?"

"I have other work to do, Ledo," the sorcerer replied smoothly. His eyes behind the mask were as silvery and opaque as the fantastic headpiece to his costume. "For now, I think you will find yourself unopposed by magic. I believe that the Archimage is exhausted by her efforts. She knows that her fearsome illusions will not deter you, and she has probably given up on trying to frighten us away. She no longer has Sight of me, and so I cannot view her. Most likely she has gone off to confer with Queen Anigel and King Antar and their snowbound provincial army."

"She will think of some other way to use magic against us," the young King said grimly, "and when she does, you had better be there to countermand it!"

"I have scried the area, and naught but the ordinary perils of battle await you on shore now." The sorcerer was reassuring. "There are only those ranks of mangonels and other catapults about the docks, and two thousand or so defenders holed up in the quay buildings and along the approaches to the palace. You should make short work of them. Take advantage of this time to gain what ground and glory you can. When the final assault upon the palace and Zotopanion Keep commences, I will be at your side."

"How far away are Antar and his reinforcements now?" Minister Jorot asked.

"They are twelve leagues off and moving with excruciating slowness in the snow. The palace will be ours and Prince Tolo installed on the throne long before they arrive at the city gates . . . if your skittish buccaneers do their job properly."

"They will," the King retorted, "if you also do yours, and make certain that we are not surprised by some deadly trick of the Archimage's."

Orogastus exploded in exasperation. "How many times must I tell you that she cannot kill — or even injure you! All she can do is seek to counter your own weapons. If you spread the fighting wide enough, you will so bewilder her that she will not know which way to turn! Now go, for I have weighty matters of magic to contemplate." And he turned his back on the King.

For a moment the furious Ledavardis seemed ready to voice a rash reply. But Jorot put a hand on his shoulder and the young monarch subsided with a scowl. He pulled his fur cloak about him and led the way to where his gig was waiting.

When the royal party was out of earshot, Orogastus sighed and said to the Purple Voice: "An insubordinate lad, our Goblin Kinglet. What a pity that I need his help so badly."

"You will not always need it, Master. Once Derorguila falls and the pirates have their fill of plunder . . ."

Orogastus glanced at the round-eyed little Prince and said hastily: "Let us talk no more of King Ledavardis, my Voice. Another king requires our instruction if he is to play his part properly in the upcoming drama. Ledo's royal saloon should be empty now. Bring Tolo along and we'll begin."

28

Haramis came out of her trance, ashen-faced with discouragement. "The Blue Lady can think of no way that we may actively oppose the invaders without compromising our archimagical principles. Like me, she is enjoined from harming a living soul, and can only use her magic in a benign or defensive manner."

The army of erstwhile rebels had halted to rest amidst snowy fields. The sun was full up, but it had disappeared behind gray clouds, and a biting wind blew from the west, where the Sempiternal Icecap covered the interior of the world-continent. Antar, Anigel, Kadiya, and their original group were taking what ease they could on the trampled road when Haramis first materialized out of thin air. She told her sisters and the King the melancholy news of her failure to stop the invasion fleet, and spoke of her extreme fatigue.

Then Haramis thought to consult the Archimage of the Sea to see if the Blue Lady could lend active assistance. Her conference had lasted nearly a half hour, and it had been fruitless.

Now, with that hope gone, Haramis sat herself wearily upon an icy rock and drank from the flask of spiced wine that Shiki the Dorok brought to her.

"Look again upon the fighting in the capital!" the King entreated. He and his wife had been whispering with Count Gultreyn and Lord Balanikar, who stood by with anxious expressions. "Have the pirates yet threatened the palace?"

Haramis lifted her talisman slowly. For a few silent minutes she passed again into a trance; then she said: "It is still secure. Those weapons of the Vanished Ones that have been brought ashore have so far proved ineffective in breaking down the fortifications."

"God be thanked!" cried Lord Balanikar.

"I would thank him more," old Count Gultreyn muttered, "if he would but mitigate this awful cold! The clouds are gathering again, and it threatens more snow. If the drifts become much deeper, neither the men nor the beasts will be able to go farther. We will all perish — and that within what would be, in normal times, a mere hour's ride from the capital."

"Can you not do anything to clear the road, Hara?" Kadiya asked her sister.

The Archimage shook her head. "I could melt some of the snow, but probably not enough to do you much good — especially if the snow begins falling again. I am so tired . . ."

"We are all ready to drop from lack of sleep," Anigel said. "All except the children, who slept in the saddle." And she glanced at Crown Prince Nikalon and Princess Janeel, who were racing about under Jagun's eye, throwing snowballs at each other.

"The foe will bring their heavy weaponry ashore soon," Haramis said. "I shall have to rest somehow, then do what I can to defend Derorguila. But I fear that the men using the weapons of the Vanished Ones will attack the palace wall at many places all at once, and if this happens, they are certain to break through in spite of all I can do. I wish I could think more clearly, and I wish I could give you more encouraging words. However, my best advice for you now is to retreat."

"Nay!" said the King, his face flushed. "I will not turn tail!"

Haramis went on insistently. "It is eighty leagues to the foothills of the Ohogan Mountains. Farther from the sea, the snow is not so deep even though the cold is intense. The pirates are unlikely to pursue you when the loot of Derorguila awaits them. You could hide until the weather improves and it is possible to go over the Vispir Pass into Ruwenda. Once there, you might take refuge in the Citadel and rally the other troops —"

Suddenly Kadiya broke in, her face alight. "Hara! I have just had a wonderful idea. I know that the Archimage of the Sea cannot actively help us with the fighting. But could not you and she work *together* to banish this horrid snow? Surely that would not violate your sacred duty."

Haramis had been speaking with her head lowered, consumed by weariness. At her sister's words she looked up, suddenly alert, and with hope illuminating her face.

"I cannot be certain ... the weather is, after all, a sign of the world's imbalance and perhaps not susceptible to our alteration. But we could try."

She climbed painfully to her feet, clasped the Three-Winged Circle, and called: "Iriane! Have you been listening? Is it possible?"

Those standing round about now cried out in amazement, for a flash of blue light dazzled them, and a glowing mass of sapphire-bright bubbles appeared, swelling larger and larger until it was taller than a man. Within it shone an azurine form sprinkled with tiny starlike points of brilliance.

The bubbles burst. There stood a plump, smiling woman clothed in flowing blue robes, with her dark blue hair dressed in a strange style and held in place with pearly combs.

"Let us see what we can manage!" said the Archimage of the Sea to Haramis. "Take my hand. Forget that talisman of yours for now. You are an Archimage, with powers of your own!"

"By Zoto!" Antar exclaimed. "She came! She really does exist."

Iriane turned to the King with a sharp sniff. "Doubt won't help your cause, young man. I recommend that you pray your heart out while your good sister-in-law and I attempt this piece of work! And you two sisters"—she nodded to Anigel and Kadiya—"take hold of your amber amulets and pray as well, even though you be not truly united as Petals of the Living Trillium. What Haramis and I attempt isn't going to be easy. We'll need your help!"

Abashed, Antar fell to his knees and bowed over his folded hands. Anigel and Kadiya followed his example, as did all of the other nobles and knights gathered round about, and even the royal children and Shiki and Jagun. Word of what was happening passed by swift whispers all through the resting army, and every man knelt in the snow and prayed beneath the heavy sky.

At first, nothing happened save that the auras of the two Archi-mages intensified. Haramis was enveloped in a corona of glowing gold and Iriane's shone blue, and where the auras mingled, the magical nimbus was a pure, brilliant green. The green light fountained up, forming an emerald lance that reached the louring stormclouds and spread through them as swiftly as a bolt of lightning.

In that instant, with success within reach, Haramis felt a malign opposition. An evil power was exerting all of its strength to foil the spell. Orogastus! She did not have to descry him to know he was there, fighting against them, striving to prevent the great cold from succumbing to the command of the two Archimages.

The green radiance suffusing the sky paled and flickered and the clouds turned dark once again. The Blue Lady, shocked by the viciousness of the unexpected counterattack, shrank away, ready to disengage from this suddenly perilous act of collaboration.

No, Iriane! Wait!

Haramis reached deep within herself, past the numbing morass of fatigue, and found a thing that was Three as well as One. Wielding it with the last of her strength, she hewed apart the smothering evil with a single mighty stroke. The Threefold dissolved then, but it had done its work. The golden glow and the blue swelled and coalesced once more. Green light engulfed the sky and there was a great clangorous peal, like a hundred giant bells.

Then the green radiance was gone.

Iriane and Haramis stood side by side, shorn of their magical auras, but with expectant faces. A breeze sprang up . . . and it was not knife-edged with chill as before but warm. From thousands of throats came murmurs of wonder. A bolt of ordinary lightning crackled across the gray sky, branching in all directions, and thunder rolled over the snowy expanse of ruined grainfields where the army rested.

It began to rain.

Blood-warm rain. A great deluge of it, like the cataracts of heaven. Huge smacking drops punched holes in the snowdrifts and ate away at the ice. Rain poured over the uplifted, frostbitten faces of the knights and men-at-arms, thawing their frozen armor. Rain like driv-ing silver lances fell from the sky in torrents, drenching the laughing

King and Queen and causing the royal children to shriek and dance for joy. The fronials tossed their heads and whickered with pleasure at the sudden rise in temperature and pawed at the puddles growing beneath their split hooves.

"To Derorguila!" Antar bellowed. He leapt into his saddle and lifted his sword. "To Derorguila!" And he trotted off among the men, who were rising from their knees and cheering so loudly that the thunder and the noise of the stupendous downpour were all but drowned out. Gultreyn and Balanikar and the other nobles also hastened to mount their fronials and prepare the men for departure.

Iriane smiled at Haramis. "Well, it worked. I'm glad. Was that your naughty lover trying to interfere?"

Haramis's face had gone quite livid from the terrible effort. The rain had soaked her garments through and her black hair was in strings, while the Archimage of the Sea looked as elegant as ever.

"It was Orogastus. Fortunately, he could have no hint of your presence, Iriane. If you attempt Sight of him, beware, for he is now able to use my own descrying to view me — and he may very well be able to do the same to you."

The Blue Lady laughed nervously. "Well! I think I'll restrain my curiosity for the time being."

"Thank you for your help. May I call upon you again if it is necessary?"

"Hmm." The pale blue brow creased slightly. "Strictly speaking, it isn't my province to assist you in the affairs of the land. But rain is not that different from seawater, so I was able to stretch a point — especially since the magic was unaggressive. I'll certainly do what I can for you in the future, but only if it be lawful. Ah — would that we were not so hedged about with rules! They make life so difficult at times."

She vanished in a small puff of indigo smoke.

Haramis now turned to her sisters, who were gathering their things together with the help of Shiki and Jagun. Kadiya asked: "Do you think we have a fair chance now of reaching the palace?"

"Thus far, only small companies of Tuzameni warriors are assaulting it," Haramis replied. "The pirate forces are engaged elsewhere in the city with easier — and richer — objectives. Yes, with the roads clearing and the great cold held temporarily at bay, I think you now may hope to gain the palace."

"Will you stay with us, Hara?" the Queen asked, looking up from adjusting the wet cloaks of her two children. The rain continued to cascade down unabated. "Will you protect us on the march to the city?"

The Archimage did not answer immediately, seeming to be lost in thought.

The King came riding back. "Still not in the saddle, ladies? Shiki! Jagun! Bring mounts for the Queen and the Lady of the Eyes and the royal children, and prepare one for the Archimage also."

The two aborigines ran off. But Haramis now said to the King: "I am wearied unto death. There is no danger facing you on the road to Derorguila. I must sleep at least a few hours so that my energies will be restored. I have strength enough left to transport myself to the palace. If you and Anigel wish it, I can take you two along with me."

"I must remain at the head of these men," Antar replied. "But I would be grateful if you would take my wife and children to the safety of Zotopanion Keep. Anigel can tell Marshal Owanon the good news about the coming reinforcements."

"Antar, I want to stay with you — " the Queen cried.

"We may have to fight our way into the palace compound," he reproved her sternly. "I cannot spare warriors to guard you. The Archimage's plan is a sound one. I implore you to accompany her."

Reluctantly, Anigel agreed. She called the Crown Prince and Princess to her, and Haramis spread wide her cloak.

But when the Queen and the children were huddled close to her, the Archimage suddenly said: "There is still room . . . Kadi! You come also. We three Petals of the Living Trillium should not be separated at this critical time."

Kadiya opened her mouth to object. But Haramis went on: "We cannot look to the Archimage of the Sea for active help in the fighting to come. I will need the wholehearted aid of you two. Without your support, I would never have been able to fend off Orogastus and bring on the rain. But our Trillium union was a fleeting one and not a firm conjunction. We will have to do better if we hope to defeat the sorcerer and his allies once and for all."

"I pledge you my troth unto death," Kadiya asserted stoutly, taking her place beneath the cloak.

But Anigel seemed oddly distracted. "The great cold," she murmured, looking up at Haramis. "It is not really gone from all our land, is it! Only banished temporarily from this small region."

Haramis nodded reluctantly.

"Then how," Anigel asked, "can we possibly win?"

King Antar said to her: "In three hours or less I shall be in Derorguila — and with these additional troops, our chances are much improved. My darling, do not be despondent!"

Haramis closed her eyes. The King had not understood the import of his wife's plaintive question, but Haramis had. She did not know the question's answer, nor at the moment did she care. She wanted only to rest. With great difficulty she called to mind a crystal image of the royal withdrawing room in Zotopanion Keep.

"Farewell!" called the King. "We will join you in a few short hours, the Triune willing."

The crystal scene turned to reality.

Haramis dared to breathe again. They had been transported safely. The children began to chatter while Kadiya and Anigel stepped away, letting the cloak fall. The chamber was chill and dreary, for the fire had gone out, and they were all soaked to the skin. Haramis wondered if she might still have a small modicum of magic left . . .

Yes. A great blaze began to roar in the hearth. Her garments and those of all the others became dry and warm. Anigel, Kadiya, and the children cried out in awed appreciation.

"I will summon the servants," the Queen said to the Archimage, "and they will prepare my bed for you straightaway."

But Haramis had caught sight of a cushioned couch. She went to it and lay down, falling instantly into dreamless sleep. The amber within her talisman glowed so wanly that it seemed hardly alive at all.

"Master! Master! Awaken!" The Purple Voice took hold of one flaccid silver-gloved hand and pressed it to his forehead. "Master, come back! Live, dear Master! Ohhh . . . Dark Powers, restore him!"

Orogastus groaned and his body, which had fallen to the floor in the royal saloon of the flagship, began to stir. The Purple Voice hastened to unfasten and remove the sorcerer's star-mask, then propped cushions beneath his head. "Don't just stand there, boy!" the minion admonished Tolo. "Get brandy!"

The Prince's instructions in kingly etiquette had been strangely interrupted, and he had witnessed an amazing magical struggle while sitting paralyzed on King Ledo's traveling throne. Orogastus had taken a brief respite to descry King Antar, and he had evidently discovered some kind of threatening magical activity going on. Bathed in a green radiance and with his eyes shining like two white beacons, he had seemed to wrestle with invisible demons, crying out and slashing at them with his talisman. And then he had collapsed. That the sorcerer could be vulnerable was an astounding new notion to Tolo, and one that bore much thinking upon.

The boy made his way unsteadily to a sideboard, slopped some liquor into a golden goblet, and brought it to the Master's assistant. "What happened?" Tolo asked. "Is he hurt?"

"Magic," the Voice said shortly. "The Archimage Haramis began to perform a colossal feat of magic — changing the weather. The Master happened to descry the event unfolding and attempted to forestall it. But . . . he failed. Most unaccountably."

"Failed," Orogastus repeated in feeble tones. His eyes fluttered open. The Voice pressed the cup of brandy to his lips and he drank a sip or two. His voice was both dazed and bewildered. "Only by chance did I think to oversee King Antar and find that the weather about the turncoat army was about to be changed. I assumed immediately that Haramis must be accompanying the force, even though I could not confirm her presence with my Sight. I exerted all of my power to maintain the cold so that the reinforcements would be hindered from reaching the city." He grimaced in sudden pain. "But I could not. And in the last moment before my defeat, I saw — I saw — "

"What, Master?" The Voice loosened the clasp of the sorcerer's heavy cape, eased his position, and helped him to another swallow of brandy.

"I saw Haramis. And . . . who was it? The other two Petals of the Living Trillium, certainly. But it almost seemed as though there was another as well." Orogastus shook his head. "But who?" His brow knit and he muttered an imprecation. "My wits are as useless as a bowl of curds!"

"Can you not resummon the blizzard?" the Voice asked. "You command the storm! The icy winds obey you, bringing ruination and despair to your enemies! Surely after you have rested and regained your strength — "

Orogastus held up his hand. "My Voice, I have led King Ledavardis and the other gullible Raktumians to believe that the devastation of Laboruwenda by the great surge of inclement weather was my doing. But with you there is no need for me to dissemble. Yes, I can command small storms, and bring down lightning, and generate whirlwinds, and create gales to speed our ships. But to cause widespread havoc through persistent bad weather is beyond me — just as it is beyond the Archimage Haramis herself. The truth is, I do not know why the climate has gone berserk. I thought briefly on the puzzle from time to time, but put it out of my mind since the tempests furthered my own plans. But this present failure of mine . . . I cannot understand it! In our earlier magical jousts today, Haramis and I seemed rather evenly matched. Then she became much fatigued and withdrew following our rupture of the harbor blockade. She should not have been able to win our encounter!"

"How do you account for it then, Master?"

"She received help from her sisters. Of that I am certain. But Queen Anigel's trillium is still blood red, and so the Living Flower lacks its full potential. And yet I was overcome."

Orogastus pulled himself into a sitting position. He took the cup from his minion's hand and drained it, then coughed and pressed his knuckles to his brow. "They conjured warm air and rain. Only in a localized area, south of Derorguila. The army of provincials will move quickly to the city now, damn them, and try to join the troops inside the palace. We shall have to go ashore immediately and take charge. The Goblin Kinglet and his men will want prodding to divert them from their plundering and back to the business of war. And I must take back my second talisman from the Yellow Voice. I will need both of them to conquer Haramis."

Again he groaned as he got to his feet, then seemed to notice Prince Tolivar for the first time since he had been stricken.

"Leave me for a moment, my Purple Voice, and take the boy. Have a boat readied to ferry us ashore. We shall need my Tuzameni bodyguard. And be sure to bring the star-box. If I do manage to find and defeat Haramis, I must take possession of her talisman immediately."

The Voice bowed. "I obey, Master." Tolo hastened after him.

Orogastus drew the Three-Lobed Burning Eye from its scabbard, reversed it, and held it upright by the dulled blade. "Talisman, answer me true."

The black lobe holding the silvery Eye opened wide. *I will do so if the question is pertinent.*

"Who were the persons who assisted the Archimage Haramis in conjuring the warm rain?"

The Lady of the Eyes, Kadiya. And the Queen of Laboruwenda, Anigel.

"Yes? Yes? I know there was a third! Who was it?"

The Archimage of the Sea, Iriane.

"By the Bones of Bondanus!" the sorcerer cried. "Another Archimage? Can it be?"

The question is impertinent.

Orogastus swore pungently. "Tell me true: How many Archimages are there alive?"

One of the land, one of the sea, and one of the firmament.

"How may I see and converse with them?"

At the present time none of them wishes to converse with you, nor will they let you have Sight of them. At some future time, if it suits his pleasure, Denby, the Archimage of the Sky, might possibly converse with you. Right now you do not interest him.

Orogastus bit back another curse and spoke in a voice of great suavity. "Convey my warmest good wishes to Denby, the illustrious Archimage of the Sky. I humbly await his pleasure."

It is done. The Eye closed slowly.

For a few moments more Orogastus thought furiously. Then he sheathed the talisman, took up his cloak and mask, and made ready to go ashore for the battle.

29

The fighting at the Derorguila waterfront had ended by the time that Orogastus, Prince Tolivar, and the Purple Voice approached in a small boat rowed by a dozen heavily armed Tuzameni warriors.

The virtually empty ships of the invasion force crowded the docks three and four deep, forcing the sorcerer and his party to scramble over them to reach the quay. On shore was a scene of the wildest confusion, upon which a gentle morning rain was falling. Acrid smoke filled the air, and the fast-melting snow was filthy with soot and blood and strewn with the bodies of invaders and defenders alike.

At the water's edge the wooden catapults that had been positioned to repel the pirates burned briskly in spite of the drizzle, the gory remains of their operators scattered amidst unused piles of rock-ammunition and overturned pots of pitch. Also in flames were those wharf buildings where the Laboruwendian defenders had made their first stand. More corpses, both Raktumian and Laboruwendian, clogged the narrow alleys among the warehouses. Most of these huge structures stood with doors wide open and windows smashed. Numbers of Raktumian seamen were hauling out booty and piling it at the dockside. Cast-off bolts of costly fabric, torn-open bales of fur, boxes of expensive knickknacks, and emptied bottles and kegs of liquor scattered helter-skelter testified to the plundering that had gone on earlier when the main body of the pirate army had passed through. Following the sorcerer's order to King Ledavardis, the Raktumians were now streaming to join their Tuzameni allies in besieging the palace.

While four of the bodyguard went off to find a cart or some other conveyance for their master, Orogastus paused beneath the stone porte cochere of Derorguila's Bank of Commerce to go into a brief trance. For the first time since his indisposition, he felt strong enough to bespeak his Yellow Voice at length.

When his silent conversation had been completed, the sorcerer's face was grim. "Queen Anigel is in Zotopanion Keep with her sister Kadiya," he told the Purple Voice. "Yellow says that the two royal children are there also, and they have let slip that the Archimage is also in the keep, sleeping off her exhaustion. Awake or asleep, Haramis remains hidden beneath the concealing spell of her talisman. But for the time being she will not actively oppose us, and we must move swiftly to take advantage of the situation."

"That is excellent news!" the Purple Voice said.

"The bad news," Orogastus rejoined, "is that King Antar is fast approaching from the south with his army of some three thousand. There are two thousand defenders within the palace grounds — mostly knights and the cream of the enemy men-at-arms. If they are reinforced by the King, we shall have a devil of a time prying them out without severe losses. Our Tuzameni troops just outside the palace have been under devastating crossbow attack from the bastions. The brave fellows are holding fast in spite of heavy casualties, but we must hasten to assist them."

"Are we any nearer to breaching the palace wall?" Purple asked. He had a firm grip on the arm of little Prince Tolivar, who listened with avid interest, his earlier fears almost forgotten.

"Unfortunately, my heavy weapons do not seem to be working very effectively. The damned curtainwall is over sixty ells thick! I must get up there quickly and attempt to break through it with the magic of both talismans. It is imperative that we take the keep and put the Queen and her children to death before the arrival of King Antar."

One of the bodyguard who had been sent off to find a means of transport came running back. "Master, the mews behind the bank are full of fancy carriages, but there is not a beast to be found."

"Never mind," said Orogastus. "I cannot wait any longer." He selected six of the Tuzameni warriors to accompany him and prepared to set off on foot for the palace, which was nearly a league inland in the midst of the great city. It was arranged that the Purple Voice would follow with Tolo and the rest of the bodyguard as best they could.

"Keep our young King well out of harm's way," the sorcerer concluded, "but be prepared to bring him forward as soon as the palace wall is broken down. We may want to use him to coerce his mother or the Archimage."

With that Orogastus was off, his silver-and-black robes glittering with raindrops and the Three-Lobed Burning Eye ready in his hand.

The little Prince squirmed in the Purple Voice's clutch, more angry than fearful at the terrible words his former hero had spoken. The minion gave the boy a nasty shake and bade him hold still, or he would fetch him a clout on his royal ear. Tolo began to weep from helpless fury. At that moment the other Tuzameni guards returned from their futile hunt, and they all set off up the steep street at a pace that made the boy stumble.

"You are going too fast!" Tolo protested. "The cobblestones are slippery! I am going to lose my crown!"

With a curse, the Purple Voice stopped and gave a command to one of the guardsmen. "Take the wretched brat on your shoulder, Kaitanus. I am encumbered with the Master's star-box."

A thick-browed stalwart with a bushy red beard caught Tolo and grudgingly swung him up. The overlapping steel plates armoring his back and hanging from the rear of his pointed casque cut painfully into the boy's tender flesh and he shrieked: "Ow! Ow! I cannot bear it! It hurts to sit on him!"

The Purple Voice cursed even more luridly than before. "Put him down." He eyed the Prince with distaste. "I suppose *I* shall have to carry you. Take the star-box then, and hold tight to it if you value your life."

Again Tolo was swung up, this time to a softer seat, and the rain-dotted glassy box with the star emblem on its cover was laid reverently in his arms. He held it to his chest as they started off again.

The smoke and flame, the shouts of the looters and screams of the wounded, and the sickening piles of corpses seemed unreal to Tolo as he viewed them from his bouncing perch behind the purple hood. This devastated city was not the Derorguila he knew; it was a nightmare place he had never seen before. Only the great bulk of the palace far up the hill loomed as sturdy and reassuring as ever.

They came into a region of once-stately mansions where fierce fighting was still going on and where mobs of Raktumians were engaged in a frenzy of looting. Tolo saw pirates draped with stolen strands of pearls and golden chains and gem-studded bracelets engaged in mortal combat with soldiers and knights of the Two Thrones. The royal forces were greatly outnumbered, however, and the Prince shuddered to see them hacked to pieces by the howling enemy. Their very blood besprinkled his rain-soaked finery as the Purple Voice trotted past, secure in the midst of the six brawny bodyguards. The Tuzameni had their huge wavy-edged swords out now and beat off those Raktumians who were foolhardy enough to challenge them for the possession of the jewel-resplendent royal child.

As they came nearer to the palace and the tumult of fighting became more intense, poor Tolo could no longer bear to look. Squeezing his eyes tight shut, he pressed his crowned head to the star-box. Dry sobs racked him and he did not care whether he lived or died.

And at that moment death nearly took him.

He felt the Purple Voice lurch and heard the acolyte's inarticulate shout. Opening his eyes, Tolo drew in a horrified breath as he saw the ornate three-story stone building above him ripple in a most singular manner. At the same time a deafening inhuman screech rang out, followed by continuous rumbling deeper than thunder that came not from the sky but from below the street. Building cornices and ornamental facades began to crumble. Roof tiles and bricks flew in all directions. Men were screaming in panic, both the battle and the looting forgotten, as they looked up to see avalanches of loose stone and entire walls falling down upon them.

"An earthquake!" cried the Purple Voice.

The Tuzameni guards were staggering and bellowing, flailing about impotently with their swords as clouds of dust and smoke billowed up. The sounds of falling masonry and breaking glass drowned out the human cries, and the rumbling reached a crescendo.

Uttering a harsh squall, the Purple Voice danced about like a maniac as the pavement began to buckle beneath him. He let go of Tolo's legs and thrust him violently away. The Prince flew through the air screaming, still clinging to the star-box. He fell, then found himself completely enveloped in something dark and scratchy which nonetheless had a springiness to it that had cushioned his landing.

For a long time Tolo only lay there amid the stunning noise and turmoil, wondering if he was already dead. But the Lords of the Air failed to appear to escort him to heaven, and the queasy movement of the earth ceased, and the crash of buildings breaking to pieces came to an end. At last he heard only the faint sounds of a few people groaning and weeping, a falling stone or two, creaks from sagging timbers, and the rain tapping on the crown that still clung obstinately to his aching head.

He was ensconced in the middle of a very large thranu-bush. Its dense, slightly sticky needles pricked his face and hands. Cautiously, still holding on to the star-box, he wriggled free and dropped to the ground, which was only half an ell beneath.

All about him was a devastation that left him speechless. Most of the mansions were in ruins, their walls cracked open to show the shattered interiors where furniture and wall-hangings now stood exposed to the soft rain. Mounds of rubble clogged the street as far as Tolo could see. The trees that had been planted in a row along the sidewalks were canted every which way. The walks themselves and the paved street had been heaved and twisted out of any semblance of an even plane. The air was full of thick dust, which the rain was fast dissipating.

Next to his lucky bush, a great pile of building stones that had once been a house wall rose almost three ells high. At one edge, protruding from beneath a granite door-lintel, was a muddy arm encased in a dirty purple sleeve. Just beyond it, half-buried, lay a dead Tuzameni guardsman, his eyes wide open and his mouth gaping in a silent scream.

Tolo climbed to his feet. He was scratched and bruised and his royal garments were a sorry mess. But no bones were broken and the ache in his head was beginning to subside. He clambered to the top of the rubble heap and stared in the direction of the palace, waiting for the murk to clear.

The fortress of the Two Thrones still stood! In the distance he heard the sound of war-horns and martial shouts, and then the peculiar thudding chirps made by certain weapons of the Vanished Ones, and the whistle of flying crossbow-bolts.

So the war was still going on.

Tolo climbed down. He unclasped his torn and dirty white fur cloak and laid it aside. He took off his blue velvet robe, then removed the crown, the royal chain, and the ornate baldric and scabbard he had worn. Handfuls of mud served to dull his gold brocade suit, his face, and his hair. He used the ruby-hilted sword to cut a length of velvet from the blue robe, and with this he wrapped the star-box. The rest of the robe and the discarded royal appurtenances he carried to the place where the Purple Voice and the guards had perished.

With special care, the Prince arranged the robe with the baldric and scabbard over it and the golden chain flung artistically aside in the region of the collar. Then he hauled many broken chunks of stone and heaped them over the garment and the other items, leaving them barely visible so that it did seem as though a small body lay beneath. As a final touch, he left the crown lying in plain sight at the edge of the pile.

Tolo put his fur cloak on again after dirtying it well. It covered both the little sword, which he had thrust into his belt, and the star-box. Then he was ready to go home.

There was a certain small, disused door in the palace wall, down on the west side near the Midden Gate. It had once been used by the muckers of the royal stable to dispose of manure, in the ancient days before that commodity was known to be valuable field-dressing. Nowadays the old muck-door was overgrown with creepers and known only to persons who worked in the stable — such as Ralabun, the aboriginal Master of the Queen's Animals.

Ralabun, Tolo's special friend, had shown him the secret door two years ago. He used it, he said, on certain fine nights when the Three Moons shone and his heart ached at the constraints of living with humankind. Then Ralabun the Nyssomu had crept out of the palace through the secret door and gone down to the River Guila; he had paddled to a certain swampy island and there prayed and sang in the ancient Way of the Mire Folk for many hours before returning.

That door, Ralabun told his young friend, was his most precious secret.

The Master of Animals had never dreamt that the door might also serve to save the life of a runaway prince . . . if he could only reach it in time.

Orogastus had only just arrived at the great square fronting on the north gate to the palace when the earthquake struck.

The square was mobbed with nearly six thousand men, most of whom had taken up positions well beyond range of the crossbows and catapults shooting from the battlements. The Tuzameni squads manning the weapons of the Vanished Ones had advanced upon the fortifications under cover of lumbering armored wagons with narrow slits at the front, through which the muzzles of the magical weapons were fired. The high curtainwall of the palace was pocked and battered but still intact. Some siege-wagons stood blackened and smoking, having been struck by cauldrons of liquid burning pitch flung from catapults on the palace ramparts. Bodies studded with crossbow-bolts lay about them. More dead men surrounded an abandoned ram standing in front of the main gate of Derorguila Palace.

When the ground began to shake and rumble, a great cry arose from the invasion force. Some men were immediately thrown to the ground while others rushed about in a panic, brandishing their weapons and screaming that the Archimage was attacking. The siege-wagons bounced like small boats on a stormy sea, and around the perimeter of the square, buildings began to topple.

Orogastus thought at first that the Archimage *had* done it. Tumbling to his knees, half-blinded by the sudden clouds of dust that arose and almost instantly turned to muddy drizzle, he held on to the Burning Eye with a death-grip and besought the talisman with all his might to calm the quaking land, to save his life and the lives of the troops. But when the earth movement continued unabated, he cried out in desperation:

"Haramis! Haramis, for the love of God! Would you destroy your own people as well as my own?"

Her reply came after a shocked instant, and he saw her, clinging to a shuddering couch in some palace chamber, not frightened at all but only resigned and spiritless.

It is not my doing. The world trembles because it is losing its balance. And the fault is yours even if you did not deliberately set about to cause it.

"What do you mean?" he cried.

But she bespoke him no more and her image faded. A few moments later the ground was firm again. With difficulty, he hauled himself to his feet.

His Tuzameni bodyguard was cursing and demanding to know what had happened, as were most of the other fighting men nearby. But as Orogastus was about to reassure them he heard a sudden strange sound.

Cheers.

Boisterous, full-throated cheers in the accents of both Tuzamen and Raktum. Men were pointing in the direction of the palace, shouting and laughing, many still sprawled on the fractured pavement or climbing woozily to their feet.

"The wall! The wall!" they roared. "Hail to Orogastus! Hail to the mighty sorcerer! Hail!"

Stupefied, Orogastus turned about and looked.

On the western side of the palace gate, the massive stone curtain-wall was riven from top to bottom. The great west tower on that side had half crumbled also, and the eastern tower at the opposite end of the fortifications sported a perilous web of cracks.

"Hail to Orogastus! Hail! Hail!"

The war-horns of King Ledavardis of Raktum blatted out the call to charge. With a mighty shout, the pirate horde rose up and began to rush pell-mell toward the new opening.

"Master, that was magnificently done," said one of the Tuzameni guards in a quavering voice. "But next time give us fair warning."

The sorcerer could only nod. He sheathed the talisman and adjusted his star-mask, which had been twisted awry in his fall.

"Master, shall we join the advance?" another guard cried eagerly.

30

H aramis turned away from the smashed window of the withdrawing room and made her way unsteadily back to the couch. The shock and the disorientation of being awakened by the earthquake and the sorcerer's bespoken shout were beginning to fade, displaced by the more horrifying reality she had just looked upon: an enormous army of howling, horn-blowing invaders massed outside the palace walls, now streaming in through the breach like water leaking relentlessly into a doomed boat.

And Orogastus was among them.

What should she do? What *could* she do?

First, she would have to cudgel her reeling brain into a semblance of orderly thinking. She sank down onto the couch and pressed her talisman to her forehead. There. That was better.

The colossal temblor that had devastated much of Derorguila seemed to have done minimal damage to Zotopanion Keep itself, aside from breaking all of its glazing and tumbling the contents of shelves and tables to the floor. Rain was blowing in the window, soaking the draperies. It was getting very cold again, as she knew it would.

How long had she slept? An hour? Certainly not two. But she did feel a little stronger. Lifting her talisman, she bespoke her sisters.

"Anigel! Kadiya! Are you well?"

A vision of them appeared. They were in the council chamber of the keep with Marshal Owanon, Lord Penapat, Chancellor Lampiar, and several other noble officers. There was much dust in the air. Chairs were overturned, and candles, papers, and other things scattered about. Kadiya was helping the venerable Lampiar to crawl out from beneath the heavy council table, which had evidently served as an improvised shelter during the earthquake. Owanon supported the Queen, who seemed dazed but unhurt.

"We are all right," Kadiya said, looking up at the simulacrum of the Archimage that hovered wraithlike in midair. "But it was a near thing when the great chandelier began to fall. Luckily, I was able to turn it aside through my Black Trillium amulet. Is this the doing of that bastard Orogastus?"

"No," said the Archimage. "He is at this time nearly as enfeebled as I. The earthquake is one more symptom of the imbalance of the world."

Penapat and Kadiya began to tend to a cut on old Lampiar's forehead, bathing it with wine. Owanon had helped the Queen into a chair. He now questioned the Archimage about the condition of the palace following the tremor.

"I have surveyed it only very quickly, but I can tell you that the situation is now extremely grave. The curtainwall has broken open near the main gate and the enemy is fast invading the palace grounds. The west tower is a ruin. The east tower is tottering, although some defenders have remained at their posts inside."

"Is the keep yet sound?" Owanon asked.

"Luckily, yes."

The Lord Marshal nodded judiciously. "Very well. I shall have to rally the troops who are outside the keep. We will try to defend its doors and maintain control of the western and southern compounds, at least. The postern gate of the palace fortifications must remain open to King Antar's forces. We had hoped he would arrive before this."

Haramis quickly took Sight of the King. "He is still an hour's march distant."

Owanon said: "Penapat, Lampiar, it falls to you to prepare the defenses within the Zotopanion itself. Let us hasten!"

The three officials and the military leaders went rushing from the council chamber, leaving Kadiya and Anigel alone with the ghostly form of the Archimage.

"Hara, what of my children?" the Queen asked.

"I will seek them out. Wait." A moment later the Archimage said: "Janeel is safe in her keep chamber with Immu. But Niki . . . perhaps he hoped to catch sight of Antar's approach, or had some mad idea of helping with the fighting. I have found him back by the postern gate barracks. There is terrible confusion, for the building collapsed in the earthquake. Niki has a scratched face and torn clothing, and he sits stunned but conscious amidst a group of wounded men. I cannot tell what other hurts he may have suffered."

"Go to him, Hara!" the Queen cried piteously. "Rescue him!"

"I — I do not think I am able to transport myself. Not immediately. The magic requires precise concentration. I am heartily sorry, Ani, but I had only slept a short time when the earthquake struck, and if I try this before I have recovered —"

The Queen started to her feet. "Then I will fetch Niki myself!"

"Go down into the midst of a pitched battle?" Kadiya was aghast.

"Yes!" Anigel shrieked wildly. "If Hara refuses to help my son, then I shall!"

Kadiya bent over the chair, took hold of her sister's shoulders, and shook her. Her dusty auburn hair stood out like a mane and her brown eyes were ablaze. "No! You shall not go! Remember who you are. Remember who the Archimage is, and the solemn duty to which she is pledged. For the love of God, Sister, put aside the fear and heartsickness that have robbed you of your good sense and integrity, and act like a queen!"

"I know what I am," Anigel wailed, squirming like a trapped animal. "I am a weakling, vile and contemptible, unworthy of the sacred office I hold!" Suddenly she ceased her struggles and slumped back, overwhelmed by desolation. "You are right, Kadi. I cannot possibly rescue my poor son. He will die and the rest of us, too — from the Conquering Ice, if not by the dark magic of Orogastus or the swords of his evil cohort."

Kadiya's grip on the Queen's arms softened. She knelt and took the smaller woman into a tender embrace.

"Dearest little Sister. You are wrong. I know that you despair over the imbalance of the world and hold yourself responsible. But so are we all guilty, insofar as we have acted selfishly and ignobly and unwisely! To blame yourself alone is merely pride."

"Pride? You do me an injustice. I have failed in many ways, but I have never been a haughty or arrogant person."

"You have always been proud, for all your gentleness. And it has afflicted you with a dark self-centeredness that has blinded you to truth. Over the years you refused to believe that anything could be going amiss in your prosperous world. You refused to recognize that any danger or injustice might exist. You only wanted to be happy, and have your husband and children happy also, and bask in sweet satisfaction."

"And is that a sin?" Anigel cried, flaming with indignation.

"It can be — when one has larger responsibilities. Your own safety and comfort, and those of your loved ones, are important — but they are not the most important things in the world. There are greater goods, greater loves. And sometimes we are called upon to make terrible sacrifices on their behalf. Sometimes we must die for them . . . or, even worse, permit a loved one to suffer or die."

A great perplexity twisted the Queen's lovely features. She did not speak, nor did she meet her sister's eyes.

Kadiya urged her: "I know that a noble unselfishness once existed within you. Find it again. Place your sovereign duty above your personal needs. Put away the bitterness and recrimination and despair that have gnawed you to a husk. Those things are worse than useless — they are poison! Love your family, your friends, your country, and the world. But love them not for your own comfort but generously — wisely, as the Triune loves us. You have not done so, but you *can*. I know it."

The Queen said: "Kadi . . . if only I could believe you."

"In your heart, you know that I speak the truth about your sin of selfishness — else your trillium would not have bled for shame."

The Queen lifted her woebegone countenance. "Not until this very moment have I realized truly what lay within me. You are right: I *was* proud of what Antar and I had accomplished under the Two Thrones. I was proud of my beautiful children and proud of myself. When it all came undone, I hated you for not understanding my pain. I hated

Hara for her lofty ideals, which were so much more noble than mine, and for her unwillingness to focus her love narrowly, as I had done. I believed that my husband and my children were the most important persons in the world — more precious than you, than Hara, than my friends and my people. As the disasters mounted I would have done anything to preserve their lives — even seen the world itself swallowed by the Conquering Ice."

"Yes." Gently, Kadiya took the Queen's hands. The two women arose.

"I was wrong."

"Yes."

"Kadi, I forgive you with all my heart."

"I know."

The sisters kissed. Then the Queen lifted her chin high. "I — I will go to Penapat and Lampiar in just a moment, and see how best I can serve our brave defenders. I am useless with a sword, but — "

The Lady of the Eyes smiled. "I am not! . . . You do what you can. In the meantime I will go and fetch that silly rascal Niki."

Pushing her straggling hair back from her face, she drew her sword and strode out of the council chamber.

The Queen now moved slowly about the devastated room. Like one in a dream she gathered up papers that had fallen to the floor and placed them carefully on the dusty table.

Look at your amulet, Sister.

Anigel uttered a surprised cry. She had completely forgotten that the spectral Archimage was watching. Taking hold of the golden chain, she drew the drop of amber out of its hiding place.

The amulet glowed richly golden, and in its depths the tiny fossil Flower was black.

The Yellow Voice had already tried four times to escape from the side of young King Ledavardis of Raktum, who was in the vanguard of his troops and showing astonishing prowess both as a swordsman and a leader of warriors. But the fighting grew increasingly ferocious as the hard-driving battalions of Raktum and Tuzamen moved into the palace grounds through the break in the wall, taking advantage of the ruined west tower, from which all defenders had fled, and the shelter provided by the well-built stone servants' quarters, laundry, bakehouse, and stables located on the western side of the keep. The pirate knights flanking the monarch used their shields not only to protect Ledavardis from flying arrows, but also to hedge in the Voice. And so the sorcerer's minion could only continue to do his job, indicating the best places to position those weapons of the Vanished Ones that still worked (most had long since ceased to operate), pointing out the path of least resistance to the advancing troops, and warning them of occasional suicidal attacks by trapped Laboruwendians.

From time to time, when he was not cringing in peril of his life, the Yellow Voice descried and bespoke the Master. Orogastus had surrounded himself and his six-man bodyguard with an invisible magical screen that turned away ordinary weaponry. But it did not assist him much as he sought to make his way through the densely packed mob of soldiers to the side of his beleaguered acolyte. By the time that Ledavardis and his knights had fought their way into the large stableyard adjacent to the western door of the keep, Orogastus had barely managed to pass through the smashed curtainwall two hundred ells distant.

It was the young King's intent to assault the great keep's western door, rather than the main entrance at the north, which was defended by a stout barbican alive with crossbowmen, archers, and numbers of domestic Nyssomu aborigines who used their blowpipes to propel poisoned darts.

A body of only thirty or forty Laboruwendian knights had massed in what seemed to be a doomed defensive action in front of the west door. They were being swiftly decimated by the Goblin Kinglet's warriors when the Yellow Voice suddenly descried a fresh group of at least five hundred heavily armed defenders swarming into the stableyard from the rear, southern side of the keep. They were led by a splendidly accoutered nobleman in a green surcoat who swung his sword with such power that the blade was a singing silver blur that wreaked death or dismemberment at every stroke. The knights and men-at-arms following this spectacular commander fell upon the Raktumians closest to the west door and caused great slaughter, bringing the invaders' advance to an abrupt halt. Some of the pirates began to run, and a rout threatened.

"Who is that great fighter wearing green?" King Ledavardis demanded of the Yellow Voice.

"He is Owanon, the Lord Marshal of the Two Thrones and King Antar's dearest friend, my Liege. He is a champion famed in tournaments throughout most of the known world."

The King addressed the knights closest to him. "We must do something about him at once. He inspires his men to fight like fiends, and he is cutting down our brave lads like heads of ripe grain! All of you! To me! Let us have at him!"

Brandishing his sword, Ledavardis burst forth from those shielding him and charged forward. After a moment's hesitation, his knights and the other pirate troops rallied, following with fresh courage.

The Yellow Voice finally saw his chance. He ducked low amidst the clangorous melee, hauled up the skirts of his wet and dirtied robe, and ran for his life toward the stables.

Hand-to-hand fighting was going on everywhere. The husky acolyte tripped over bodies and dodged the weapons of friend and foe alike before gaining the great stone structure. Its outer precincts were crammed with wounded Raktumians who had sought shelter from the incessant shower of bolts and arrows pouring from the keep's battlements. Deeper within were many slaughtered stablehands, and a handful of pirate corpses, one with a pitchfork in his throat. The wielder of this weapon lay sprawled atop his victim, a dagger sunk in his back. Strangely, he was not a human but a dwarfish Oddling dressed in exceptionally handsome brown leather garments.

As the sounds of the battle echoed distantly behind him, the Voice came to the grooms' quarters, where he discovered a windowless chamber that could be locked from within. A refuge at last! He darted inside and closed the door softly. Then, leaning against the thick planks, he waited for his heart to stop pounding and his breath to slow before bespeaking the Master.

Unlike the sparsely furnished and doorless dormitories around it, this place had a degree of luxury — a table, small chairs, a bed with fine blankets, rugs on the floor, and a fireplace in which coals still glowed and a pot of stew hung from its crane, steaming. On the table was a clean wooden bowl, a spoon, a heel of bread, a crock of beer, and a pewter canikin.

A refuge indeed!

Postponing his duty for a little while longer, the famished and thirsty Yellow Voice heaved a grateful sigh and went to help himself. He was ladling the delicious-smelling stew into the bowl when he felt a sharp prick in his back.

"Stand still!" a voice hissed.

The Voice froze.

"Drop those things!"

"I meant no harm," the Voice said. But the blade thrust at him, breaking the skin, and with a cry of pain he let the bowl clatter onto the hearthstones and the ladle drop into the pot. "I am only an unarmed townsman, caught up by mistake in the fighting —"

"Silence — or you die! And do not move." The whisperer withdrew the blade and the Voice felt blood trickling down his spine.

"I will stand quite still. I would not dream of moving —"

The Voice's conciliatory babbling died in his throat as he felt his hood whisked suddenly from his head. Out of the corner of his eye he saw a narrow blade flash past his ear. Cold metal touched his scalp where warm metal also lay. His heart stopped as he realized what was happening.

"Great God, not the talisman! *Master! Help me —*"

But the silvery circlet was already plucked from his head, spinning through the air, striking the floor with a musical clink. The Yellow Voice whirled about in desperation and flung himself upon his assailant with a hoarse bellow. But where was he? There was no man in the dim room, only a small dark figure that scarcely reached the burly Voice's waist. Another Oddling?

The acolyte fell upon the tiny form. It shrieked — but its cry was drowned out by the Voice's own agonized scream. He felt a sudden coldness beneath his ribs. It was amazing, how the cold hurt him. He thrashed about, trying to pluck at it, suddenly blind to everything around him, seeing only the face of the Master.

Eyes like white beacons, shining from the star-mask. And then the eyes of the Voice himself flared bright, and he ceased trying to pull the cold thing from his breast . . . from the breast of Orogastus himself.

The small assailant had wriggled free. Fighting to counter the hideous pain, the sorcerer listened. He heard panic-stricken breathing turn to sobs. His attacker was in the corner, trapped! Now all Orogastus had to do was turn his head in order to see who the killer-thief was. Turn only a little more so that the one hiding in the dark would be illumined by the eyes of enchantment and identified. Turn before the blood-starved brain died. Turn! Turn—

The shining eyes found their target and flickered out. For the briefest moment the Yellow Voice himself saw Prince Tolivar crouching in the corner. Then the acolyte lay dead on his back with a small ruby-hilted sword run through his heart like a skewer.

"I didn't mean it," Tolo said after a long time. But the Yellow Voice was utterly still.

The little Prince climbed to his feet and wiped his streaming eyes and nose on his golden sleeve. Swaying, he looked down upon the body. Rubies winked in the folds of grubby yellow cloth. Tolo took a great breath, bent down, grabbed the hilt of the sword with both hands, and pulled. It slid free with surprising ease.

He wiped the blade on the dead man's robe and then walked shakily to the opposite side of the chamber.

It had rolled under the bed.

Tolo fished it out with the sword, lifted it, and carried it at arm's length to the table. He drew up one of the chairs, sat down, and stared. It had a many-rayed star at its front and three grotesque heads that seemed to snarl familiarly at him in the firelight.

It took him a long time to work up courage; but at last he went to where he had hidden the star-box, unwrapped it, and brought it to the table. He opened the dark, glassy lid. Inside was a bed of metallic mesh, and in one corner a set of flattened, many-colored jewels.

Tolo had read the little red book. He, not the Black Voice, had taken the star-box without permission and studied it.

Using the sword again, he gingerly tipped the Three-Headed Monster into the box. There was a dazzling flash. Tolo fell back with a cry and almost fled then and there. But instead he looked into the box and saw that the Star had vanished from its former position beneath the central monster head of the talisman. It no longer was bonded to Orogastus.

Tolo pressed the blue gemstone.

It lit, and a gentle musical note sounded.

Then he pressed the red, the yellow, and the two green ones. They also glowed tunefully. There remained only the white gemstone. When he pressed it, a louder musical chime sounded, then all of the lights winked out.

Through the thick door Tolo heard shouts and the clashing of swords. He had not noticed any noise before. The fighting must be getting closer. Ralabun had made him promise to stay hidden in his room until he returned, but Tolo had a feeling that his Nyssomu friend would not be coming back.

"If the magic didn't work," he whispered to himself, "I'll die if I touch the talisman. But if the pirates get me, I'll die anyhow."

Trembling, he reached into the box.

T**olo! By the Bones of Bondanus — the brat was not only alive, but he had also bonded the Three-Headed Monster to himself!**

Halted in the midst of pandemonium, with weapons clanging on all sides like the hammers of hell and his guardsmen yelling as they fended off attackers, Orogastus felt his heart sink as he lost Sight of the little Prince. It would be futile to go after Tolo now. Wearing the talisman, he would certainly conceal himself somewhere in the sprawling stable or in one of the adjacent buildings of the courtyard, and no sorcery would be able to pinpoint him. That much of the coronet's working required no effort on the boy's part.

But surely he would be unable to command the Three-Headed Monster. He was half-frightened to death. No, Tolo would only hold fast to it — and to the star-box as well, sly little wretch that he was! — and cower in some hidey-hole until the battle was over.

Orogastus knew with sickening certainty that the Three-Headed Monster was lost. But at least the Archimage and her sisters did not have it. Tolo would never turn it over to them. Not after having killed for it. What a grotesque end for the poor Yellow Voice . . .

All three of his acolytes were gone now, along with the hope that the Star Council might be resurrected and the Cynosure destroyed. But he still had the Burning Eye, and the battle was going very well, and Haramis was proving to be more inept an opponent than he had ever dared to hope.

If he could win this war, there would be time to think of ways to trick the little Prince into surrendering his talisman . . . time to recruit new followers and initiate them into the Star . . . time to master the operation of his own talisman and either win Haramis over to his side or destroy her —

"Master!" One of the Tuzameni guards pointed to the western side of the keep. "Listen to the pirates cheering. Something has happened over there!"

"I will scan it with my Sight." The sorcerer used his talisman to oversee the entire palace courtyard from high in the air. He saw that the invaders had thrown open the main gates of the fortifications, so that overwhelming numbers of them now swarmed about the grounds. Most of the pirate warriors kept back from the massive keep and concentrated on the many other palace buildings, doing more looting than fighting.

Only on the western side where the noise was coming from was any serious attempt being made to penetrate the stronghold. Most of the defenders were concentrated there, before the vulnerable west door. The Raktumian attack against them was being spearheaded by King Ledavardis and his mob of noble cutthroats, and a rather good job they were making of it! The King . . .

Almighty Bahkup! What did Ledo think he was playing at? Challenging Marshal Owanon to single combat? The young lunatic! He would surely be slain, and the pirate army would dissolve into chaos.

"Quickly!" Orogastus shouted to his bodyguard. "I must reach a high vantage point where I can work my magic."

"The bakery there has a stout roof with a parapet," a guardsman said, "and it is beyond the range of the shooters in the keep."

They pushed and slashed their way to the structure, hewing down even those Raktumians who were not quick enough to get out of their way. The bakery interior was a welter of corpses, moaning wounded, smashed tables and racks, and blood-splattered walls; but the main press of combat had passed it by. The sorcerer found the ladder leading to the roof and climbed it with alacrity, leaving his guards below. From on high, he had a perfect view of the fighting going on around the west door of the keep.

The squat young King of Raktum and the tall Lord Marshal were hacking at each other with a will while knights of both nations now stood with lowered swords, watching and cheering. The teenaged monarch was strong and agile for all his ungraceful shape, but it was plain to the sorcerer that Ledo was outclassed by the older man. Owanon had the King in retreat, backing toward the line of Raktumians. Ledo was certain to be downed at any moment.

Orogastus lifted his talisman with the three-lobed pommel upright. Never before had he dared deliberately attempt what he did now. If he miscommanded, he knew there was a possibility that he himself might die. But the chance had to be taken.

Three-Lobed Burning Eye, smite Owanon unto death.

The three eyes of the pommel opened. From them blazed a tricolor beam — white, green, and gold. It struck the Lord Marshal upon his breastplate and spread over his entire armored form in entwining bright streams. His body was enveloped in glowing smoke. His sword dropped from his hand and he fell at the feet of the astounded King of Raktum. Plates of scorched armor rang on the pavement, together with blackened bones.

Three-Lobed Burning Eye, blast open that door!

Again the ray flashed forth, this time dazzling white, striking the iron-bound gonda planking of the heavy portal. The metal turned incandescent and the wood burst into roaring flame. An instant later the door dissolved in a cascade of black cinders. The Raktumian warriors gaped, not believing their eyes. But King Ledavardis screamed jubilantly: "Forward!" The men gave a shout and surged toward the narrow entry.

His heart soaring with exultation, Orogastus turned and brandished the wondrous weapon at the main door on the north side of the fortress.

Three-Lobed Burning Eye, now blast this door!

Again the beam of light lanced out, and the wide main entrance to Zotopanion Keep lay wide open before the invading horde.

Haramis! the sorcerer cried. *Haramis, surrender! I can command my talisman to kill! I have killed the Lord Marshal of Laboruwenda and I will kill anyone else who opposes me! Order the keep defenders to lay down their arms. Order Queen Anigel to come forth and submit to King Ledavardis. If you do this, I will spare the lives of everyone in Derorguila. If you refuse, they will all be slain. Haramis, surrender!*

There was a movement in a window at the topmost level at the front of the keep. With his own naked eyes, Orogastus beheld a distant figure clothed in white. She said:

No.

Burning fury fountained up within him. Damn her to the deepest of the ten hells! She herself would be the next to die!

He lifted the talisman . . . then cried out as the Sight of her face filled his mind. He could not give the command.

Damn her! Damn her! He did not love, could not possibly love her! He hated her from the very depths of his being, with all his heart and soul and strength. Why then did he feel enchained to her — drawn to her irresistibly, fatally?

"I will be free of you!" he groaned aloud. He obliterated her face and filled his mind only with the image of the magical pointless sword.

Three-Lobed Burning Eye, I . . . I command you to smite Haramis unto . . . unto death!

Wrong! He had done it wrong, faltering in resolution, betrayed by that personal flaw he detested so fiercely. Betrayed by love.

He felt the rage of self-hate burning inside of him merge with a tricolored ray. It lashed out at her, and when it reached the window opening, it fragmented into a thousand glittering, ringing fragments, as though it had turned to solid crystalline ice or a mass of refulgent diamonds. In his own gloved hands, the talisman was burning hot. He dropped it with a cry of agony and it clanged onto the parapet at his feet and lay there, dark and dead and eyeless. His silver leather gloves were smoking. He ripped them off and cast them away with an oath.

The figure at the window was unhurt. She seemed to magnify and hover not two ells before him, tall and lovely, with a face sad but full of determination. One slender hand held the wand called the Three-Winged Circle.

I must go to the aid of my people, Star Man. Then I will come to you and we will finish this.

Unwilling to waste her uncertain energies by transporting herself to the ground floor of the fortress, Haramis now ran down eight flights of stairs to where the fighting was going on inside the keep. But by the time she reached the second level, so many invaders had poured in through the two open doors that the great hall below was a riot of combat, with the stone floor flowing with blood and the antagonists so crowded they could hardly swing their swords.

Anigel and young Princess Janeel had taken refuge in a heavily guarded strongroom adjacent to the ornate presence chamber on the keep's second level and were secure enough for the moment. Kadiya had found Nikalon only slightly injured. She and the Crown Prince were now hurrying to the sanctuary via the backstairs.

Haramis made her way onto a minstrel's balcony above the main entrance to the great hall, hoping to use her magic to reclose the two doorways. But each time she materialized a new barricade, the sorcerer outside blasted it open again. Finally, she was so exhausted by the futile efforts that she was forced to hold off.

I am really unequal to him in magical strength, she said to herself. For all my training, he is the stronger enchanter. We are unable to kill one another with magic, but he is certain to win this war. Lords of the Air! How will it end?

Standing in the shadows above the carnage, she watched the valiant, outnumbered Laboruwendians try to stave off the enemy forces pushing up the grand staircase toward the throne room and the Queen. The stairs were opposite the main entrance of the hall and had been one of the palace's most famous features — an expanse of white marble twice as wide at the bottom as at the top, carpeted with scarlet and ornamented with golden banisters and silver-gilt lamp-standards. At solemn court functions the stairs were lit by thousands of candles and formed a promenade for gorgeously dressed men and women. Now they were a stage for butchery, running with blood.

The palace defenders were concentrated there, directed by Penapat the Lord Chamberlain. The heavyset nobleman bounded from one side of the broad stairs to the other, shouting commands. As one group of knights fell vanquished another pressed down the stairs from the anteroom of the presence chamber, fighting to the death to defend their Queen.

Poor souls, Haramis thought. They still have hopes that I can turn this monstrous throng away, and then King Antar will arrive and win the day. But they are doomed . . . doomed. Ah, God! If I could only think properly!

As she tried to recover, Haramis gave what aid she could to the crucial defenders on the staircase. In her weakened state, she was able to deflect enemy sword-strokes from this man or that, but she could not protect all of them. One by one the knights at the forefront of the affray succumbed. The advancing enemy threw their bodies and those of their slain comrades over the banisters onto growing heaps of dead men down below.

King Ledavardis of Raktum, slightly wounded in his sword arm and no longer able to take the field himself, surveyed the battle from the safety of an alcove at the right of the stairs. Hedged round with armed protectors, he now urged his men on with a mighty shout:

"The Queen! The Queen! She is up there in the throne room at the head of the stairs! Half the loot of Derorguila to the man who takes Queen Anigel!"

The pirates responded with a thunderous roar and a renewed surge of bodies. There were over nine hundred men in the great hall and three quarters of them were Raktumians. A fresh lot of La-boruwendian knights came forth from the anteroom at Penapat's command and arrayed themselves in a position to charge.

Haramis touched her talisman. She saw that Kadiya and Nikalon had reached the strongroom behind the thrones safely. Antar and his army had arrived at the postern gate at long last, but it was now securely held by a huge force of the enemy. The King would be forced to march around the perimeter of the fortress to the break in the wall, where he would inevitably meet the right flank of the pirates and be fought to a standstill. His plan to reinforce the keep defenders had failed.

"Oh, God, it is hopeless!" Haramis was now near to weeping from grief and frustration. "I do not even have the strength to take Anigel and Kadi and the children to safety . . . Iriane! Iriane! Is there nothing *you* can do?"

A froth of blue bubbles materialized beside her on the balcony with commendable swiftness, and the Archimage of the Sea stepped forth from the midst of them. Iriane frowned as she looked down upon the insane tumult in the hall, and she shook her head.

"There are so many of them, and all in a frenzy of blood-lust. We could try new illusions, but I seriously doubt that the ruffians would be distracted. What you really need are more fighters on your side."

"King Antar cannot get into the palace compound from the south. The pirates hold the postern gate. It would be useless for me to try to transport him and his knights here a few at a time, even if I had the strength to do so . . . which I do not."

"Well, I can't do that particular trick at all," Iriane admitted. "I am only capable of transporting myself." She pursed her cyan lips and narrowed her indigo-shadowed eyes in thought. "Hmm. Fighters . . . fighters. You know, my dear, we Archimages were not always at the mercy of the ungodly. Back in the old days, when the Star first threatened the world, we had the Sentinels of the Mortal Dictum as the ultimate defense. They *could* take the lives of those rational beings who persisted in evil aggression."

"But only the entire Archimagical College could order the sindona out," Haramis retorted bitterly. "The Teacher in the Place of Knowledge told me so. And those ancient Archimages are long gone safely beyond."

Slowly, Iriane shook her head. "The College still exists. Only three members are required for its functioning. You and I and—"

"Denby!" Haramis broke in, fresh hope electrifying her. "But would he?" Without waiting for Iriane's reply, she threw back her head and cried out at the top of her lungs: "Denby! Help us! Let us have the sindona!"

When nothing happened, she called his name again, wild with desperation. "Denby! Archimage of the Sky! Dark Lord of the Firmament! You pretend to be aloof, but I know you have been watching from above. I know you have been involved in this from the beginning, long before my sisters and I were born. Help us!" She grasped Iriane's cool blue hand. "We, your fellow-Archimages, entreat you in the name of the Triune!"

The terrible sight and sounds of the battle softened and dwindled away. Haramis saw Three Moons, full and silvery gold against a serene and star-spangled sky. They were not small, as the Moons had always seemed to be when she saw them sailing overhead, but large enough so that their globes almost filled her vision.

One of them seemed to have the face of an old, old man. His wizened brow was knit in an attitude of annoyed perplexity.

"Denby!" Haramis exclaimed. "Remember your sacred office and help us to summon the sindona!"

The land and the sea are not my charge, said the Moon peevishly.

"You are an Archimage," Haramis said. "You belong to the College. Iriane and I make this most solemn demand of you!"

Oh. Well! I suppose I must, if you put it like that . . . but it won't solve things permanently, you know!

The Man in the Moon and his two inanimate counterparts vanished.

"Look!" Iriane crowed joyfully. "Oh, look!"

A phalanx of fifty pale ivory statues had appeared on the grand staircase just behind the row of faltering defenders. They were far taller than men, and wore glittering crossed belts on their breasts, and iridescent crown-helms. Each one carried a golden skull tucked under its left arm. They marched slowly down the bloodied staircase in remorseless order, five abreast, and the dumfounded Laboruwendians fell over themselves scrambling out of the way.

Those warriors of the invasion force who had caught sight of the descending Sentinels of the Mortal Dictum — and this included most who were fighting within the great hall — ceased their clamor and contention and stared at the odd spectacle in startled wonderment. For a moment the hall was nearly silent.

Warriors of Raktum. Warriors of Tuzamen. Lay down your arms in the name of the College of Archimages.

The voice was very soft, almost maternal, and it came from the air and not from the motionless lips of the sindona.

For an instant the pirates were too petrified with surprise to act. Then a scarlet-smeared Tuzameni warlord in the front rank of those at the foot of the stairs brandished his wavy-edged sword and yelled in a coarse voice: "I'll be damned if I surrender to a pack o' naked spooks!"

One of the leading sindona looked down upon him, lifted its arm, and pointed.

The knight vanished in a puff of smoke. A polished white skull bounced to the floor where he had stood and rolled about on the gory flagstones. A murmur of awe and fear went up from the men nearby.

But the invaders did not yet understand what was happening. As the sentinels continued down the stairs numbers of the emboldened foe just ahead of them began to attack, hewing at the moving statues with swords and battle-axes and spike-studded flails. The iron bounced harmlessly from the smooth ivory bodies. Crowned heads turned and fingers pointed. A cascade of death's-heads went clattering and bouncing down into the mob.

A quick-witted bravo cried out: "It's only a trick, lads! They're phantoms cooked up by the Archimage! Pay 'em no mind!"

A howl of relief and fury went up from the pirates as they pressed their attack with fresh vigor. But moments later the ranks of sindona reached the floor of the great hall and fanned out among the fighters, pointing their deadly fingers at one foeman after another. The skulls multiplied, and the invaders who survived could not help but crush them under their mailed feet. It slowly came home to them that their comrades were dying on all sides in quiet little wisps of smoke. Many Raktumians ceased fighting and began to look about for a way to escape.

The sindona were quite invulnerable to human weaponry. With their majestic, carven faces calm and gently smiling, they did their necessary work.

The more intelligent among the invaders now moaned in growing terror and sidled toward one of the crowded doors, causing the Raktumian leaders and the Tuzameni warlords to cry out: "Nay, men! Those things are only illusions! Forward! Do not fear! To the throne room and the Queen!"

In his alcove, the Goblin Kinglet was about to echo these courageous sentiments when he caught sight of a woman in white standing on the musicians' gallery high above the main entrance of the hall. It was the Archimage Haramis and she was looking directly at him. He heard her voice as though she stood only an arm's length away.

"King Ledavardis of Raktum! The beings you see are called the Sentinels of the Mortal Dictum. They are not illusions. They are real, and they are putting to death those of your warriors who harbor thoughts of killing in their hearts. In this hall there are fifty sentinels. There are many others outside the keep, equally deadly. Surrender, or you and all of your people will die."

The quailing young monarch managed to say: "You are lying!"

She pointed her talisman at him. "See for yourself." And into his mind sprang a horrific scene: Tall pale forms with golden skulls tucked under their arms were gliding through the battling throng in the palace grounds, leaving death and stunned bewilderment in their wake.

Do not falter, Ledo! I am here!

Orogastus appeared at the western door, his silvery star-mask and robes gleaming and the Three-Lobed Burning Eye held high.

"Kill those things!" shouted the King frantically to the sorcerer. "Kill them before more panic spreads among the men!"

But a rout had already begun. The invaders inside the great hall were racing out of the main entrance, shrieking: "Demons! Demons are coming! Run for the ships!" Their terror spread swiftly, infecting the throng of invaders outside.

Orogastus lifted his talisman and cried out a command. A tri-colored beam of light struck one of the sindona and it exploded with a deafening report, the fragments of its rock-hard body peppering the fleeing pirates with tiny missiles and making them scream and run even faster.

"Stop!" Orogastus admonished them, in a voice like thunder. "Come back, you fools! Look — I am killing them!" And he slew a second living statue.

At the death of the first sindona, the others had turned and gazed impassively at the sorcerer. Now they pointed in unison at him, and Haramis cried out in spite of herself and felt her heart plummet.

But no dissolving puff of smoke appeared. The skull of Orogastus remained secure within its flesh, wearing its awesome star-mask. He cried out in triumph and began to blast them to shards, one after another. The noise of the explosions was stupendous, and it served only to demoralize the invaders still more.

The knights of Laboruwenda, on the other hand, now came stampeding down the staircase, led by Lord Penapat, to pounce upon King Ledavardis and the thirty or so men surrounding him. Trapped in their alcove, the Raktumians put up a fierce resistance.

All of the sindona within the emptying great hall now converged upon the sorcerer, seeming to ignore the extermination of their fellows. Haramis remembered that the spirits of the destroyed statues passed into those still whole. The detonations were deafening as the sorcerer slew sentinel after sentinel; but they still marched inexorably toward him, now holding the golden skulls before them with both ivory hands. Orogastus waved the talisman wildly, killing one after another. Still they came closer — and more now appeared at the two open doors, also advancing.

"Iriane!" Haramis cried. "Can you lend me some of your strength?"

"Well, I could give you a little," the Archimage of the Sea replied, "but certainly not enough to restore you completely."

"I only need sufficient magic to transport myself one single time."

"Let's try it." The Blue Lady took Haramis's head in her hands, drew her down, and brought their brows together. Haramis felt a burst of blue light behind her eyes. A new vigor infused her mind and body.

"Thank you! Now pray for me!" And with that, Haramis clasped her talisman and vanished.

"Dear me," Iriane murmured, shaking her pearly coiffure. "What can she be planning to do?" She gazed upward with eyes momentarily blank. "Denby? Are you watching?"

But there was no reply from the aloof firmament.

"So much the worse for *you,*" said the Archimage of the Sea.

She lifted her skirts and began to trot along the encircling balcony toward the western side of the great hall, where Orogastus was still shattering one sindona after another. The view of the final confrontation would be much better from over there.

32

The strongroom behind the thrones in the presence room was intended to store the great treasures of the royal regalia, and to provide a convenient withdrawing room for the monarchs during tedious court functions. It was all but impregnable, but it was also small and crowded with coffers of jewels, and had only the one door, and was freezing cold. No one could remain within it indefinitely.

Lord Penapat had hustled Anigel, Janeel, and the old Nyssomu nurse Immu into it when the keep doors were sundered. It was not a place the Queen would have chosen. Anigel realized that she could not fight, but it was maddening to be so helpless, and not to know what was happening.

She was overjoyed when the strongroom door opened after a short time and Kadiya entered with Nikalon. Immu made a quick examination of the boy and pronounced him healthy enough except for a few bruises. He was crushed by shame for having forced his aunt to rescue him.

Kadiya gave her sister a lively account of how she had gone invisible, with the aid of her Black Trillium amulet, and collected the Crown Prince from the fallen barracks. Not wanting to deprive Anigel and the others of hope, Kadiya did not mention that she had found the area behind the keep crowded with hundreds of enemy troops. But the Lady of the Eyes knew full well that there was no chance at all of Antar being able to bring in his reinforcements through the postern gate of the fortifications.

And unless Haramis produced a miracle, those of them hiding

within the strongroom would soon have to choose between surrender and a slow death by starvation and thirst.

They settled down to wait. Kadiya sat by the door, sharpening her sword, while the others wrapped the ornate coronation robes around themselves to keep warm and huddled in a close group.

"I am more grateful than I can say for your having restored Niki to me," Anigel said to Kadiya. "At this terrible time it is a comfort to know that at least two of my dear children are safe."

"Dumb Tolo's probably safe, too," Princess Janeel said disgustedly.

"We will not speak unkindly of him." The Queen was mildly reproving, but her eyes suddenly misted at the thought of her youngest son. "Tolo is too young to know the terrible thing he did. If he were restored to me, I would clasp him to my bosom and forgive him with all my heart. And so should we all."

"Without even *punishing* him?" Niki was scandalized.

"Yes," said the Queen.

The Crown Prince muttered at that, and Princess Janeel began to speak callously of Tolo's bleak future in the clutches of the awful sorcerer until Immu bade them both to be still, and think of better things.

"What better things?" the little Princess asked. "There are none."

"Of course there are!" Immu scolded. "Silly child!"

"The pirates will capture us . . . and I shall have to wed the Goblin Kinglet after all!"

"Now, sweeting, hush. There is still hope. Things may not be as bad as they seem . . . Ah, they were much worse during the terrible battle for Ruwenda Citadel. What situation was more hopeless than that? Yet we won out — and Black Trilliums bloomed in Ruwenda for the first time since the withdrawing of the Conquering Ice."

"I remember." Queen Anigel tried to smile. But Immu's mention of the ice made her shudder.

"Yes, it was the greatest battle ever fought in Ruwenda," Kadiya said. "Perhaps the greatest ever fought in the known world! Humans and Folk and even Skritek were the combatants, and good magic and bad made even the Three Moons themselves tremble."

"But the three Petals of the Living Trillium brought about a great victory," Immu said to the Prince and Princess. "Your mother and Aunt Kadiya and Aunt Haramis won the battle and won the war even though it seemed hopeless."

"Tell us the whole story again," the Princess begged, nestling further into her extravagant covers.

So Immu did. She spoke of how the Archimage Binah arrived just in time to help the Triplet Princesses of Ruwenda be safely born, and then related how each girl grew up and went on her quest and found her magical talisman.

The old Nyssomu nurse was just about to tell how Ruwenda was saved when the Archimage Haramis opened the strongroom door.

"Sisters . . . come with me."

Kadiya sprang to her feet, her face alight. "Hara! Is there good news?"

"Put down your sword, Kadi. You will need another weapon for the fight that we now face." The Archimage was nearly as pale as a sindona. Silhouetted in the door, her cloaked form had a faint rainbow radiance shimmering about it. She looked unfamiliar, even fearsome.

Queen Anigel cried out, stricken. "Then we have not won the battle?"

"The pirate army is in full flight toward the harbor," Haramis said. "Antar and his men are in hot pursuit of the stragglers. Ledavardis, King of Raktum, is at this minute the captive of Lord Penapat and his knights — "

Niki and Jan let out a happy cheer.

" — but the battle is not won. Orogastus remains. I summoned the sindona, and they are contending with him. But he is speedily destroying them, and the time has come for us to confront him. Come with me now! The only weapons you will need are your amulets."

Kadiya threw off her sword-belt. The Queen rid herself of an encumbering heavy cloak. They rushed through the empty presence room, past the antechamber, and out to the broad foyer at the head of the grand staircase leading down into the hall.

"Great God!" breathed the Queen.

Kadiya was incapable of speech, so strange and terrible was the scene spread before them. The enormous room, a full one hundred twenty ells long and equally as broad, was full of smoke. Wall torches flamed eerily among the ancient banners hanging on their staffs. Bodies were heaped everywhere, and dotted among them like red-stained white fruit fallen from some invisible tree were hundreds of human skulls.

From minute to minute blinding explosions came from the side of the hall to the west of the staircase. Kadiya and Anigel saw ghostly pale figures massed shoulder to shoulder there. Sindona — perhaps a hundred, perhaps less. The sorcerer was presumably among them, although nothing of him could be seen.

Haramis lifted her talisman with the trillium-amber glowing within. "Stand close to me," she bade the others. "Take the Black Trillium in your hand. Abolish all fear, all hopelessness, anything that has ever diminished your love. Give yourselves freely to each other and to me. Trust . . . and then follow where I will lead."

Kadiya and Anigel stood on either side of Haramis in the middle of the flight of stairs. The gloom and the smoke were suddenly gone and the great chamber seemed flooded with pitiless light. They saw Orogastus clearly. He wore his Star vestments and gripped the Three-Lobed Burning Eye by its dulled blade, but so tightly did he have hold of it that the dark metal had sunk into his flesh, and his hands were covered with blood. The lobes of the talisman's pommel bore three glaring eyes that flared green and gold and white, and at each triple pulsation a sindona vanished in a great concussion of sound and light.

Fragments of destroyed statues covered the ground around the sorcerer like coarse snow. The sindona had formed a ring about him, three deep, with the innermost of the crowned sentinels about six paces away. Each held a golden skull before it. They were immobile, seeming helpless as he swung giddily about, blasting them on all sides.

The Queen and the Lady of the Eyes suddenly felt themselves soaring, even though they knew at the same time that they stood firmly on one of the wide stairs. They hung above Orogastus, together with Haramis, and looked down upon him.

He looked up and saw them. His face, half-hidden by the mask, was framed in the rays of a great silver star. His lips parted and he cried out a single word. "Haramis!"

I am here. We are here. We must end this.

Orogastus lifted the Three-Lobed Burning Eye toward them, ready to command the annihilation of the Living Trillium. But he hesitated, remembering what had happened before, how the talisman had failed — and in failing, forced him to drop it. If he dropped it now, the sindona would be upon him in an instant, crushing him beneath their heavy bodies.

Was his will strong enough to kill her this time? Before, his concentration had wavered, distracted by his cursed love for her. But now one or another of them was sure to die . . .

Or would he?

Soul-shrinking terror washed over him. No! She would not kill him. She would do worse: exile him to a living death in the Chasm of Durance, in the bowels of the earth. The Cynosure would draw him there, as it had drawn him to the Kimilon, and he would be imprisoned alone until he breathed his last breath.

"No!" he screamed. "You shall not!" Holding the talisman high above his head, he emptied his mind of all thought, then formulated the command.

The Archimage said: *Kadiya, Anigel, now cleave unto me with all the loving strength you own, for we must turn back upon him what he would wreak upon us.*

The pommel of the Three-Lobed Burning Eye seemed to swell to titanic size, hiding the Star Man beneath. The three women saw the brown human eye, the golden eye of the Folk, and the silver-blue eye of the Vanished Ones stare hugely at them for a brief moment. Then the eyes were slowly transformed. They became three golden Moons, orbs slowly eclipsed by darkness, becoming black globes fringed with a luminous golden corona. The globes changed in turn, blooming, becoming a great three-petaled Flower the hue of night. Standing within its golden center was a man, and upon the petals of the Black Trillium were three women.

Haramis! You cannot do this! Not to one you love!

The man held a dark sword. Beams of brilliant starlight shone from his eyes. He said very clearly: *Smite them all. Smite the Living Trillium unto death.*

And the magical energies flowed.

Out from the center of the Flower where the Star now blazed came a twisting funnel, a whirlwind of light. Before it engulfed all of them, they saw the Trillium itself divide into threefold form: golden, green, white, with a starry heart in each. A great roaring brightness surrounded them. They seemed to fall head over heels, flying through the air like leaves, a blizzard of coruscating tricolored sparks swirling around them.

The Archimage of the Sea said: "Love is not only permitted, it is required."

The Archimage of the Firmament said: "It is also very inconvenient."

There was a thing ahead of them in the rushing storm of light. It was hexagonal in shape and dead black. They pitched and reeled and tumbled toward it, and it grew until it was immense and the volume of mind-shattering sound insupportable.

The Archimage of the Land said: "Do not be afraid!"

But I am afraid! So afraid . . .

Haramis, Kadiya, and Anigel were stunned by silence.

Standing in a row on the stairs.

Haramis between her sisters, head bowed, arms limp at her sides, the amber in the talisman at her breast throbbing to the rhythm of her heart.

Their own amulets also luminous and pulsating.

Alive.

Kadiya uttered a great sigh. She descended the stairs with Anigel trailing after and made her way cautiously through the pathetic human remains of the battle to where the remaining sindona stood. There were less than two dozen of them left, still in a perfect circle, still holding the golden skulls before them and seeming to smile serenely.

Within the circle lay the Three-Lobed Burning Eye, and nothing else.

"It was my talisman," Kadiya murmured. "Then it was his. Whose is it now?"

But the Sentinels of the Mortal Dictum did not answer. As the sisters watched, their forms became as insubstantial as mist, finally melting into nothingness.

"I suppose the sorcerer hid the star-box somewhere," Anigel said. "We shall probably be able to find it, and then one day you will be able to use your talisman again."

"I am not at all sure that I want to," said the Lady of the Eyes.

Anigel's eyes were watering — perhaps from the smoke that still filled the place. "I'm certain that I don't want to use mine."

They looked back for Haramis, but she was gone. No other living soul was to be seen in all the great hall.

"Let us go out into the clean air," Kadiya said, taking her sister's hand.

Together they passed through the western door of the keep and into the courtyard. There they found the sun brightly shining, and the air astonishingly sweet and warm. A crowd of battered and blood-stained Laboruwendian knights and men-at-arms hailed the two women with cheers and merry shouts. Lord Penapat cried out: "The foe has turned tail to the last man — save one!"

And the throng opened to show King Ledavardis of Raktum seated upon a stone mounting block.

He rose, smiled sweetly, bowed, and said: "The Goblin Kinglet begs mercy of Queen Anigel and the Lady of the Eyes, and herewith he surrenders."

"You treated my imprisoned children with kindness," Anigel said. "I will treat you the same. It is my will that you now leave my country."

"That — that is all?" Ledavardis regarded her with amazement.

The Queen nodded, then said to Penapat: "Take your men, and escort the King of Raktum to a ship, and see him gone."

There was some murmuring, but then most of the warriors began to laugh, and they set out for the palace's north gate. Queen Anigel seemed not to see the dead men lying all around, nor the blood, nor the ruins of Derorguila Palace. As if in a dream, she looked up into the blue heavens where a few white clouds sailed. It was a Dry Time sky, and a warm wind came from the sea. Finally she spoke.

"Kadi . . . I think the balance of the world is restored."

"You may be right. Let us pray it is so. Haramis will know for certain, but I think we should wait until later to ask her about it."

"Yes. She must be very tired."

Kadiya straightened. "There is much work to do. We must tend to the wounded, and we will have to arrange food and drink for our victorious fighters. I will go to the upper levels of the keep and roust out the noblewomen and whatever servants can be found. Then we can —"

She broke off. There was a trumpet sounding, and a chorus of joyous shouts, and the loud drumming of fronial hooves.

"Antar!" cried the Queen. "Antar!"

She went dashing to the forecourt with Kadiya close behind. They saw the King of Laboruwenda and his men riding in through the main gate. And sitting behind the King was a small figure that Anigel first mistook for either Jagun or Shiki. But those two valiant aborigines were on their own mounts just behind Antar, waving.

"Who then is he carrying?" Anigel cried out to her sister. She stumbled to a halt, out of breath. The King caught sight of her, spurred his animal, and came galloping toward her. Finally the Queen saw who sat behind her husband and burst into tears of joy.

"My baby! Oh, thank God! Tolo! My darlings, you're both safe!"

The smiling King reined in, leapt from the saddle, and took his wife into his arms.

Kadiya stood, hands on hips, and looked up at little Prince Tolivar with a wry expression. "Well, you'll have quite a tale to tell, won't you, young man?"

Tolo shrugged, letting her lift him down. "Nothing much happened. I escaped from the sorcerer during the earthquake. Papa found me. It was almost like magic."

"We have had enough magic to last us for quite some time," the Queen said to her son. "And I dare say you have, too."

"Yes, Mama," Prince Tolivar said.

He let her hug and kiss him, and then his father picked him up, and they all walked slowly back to Zotopanion Keep in the bright sunshine.

Haramis mounted the stairs. All over the upper floors of the palace stronghold the noncombatants were beginning to emerge like timid lingits shy of coming into the light. The Archimage spent a short time on the third level reassuring those she met, telling them that the war was over and Laboruwenda victorious. Then she asked to be shown to a quiet place where she might rest. An aging noblewoman took her to her own quarters, saying she would be honored if the Archimage used them. After thanking her, Haramis gratefully closed the door and locked it.

The chambers were not large, and of course the casements had been broken in the earthquake. But only soft breezes blew in through the paneless windows now, and the bed was dry. Haramis knew she would be able to sleep.

She took off her shoes, loosened her clothing, and prepared to lie down. But then she sat bolt upright, realizing that once again she had failed in her duty. She must be sure . . . sure that he was banished.

She took up her talisman for the last time on that long day.

"Show me the Chasm of Durance."

The vision was hard to fathom, and only slowly did she understand the meaning of the mass of chaotic broken stone that filled her mind's eye. When she did understand, she was too weary even to weep.

The earthquake had done it, of course. It had shaken all of Labornok and Ruwenda as well. The deep shaft below the Place of Knowledge had collapsed during the great tremor, burying the cavern below and the Cynosure within the cavern under an unimaginable burden of rock.

"Where . . . where is Orogastus?"

He has gone the way of the Vanished Ones. He is no longer in this world.

She had banished Orogastus into that rock-clogged, airless hell without knowing, and now he was dead.

Had Iriane known? Ah, but it was an affair of the land! Even if the Blue Lady had been aware of the Chasm's collapse, she was under no obligation to tell. The sorcerer was gone and the archimagical principles remained unsullied.

"It is finished," she whispered. "I am only sorry he was so afraid at the end . . . Who would have thought that he would be afraid?"

She closed her eyes at last, and gave herself to dreaming.

Epilogue

When Orogastus awoke, it was dark as night all around him. Every bone, every muscle of his body cried out with pain.

The pillow beneath his head felt soft. Wondering, he let his fingers steal over the blankets that covered him. They were pleasantly warm and silken. Dimly, he was able to discern a tall oblong nearby. But surely there were no windows in the awful Chasm of Durance . . .

He sat up, slipped from the bed where he had been lying, and discovered that he was naked except for the old Star pendant hanging from a chain about his neck. The oblong shape was a window indeed, covered with thin draperies. When he swept them aside, he drew in a shocked breath.

Stars. More than he had ever seen in the sky. And not twinkling white, but blazing steadily in every color imaginable. A great triple river of infinitesimal faint stars flowed amongst brighter ones. Were those the constellations he knew? . . . Yes. But he had never seen them so gloriously drawn.

"Then I am dead after all." He turned about in a daze and bumped into a small chair. Starlight now bathed the room in silvery radiance, and he saw a robe flung over the chair and put it on without thinking.

There seemed to be a door beyond the foot of the bed. He limped toward it — then stubbed his toe painfully on something that lay on the floor.

A black hexagon.

A sudden vertigo seized him. He staggered and nearly fell. Taking hold of a bedpost with one hand and the Star pendant with the other, he waited until the terrible flush of mortal terror subsided. Then he knelt and dared to pick the black thing up. It was flat, perhaps half an ell wide, and made of smooth metal. The Great Cynosure.

Still holding it, he opened the door.

Beyond was a cozy, book-crammed study. An old, old man with a dark face looked up from his reading, lifted one white eyebrow, and waited.

"Who are you?" Orogastus whispered. "And why — " He held out the Cynosure.

"You won't need that thing," the ancient said. "Just throw it in the corner. Then come and sit down." He gestured at a dusty sideboard. "Take a drink if you like. Don't mind my bad manners. I don't often have visitors. As a matter of fact, you're the first in a long, long time. But the urge to meddle just came over me!" He chuckled craftily. "Very odd. But so's this whole affair."

He went back to reading his book, just as though he were the only one there.

Above the sideboard was another window on the stars. But something else was floating out there, too — a shape like a half-moon painted a brilliant blue and white. For many minutes Orogastus stared at it in mute incomprehension.

"You'll get used to the view," said Denby Varcour. "It's one of the best things about this place."

©1992 Claudia Carlson

Iriane

ERNAL

CAP

BRANIA

GALANAR